CONVERGENCE

AN ELLEN DUST TIME BREACH FANTASY - BOOK 1

C.J. EMERSON

Copyright © 2022 by C.J. Emerson

ISBN: 978-0-9565679-5-6

All rights reserved.

No part of this book may be reproduced in any form or by any electronic or mechanical means, including information storage and retrieval systems, without written permission from the author, except for the use of brief quotations in a book review.

For Kirby and the Kids

CHAPTER 1

Leaving

A CHANGE IS COMING

Another child had been taken. Ellen listened to the conversations as she threaded her way through the market stalls; instead of the usual hubbub of voices, people were whispering as if unwilling to disturb the air. Even the dust kicked up by her skirts seemed reluctant to rise.

That made three this week, disappeared without a trace and always at night. Javer was the latest, someone said, son of the blacksmith's widow. Thirteen years old but big for his age and already working at the forge with his uncle. A good lad, everyone said. If Javer could disappear, no-one was safe.

No apples today either, even though it was September and the trees had been bowed down with fruit after a wet spring and a hot summer. They'd lost more land as the river changed its course again. The orchard that stood since before she was a child, the orchard she'd stolen from more times than she could remember, had been swallowed by the water that no-one ever crossed. And no-one seemed to care.

Change was in the air. She'd sensed it for a while, the way she could smell a storm coming. And not all change was for the better.

She checked the city clock on the tower of the Assembly building; it was time to go home, but although there was an unseasonal chill in the air she wasn't ready to find herself enclosed behind walls, not yet. She left the marketplace and made her way to the track that led towards the estuary. A longer way round, but she'd long since learned that the journey was at least as important as the destination. The path took her through a narrow alley away from the centre of the town, then left the buildings behind as it curved past the tavern on the corner. Packed earth now rather than stone, it weaved through tall grasses on towards the small harbour where the river widened on its journey to the sea.

She'd loved this place since she was a child. When she wasn't hustling for food, she'd come here to see the masts and hear the shouting, to watch the crates and bales being unloaded and breathe the smells of tar and salt, to taste cinnamon and nutmeg in the air. But today the wharves were empty, as they had been for months. Just two lean men with fishing lines who looked over with no sign of recognition or greeting, and then turned back to their contemplation of the water.

She stood for a moment on the cobbled edge of the dock, looking down at grey ripples and through them to the mud beneath; when had the last ship slipped its moorings? There must have been a final brig that sailed away, but who knows in advance when the last time arrives; the last ship, the last kiss, the last breath?

The horizon was a grey blur as always, where the sky and sea seemed to melt into one another. One of the fishermen pulled in a catch, swore, and threw it in disgust across the cobbles in her direction. Not a fish, then. She walked over to the object and picked it up, wiping away the coating of mud and weed. It seemed to be some kind of rule, about a foot long and three inches wide, made from a substance she'd never seen before. The body of the rule had been white once, she guessed, but was now the colour of pale cream, hard and with a sheen like silk. Running along the centre, one section slid backwards and forwards, covered with tiny numbers and symbols, with another slider across the whole depth of the rule like a piece of glass, transparent apart from a thin line from top to bottom.

She knew about the measuring rules used by carpenters and stonemasons, but this was different. And she was pretty sure that no-one in Haefen had seen anything like this before.

A raindrop landed on her cheek, then another, and she watched as a dervish of wind span across the water, bringing a flurry of spray. Time to turn back before the rain set in. Appearance was the least of her concerns; a childhood on the streets had taught her other priorities, and now the world could think what it liked about her, but she preferred not to become soaked. She placed the strange rule in her basket, arranged the shawl to cover her hair, and turned onto the track leading back to town and the house on Silver Street. Tollin would be ready for his midday meal; she'd long since learned that old men lived by their stomachs, and there was little else for him these days.

There weren't many men for whom she felt any fondness, but Tollin had given her a home when no-one else would, seventeen years ago, when he was still Chief Magistrate for the City Assembly. If anyone thought the worse of a middle-aged widower for taking in a brat from the back streets, they didn't say so. At least, not out loud. But popularity was fickle, especially in a city that preached morality even while the practice was something else, and in the elections three years after Ellen came to stay, Tollin lost to a younger man who painted her friend as a relic with questionable morals, lucky not to be denounced and exiled.

Why was she thinking about the past? The unsettling sense of change, perhaps. Not just change, but loss and decay. *We fade too soon when our purpose deserts us*, she thought, wondering if she would ever find her own role beyond caring for an old man in a house that used to be a thoroughfare, but had turned into a living grave. No-one visited now that Tollin was out of favours to give. No influence. No power. She made a vow as the drizzle turned to rain, and prayed to the gods she didn't believe in that she would never allow herself to become so diminished.

THEFT

For three hours now he'd been waiting, hunkered down behind a cluster of ornamental bushes that formed part of the campus landscaping. The car was half a mile away; security was tight, and he hadn't bothered to forge a pass. The old ways were more fun.

Lights still burned in Laboratory 313, Department of Experimental Metaphysics, University of Mittani. He could wait, he was a patient man. Had to be in his line of work. This job might be a little old school, but that was academics for you, precious about their research, jealous of the competition. Life would be so much easier if people trusted each other. The professor wasn't in there herself. Earlier in the day he'd tracked her back to her apartment on the other side of the park, an easy walk to the campus. A nice low-rise block with communal gardens and reserved parking, not that she needed it. He imagined how it looked inside; perhaps he'd check it out for himself one day. Clean lines, muted colourways; he was betting on greys or taupe. A kitchen full of heavy pans that had never been used, ditto a range cooker big enough for a family of six. He was still open as to the possibility of a cat. He liked cats, kept *themselves to themselves. The world would be a better place if more people were like cats.*

As for the bedroom; a king-size bed with pure white linen and only one set of pillows. A couple of formal dresses in the wardrobe for official functions, but casual clothes and comfortable shoes for work. Academics always cut themselves some slack when it came to appearance. They should try living in the real world with customers to entice, investors to satisfy.

At least it wasn't raining.

He pulled back behind the bushes as a couple of people passed by on the walkway between him and the building. The university had doubled in size over the last few years, and the buildings formed one of the signature developments in the new Natural Philosophy Park. Five years ago it was a car park; that was progress for you.

What would it be like to study here? Not that he ever had the chance with feckless parents who never saved for his education. But he'd done all right, even if it meant getting cramp while waiting for some over-enthusiastic postgrad to let him get on with his job. She should stop trying to impress her boss and go wherever people like her crawled to at night.

This little project was simple enough. Break into the lab, hack into the database, and copy the results of three years' research, all without leaving a trace. He would have done this from the comfort of his home once, but these days people were more diligent about cyber hacking. No-one networked sensitive information, especially the quality of work the client had tasked him to find. Not to worry; he liked a bit of analogue; it kept him in practice.

The lights went out in Laboratory 313, the last in the building. A few moments later he saw the main doors open and a figure walk out. Even in the gloom he could make out the green hair of Danu Khepa, research assistant. Green; sometimes he despaired of the modern world.

Bribery, he thought, is a wonderful tool, like a universal key. You need something unlocked, bribery will get you in ninety-nine times out of a hundred. The hundredth time is likely to be a little messier. Luckily, the security guard on duty tonight had several interesting and absorbing hobbies he preferred not to trouble his wife with. A woman of limited imagination, apparently. It took all sorts.

The man checked that he was alone, then left the shelter of the bushes and walked quickly to the main glass entrance leading into a five-floor-high atrium. Trees, easy chairs, and a coffee shop; nice work if you can get it.

Locked doors. Not to worry, he'd expected this. He rang the bell, an insignificant device for such a grand building, and watched as the security guard left his office, walked slowly across the foyer and opened the door. A cheerful chap, by the look of him, happy in his work. But the wrong man.

Now he had a problem. They both did.

He knew about the strict protocols in place for letting people in without passes. A sad reflection on society when even guards at universities carried guns.

In life there's a time for words and a time for action, and words, he'd always felt, were precious and not to be wasted. The guard folded in two with a sudden and unexpected punch to his solar plexus, and opened up again like a flower with a kick to his jaw. He was already unconscious as he fell backwards, hitting his head on the edge of a step.

The man checked for a pulse in the neck - nothing - then dragged the guard's body through the lobby and into the security office. A smear of blood tracked across the floor, but there was no time to clear it up. This place was shut for the night, no-one would be in until morning and by then he would be long gone. He couldn't conceal the break-in now, but it would take days for anyone to discover what he'd taken. If they ever did.

He ignored the lifts and took the stairs to the third floor, two at a time. Why miss an opportunity to keep in shape? He found Laboratory 313; the electronic lock was laughably simple to bypass, almost an insult, and he was in.

Time to get to work.

RUINS

By the time she reached home the rain had soaked through her cloak and shawl, and with every step water squelched from her shoes. The sky had been clear when she left for market that morning, and it wasn't yet the season for boots.

Within four hours what remained of the daylight would fade, and no-one wanted to be out these days after dark. Ellen closed the heavy wooden door, bolted it behind her, and emptied her basket onto the table. The strange object first, then cabbage and roots, dried beans to replenish the store cupboard and a small bony fish for Tollin, the best she could find. Perhaps, she thought, I should join the men at the dock tomorrow and try to catch something better myself.

Last out of the basket were candles for when it got dark. Tallow again. Tollin would moan about the reek, but she hadn't been able to find beeswax for weeks.

She heard movement in the room above as she stored the goods away, and then the old man's voice calling down. 'Ellen, is that you, girl?'

As if it would be anyone else. 'No Tollin, just the burglar come to rob you of all your immense wealth.'

'That's a relief. But before you fill your sack and leave me destitute, could you make me some lunch? You women live on air, a man needs food.'

'I bought fish; at least, I assume that's what it is. But I need to show you something first.'

'You think my stomach can wait? What's so important that you keep a man from his meat?'

She covered the fish with a plate. A stray cat, grey and white with only one ear, had been coming round for the past few weeks. Even with all the doors and windows shut, it always found a way in, especially on market days. She had searched once, with little enthusiasm, to find its secret entrance, but it was so thin and she tried not to be cruel.

The solar on the floor above had the largest window in the house. Tollin was on his feet, looking down at the street, as usual. He hadn't noticed her come up the stairs. *'Like a ghost you are,'* he'd said more than once. 'Light on your feet' might have been a better compliment, but ghost would do.

Ellen looked at the man who'd been a father to her for as far back as she could remember. Her parents had become ghosts long since, and she'd gleaned the frail memories of them from stories Tollin told, about the days when they'd all been young and friends and the future hadn't happened.

Then she'd been born. There must have been a life with her mother and father, all three of them living somewhere. Perhaps they'd held her, laughed and hugged. Perhaps they'd loved her. Those were the days she couldn't remember, so they could be whatever she wanted. And then her parents died, but that was another memory she'd lost, and Tollin wasn't telling, and some memories were best left alone. At seven years old, she was living on the streets. Perpetually hungry, part of a gang of orphaned brats that stayed alive by stealing food and sleeping wherever they could find shelter for a night or two. Strange how she had no problems remembering that life.

Tollin was married then and his wife wasn't about to give a home to a wild urchin from the alleys, that was his excuse for failing his friends. But after she died giving birth to a stillborn son, he'd spent nights asking around the tenements and searching the side alleys. Ellen was fifteen by then. He found her one night in the place she slept near the Shambles, a wreck of a building that bordered the small square where the executions were carried out. Monthly entertainment for the masses. But screams never bothered her, and it was better than sleeping in the open.

Just another bastard who assumed he could buy her, she'd thought as he asked her name. Wouldn't be the first, probably not the last, but none tried twice; she was quick on her feet and quicker with a knife. But he returned the next night with food that she didn't need to steal and clothes that weren't rags, and eventually he persuaded her to live in his home, a mixture of daughter and companion. And now a friend.

Ellen watched as he stood by the window with his back to her. His hair, once a copper gold, was now as white as his beard. The pair of spectacles he needed for reading dangled from his fingers, and his head - always held so high - now seemed too heavy for his shoulders.

Tollin turned and smiled. 'So what do you have for me, Ellen? What's so important that you leave my food in the kitchen to be scavenged by marauding beasts?'

'It's a cat, Tollin. I like cats. We should have one of our own, keep the mice in check.'

'Perhaps I like the mice,' he said. 'Small, generally keep out of my way.'

'True. And they're not given to wailing when their bellies are empty, unlike you.'

She joined Tollin at the small table by the window. 'Another child was taken last night. Javer, Widow Smith's son.'

'Taken? Not stayed out all night with some lass?'

'He's just thirteen and his mother would flay him if he tried anything like that. No, they found a boot and some scraps of his clothing by the river. And there was blood, someone said, a pool of blood.'

'No-one saw what happened?'

'Rafe, the grocer from Mewling Lane, said he saw a large animal the size of a young steer, dragging something across the meadow towards the riverbank. Black as night, he said, with yellow glowing eyes. But he'd been drinking at the Market Tavern all evening, as usual, and we've sat through his stories before.'

'If this was my great-grandfather's time I'd say it was a wolf,' said Tollin, 'but no-one's seen them around here from before I was born. Fearsome buggers, wolves, but not that big. Who knows what he saw.' He sat, scratched his stubble and looked up at Ellen. 'How many is that now?'

'Three this week, eleven altogether since the first one disappeared at the start of the month.'

She'd been putting off this conversation, but it couldn't wait any longer. 'Something's wrong, Tollin, and not just the children who go missing.'

'What else then? It's not like you to worry about what happens to other people. They make their own choices, you always say.'

'Children don't choose to become a wolf's supper. And I went to the harbour on my way home. When was the last time a ship arrived? We hear half-hearted grumbling about the scarcity of spices or decent cotton, but nothing more. People in this town keep their heads down and accept whatever happens as if it's fate. As for the Assembly; if you were still in charge, you'd put patrols on the streets and you'd do your damnedest to find out why the ships have stopped coming to Haefen.'

Tollin sighed. 'It isn't that people don't care, but the Assemblymen are more concerned with keeping the city's silver in the vaults or their own pockets, rather than spending it on imagined threats. Patrols cost money and elections are around the corner.'

'We're talking about people's lives.'

'They could police the streets, I'll give you that. But as for the ships, what do you expect them to do? Magic up a flotilla from nowhere?'

'No, but at least try to find out why they don't sail here any more. And it can't be beyond the wits of people to look after their children better.'

'Young ones always go missing. Sometimes from accidents, sometimes not. You know better than most what men are like. Three in one week seems like too many, but it could be a coincidence.'

'Really? If it's wolves, why have they come back? And another thing; when did you last look at the river? A month ago it took thirty minutes on foot to reach it from the last house. Now it takes ten. The river's three times as wide as it was a few weeks ago. You've seen Hubert's place; he relied on that orchard. Now it's gone.'

'The river always had a mind of its own.'

'But when does it move further away? Never. It's a noose, tightening around us. The river on one side, then the sea, and the hills behind us. We're trapped in a shrinking world.'

All her life she'd known that they kept to their city boundaries. The river was too dangerous to cross, and why bother when the other side was an impenetrable forest? No-one climbed the treacherous hills to the south and no-one knew of any passes. Occasionally someone might travel east to Lannick, but that was a week at least each way, and what was the point? Haefen had everything people needed, so travelling was pointless.

These were facts of life, something everybody knew and nobody questioned. Ships arrived with goods, but no-one from the city ever took passage to sail away. They'd become complacent in their own little world, even as it shrank around them.

Tollin noticed the rule in her hands. 'What's that, girl? Become a rubbish collector? It's from the harbour, the stink of mud gives it away. Couldn't you wash it properly like a civilised woman?'

'A fisherman pulled it out.' She placed it on the table and showed him how the different parts slid past each other. 'I've no idea what the symbols mean. Have you ever seen anything like it?'

'Never.' He picked it up and turned it over in his hands. 'And what by all the gods is it made from? Some sort of wood?'

'It's a wood that doesn't float. And where's the grain? This is as smooth as glass.'

Tollin put on his spectacles and slid the different parts around, squinting at the tiny numbers and symbols. 'Fell from one of the ships,' he said. 'Perhaps you could sell it in the market, someone might want it as a curio.'

But if this was ever on a ship, it wasn't the sort that came to Haefen.

Tollin placed the rule back on the table. 'While we're discussing strange things, was there any gossip about Walter, the butcher's boy? His father came round this morning; Johan's been a good friend, even if the other fair weathers can't be bothered.'

'What about his son?'

'The lad's always been touched, a kind soul but strange

notions. Took it into his head to go to Lannick, gods know why. He came back three weeks ago, said that where the town used to be was just ruins, old ones at that. Trees growing where walls used to stand.'

Ellen looked at his face for signs that he was having fun with her, but his face was serious. A kind man, Tollin, but not celebrated for a sense of humour. 'That's ridiculous,' she said. 'He must be making it up. Or more likely he got lost and went somewhere else. You said he was touched.'

'But not like that. Strange, but not a fool. I remember him at four years old, looking at books in the new library. If you quizzed him later, he could tell you exactly what was written on any page, word perfect. If Walter said he saw something, I believe him.'

'Lannick's not much smaller than Haefen. And weren't you there earlier in the year?'

'Two days at the Boar Inn, ale to match any here, shops full of goods. How could a town like that fall into ruins in just a few months? Even if it had, where have all the people gone?'

'So it can't be true.'

'That's what I thought. But after the boy got home, his father decided to make the journey himself. Good thing he took enough food for the trip there and back; his son was telling the truth. Johan traced where the streets used to be, and a few buildings still had a couple of walls standing, but it looked for all the world as if the town had been abandoned more than a century ago.'

AN OLD FRIEND

The next day, and a pale winter sky outside her window. Ellen barely slept, unable to block out the thought of children being taken for food, or the river swallowing the town. Tollin wanted a quiet life, any fire in his belly had long since been damped down to a gentle glow. If something was to be done, Tollin would be no help.

But where to start? Raise a militia to patrol the city limits? That felt like a forlorn hope. People preferred the safety of their beds at night; whether it was monsters or wolves crossing the river, no-one would want to put themselves in the way of a possible mauling.

As for the disappearing land, who would build dykes to keep the river back? And what use would such a barrier be when the waters rose so quickly and without warning?

She dressed, ate breakfast before Tollin was awake, and made her way across the city to the home of the only person who might take her seriously. The moon was still visible above the empty streets, a pale crescent hanging over the rooftops. Easy to imagine a monster roaming here in the night, looking for prey.

Annegret's house stood in the second-best part of town. Not as grand as Tollin's but comfortable enough, with two bedrooms upstairs and a yard at the back for chickens and a goat. We're the lucky ones, Ellen thought. Both street rats, both escaped to a better life. Most of the kids she grew up with had escaped life altogether before they left their teens; life in the back alleys of Haefen was hard and dangerous. But Annegret found her man and married him, and if there wasn't much love, at least there was companionship and respect. Who could ask for more?

The oak door opened before Ellen could knock, and Annegret pulled her inside. 'I saw you from the window, striding along as if you had a bone to pick with someone. Not me, I hope.'

'Not you, my friend. But I would dearly love to talk to you about something. Is Will at home?'

'Gone this last hour. Helping a neighbour repair a collapsing barn, don't ask me whose. He keeps his counsel, I keep mine. Works best that way.'

'No change in your relationship then?'

'I'm happy enough, Ellen. Why wouldn't I be? A roof, a warm bed, a man who puts food on the table.'

'Nothing comes for free.'

'If I pay, it's a price that seems fair to me. To be blunt, he doesn't ask for a lot, usually too tired. And at heart he's a good man, as much as any of them are. We both know how this world works.'

Annegret poured them each a mug of small beer. 'So will you tell me what's brought you all this way on a cold morning? Not to discuss the state of my marriage bed, I'm guessing, and knowing you, there's a mission in your sights. Something to do with the children disappearing?'

Ellen sipped the beer. 'I always said you could read my mind. Tollin told me not to worry, but this isn't normal.'

'You're talking about animals crossing the river. But unless they've learned how to build boats or bridges, the river would sweep them away.'

'But a creature like the one Rafe described could make it,' said Ellen, 'especially if it was hungry and hunting for food. And there are other things: no ships coming in, the way the river's growing and eating away at our land. Lannick falling into ruin almost overnight. I tell you, something is very wrong in Haefen.'

Annegret shook her head slowly. 'You need to speak to the Assembly. Perhaps Tollin's lost the spark, but there must be others who see what's happening.'

'The Assembly? You know what they call me; the witch of Silver Street. I've heard the rumours that I want to steal Tollin's house from under him. That I'm unnatural for not being with a man.'

'Half those Assemblymen tried their luck when we were on the streets. I bet if you look under their silks and furs some of them still bear the scars.'

'Aye, we had fun sometimes. But maybe you're right, I can't do anything alone. Every citizen is entitled to an audience. If the Assembly agrees to hear me, we just might be able to do something.'

THE SUN HAD REPLACED the moon above the rooftops as Ellen made her way back across town. For Annegret's sake, and Tollin's, she would stand up in front of the men who'd treated her like an animal, and alert them to the threats to their city. What was the worst that could happen?

THE CITY ASSEMBLY

The Assembly met in the Court House, a large, timber-framed hall supported on stone pillars above the old exchange. When Tollin was Chief Magistrate she'd sat in the public gallery during the trial of an itinerant teacher who denied the existence of the gods. Given the choice of death or exile, he'd packed his belongings and left the next morning.

'Good thing they don't ask my beliefs or I'd be on the road with him,' she'd said to Tollin later.

'It wasn't so much what he said as how he said it,' Tollin told her. 'He mocked people's beliefs; I know our rulers take themselves too seriously but no-one likes to be made fun of.'

That trial was five years ago, and now she was climbing the steps to the chamber to plead her own case. At least no-one had accused her of anything, even if more than a few wished they could.

The semicircle of members' seats overflowed with Assemblymen in their ceremonial robes of crimson velvet, and fifty pairs of eyes fixed on her as she walked in. She looked around at them, meeting every gaze; hungry men at a dining table, dribbling as they caught the scents of food from the kitchens.

The public gallery was less colourful but noisier. Widow Javer in the front row next to Johan and his son, and a few other faces she recognised, the mothers and fathers of the children who'd disappeared. Hubert sat near the back, the skin on his face sagging and creased as if the fat underneath had been dissolved away. Most of the others were strangers, come for entertainment.

The Chief Magistrate made his entrance into the Assembly Hall after Ellen reached her supplicant's podium. Vlakas, the one who'd deposed Tollin, a swollen cockerel of a man. He stood in front of the Speaker's seat, called the Assembly to order and waved a document in the air as if he'd just pulled it from a pile of shit.

'We are gathered to consider a petition by Ellen Dust. A woman known to you all, I believe.' Someone in the gallery stage-whispered "We all know the witch of Silver Street," and a ripple of laughter rolled around the hall. Vlakas smiled and nodded as if in agreement. 'She alleges that we are taking insufficient care in the face of certain events. To wit, that we have taken no steps to prevent our children from disappearing.' Pause. 'That we have failed to investigate the lack of ships bringing goods.' Pause. 'That we have taken no steps to protect ourselves from the incursions of monstrous beasts from across the river.' Longer pause. 'And that we are allowing the river itself to threaten our city.' He shook his head as if in disbelief. 'Mistress Dust, what grounds do you have for making such censorious claims against the City Assembly, against these men who spend their lives caring for the citizens of Haefen as if they were their own children? Why do you promulgate such calumnies?'

Half the gallery wouldn't understand what he meant, but

she had to admire him. Straight on to the attack with no chance for her to make her own arguments.

'I said nothing against the members assembled here.' Be respectful, Tollin had counselled. You need all the goodwill you can garner. 'I only request that you recognise the threats to our city and take action to prevent worse.'

One of the members levered himself to his feet. She recognised him from the past; he'd been a pretty-boy with too much of his father's fortune, and she'd deflated his pride more than once. Funny how the handsome ones always turned to fat; now he looked like a prize hog, fattened for the spit.

'I know you, mistress,' he said. 'A vicious renegade from the streets, where you belong. Not in this august place for honest citizens. You try to fill our heads with impious thoughts of creatures and inundations and stolen children. Let me be clear, Ellen Dust; if there is any danger in our city, then it comes from you. Your words are deceitful. Your words are vengeful. Your words are poison. And you are no more than a vicious slut.' He held up his hand to silence the murmuring from the gallery, then chopped it down like an axe. 'Ellen Dust, I denounce you.'

The murmuring turned to gasps; a denunciation. Unexpected, but not in a good way. She must be losing her touch, to let them waylay her like this. If they found her guilty, there was no limit to the penalty they could impose, and while screams didn't bother her, it would be a different matter if they were hers. The execution square near the Shambles never quite lost the odour of burning female flesh.

A muttering started up in the gallery again, and she couldn't decide if they were for or against her.

'We have a denunciation,' cried Vlakas. 'How does the Assembly find in this matter?'

One by one, some more slowly than others, the members

stood, stretched out their right arms and then let them drop to point at the ground. Ellen looked around the chamber; not one had pointed up towards the roof in her favour. They'd turned her petition into a trial and she had walked into a trap of her own making.

'Mistress Dust, the decision of the Assembly is unanimous,' said Vlakas, looking as though he'd just found a purse stuffed with gold. 'They have denounced you as an enemy of the city of Haefen. No domain allows enemies within its bounds, and the sentence specified for denunciation is death.' His voice dropped; he'd always had a taste for drama. 'But we are humane men, and out of respect for your protector Tollin, you may choose exile. I grant you seven days to decide. If found in our city after that time, you will be taken and executed in the prescribed manner for women of your sort. You will be put to fire at the stake. Do you understand?'

They were smiling now, those smug men in their robes with their fat wives at home. No matter. She should have done this years ago; leave Haefen.

A BEAUTIFUL KNIFE

Annegret took her hand and squeezed it gently. 'It's my fault. I suggested going to the Assembly but I should have realised how much they hate you. Gods know, they waited a long time for this revenge.'

They were back in her home the morning after the Assembly, sitting close to each other at her table. 'Maybe it's for the best,' said Ellen. 'We both know I've never really belonged here. Of course, if you fancy a break from Will…'

Annegret smiled, and shook her head sadly. 'What, two street rats together against the world, just like the old days? I don't think so, my friend, I'm sorry. We had each other's backs more than a few times when we were young, but that was then. You're right, though; if you're leaving Haefen you should choose yourself a companion, even if it's a man.'

'Don't worry, I'll travel faster on my own. There must be towns or villages beyond the forest, and just because no-one's travelled there doesn't mean they don't exist. Perhaps I'll find someone who can explain all this shit.'

'You can't be serious. Those beasts come from the forest.

Wolves or monsters, you don't want to face them on your own.'

'The forest doesn't go on forever. As for wolves, I'll take my chance. My time here's over and I can't sit back and wait till the water's around my waist.' She stood and brushed down her skirt. 'You've been a good friend, Annegret. Look after your man, don't pay more than seems right to you no matter how warm the bed. And think of me.'

THEY'D HAD their disagreements before, but nothing like this. After she gave Tollin the news about her exile, they'd argued into the night, and when they declared a truce for food, she found the plate in the kitchen knocked aside and that day's supper disappeared.

Now, back from seeing Annegret, the tension in the house was still palpable. She rehearsed with Tollin the case she'd made to Annegret. There was no point in travelling to Lannick to look at ruins, and no-one ever found enlightenment by keeping their head down and ignoring what was happening. Someone had to leave Haefen to look for answers. Now the Assembly had made the decision straightforward; that someone would be her.

It wasn't simple to counter Tollin's arguments. They were the rational ones she would have made if the tables were turned. 'Let me go back to Vlakas,' he said. 'He's a pompous bastard, but he'll listen to me. I'll ask for commutation of your sentence; if you apologise in public to the Assembly and stop talking about threats to Haefen, he might persuade the others to let you stay. A day in the stocks might injure your pride, but not much else.'

'Can you hear yourself, old man? I'm better off accepting exile. I love you for giving me a home when no-one else cared and I'll be sorry to leave you, but there's no other way.'

'You're a strange woman, Ellen, not like the rest of us. But I'm begging you; let me speak to Vlakas.'

'If I do nothing, the day will come when you find yourself staring into the eyes of one of Rafe's creatures, and no-one will be left to help. I love you too much, old man, to see that happen.'

Tollin finally gave in. 'But if you don't want to get yourself kidnapped or killed, you have to be prepared. Something happened to those children and you'll need to defend yourself.'

She sometimes wondered what he saw when he looked at her. Men found her attractive, always had. Long hair; someone once told her it was the colour of a raven's wing, but it just seemed black to her. Ice-blue eyes, true, and pleasant enough features. But even Tollin had no idea how many she'd fought off ever since she was twelve years old. Men who thought they could take what they wanted, and went home carrying less than they started with.

She'd never seen herself as brave, but people taking what didn't belong to them never sat well. Especially when it belonged to her. Especially when it *was* her. And right now, something or someone was taking their children and, little by little, field by field, taking their city.

Tollin returned from his bedchamber with an object wrapped in scarlet silk, unwrapped the package and handed her a dagger in an ornate leather scabbard. 'Belonged to your father. Years ago, before you were born, one of the sailors fell between his ship and the side of the dock. Couldn't swim, like most of them. Your father jumped in even though the brig was swinging back, and pulled the fool to safety. Another few moments and it would have crushed them both to death. The sailor gave him this by way of thanks.'

She took the scabbard from him. Black with silver around the top and the base, and heavier than she expected. She drew out the dagger by its handle, topped by a circular silver pommel with a ruby set in the centre. The cross guard was engraved on each side with words written in an unfamiliar script.

'This is beautiful.'

'It's deadly. Keeps an edge like nothing I've come across before or since. I took it to the blacksmith, he'd never touched steel like it.'

'This is yours, my father gave it to you.'

'Ellen, you might think me an ancient fool, but I know a little of your life before I found you. This won't be the first knife you've used in anger, and I'll feel happier knowing you have something to defend yourself.'

He was right. And though she was better fed now than the old days on the streets, she wasn't as fit. Lost the ability to see hidden dangers, the edge that had kept her alive. And so for the little time she had left she ran, late in the evening or early morning when no-one was about, getting used to the feel of the woollen leggings she'd made to wear under her skirts. She practiced with the dagger; the weight was perfect for throwing and it sliced through a side of mutton as if it was warm butter. Her muscles might be older, but they still remembered.

The days were drawing in as autumn threatened to give way to an early winter. Tollin's fears had redoubled.

'Why go now and add to the danger? I'll ask Vlakas to delay sentence a few more months until spring. The roads will be easier then.'

'He'll say no, and I don't want to give him that satisfaction.' She'd wasted too much time already, even though she shared his worries and had no illusions. Rain and snow would be the least of her problems once she left Haefen.

CHAPTER 2

Exile

WOLF AND BABIES

A squall of rain hit the window like an attack as Ellen looked down onto the street below. The stream of people had thinned as evening approached, leaving the flarelit cobbles glistening. Further up, towards the river, the entrances to alleyways were black holes; there was no money to light the damp, gimcrack tenements that she knew only too well.

'I still say it's madness.'

It was hard to hear the defeat in the old man's words. She turned to face him, smiling to soften what was about to happen, but he wasn't looking at her.

'This won't be like a summer picnic,' he said. 'You get across the water and into the forest, and that won't be the end of it. Even if you're not taken to become some creature's supper, you'll be on the road for months and in search of who knows what?' He sighed and shook his head. 'Your father was an impetuous fool and you're his daughter. I tell you girl, if I were younger…' The words disintegrated into a hawking cough which he tried to stifle with a blood-specked rag.

'But you're not younger,' she said, 'and I'm not a girl. I have more than thirty years behind me and you of all people should know, I'm not exactly standard issue.'

'That you're not.' He brushed imaginary dust from the cover of the pocketbook in front of him, where he spent his days recording the journal of his life. An old man's hobby. 'Doesn't seem right, a girl like you trying to…' His voice faded to silence.

'Trying to do what?'

'Trying to save us, and I don't know what from. Why you, Ellen?'

She took his hand in hers, velvet on parchment. Over the past few weeks, she'd noticed his skin becoming ever more translucent. It reminded her of a chrysalis nearing term, so thin and frail that it seemed any touch might slough it away.

'This is my responsibility, Tollin. My duty. Did you ever turn away when people relied on you? And would you rather watch me burn if I stay?' She turned back to the window so as not to see him wipe his eyes.

'When will you leave?' he asked. It was hard to hear him like this, speaking with the plaintiveness of an old man, seeing yet another loss creep up on him.

'Tomorrow. Any longer and they'll have me tied to the stake. The year's late enough as it is, but at least I'll be heading south.'

Her body might be in Haefen, but her spirit was already on the road. More children, and older, had disappeared, and Rafe wasn't the only one who'd seen strange creatures prowling the edge of the city at night. Whatever waited for her on the road, she couldn't stay any longer in a home which was anything but.

. . .

THIS FELT LIKE A LAST GOODBYE. By the time she returned, if that ever happened, Tollin would be long gone. She would never see him, hear him, hold him again. The next morning she made one final check that the dagger was in her pack and, with one last, heart-wrenching hug, she was gone.

She hurried away from the house along the empty street. Never look back was part of her creed, regrets led nowhere, but at the entrance to one of the alleyways she turned to see Tollin at the window with one hand pressed against the glass. She waved, turned and slipped into the alley. All Tollin would have seen was her shadow as it merged with the darkness.

She'd set off before the sun, wanting to get away without attracting attention. She kept to alleys and back streets until, where the houses thinned and the streets became dirt, the fields began. Beyond the fields ran the river that circled the village like a moat. The forests that rose from the opposite bank stretched for miles until they met high, distant moors that turned purple in autumn and white in winter. To people in the city, it was a bleak wilderness full of dangers to frighten children. Who would want to go there?

She left the silent streets behind and made her way to a field that led down to where the river was at its narrowest. Easier to cross, if the fates were on her side. This field had been planted once, but now it was covered with stands of copper bracken that reached above her head, blocking her view. An undergrowth of brambles covering the ground seemed to grab at her feet, as if trying to hold her back. The ground was clearer near the hedge line, but eventually she had to strike out, almost swimming through the bracken towards the sound of running water. With the steepness of the slope and the fronds of vegetation blocking her view it wasn't until she was a few yards away that she saw the remains of a bridge rising from the bank opposite, nothing more than a few stone steps that climbed and stopped at emptiness, hanging almost impossibly in the air. The stone was dark with age and mottled with blotches of orange lichen. The broken edges of the stone dripped with moss where the original span across the water had collapsed, but if there had ever been a twin on this side, the river had long since carried it away.

Now to find a good place to cross. The river was at least a hundred paces wide and the blue-grey water eddied with whorls that spiralled in and stretched back with hidden currents, foaming and dancing around the rocks that reached up from the surface. This was impossible. She looked along the river in both directions for somewhere that might be easier, and noticed tracks along the bank, heading upstream. Paw prints in the mud, large paw prints, and not from any dog. Still, this could be her best option. She followed the track until it curved towards the water and disappeared. Wolves with wings? But as she looked more closely, she made out the shadow of a wide path under the surface, nothing more than a change in the water's texture where it was choppier, running shallow over stones. This had been a ford once, the way out. Perhaps it still was.

She stood by the edge of the water for a moment, aware that her heart was beating faster than it should. The trees were little more than tall shadows on the other bank, while back towards the village, the sky was already lightening; people would be out of their beds soon and moving about the streets. She had a home there, a comfortable room, company. A few friends. And a stake near the Shambles with her name on it.

It was time. She turned back towards the river, away from home. There was no point in waiting any longer. She unlaced her boots, tied them together and strung them round her neck, then stepped out into the water. How could something that wasn't ice be this cold? The stones underfoot were slippery and she almost fell at her first step, but she steadied herself against the current that sucked at her feet and calves as she picked her way across.

A mottled layer of ash, oak and birch leaved covered the opposite bank, sloping up towards the borderline of skeletal trees. Not far behind them, the deep green of the permaforest stretched away into the distance. Ellen dried her feet as best she could, laced up her boots and looked back across the river, beyond the fields and on to the distant roofscape of the city that was already retreating into mist. In all her life she hadn't been this far from the streets and alleys of home, from the sour odour of bodies and the crush of other souls. Now it was as if someone had hacked away a limb.

A faint track led up from the riverbank and into what looked at first like impenetrable undergrowth. She'd fought off wolves before, even if those had been human, but all the same she took the scabbard from her pack and strapped it to her belt.

After four hours following the faint trace of the path, Ellen realised that the forest was home to more than wild creatures. There were animal tracks for sure, some larger than she liked, but also the clear imprint of boots in the mud by the side of the path. Snagged on a thornbush, she found a fragment of cloth which had once been red but had faded to rainwash pink. There were other humans amongst these trees, and they wouldn't have come from Haefen.

While she walked, the only sounds were her own breathing and the unsteady beat of her footsteps, but gradually she became aware of a muffled keening, like something trying to hide its pain. And another sound, a low, wet growling that rose and fell, snuffling to silence, then rising again.

The sounds were coming from ahead of her, she was sure, in the direction of travel. Now would be a good time to have the dagger to hand. She crept forwards, worried that whatever was ahead would hear her heartbeats.

There was something else in the air now, not only the sounds but a familiar smell that reminded her of the Shambles at the edge of the town, where both animals and people were turned to meat. The sweet stench of fear, and the metal rust of blood. And without warning, in a small clearing ahead, she came upon a carnage scene. A young woman, little more than a girl, lay as limp as a rag doll at the edge of the trees. The woman's arms and legs jutted out at impossible angles, and her blood-soaked clothes were little more than shredded rags. On the ground next to her, something that used to be a man spasmed as if it was still alive while the animal astride him snuffled, burrowing into his guts to tear off another piece of his entrails. Rafe had exaggerated, but not by much. She'd never imagined a wolf could be this huge, nothing like the dogs that ranged around the town. Ellen watched the creature as if mesmerised, at the beauty of its sleek black fur rippling as it gulped down the warm flesh.

Don't move, she told herself. There was nothing to be done for these people, so she started to back away slowly, hoping the creature was so engrossed in its meal that it wouldn't hear. But what would prevent it from finding her later, perhaps while she was sleeping?

She stopped moving as the wolf paused, looked up to sniff the air, and turned to stare straight at her. They were, at most, thirty feet apart and the luminous amber eyed locked onto hers, holding her still for what seemed like an eternity. She felt no fear now, no excitement, only peace. And then, in one flowing motion, the wolf covered the space between them and launched itself into the air. The spell broke and she had barely enough time to step sideways and out of its path. She braced herself to fend it off but felt its teeth sink deep into her left arm, below the shoulder. She'd twisted away far enough to prevent its full weight toppling her to the ground, and she was still standing as the creature landed, turned and lunged at her. There was no need to think about what to do next. Her muscled reacted as if they had rehearsed this a hundred times. She sidestepped again as if time had slowed, switched the dagger to her other hand and stabbed up into the base of the creature's throat. A shallow cut, but even so it fell to the ground with a bubbling scream, rolled over and tried to rake her with claws as long as her hand. She slashed again, more strongly this time, catching one of its forelegs.

One last snarl and the thing was gone, limping away along the path that had brought her there. She listened as it crashed through the undergrowth; the sounds growing fainter until the clearing was silent. Had she done enough to kill the animal or was it only wounded, waiting for a chance to finish what it started?

Time to take stock. No pain, not yet, but blood was seeping through her torn sleeve. She knew wounds; this was going to hurt, and hurt badly.

She'd been so intent on the creature and its victims that she hadn't noticed another figure, sat apart from the rest and propped against a tree at the opposite side of the clearing. The woman's legs stretched out with skirts rucked up towards her waist. Ellen ignored the wound in her arm, ran across and knelt beside the woman. She looked unmarked, but pain and exhaustion had twisted her face into a rictus of misery. Something moved on the ground between her legs, partly hidden by the skirt. Ellen pulled the material aside; a baby, barely more than a few days old. And something else, a pool of blood from a wound in the woman's side.

Blue veins pulsed beneath the translucent skin of the woman's face. Ellen had no experience of newborns but death was always present in the city and he was here now, sitting by the woman's side, waiting for his moment. One soul or two?

The woman reached out silently, and Ellen placed the child in her arms. The tiny creature squirmed as the woman stroked its head, kissed its hand, murmured softly and offered it back like a gift. She tried to speak, but the effort proved too much.

'I won't leave her here, I promise,' Ellen told her, not knowing what else to say.

The woman tried to smile, but then her body stiffened and relaxed, her eyed closed, and as she slumped back the baby in Ellen's arms twitched, kicked and gave a small, angry cry.

NIGHT IN THE FOREST

The baby squirmed in her arms. She had nothing for it to eat other than the bread and cheese in her pack, and a newborn couldn't survive on that. Her only choice was to turn back the way she'd come, cross the river, and hope the child lived until she could get it back to the city. She'd have to take her chances with Vlakas.

Her arm was throbbing where the wolf bit her. She used precious water to wash the wound, cut a strip of material from the hem of her skirt and wound it round her arm as a dressing. Time to leave. She packed everything away and picked up the baby, which looked at her with such trust that something in her guts twisted. And then it started to cry. No creature that small had a right to make such a sound.

As she made her way around the edge of the clearing, Ellen jiggled it up and down, the way she'd seen new mothers do with their infants, but the wailing continued. With all the commotion, she'd lost her bearings in the clearing, and there was no sign of the track that led home. The only path she could find climbed up into the forest, and the path that led her here had also been climbing. Her way back should be downhill, in the direction the wolf took as it slunk away.

Time to calm down and reassess. She was wounded and alone in a forest with a newborn baby, a damaged creature that was possibly waiting for its revenge in the undergrowth, and three dead bodies, one of them half-eaten. On the plus side, she was still alive.

Ellen looked over at the corpses, already attracting clouds of flies, and considered covering their bodies with fallen leaves and branches in a futile attempt at burial. That would be for her sake more than theirs and sentiment was for other people. Death was the end; no dreamless sleep, no awaking to a new life, no torments by sadistic gods. One moment warm and breathing, the next a soft sack of meat waiting to decompose. And if those bodies provided an easy meal for a hungry wolf, she might have more time to get away.

She looked at the remains again, dispassionately. She'd seen corpses before; some had even been of her own making, but the patterns on their clothes were unfamiliar and even through the pallor of death, she noticed that their skin was a different tone from people in her city, like honey from the red clover meadows. What brought them to this place? What caused a woman with a newborn baby to risk everything?

Her plan was to find a village or town within a few days. But these people had been trying to get away from something. Perhaps the very thing she was heading towards. It didn't matter; she had to move, and quickly. If the way back wasn't an option, and blundering through the dense undergrowth trying to find it would be a step too far, the only option was to go forward. If the child stopped its wailing and held on to life long enough, she might yet save them both.

. . .

The light was fading fast in an already dark forest, with the sky only just visible through the tops of the towering trees, but this was a sudden change and the temperature had dropped. She had no idea how far the forest stretched, but it seemed unlikely that she would get to the edge before nightfall. They needed somewhere safe to spend the night.

There was nothing for it but to strike out and hope. If she'd believed in the gods she would have said a small prayer, but she's always though that submission to a deity was very overrated and with no discernible benefits. *'How do you know that your god is the real one?'* she'd asked a priest in Haefen. *'That's the point,'* he'd explained as if she were stupid. *'You can't know, you have to believe.'* She preferred to believe in herself; more reliable and always around, even if she was given to the occasional bout of smiting when people got in her way.

Ten minutes after she left the clearing, a sudden flash of lightning turned the trees into silhouettes. Seconds later, a crash of thunder shook her body as the first raindrops negotiated their way through the canopy of leaves. The baby was lighter than she'd thought and she held it close, wrapped in its mother's shawl to keep it as dry as possible.

The path continued to climb. She hadn't noticed at first, but the ground alongside had changed, the vegetation giving way to stone until she found herself walking through a gully with walls of rock on each side. Tactically, she knew, this was both a good thing and a bad thing. On the one hand, she was protected on two sides, on the other she was trapped with only two ways to run. If there were more of these wolves and they hunted in pairs, her journey would be over before it had begun.

The twilight would soon turn into night. A little further along the gully, on her left, she noticed a darker patch about fifteen feet up the rock face. Some sort of opening with a narrow ledge; not quite a cave, but at least it would be protection if she could find a way up. Spending the night on the ground was asking to die.

The rock was rough; not worn away and smooth, but as if a giant hand had used a hammer and chisel to hack out the gully. With luck she would find enough handholds to help her climb out of reach of any animals. But not holding a baby. Ellen tucked her skirt into her belt and then said a quiet 'thank you' to Tollin for the coil of rope he insisted she pack. Old, but practical.

'Don't worry, little one, I'm not leaving you here for long.' The child had long since stopped crying, but her eyes were still open. Ellen tied one end of the rope around its swaddled body on the ground, knotted the other around her waist, and then began to climb. Even though the opening wasn't far above, after ten minutes on the damp rock face she was only halfway there. Her injured arm was burning, and she learned not to put any weight on it. More than once she hung by her fingertips, kicking around for a toehold. Despite the cold, her back and face were damp with sweat. Rivulets ran into her eyed as she focussed on the way up, and not back down at the bundle on the ground.

At last she pulled herself up onto the ledge and rested for a few moments to catch her breath. The opening into the rock was perhaps three yards deep. Not high, but enough for her to sit or crouch or sleep. Now to retrieve the child without smashing it into the rock face. She'd done what she could to cushion its tiny body and pulled in the rope, inching the bundle up so that it didn't gain momentum and swing about. At last it was at the top; she reached over the ledge and pulled the child into the safety of the small cave.

She had no fuel for a fire, even if she was prepared to take the risk, but at least they were out of the wind and rain, and safe from attack. The darkness was almost complete now. If not a fire, then perhaps a little light would be permissible. She rummaged around in her pack for a candle and Tollin's other leaving gift, a fire kit with a flint and some gauze to use as kindling, enough to help her light the candle. Her shadow swooped across the walls as she examined their shelter for the night, but apart from a few bird droppings there was no sign that anything else would share the space with them that night.

Ellen drew back the shawl from the child's face and touched its cheek. The skin was warm and the eyelids fluttered, but still no crying. Not a good sign. Even she knew babies cried, one of their purposes in life. The little soul had to be be hungry and thirsty so she moistened her finger with water, something for it to suckle. It would be merciful to press the shawl back over its nose and mouth and help it out of the world, but the day had been harder than she ever imagined and taking the baby's life would be a kindness too far. The poor creature deserved one more chance, and she'd seen enough of death that day.

A BROKEN PROMISE

She woke to a pale, grey light, still wrapped around the baby to keep her warm. But this time the child's eyes stayed closed and her face was cold, and Ellen knew she was alone again.

The rain had stopped. The air was warmer but outside the entrance of the shelter every feature, even the other side of the gully, was hidden in the mist as if a cloud had sunk to earth. Ellen breakfasted on bread and cheese with a little water. There was enough left for a couple of days, but she'd need to find more. It was easy to be confident back in Haefen, telling Tollin how quickly she would find another settlement. But although her home was less than twenty-four hours away, it might as well be somewhere beyond the stars.

As far as she could tell, she'd been following the right path out of the forest. There hadn't been a choice. Now she had another decision to make. She could leave the body of the baby there and hope no animals would find it, but a promise was a promise and she wasn't ready to let go, not yet. So it was time to reverse the climb of the day before, lowering the child's body first and then scrambling down herself. She was nearly at the bottom when her foot slipped and she fell the last few feet, just missing the small body and landing on her injured arm.

She sat up slowly and checked herself. Nothing broken, although the wound had started to seep blood again. A lucky escape this time. The child would be a burden and she looked around to see if there was anywhere she could bury the corpse safely. She was surrounded by rock, and she considered collecting stones to build a burial cairn but couldn't see anything small enough to lift easily. She would have a companion for a little longer.

The path through the gully was just visible, although she couldn't see more than a few yards ahead. Not that it mattered, there was only one way to go. She strapped the child's body to her pack and started to walk. Even though she'd tied back her hair, it was growing heavy with moisture from the air. Walking through the mist was more like swimming through a cloud, and she shivered as her clothes become saturated. No matter, she told herself, I'll be warm enough once I find my stride.

The path rose more and more steeply and, without warning, she was out of the mist and into clear air, with blue sky above. The forest stretched behind her and she found herself standing on the edge of a high moor.

Yesterday's storm had circled round and was waiting on the horizon. Ellen stopped for a moment and looked across the moorland at the massing clouds, purple in the late morning light. And at something else shimmering in the far distance. It might be her imagination, or hope was playing tricks with her eyes, but it looked like buildings glinting in the sun.

After an hour, always climbing, the path met a larger track with rain-filled potholes and ruts that looked as though generations of carts had carved them. She hitched up her skirt; the hem was heavy with mud, ragged and torn.

Her back ached. She wasn't used to carrying such a weight for so long, and she shifted the pack from one shoulder to the other. It was no better, her muscles were complaining and the skin was sore where the straps cut in, but this felt even worse and she moved it back. Her arm would need looking at again, and soon; please the gods, the wound wasn't rotting.

Everywhere she looked, large stones studded the landscape, rising from carpets of heather. Some stood like giant grave markers, higher than a tall man, others had tumbled on their sides. Hours had passed since she started out that morning and she felt faint, whether it was from hunger or the effect of the bite. She started counting her steps as if it made a difference, and after five hundred paces along the track, she noticed a flat stone not too far away. Somewhere to sit and rest, to allow herself something to eat and drink.

She shouldn't be this tired. It was as if the animal bite had drawn all her energy, leaching it away from her legs. Ellen turned off the track and picked a way through the heather, but while she was only a couple of yards from the flat stone she stepped onto a stretch of brighter green and sank up to her calves. Stupid, stupid. She set the pack with its small body onto firm ground and tried to lift one of her legs, but the more she moved, the more the bog sucked her down. She stopped struggling and took deep breaths to calm her heart. Her entire body was tilted to the side where one leg had been pulled lower than the other, but at least her arms were still free. As slowly as possible, she twisted around to the firm ground that was just within reach to one side. She stretched, reaching out to her limit, then managed to grasp the base of a gorse bush and pull herself out, hoping that the plant's roots would hold. Little by little her legs came free, and then with a final sucking sound the bog gave up the fight and she was lying on the ground, stinking of rotting vegetation. On the road for less than two days, and already she'd come close to death twice. She was, without doubt, out of practice.

Ellen waited until her breathing slowed, then skirted the bog and headed for the fallen rock where she swung her pack to the ground. Surely it was heavier, and not just from the body and the rain and mist that had soaked it through. Perhaps, she thought, some unknown presence had been walking behind her, slipping in rocks to weigh her down.

Her left arm was throbbing in time with her heartbeat. She shrugged off her cloak and jacket, unwound the rough dressing and sniffed at the rag. The musty smell of blood, but also what she'd feared, the sweet perfume of decay. She probed the edged of the gash, ragged where the animal's teeth had ripped and torn at her flesh, and wiped away the greenish pus seeping from the wound. Only yesterday, but already the attack might as well have happened in another life.

She needed to clean the bite and got to her feet, wary of the dizziness returning. Last time she'd used material from her skirt for a dressing, but it was stained and covered with mud. The baby's shawl would do, the poor soul had no need of warmth now. She tore a strip to make a new bandage and wrapped it around the wound. At home she would have used a honey paste to help with healing, but this was a wilderness and home was somewhere else.

AFTER FOOD and a few more hours the light began to fail, and Ellen realised that she'd been veering from side to side on the track, stumbling even when there were no potholes. The purple clouds from the horizon were billowing towards her like an aerial army, and the distant thunder was a constant vibration throughout her body rather than just a sound. If the storm caught her here, the only respite would be in the lee of one of the larger standing stones.

There had to be a way down from the moor, and soon, before the light disappeared and the storm hit. The distant shimmer of buildings that she'd seen would take hours to reach, always assuming they were real. If she could drop low enough and back to the tree line, perhaps she would find an outbuilding that was open and unguarded. She'd noticed a few piles of fresh sheep droppings dotted about on the heather. Where there were sheep, perhaps there would be a shepherd, or maybe a bothy where she could take cover.

While she was weighing up the relative dangers of staying on the moor overnight, or finding a shelter, she came to a split in the track. Just one problem, there was no way to tell which was the right one to take. Perhaps it didn't matter, she thought, perhaps both tracks led to the same place.

But first there was one task she couldn't put off any longer. She should have done this yesterday, back in the clearing, so what had stopped her? Emotion? Distaste? Or just that she didn't like breaking a trust?

She looked around. Fifty paces off the track a patch of brighter green was too welcoming to be safe, but perfect for what she needed. She chose her way across, testing each footstep to ensure solid ground. At the edge of the green patch - she'd guessed right, an area of bog - she lay down the pack, untied the body and unwrapped the shawl. The corpse seemed to have shrunk, with grey, wizened skin.

She reached down and traced the line of the tiny lips. Hardly drawn a breath, never would again. Perhaps she should feel upset, maybe even shed a tear or two, but after all this was just another death out of so many. Of all the possible futures for the child, this was the one it drew.

And now she would have to break her promise at last and

leave the child behind. She collected a few stones and placed them next to the body on its shawl, wished that she could remember some prayers, just in case, then wrapped the bundle and threw it as gently as she could out into the bog. For a moment it floated and her heartbeat quickened, and then the bundle tilted and sank below the surface.

WAKING DREAMS

Ellen picked her way back to the main track and considered the two paths forking off in different directions. Left or right? Go wrong and she'd have to leave the track and strike out across the featureless moor. Not an attractive prospect.

She knew people who would wager on anything. Flies crawling up a window, leaves falling from a tree. Sinking a yard of ale the fastest. Wife tossing. But those were all a fool's way of losing money and life was hard enough without throwing it away. Now she had no choice but to take a gamble, with more at stake than the loss of half a week's housekeeping. The clouds rolling in from the horizon were a bruise spreading across the sky. Time, she thought, is a luxury I don't have.

The fork stood on top of a slight rise but the right-hand path seemed to veer away from where she'd seen the buildings in the distance. Left it was.

The pain in her arm was worse. She pulled back her sleeve; below the bite, the skin was swollen and mottled with red and white blotches. The light was fading fast now; she would never reach shelter before the storm arrived. It was a three-way race between her, the thunder and nightfall, and she was in last place. But losing wasn't an option; in the dark she could easily miss the path and end up in another patch of marshland, sinking out of sight like the child's corpse. She walked faster, wondering what happened to the bones of creatures that were sucked down into the bogs. Did they disintegrate, or collect somewhere beneath the surface in a dark wet catacomb? Did they float back to the surface when the flesh had rotted away? Or did the bodies stare sightlessly at the sky, preserved for centuries?

She'd often considered how she wanted her life to end. Not like some she'd seen with the bloody flux, a long, slow sickness, painful and without dignity. Better to go in the twinkling of an eye, an accident. One minute laughing, the next in the ground. The details didn't matter as long as it was fast and she didn't see it coming; she'd knew that the fear of death was worse than dying. Death was sometimes kind, and she'd known people greet him with relief. But not her, not today.

After an hour, she was forced to stop. The dizziness was worse, and twice she'd stumbled and nearly fallen. A night on the moors in a storm with a broken ankle, not part of her plan. But she needed to rest. The path had been losing height but the fallen monoliths still surrounded her. One of them had toppled onto another, forming the semblance of a shelter, and she propped herself against the upright. The temptation to lie down and sleep was overwhelming; she forced down a little water and stretched out on the heather, just for a moment or two.

SHE WOKE to find herself soaked through and lying in a small pool of water. The storm had come and gone while she slept, and by the position of the sun it was the next morning. Ellen forced herself to sit, shivering even though it was warmer than normal for the time of year. Sharp pains stabbed down her injured arm; the swelling was so bad now it was impossible that the skin hadn't burst, and angry red veins had spread from the marks of the animal's fangs.

There was no point in blaming herself. Falling asleep had been stupid, but self-pity solved nothing. She managed to stand and waited until the tremors in her legs subsided, then made her way back to the path and carried on towards the place where the buildings had glimmered the day before. Unless they'd been an illusion which, given the way she was feeling, seemed all too possible.

After a while, she noticed Tollin walking beside her. She talked to him, chattering about everything that had happened as if it were just another morning at the market. The next time she looked, he'd turned into the mother from the clearing, holding her dead baby. So what if they were only in her mind; if she could imagine them, didn't that make them real? And now the promised sheep had appeared, dotted about the moor like small bales of cotton on legs.

Tollin returned, but he looked different this time; younger and taller. He seemed concerned, but when he spoke his voice sounded far away. He reached to take her arm but she shrugged him off. Have to keep focus, she told herself, don't give in to the phantoms. The man took hold of her arm again and caught her as she collapsed to the ground. Was she imagining touch now? The last thing she remembered was being lifted over his shoulder, thinking how strong his arms were for an illusion, and that Tollin had never smelt of sheep.

CHAPTER 3

Espionage

HANDLES AND MANIFOLDS

~~~

I used to love this walk in the morning. Along the street from my apartment, through the park to the lake, across the bridge and onto the campus of Mittani University. The day after the break-in (not that I knew about it yet) I stood on the bridge for a moment; its wooden boards were a deliberate anachronism, like an echo of an imagined past. The University was in front of me but I turned and looked back at the city; I liked to imagine the buildings of downtown as shards of crystal and steel reaching up to pierce the sky. There's nothing to say scientists can't be poets too.

The city wasn't perfect, and the government had no answer to the beggars' camps outside the downtown offices, but there wasn't anywhere on the three continents to match Mittani. Not for her towers, not for the smell of cinnamon from bakery stalls in the morning rush, not for her sheer beauty. Who would be anywhere else?

I've always preferred to live alone, although in a city you're never more than a few metres from the nearest person. Or is that rats? And I never needed to wake up alone if I didn't want to. Female, single, attractive enough and not too eccentric; there would always be someone. Clever too, although for most men that falls on the debit side of the balance sheet. But people are so difficult. One night of fun and they think they own you; or worse, that you own them. Neither option has ever appealed. Equations, on the other hand; you know where you are with numbers. Never needy, and always obey the rules.

Shalmar Eser took a different view, of course. Ever since the day we graduated together, fifteen years ago, he'd tried to recruit me either to his corporation or to his life. He couldn't understand why anyone would choose a life of research over one turning technology into money. And he'd done that well enough. Of all those towers of crystal, the tallest was owned by Eser Corporation. Unquestionably beautiful; from where I stood it seemed far too slender, balanced on its point like a needle glinting in the sun.

Exactly a week before the day after the break-in, on the day the building was commissioned (I like to be precise when it comes to time), I turned up at Shalmar's party.

'Exclusive, darling, very,' he'd told me. *'People have already ransomed their mothers to be here.'* I've never been tempted by exclusivity, but Shalmar Eser events were hard to resist and there would be an announcement, a new product to dazzle the investors and bewitch the crowds who always queued for days and nights to be the first to immerse themselves in the latest Veeyar.

Usually, hints and rumours leaked out. Some were deliberate, part of Shalmar's strategy to parlay up the share price and go viral. Some were a mixture of fantasy and hope. This time, though, there had been an uncharacteristic silence. I remember thinking through the possibilities, guessing which direction Shalmar would take now. An impossible task. All you could rely on Shal to do was the unexpected, and I had given up speculating. But he was a friend, of sorts, and so I decided to be there for the reveal and join the acclamations and applause to build his ego even higher. I know I shouldn't be, but I'm still surprised by the way men need constant praise and reassurance to prove to themselves that they're the best. Alpha plus. Hormonal creatures, men, and Shal's switch was permanently set to 'on'. Must have been exhausting.

BUT I WAS WRONG, there was no announcement. Just a toast when we raised our glasses to the new headquarters and some disappointed mutterings in the crowd.

A little before the party broke up, I stood outside on the viewing platform, looking across the cityscape to the far plains of Shukanni. Shalmar joined me with a bottle from his private cellar; I recognised the label.

'What do you think?' he asked.

'The wine or the building? Very impressive, both of them. But I expected you to boast of your latest way to prise money from hard-working people who should know better.'

'You're a cynic, Ash. Always were. I give people what they want and I make them happy. What's so wrong with that?'

'You're a clever man, Shal. Not a genius like me, but not bad. You could have advanced the frontiers of knowledge, and instead you exploit others.'

'I've advanced a few frontiers in my time, and I'm not finished yet. And if you're the genius, how come I own three houses and a yacht and you live in an apartment block just off campus?'

'Integrity?'

Shalmar filled our glasses. 'There is no such thing. And don't forget, my offer of a job still stands.' He waved his arm to encompass the city. 'All this could be yours.'

'In exchange for my soul? I think I'll pass.'

THAT WAS THEN. On this day, standing on the bridge by the ornamental lake, a man brushed by me so closely that for a moment I worried I might topple over the railing onto the patches of waterlilies. I thought he was about to apologise, but he cracked the slightest of smiles and then hurried on.

I sensed something familiar about him, a small tug on a skein of memory. Not a colleague, too well dressed for an academic. A neighbour, perhaps? To be honest, I have no idea what most of the people in my block look like. I checked my purse out of reflex but nothing was missing, likewise the pockets on my jacket. A prick in a hurry, nothing new there.

But the encounter had unsettled me, on this of all days. Now I was the one in a hurry. After years of work, today my postgrad and I were finalising the stress-tests of the theory Danu was already calling the Ashira Field. I hadn't complained. Knowing Danu, she would have been there for a couple of hours already, with her carefully crafted, just-tumbled-out-of-bed look that sent men into a state of hormonal overdrive. And women. I'd already turned down a not-very-subtle invitation from Danu for a night together, but I had been tempted. Boundaries existed for other people and in a choice between Shalmar Eser and Danu Khepa it would be no contest.

IT WAS TOO EARLY for students, except for a gaggle of Niyan girls who giggled past me. I recognised a couple from my course on Quantum Teleology; sat together, never asked questions but always achieved firsts in their essays. Work ethic - not so much of that in the Mittanese students but for

Niyans and Shukkanians, being here was something their parents never dreamed of.

As I got closer to my building, I saw something happening. Four security guards with guns, checking everyone's IDs.

'What's going on?' I asked.

'Break-in last night, the guard was killed. Sorry Professor, can't tell you any more than that.'

I tried to remember who'd been on duty the day before. I knew most of them to have a joke with, but I'd left before the night shift came on. I picked up a coffee from the cafe on the ground floor and took the stairs to my laboratory. There it was again, the small thrill whenever I saw the name on my door; Professor Ashira uit Banipol, Head of Experimental Teleology. Perhaps not a meteoric career, but at twenty-nine I was still the youngest professor in the University, with a salary of five hundred marks a month. Not much compared with what Shalmar would pay me, but I got to sleep at night, and being the boss had its perks.

I found Danu in the lab, hunched over a terminal screen. Green hair again, that was two days in a row, and shaved even shorter on one side. Leather jacket over a purple sequinned top, and humming along with some music on her headband.

She looked up and smiled, her lipstick matching her hair. 'Mornin' boss. Wanted to go through the handle decompositions of the manifolds. We worked them through a hundred times, but I wanted to check again, to be sure.'

'You're worse than me. The equations stack up and I already wrote most of the paper. We run with everything as it is, the way we planned. If there are still no unexpected anomalies, we're good to go.' My coffee was thick, black and bitter, the way I liked it. The on-campus franchises never let us down.

'Did you see the guards?' I asked. 'They said a guard was killed last night.'

Danu straightened up, her smile gone. 'Must have happened soon after I left. It was Tudhal, nice guy. His wife just had their third, a girl.'

'Why would someone do that?'

'A break-in, but no-one's reported anything missing. Our lab was still locked and I couldn't see anything wrong.'

'What about CCTV?'

Danu laughed. 'Are you serious? The cameras haven't worked for months. I think the bastard who broke in panicked when they killed the guard. Looks like Tudhal was attacked when he went to the main door and then fell and hit his head.'

Industrial espionage, that was my guess. Half the corporations in Mittani made their money exploiting research that came out of the University. It was one reason I kept my work secret until the day I was ready to publish and stake my claim. The Dean didn't like it; '*You can tell me, Ashira,*' but she had a suspiciously sumptuous house.

Do you understand how universities work? Forget any notions of ivory towers filled with gentle souls seeking the truth. If it wasn't a corporation trying to steal my ideas, it would be another academic trying to freeload. And this latest piece of work was a game changer, I'd known that from the start. My name would be remembered for generations, funding would never be a problem again and Shalmar would bow down before me. I might spend the night with Danu, just to say thank you. Might even be fun.

THE MARKDOWN

All in all, it had been a good day. There were no surprises as we ran through the work one last time; now all I had to do was complete the paper.

I'd talked it through with Danu. What I would have done without that woman I can't imagine, and we both agreed that my best option was to read the paper in person at the next meeting of the National Metaphysics Society, to prevent any details being leaked beforehand. Publication could come afterwards; journals would beg to have it.

Once the minor hurdle of peer review had been cleared - and I had no doubt it would be - I'd apply for funding for the experimental phase of the project. If you're not a mathematician, you won't understand how elegant and beautiful equations can be. But seeing them translated into something concrete that affects the real world is sublime.

Danu had left early for an evening of rock climbing on the limestone gorge outside the city, and I wasn't ready to go home. In a few short weeks all the secrecy would end, all would be revealed to the world, and once that happened my privacy would be gone. So what to do with one of the few nights left when I still had some chance of anonymity?

Just off campus is Old Market Street. No shops or stalls these days, just half a mile of bars and clubs and street food. Whatever your predilection, it can be satisfied somewhere on Old Market Street; I'd pushed my own limits a few times. But I wasn't in the mood for exotic, just a few drinks and maybe someone to take home for an hour or so. I felt that I'd earned it.

The Markdown, that would do. Too expensive to be fashionable with the students, too bohemian for the faculty. Perfect. The cocktails were exquisite, and I was in the mood for something punchy to get me where I wanted to be, and quickly.

The bar was still relatively quiet when I walked in. The main crowd wouldn't arrive for another couple of hours, and I intended to be long gone by then. The lighting was a subdued indigo that night, smoothing out features on faces. Not that I needed that sort of help. I took a stool by the bar and ordered a jug of Mule Kick. A Markdown special and mouth-puckeringly bitter. It would do the job perfectly.

A man further down the bar caught my eye. He'd walked in a little after me and looked barely out of his teens. Always hard to tell with Niyans, though; the white-blonde hair and beard were the giveaway. He raised an eyebrow in the usual question, but I shook my head to show that I wasn't interested and he turned back to his drink. Not that I mind them young, but I like a choice.

Someone had slid onto the stool next to me while my attention was elsewhere. 'Seems like you're set up for the evening.' He looked, and smelt, like a salesman who'd spent too much time on the road that day and not taken the opportunity to freshen up.

'I'm sorry?'

'The jug. I like a woman who doesn't stint herself.'

'Thanks, but no thanks.'

'You waiting for someone then?'

'No. Maybe.'

'You're into women? I don't mind, you can bring her along.'

What is it about the word 'no' that men don't understand? But perhaps it was a salesman's reflex, talking even when the door had been slammed in his face. I try to be charitable sometimes, believe it or not. I took the jug and my glass and walked over to the first man whose face said that it wasn't only his ship coming in, but the whole fleet plus auxiliaries.

'Hi, I didn't think…' The accent, definitely Niyan.

'That's ok,' I said. 'Sometimes thinking is very much overrated.'

His drink looked like house wine, so I slid his glass down the bar, called for a fresh one and poured from the jug. I like sharing.

'Drink up boy,' I said, 'you've got some work ahead of you tonight.'

THERE IS something to be said for younger men. They're energetic and grateful, which are both qualities I value in a lover. We began in the elevator to my sixth-floor apartment, an amuse-bouche, before we settled down to the meal. First course in the living room, taking in both the sofa and the rug by the glass door to the balcony. Main course in the unused kitchen and dessert was food on the go, finishing up in the bedroom.

When we came to a natural break, I propped myself on my elbows and looked at him as he tried to catch his breath. I had considered the possibility of keeping him around a little longer for a late-night snack, but he was already giving me the puppy dog eyes. Time to close out.

As I climbed from the bed and began to get dressed, he said 'my name's Mack' and, rather incongruously, offered me his hand to shake.

'Thanks for sharing, Mack, but I hadn't asked.'

Names are like hooks, I try to keep away from them when I can, especially with men.

He started to speak again. 'Wanted to say that I had a great time, thanks.'

As if I'd done him some sort of favour. One small step away from asking how much. But there was no need to be too impolite; he was young after all, and I did say that I try to be charitable.

'Me too,' I said. 'But all good things have their season.'

'You sure you don't want to try the bathroom, make it a full house?'

'Been there, done it.' But the bathroom was a good idea, if not for what he had in mind. I turned on the shower and shouted, 'You're a nice guy, Mack. Make sure you close the door on your way out.'

'Leave you my number?'

'And then what? You'd mope around all day waiting for me to call, which I wouldn't. Then you'd forget the fun bits and resent me and neither of us wants that. Trust me, I've been down that road before and I know where it leads.'

'You said earlier that you liked doughnuts. I could get us a bag to share, there's a great place near the Markdown.'

'Fine Mack, you go get some doughnuts.'

'You'll let me in when I get back?'

'No, that's the point.'

Silence for a few moments, and then I heard the apartment door open and shut. At least he hadn't slammed it.

SOMETHING MISSING

'*I* told you to use biometrics. No-one's going to steal your eyes. Well, probably not.'

Danu was right. If I'd used facial scanning instead of my old school physical encryption key, the bastard from last night wouldn't have been able to steal it. And if he'd tried to hack out one of my eyes or cut off a finger, at least I'd have noticed. It probably happened while I was in the bathroom saying no to doughnuts or any other late-night snack. Always assuming it was him, of course.

What about the man who bumped into me on the bridge the day before? I remembered checking my purse, but not the compartment where I kept the key. Now I thought about it, I hadn't looked at the project drives yesterday. Danu had her own access.

'The key's not much use without the data,' I said.

Danu's face had drained of colour. 'The break in, night before last.'

'You said nothing was taken.'

'I said nothing was missing. Gimme ten minutes boss, I need to check something.'

A coincidence or something else? It was public knowledge that I was presenting something at the Metaphysics Society in a few days but no-one would have any idea what I'd been working on and ninety-nine percent of people, even those in my field, would have a hard time making sense of the data and the equations. They'd have to be a genius, and there aren't many of those around.

Danu sat back from her screen and shook her head. 'Not good news, boss. Sorry. I should have looked deeper yesterday.'

'Give me the headlines.'

'Someone copied the data on the encrypted project drive. They took everything on macro QE, everything.'

'But they couldn't read it, because without a key it's just bits and bytes.'

'But now…' I knew she felt let down when she reached out to squeeze my arm. 'We talked about you taking strangers back to your apartment. Even I could knock you over with one finger, you put yourself in danger every time. Someone could take far more than a key; message me at least.'

'I have an alarm. And perhaps I need some excitement in my life.'

'You're about to change the word! That isn't exciting enough for you?'

'Somatic excitement. I like my body to fizz, not just my brain.'

'So take up rock climbing.'

'Bit late now. So what are our options?'

Danu played with the piercing in her bottom lip, the way she always did when something worried her.

'You're due to present your paper in four weeks. Then the world will know.'

'Not all the details though, that won't come until I publish.'

'Someone wants a head start. This was a professional operation. Someone was prepared to kill to get your data, which means there's a lot more than just a reputation at stake.'

'So not someone from the University.'

'There has to be money involved, and a lot of it,' said Danu. 'That means one of the corporations.'

'But why me? There's research going on all over the shop. The only people who have any idea what we're working on are you and me.'

'I promise boss, not said a word.'

'As if. Me neither. But someone guesses how valuable our work is.'

'How? What we developed is a theory,' said Danu. 'We still need to prove the concept in the next phase, and that's a tricky game to play. Some of the technology doesn't even exist yet, we're going to invent it.'

'But if somebody who doesn't realise all the implications tries to use this…' No-one knew, not even us, what might happen but it could be disastrous in the wrong hands.

'I'm not having another go,' said Danu, 'but that guy you picked up in The Markdown, you said he was Niyan?'

'Pretty sure. I didn't get round to questioning him on his ethnic antecedents.'

'They're a close-knit community. Niyans are in demand as muscle for anyone who needs a bit of protection. Or dirty jobs carried out.'

'And you know this how?'

'I lead an interesting and varied life. But I'm thinking, are any of your students Niyan?'

'Some. The good ones are female. Never ask questions in class, but always turn in excellent work. Mind you, their government pays all the fees so they don't need to take jobs as well as study.'

And then I remembered. 'A few months ago one of them came to see me by herself after a tutorial, which was unusual in itself. They tend to hunt in packs. She was asking questions about modular ontology, we'd been covering it that semester. I'd mentioned entanglement in passing and the possibility it could happen at a macro level, not only with elementary particles. A throwaway, nothing detailed.'

'Please tell me you said nothing about the research? Or about entanglement between pre-existing entities?'

'It was months ago, I can't remember every detail. Only an expert in the field would be able to work out the truth from anything I said.'

'You should talk to her.'

'That might be difficult. Now I think about it she hasn't been in class since.'

'So what happens next?'

'We should tell the college police.'

'They won't find anything,' said Danu. 'We'll simply put our project in the spotlight and make people wonder why we were singled out.'

'Perhaps we weren't. We have no idea who else was hacked. And anyway, they might be able to find some clue here; whoever took our data must be the same person who killed the guard.'

Danu laughed. 'Come on, boss, join the real world. If the police haven't found any leads from the mess the killer made of the guard, they won't find anything up here. If we want to discover who did this, we're better off doing it ourselves.'

'I'm a quantum teleologist, not a detective.'

'Leave it with me, I know people who know people.'

'Do I need the details?'

'No. But if I find anything, you'll be the first to hear.'

CHAPTER 4

The Priory

THE INFIRMARY

❦

She was woken by a shaft of sunlight from a high window in a wall of grey stone. No hazy swimming up from sleep, but instant awareness. Ellen pushed herself upright with her good arm and looked around. She was in a bed, in a room with five others, all empty. Someone had bandaged her wound with clean, white gauze and the skin below was back to its accustomed colour. Her clothes were folded on a chair next to the bed, looking cleaner than she remembered, and now she was wearing a simple white shift. No sign of her dagger.

Living on the streets as a child had taught her that three things were paramount for survival: food, shelter and control. And the last of these was the most important. If you were in control of your life, the rest would follow, and her current situation didn't fit that definition. Even when she'd been backed up against the far wall of a dead-end alley by a gang of drunks fancying their chances, she was the one in control. Practice makes perfect, and the odds had always been in her favour.

Now they weren't. Injured, unfamiliar place, no memory

of how she got here. The antithesis of being in control. She needed to get to her feet. Better to face something bad while standing up, even if her knife had disappeared, than lie supine in a bed, waiting for her fate. She pulled the bedsheets aside and swung her legs out, but they refused to take her weight and she fell back, her heart pounding with the effort.

She was about to try again when a man entered through a door at the end of the room. He was taller than most she had known, and lean. About thirty years old at a guess, her own age, and as he came closer she saw pale grey eyes in a face that had weathered to the colour of walnuts. The sandals under his dark brown cassock made slapping sounds on the stone floor and the rope which tied the robe around his waist swung like a pendulum. He was carrying a small flask of water.

'I guessed you would wake today, and it seems I was right. How are you feeling?'

'Where am I?'

'Ah, she speaks! You're in Fenmaen Priory, on the edge of Fenmaen Moor. And you're lucky our shepherd found you. A little longer and I couldn't have saved your arm, let alone your life.'

'How long have I been here?'

'Five nights and half a day.' He pulled a chair across from one of the other beds and sat, folding himself down as if his limbs were precious. 'I am Brother Thomas and this is my infirmary. We had one other patient when you arrived, but I discharged him to give you privacy. A good man, Brother Albertus, but he prefers our beds to the simple cot in his cell. I indulge him occasionally, although not for too long, even though he berates me for being a young whipper-snapper.'

'You have cells? Is this some sort of prison?'

The man laughed, showing small white teeth. 'Cell is the

word we use for our rooms. We need nothing more than a bed and a small table.'

That sounded like a prison to her.

He handed her the flask; not water but a cool, sweet liquid with a bitter aftertaste. 'A cordial that I sometimes use, but not too potent. It should restore your strength; something tells me you've had a taxing time.' He reached across and before she was able to protest, took her wrist for a few heartbeats before releasing it.

'Will you tell me how you came about the wound? I treat many cuts from accidental falls, some of the brothers forget they aren't so young anymore. But that injury to your arm was no accident. The bite of a wolf, I would guess, and a large one. But no-one's seen one of those creatures here for a hundred years or more.'

'Some sort of wolf, yes. And huge. It attacked me in the forest.'

'Ah. Whatever it was, there was poison in its fangs and you were having visions when our man found you. But I drew out the venom with poultices and I believe you'll recover well.' He paused for a moment. 'You're suspicious, I think. So would I be if I woke in a strange bed in a strange place, with a strange man asking me questions. But I give you my word that you'll come to no harm here. This is a place of learning, not a prison, and you're free to leave whenever you want. But I would counsel you to rest for at least a few more days.'

A few more days. If he was telling the truth, then she'd been here longer than she'd been on the road.

'Perhaps you could tell me a little about yourself,' he said. 'I'd like to know what to call you other than "the woman".'

'Ellen. Ellen Dust.'

'No-one wanders on Fenmaen Moor for recreation so I wonder where you came from, and where you're going.'

The first part of the question was easy, the second impossible to answer in a way that wouldn't sound ridiculous. 'My home's a city called Haefen. A two-day journey from here, the other side of the forest.' Just two days away and yet no-one had ever mentioned this Priory.

'Haefen. Hmm. Going by your clothing and the provisions in your pack, you can't have been on the road for more than a few days. But Haefen?'

He stared into her eyed without blinking, as if he was searching for a different answer. 'Forgive me if I ask you again,' he said, 'but where have you come from?'

'I told you, Haefen. I was born there, I grew up there.'

'So why leave your home?'

Telling a stranger about being sentenced to death or exile was, she decided, not the best option right now. 'Strange things were happening in my city. I came looking for answers.'

'And you expected to find them here?'

'I didn't know you existed. I've never heard of Fenmaen Priory.'

'Yet you took yourself onto the moors in a storm where a dagger, no matter how beautiful, would have been little help. As you found.'

The man sat back, with no expression on his face. 'May I tell you something? You might not have known about our community, but we have heard of Haefen. And from what we know, the inhabitants abandoned it to the sea centuries ago.'

Was he lying, or trying to play games with her? 'You must be talking about somewhere else,' she said. 'I was there within the last week and it was the same place I've known all my life.'

The man unfolded himself, walked across the room and looked out from a long window that stretched almost from floor to ceiling, rising to a pointed arch of stone. Beyond him, Ellen saw a patch of blue sky and the top of a large tree, its pale green leaves speckled with sunlight as they fluttered in a breeze.

There shouldn't have been any leaves that colour, not in late October.

The man looked down at the floor as if contemplating. Or praying. Then he returned back to her bed and sat again.

'So, Ellen Dust, you need more rest. I'll arrange for food to be brought here, and I'll return later so that you can tell me about Haefen. Your Hacfen.'

A CHANGE OF SEASON

The food, when it came, was thick soup and a hunk of dark, sweet cheese to go with a mug of ale.

Thomas had been right, she still needed rest. She lay back after she'd finished eating but woke, judging by the colour of the sky, in what must have been late afternoon. Ellen swung herself out of bed, stood and walked around the infirmary, gingerly at first but then with more confidence as she felt her legs getting stronger.

The bite on her arm had been bandaged well but she wanted to check for herself, and had just started to unravel the dressing when Brother Thomas entered and hurried over to stop her.

'It won't be healed yet. I told you that the wound was poisoned and the distemper was spreading. The poultice I applied has helped, but it will take time.'

He tied the bandage back on. 'When you arrived, I was worried you would lose the arm. I thought we might lose you altogether, but you're stronger than you look.'

'Strong enough not to want this bed any longer.'

'I agree. Your clothes are there, cleaned and mended as best we could.'

'What about my pack?'

'Safe in our storage, nothing has been touched.' He paused. 'Your dagger appeared to have been used in anger. The wolf?'

'I wouldn't be here without it.'

'We don't allow weapons inside our walls. It's yours when you leave. And when you're ready, I shall take you to the library. It looks out on to our kitchen garden, a place both beautiful and useful. As all things should strive to be, wouldn't you agree?'

He turned his back while she dressed as quickly as her arm would allow. When she was ready, Thomas led her from the infirmary to a covered walkway outside, surrounding a square space paved with slabs of stone. They walked around two sides and then back into a room with shelves reaching twelve feet or more up the walls, filled with lines of books. Thomas led her past islands of small desks along the centre of the room, and over to two chairs by a window that reached almost to the floor. A garden of herbs and vegetables outside was flourishing. The way it would in summer.

'Normally several brothers would be here. We study and we used to teach, when there were students. But I have arranged privacy for an hour or two. The head of our order, Father Unselm, wants to meet you.'

'But do I want to meet him? You say I'm not a prisoner, but I still don't know what you do here.'

'Father Unselm will answer your questions. But before he joins us, will you tell me about these "strange things" happening to your city? My curiosity is piqued; we're visited by so few people from outside.'

Thomas seemed like a child, hungry for information. And why not? Whatever else these people were, they didn't seem dangerous if he was typical. So she told him about the disappearing children, she told him about the ships that no longer sailed to the harbour. She told him about the Assembly and exile, about the start of her journey into the forest. She told him about the people she found, about the mother and child. The creature that attacked her. She told him that when she left her home, less than a week ago, it was late October.

'You must be mistaken,' he said. 'The month is July - look outside.'

'I was on the road for two nights, nothing more. Once in the cave with the child's body, once on the moor when I slept through the storm.'

'You were close to death. Perhaps you're confused about when you left home or how long you've been travelling.'

'I started out with enough food and water for only a few days because I had faith I would find a village or a town. And I know what season it was when I left. Trust me, Thomas, my mind is no more confused than yours.'

'There must be an explanation.'

'That's one reason I left Haefen, to search for answers.'

Thomas studied his hands and scraped some dirt from under a fingernail. 'Forgive me, we all take our turns with the weeding and planting and I had hurried back to see you.'

She recognised when someone had something they didn't want to say. Something hurtful or shaming. Or something they couldn't explain. But Thomas was pointing out at the garden with a look of shock on his face. The leaves, the plants and the earth were turning white.

'This can't be, snow in high summer.'

'In Haefen, winter was almost upon us when I left. Two weeks ago.'

Thomas waved his arms as if to bat away her words. 'I should find the Prior and tell him we're ready,' he said. 'And don't touch the books, they're worth more than the sum of everything else in the Priory.'

After he left, Ellen walked over to the window and pressed her palm against the glass, cold to the touch. She'd become inured to surprises. Seven days ago she left Haefen as winter arrived, travelled on foot for two days, was rescued and brought to the Priory in high summer, and now winter had found her again as if it had been tracking her footsteps.

SHE WAS WONDERING if Thomas would ever return when she heard a sound behind her. Again the double tap of sandals on stone. She turned to see Thomas and a much older man, bald and smooth-skinned as a young girl.

'We don't entertain many women here,' he said, 'unless there are students. But this last year we have experienced a strange isolation.'

She began to stand, but he waved her back to her seat and then turned to his companion. 'Thomas, you may leave. No doubt you have herbs to crush, potions to distil, and malingerers to indulge. And be so kind as to ask Brother Sera to join us in about thirty minutes.' He started to lower himself into the seat where Thomas had been, then stopped and shouted after him. 'And get someone to light the damned fire in here.'

The Prior settled himself into the chair next to her. 'I'm Father Unselm, Prior to this order, but you already know that. And you are Ellen Dust, of Haefen, a town which disappeared into the ruins of time many years since. Yet I hear it was thriving less than a week ago, when you left. So either you are not who you say you are, or the reports of Haefen's demise were premature. Or something strange is happening to the world we inhabit. Which do you think it is?'

In spite of the polite way he talked, he was calling her a

liar. 'I can't answer for what you've heard about Haefen,' she said, 'but I left because it was threatened. No-one believed me then and it appears that no-one believes me now, which is both tiresome and annoying. You might not be used to women, but you really don't want me feeling annoyed.'

While she was speaking, the Prior continued to stare out at where the garden was being covered with an undulating white sheet. The gentle snowfall of a few minutes ago was now a blizzard, so many large flakes tumbling from the sky that the world had shrunk to a curtain of grey and white.

'And yet you arrive here from a city of myth,' said the Prior, 'bringing a change of season on your heels. I think, perhaps, there is a connection.' He sighed and turned back to her. 'I'm an old man, Ellen. Like most old men, I prefer certainty in my life. I take my meals at the same time every day, I take the same familiar paths through the grounds for my exercise. I know the faces and quirks of all my brothers. I could recite to you the title of every book in this library. I anticipate with pleasure the waves of students that run up to our cloisters each spring, and recede just before winter. I especially like the certainty of knowing what season it is. You will have noted the disappointment in my voice, at having some of those certainties dashed.'

'And perhaps, Prior, you will note the disappointment in *my* voice when I tell you about the children and young people of my town who are disappearing, taken by wolves that cross the river at night to feed. When I tell you about the river that eats away at our land, field by field, closer and closer to our streets. Are we comparing disappointments? Is this a competition?'

He looked across wistfully at the dark, cold hearth and turned back to her. 'Forgive me. You fought for your life against one of these creatures, and I complain about an unlit fire. Believe me, I'm not uncaring, but I have based my entire life on order and routine. You've brought the first rustling of wind in the trees, but I fear a storm is coming to sweep away everything I love, and I don't know how to protect myself or my brothers.'

He paused for a moment. 'Old men always point out to others their relative youth, as if one or the other were a badge of honour. I'm not sure which. You are young, and in my experience the young have little time for tradition; that appreciation comes with age, like a taste for fine wine. Take this Priory; our order came into being centuries ago, dedicated to learning and teaching. I took vows to devote my life to knowledge, as the others did. Thirty of us living off the land, our fish ponds, and the sheep we keep on the moor.'

It was as close to an apology as she was likely to get. 'Thomas mentioned students. What happened to them?'

'It started a year or more ago. We've always taken in the sons and daughters of the wealthier families from Kharuna or Hattila. They stay for a few months at a time, learning the skills they'll need in a civilised life. Rhetoric, disputation, debate. Using words to win an argument. We teach them what it means to live a good life, what is beauty, or justice. We teach them to think beyond the confines of trade or power to some of the eternal truths. Our gift to the world.'

'So what happened?'

'The start of a new term and no-one arrived. We waited for days, then weeks. At first we thought something had happened to the roads, but to all of them at the same time? We had no messages and although those of us who took vows are forbidden to leave the grounds of the Priory, we have lay people who work for us, like the shepherd who found you. We sent one to find out what had happened; he should have returned within a week, but we never saw him again. We tried again, in a different direction but with the same result. We sent no-one else.'

'So what now? You just wait to see what happens?'

'What can we do? If fate has cast us adrift, then we must submit and accept our fate. We've seen no-one for months, as if this Priory is an island and the moors an ocean that no-one is able to cross. Except for you.'

'I can't believe you'd just give up when you realised you were alone.'

'We are men of learning, not action. We searched through the writings of the ancients for answers, but there was nothing.' He looked beaten. 'I confess, I miss the young people. They can be a trial sometimes, with their noise and their running; why do young people feel the need to move so quickly? But they brought colour and the scent of another world.'

This place was his sanctuary, she realised, his safe harbour from the world. For all his professed love of knowledge, everything he experienced was in his mind. He knew nothing outside the covers of his books; words, just words. How would they save him if his Priory was experiencing the same shrinking boundaries as Haefen?

The room had become dark while they were speaking, even though it couldn't be much past mid-afternoon. Snow was still falling outside, some flakes settling in the leaded corners of the windowpanes.

Another of the brothers joined them, his face lit from below by the candle he carried. Trying to keep up behind him, a boy in his teens struggled under the weight of a basket of logs.

The Prior rubbed his hands together. 'Ah, Brother Sera, as ever a spark to cast away darkness.'

'Father Unselm. Let me set some more candles and supervise this child. I'm sure we would all prefer flames and warmth to suffocating in smoke.'

He circled around the library lighting candles, whose

warm glow reflected off the gold tooling on the green and red leather spines. By now the boy had coaxed a flame in the hearth and was persuading it to spread with a pair of bellows while Sera stood over him like a hawk preparing to stoop.

'You can go now, boy. And don't forget you have a disputatio to prepare for tomorrow. Do not let me down!'

When the child had left, Sera pulled up a stool. Ellen tried to guess his age; older than Thomas, she thought, but it was hard to tell. In his later thirties or early forties and tall, but bent as if he spent a lot of time in small rooms. He studied Ellen with dark, sad eyed set deep above a hooked nose, and his hands looked as if they managed to evade the mandatory garden duties as they swept back his long hair, black with streaks of grey, from his forehead.

'Brother Sera,' said the Prior, 'may I introduce Ellen Dust of Haefen.'

'So it's true, we have a visitor from the past. How intriguing.' Sera selected a book from one of the shelves and brought it over to Ellen and the Prior. 'A volume of travellers' tales,' he said. 'Sifting fact from fiction is an art but the bones of the stories are reliable.' He leafed through until he found the page he wanted. 'Marcellus of Hattila, describing a journey he took four centuries ago. People travelled then, unlike today.'

'Perhaps they were restless,' said Unselm, 'dissatisfied with their lives. We have no need to leave our home.'

'Or perhaps, dear Father, they weren't content to read about the exploits of others and wanted to experience the world and its truths for themselves.'

'The ancients discovered what was true. Their writings are all we need to understand our world.'

'But surely a fact is a truth known by experience?'

The Prior turned to Ellen. 'You will have gathered that

Brother Sera would prefer to be writing books about his own exploits rather than reading about the travels of others.'

'Although in this case dear Father,' said Sera, 'even I will allow that a book might be of assistance. See, this is a passage where Marcellus describes part of his journey.' He began to read:

'On the eighth day of the third month just before noon, two days after leaving the desolation of the high barren moors, we reached the edge of the forest and came upon an arm of the sea, glittering towards the horizon. The tide was retreating and as we rested where the water met the land we saw a narrow causeway appear, leading to an island lying a few hundred yards from us. We crossed carefully, seeing on each side the remains of old stone buildings under the water. The island itself was covered with the ruins of what must once have been a thriving town, but long since abandoned as the sea claimed the streets and houses. Where the people went, I know not. If ever a town was misnamed, this one was. Our guide had told us the truth and brought us to the ancient remains of Haefen.'

BROTHER SERA

❦

She wondered if this was all an elaborate hoax, although why would they want to persuade her that her home was gone? It would be easy to prove them wrong; retrace her steps across the moors, back through the forest, across the river, and there would be the town, the marketplace, the harbour. There would be Tollin, fussing and delighted to see her again. Little over two days, barring accidents and attacks by wild animals. As well as the need to stay out of the way of Vlakas and everyone from the Assembly.

It would never happen. If Haefen still existed, she would gain nothing by going back. If it was gone, she'd be no closer to understanding. And unless she found her way home, while she had no proof either way of his fate, Tollin would still be alive.

The Prior and Sera were waiting for a reaction.

'Is this meant to be proof of something?' she said. 'A story in an old book; he could have made it up or been talking about somewhere different.'

Sera turned to a series of drawings at the back of the volume. Ellen recognised a map with Lannick near the top, a large dark area labelled Fenmaen Forest leading to another called Fenmaen Moor, and along the top edge of the forest was a river, widening as it reached the sea, meandering on its way to encompass another town. Haefen. She was looking at her home.

'This was what Marcellus expected to find,' said Sera. 'The reality was something different.'

'When did you say he wrote this book; four hundred years ago? Perhaps the town had disappeared when he arrived but was rebuilt later.'

She heard the defeat in her voice. She'd seen it for herself, the river widening and swallowing land, cutting them off. But not four hundred years ago.

'I need wine,' said Unselm. 'Brother Sera, perhaps you could bring us a bottle, and none of the Hattilan vinegar we keep for the students. My private cellar, a Kharuna red.'

When he'd gone, Unselm sat for a few moments, staring out of the window. The moon was out, reflecting off the billows of snow that covered the ground and weighed down the branches of the trees.

'You said that no-one believed you, but I do,' he said. 'While I ate my luncheon, the Priory was enjoying high summer. Now we languish unprepared in the depths of winter. Time and the seasons have gone awry, somehow.'

He shuffled around in his chair as if his clothes were an irritant. 'I am a scholar. I respect our predecessors, who mapped the bounds of human knowledge. But nothing I've read encompasses this.'

He sounded lost. Just like Thomas, he was finding it hard to believe the evidence of his own eyes.

Sera arrived back with a bottle and three glasses, which sparkled in the candlelight.

'You're welcome to stay with us,' said the Prior, 'but I suspect that is not your plan. However, rather than wandering at random as so many exiles do, might I suggest a useful destination? The port town of Coria is about two weeks away. Not a straightforward journey, and we have little contact with them. But the town was - or is - a busy port with many ships. A good place to start, perhaps.'

He was right, she had no intention of staying. These beautiful books were ornaments, not answers. Not that she'd ever had much time for words.

'I shall prepare a map for you and lend you a companion,' said the Prior. 'Brother Sera would never forgive me if I kept him here while you continued your journey, so I hereby give him a dispensation to leave the Priory and travel with you, at least as far as Coria. If you find nothing and wish to return, he will accompany you back here.'

Ellen glanced at Sera, who failed to suppress a grin. Give him time to find a cloak and boots and he'd be on the road within the hour. She'd told Annegret she preferred to travel alone, but after her experiences so far, a companion for the next stage felt like an excellent idea.

'If I understood these recalcitrant seasons, I'd suggest waiting a few weeks until spring,' said Unselm, 'but for all I know that could arrive tomorrow, or not at all. You should stay awhile to let your wound heal under the care of Brother Thomas. And then, if you still wish to go, I shall bid you both farewell.'

A PLAGUE OF WORMS

Whether it was the wine, the effects of the wolf's bite or simple weariness, Ellen fell asleep as soon as she was shown to a simple cell with a bed, a chair and a small table with a basin and pitcher of water. She woke with a start from a dream that faded before she could catch it, and lay there for a few moments thinking about the day before. At least the next stage of the journey was clear. Please the gods that Sera would be what he promised, open to finding answers in the actual world and not just in meditation and books.

In a corner of her cell, between the wall and ceiling, a spider was waiting in the centre of a beautiful web that shimmered in the pale morning light. Like the brothers, she thought. They constructed cobwebs of learning, fine and beautiful in themselves but liable to disintegrate in the slightest breeze. What constructions they would make if they exposed themselves to real life.

She'd only been twenty-four hours in the Priory, but already the urge to escape the cold stone walls and the certainties of the brothers was almost irresistible. She dressed and left the cell, searching for a way to fresh air outside the walls. As she walked towards the corner of the corridor, she noticed a sweet odour, something familiar. She recognised it from home, the time a rat died under the floorboards of her room and rotted as maggots fed it on it.

She reached the corner and saw, a few yards away, one of the brothers sitting on the floor with his back propped against the wall and his legs straight out in front. His head was tilted to one side, away from her, but his eyes were closed.

At least she'd found the source of the smell. A liquid had soaked through the brother's habit just below his chest, turning the rough brown cloth a darker shade, almost black. At least he was still breathing, the body was moving slightly. But this wasn't the rhythmic rise and fall of his lungs, more of a squirming movement by his stomach, as if something wanted to escape from the folds of cloth.

She moved forward, cautiously. As she came closer his head tilted back towards her and she only just resisted the urge to vomit. The man's right eye had become a mound of creamy white worms, each about two inches long, spilling from the socket like a stream of pale tears flowing down his cheek.

More creatures were crawling out from his wide sleeve and dropping to the floor. Ellen was about to call for help, when the man opened his remaining eye and looked into hers. He worked his mouth as if to say something, and she leant in a little closer as he tried to moisten his lips with a grey, pitted tongue. He gave a slight cough, then another that sprayed her with spittle. She moved back just in time. A final spasm gave way to a choking sound as more of the worms cascaded from his nose and mouth.

Ellen used her sleeve to wipe her face clean and looked back at the man. He was still alive and trying to breathe; the look on his face was pure terror and supplication. Yet there was nothing she could do for him. The thought of touching his clothes or his skin, of getting close to the worms or maggots that were still pouring from his eye socket and crawling out of his mouth; she would choose fangs and claws any day over that.

She heard a shout from the other end of the corridor and Thomas ran towards her, his cassock billowing.

'Get back Ellen, I beg you.' He stopped a few feet away. 'Please tell me you haven't touched him.'

'I found him like this, he's still alive. Can you help?'

The man on the floor slumped a little further as Thomas stepped closer. The squirming movements under his habit, above his stomach, were more frantic.

'Brother William.' Thomas's voice was soft, as if soothing an infant. 'Brother, do you hear me?'

The man moved his head slightly to face Thomas, although it was hard to know whether that was his intention or a result of the movements of the grub-like creatures.

'I am sorry, dear friend, that this is your fate. But you know how it ends. It will be soon now, the torment will be over.'

Brother William spasmed with another muffled cough, spewing out an eruption of worms. His remaining eye looked past Thomas and then lost its focus.

Thomas sighed. 'Go to your room now, Ellen. I have arrangements to make and it isn't safe here. I must tend to Brother William first, and I'll come for you as soon as I can.'

'Not until you tell me what's happening.'

'Go! And wash yourself, your face and your hands. Check your clothes, make sure that none of these parasites have found a way to you.'

That was enough. She ran back to her room, pulled off her clothes, filled the basin with water and soaked her face and neck, rubbing away at the skin until it became too tender to touch.

Then her clothes. She examined every fold and crease, looking for any sign of movement, any sight of a string of creamy white. Nothing. She dressed again and was about to pull on her boots when she saw something inching its way up from the sole, heading for the top where it would have fallen in. Ellen kicked the boot over and pressed down on it hard to squash the worm, then set it upright again. She wet a corner of her bedding and used it to clean the boot, then checked the outside of each of them and sluiced out the insides with water. Better to have wet feet than the possibility of being infested like Brother William.

That morning the Priory had felt claustrophobic but safe. Now every breath was dangerous.

ONWARD AND UPWARDS

The sound of someone knocking on her door broke her reverie and Thomas entered with a tray of food. He looked worried. No, more than worried. Scared.

'I've brought you something to eat. When you're finished, I'll take you to Unselm. You leave today, this morning, as soon as possible. You have a long day ahead.'

He was standing close to the door. 'Three more were taken ill in the night, with the infestation you saw. It's been years since we last suffered this affliction; there is no cure and we're all wondering who will be the next.' He seemed uneasy. 'Unselm believes you might have brought this to us. You're the only person from outside the Priory in months.'

'You think I'm carrying these creatures? That's impossible; why haven't I fallen ill like the others?'

'Believe me, you don't want to. This plague starts with a cough, like many ailments, but then swellings appear in the groin and under the arms. Red at first and turning purple as they grow, as if they have a life of their own. As, indeed, they do. But there are other swellings inside the body. The stomach, behind the eyes. Eventually they ripen and release the worms that smell of rotting meat. When the internal boils split as the creatures eat their way out, the man dies. In pain, and there is nothing I can do to ease it.'

'What happens to the affected brothers?'

'Confined to their cells until they die. No, don't look so disgusted. We need to isolate them as well as we can. When they die, we burn the bodies and use smoke to fumigate the cells, which we leave unused for at least three months. We place any recoverable bones in the ossuary to join the brothers who went before.' He edged further towards the door. 'I'll come back for you in half an hour. Be ready.'

She ate quickly. If she were the carrier of this plague, why wasn't she ill like the others? Perhaps the people in the clearing had been diseased. When she tried to help the woman with the child, her hands had become covered with blood. As for the other victims of the creature, their mauling would have disguised any signs of the sickness.

When Thomas returned he led her through the cloisters to Unslem's study, a high-ceilinged room as large as five or six of the brothers' cells. Thick rugs patterned in reds and golds covered the stone floors, and the upholstered chairs had been carved from a type of wood she'd not seen before, a reddish brown flecked with a grain like veins of gold. The arms were turned in shapes of fantastical creatures with talons and wings, and she thanked the fates that she hadn't met one of them amongst the trees.

Sera was there too, dressed for the road, his habit replaced by loose woollen leggings and a leather jerkin.

The Prior looked across at Thomas, who nodded his head. 'I see Thomas had told you. Please understand. In our community, any illness spreads like weeds in a field. Those worms you saw in Brother William ride around in clothing or hair until they decide to enter the body through some orifice. Once inside, they multiply and… Well, you have seen the results for yourself. And whatever the cause, it is safer for us all if you leave now.'

He handed her a rolled parchment. 'I prepared a map, although who can guarantee its accuracy, with the world outside these walls moving and changing, and we have prepared provisions for two weeks at least. By then you should have reached Coria or found a civilised place to replenish your supplies.'

She'd set out with just a few day's worth of food when she left Haefen, and her pack had been as heavy as she could bear. 'Even two of us couldn't take that much food and water,' she said, 'unless Brother Sera can carry the weight of another man.'

'Which is why you have another companion. He's waiting for us outside, near the main gate.' Unselm led the way to a heavy oak door which opened out onto a courtyard she hadn't seen before, surrounded by a high wall whose length was broken by a gatehouse. Standing in front of them was a mule, dark grey except for white around his nose and his right ear. Ellen noticed her own pack strapped to the bulging panniers on his flanks.

'Meet Hob,' said Unselm. 'Stubborn sometimes, but strong and willing enough if he likes you. A loan, I am afraid, Hob's too valuable for us to lose. Brother Sera will return with him when you find what you're looking for. I simply hope he finds the Priory still standing and some brothers to welcome him home.'

The mule flicked his ears as he turned to look at her, and Ellen wasn't sure if his expression was anticipation, resignation or contempt.

CHAPTER 5

On the road

CLIMBING TO THE PASS

The door in the main gate swung shut behind them as they set out along a wide track which stretched out in a curve towards the horizon, and away from the pestilence.

Unselm's map seemed simple enough, with their route traced out and a few landmarks shown. The path would take them to a river, possibly the one that flowed to Haefen and was consuming her home. Or had consumed. Flooding or flooded, present or past. Don't believe what you're told or what you see in books, she reminded herself. Wait for the evidence of your own eyes.

The course of the river would be their guide as it skirted the bottom edge of the moors. Then they would need to reach the other side as their path rose towards the mountains.

The mountains. Sera had pointed them out before they set off, a jagged line of white in the distance. Unless he'd told her what they were, she would have taken them for clouds. Haefen didn't have mountains.

For the first few hours they walked in virtual silence, one

on each side of the mule as if there were an unspoken agreement to keep apart. Perhaps Sera thought she was tainted, or wanted to protect her in case he was the one carrying an infestation.

The walking was comfortable enough, and she guessed that Sera with his longer legs was matching his pace to hers. They passed drifts of snow in the lee of the rocks scattered either side of the track, but the sky was clear and high. The winter of yesterday had disappeared as quickly as it arrived, leaving just the detritus of its presence.

Ellen looked over at her companion when they found a place to stop for food. She was right, he was unlike Thomas or Unselm or, she guessed, any of the other brothers.

'How long have you been at the Priory?' she asked.

'Close on ten years. Most of the brothers arrive as students and never leave.'

'And you?'

'I had a life before.'

'Is that all? If we're going to be travelling together, shouldn't I know at least as much about you as you do about me?'

'I was a different man then. When I came to the Priory, I left him behind.'

'You reckon we can leave our past behind?' said Ellen. 'I'm not so sure. It's a part of us. It defines us.'

'So every mistake I've ever made will follow me round forever? I'm not sure I like that idea. I have faith that we can remake ourselves if we want.'

'To an extent. But surely we're the sum of all our experiences. All the pain, all the anger. And some joy.'

'Some joy?'

'My life wasn't a complete disaster. What about you, why were you so keen to remake yourself?'

The hobbled mule had found a patch of yellowing grass

and tore off clumps to eat, rolling them round in his mouth before swallowing.

Sera studied Ellen as if she was some kind of exotic beast. 'You're a strange one, not like other women I've known. They spend their time looking after their men and their children. Cooking, washing, chattering. I don't know any who would attempt a journey like this, let alone without knowing what they're searching for.'

'I've done my share of the cooking and washing. But I don't need a man. I had enough attention from them when I was barely more than a child. As for children of my own… No, I'd rather go back to fight the wolves in the forest than trap myself like that.'

'You think children are a trap?'

Ellen sighed. 'Maybe not for men. You go off and carry on living your lives. But for women… I've seen drudgery happen too often. I've watched mothers lose themselves in the lives of their husbands and their children. Not going to happen to me. Not now, not ever.'

'You are… singular.'

'And you have evaded my question.'

Sera grunted. 'It's not a secret. I was a mercenary. I fought for whoever paid the highest price, sometimes against men who were my friends and comrades only weeks before.'

That explained a lot. 'Why did you stop? Were you a terrible soldier?'

He smiled. 'I was good, one of the best. But I was also proud and I was arrogant. Why not? I had money, I had women. I had it all.'

'No you didn't or you would have carried on with your life. Something happened that brought you to the Priory.'

'A conversation for another day, Mistress Dust. And you'll need to trade more of your history if you want to hear more of mine. I bet you have a few interesting stories to keep us amused around an evening fire.'

The mule had wandered off the path, heading for a patch of vivid green grass. 'Hob! Hob, come here.' Ellen dusted pieces of dried grass from her skirts. 'I know we're on a path, but the land is still marshy off to the sides. I only just pulled myself free from a bog when I was crossing the moor. Mind you, I was carrying the corpse of a baby at the time so I had other things on my mind.'

'I won't ask. And don't worry about Hob. He could pick out a safe path across the moors on a moonless night. But we should be on our way.'

The mule had already turned back, either because of Ellen's call or because he'd changed his mind about the grass, and ambled his way towards them as if he were out for an afternoon stroll.

THE MOUNTAINS WERE CLOSER. Those shimmers of white on the horizon had resolved into sharper edges of snow-covered peaks. The path had dropped to the river some hours ago, and the course took them along the bottom of a shallow valley. On the other side of the water, heather-covered slopes rose from the riverbank in shades of white and purple.

They walked in single file as the rocky path climbed and fell, sometimes dropping down into the margins of the water, sometimes taking them up and through thickets of brambles that Sera cleared with a machete. At least he hadn't forgotten all the skills of a soldier.

After they'd been walking for half a day, they heard rushing water, like distant thunder getting louder by the minute. The river itself had been widening, running faster and foaming around half-submerged rocks, and then around a curve in the path, they saw the cause of the sound. The river tumbled over the edge of a precipice to fall hundreds of feet, sending up a mist of spray that soaked their clothes.

Ellen was last in the line, walking behind Hob. She retrieved Unselm's map from her pack; this was where they needed to cross to the other side and begin the climb into the foothills of the mountains.

Sera joined her. 'This is madness,' he said. 'there's no way we can get over this.'

'A ford maybe, further back? Not that I remember seeing one. Or stepping stones?'

'In this current? I don't think so. One slip and you'd be carried over the falls. And Hob would never make it. Moors yes, torrents of water, no.'

The mule heard his name and turned to look at them, his ears twitching.

'You're right. Even if we find a way across, we can't leave him behind.'

The river flowed to their right, while to the left the rocky wall was partly hidden by bushes and brambles. 'The river's swollen by snow from the hills,' said Sera. 'If this were summer, as it's meant to be, the water would be lower.'

'Perhaps. But we can't wait here for the seasons to change. There has to be another way.'

They made their way back, Ellen in the vanguard now. She scanned the water, hoping for a ford like the one she'd used to leave Haefen. The alternative was to retrace their steps until they came to a narrow section, and the possibility of getting across to the other bank. But there would be no track to follow and who could say what other obstacles they'd find.

She realised that the familiar pattern of Hob's hooves had stopped. A few yards back, he was waiting by a bush growing against the rock face. 'Come on boy, what's the matter?'

Hob brayed and pawed at the ground. 'He's an intelligent

lad,' said Sera, catching them up. 'Perhaps he knows something we don't.'

Ellen peered at the bush where Hob had stopped. 'There's an opening here in the rock,' she said.

Sera joined her with the machete and hacked at the scrub, clearing the opening. 'It looks like a cave, but it goes a long way back. You want to toss for who investigates?'

'The honour's yours, I'll stay with Hob. But you'll need a light.' She found one of Tollin's candles in her pack and lit it with the flint. 'Take this, and take care.'

Sera pushed through the remains of the vegetation into the cave; the glimmer of the candle drew fainter and then disappeared.

Ellen's feet ached after the long walk, and the bite on her arm was throbbing and sore. She sat on the path next to the cave entrance as Hob nuzzled her with his nose. How long had Sera been gone? Only ten minutes, but it felt like hours. Real time versus perceived time; which really counted?

After a few more minutes she heard a faint echo and looked back into the opening. In the distance a small, wavering light was growing stronger as Sera made his way towards her, soaked to his waist and out of breath.

'It's not a cave, but a tunnel. Bends round and heads under the river. I didn't go all the way, I thought you might be worried. But this has to be our best option. Trouble is, we have to negotiate a flooded section and the water's getting deeper. It's a risk. If we're going to try, we should go now.'

He led, forced to crouch even though he wasn't much taller than her. The walls were soft and green with moss in some places, slick with a sheen of water in others. And she'd felt claustrophobic in the Priory. The mule seemed unconcerned, plodding between her and Sera. The tunnel was curving now, back towards the river, and drops fell from the roof onto her hair and face.

Sera stopped. 'We've reached the flooded section. Let me go first; if it's no deeper we'll carry on.' The water rose to his knees, then his waist, then a little higher as he waded across while holding the candle above his head.

'It's deeper, but not too much. Do you want me to carry you?'

'Ask a question like that again and it will be your last, I promise.'

Hob followed Sera, still unconcerned, and Ellen watched as they rose out of the water at least twenty yards away. Now to make good on her boast. Boots tied around her neck and then a careful step into the ice-cold pool. The surface under her feet was peppered with sharp points of rock; perhaps the boots would have been a good idea after all.

The water reached higher than she expected, up to her breasts, and the faster she tried to move, the more it tugged at her clothes. And then the ground rose, and she was on the other side, shivering.

THE DRIPS WERE MORE like drizzle now. Sera stopped and she heard him swear.

'What is it?'

'Rock fall. I didn't get this far the first time.'

'A rock fall in here?'

'Looks like part of the roof has crumbled. I'm guessing there's only a few inches now between us and the bottom of the river bed.'

'Can we get through?'

'It would take hours to clear this, and we might provoke another collapse. If the roof gives way we'll be drowned within seconds. We need to find another way.'

Once again they retraced their steps, Ellen carrying the candle now, until they came to the flooded section. It was wider than last time, much wider. Which meant deeper. Sera began to wade through, but the water rose past his chest and up to his neck before he turned back.

'Can you swim?' he asked.

'Yes. No. Perhaps. Is it difficult?'

'We could probably get across. I can help you if you're not too proud, and then ferry the packs.'

'Do mules swim?'

Hob was already making his way back towards the rock fall in the distance.

Sera shook his head. Even as they stood there, the level of the pool was rising. 'I'm damned if I'll leave the mule. There's no other option, we have to clear the rocks.'

Perhaps he was right. But if they failed, they'd be trapped there until the water level went down, if it ever did. Assuming it never reached the roof.

'I've heard that drowning's a peaceful death,' said Sera.

'A theory I have no intention of testing. We should hurry.'

They followed the mule back to the rock fall. Some of the stones were little more than rubble, but the boulders posed more of a challenge, and Ellen looked up to where the roof of the tunnel arched fifteen feet above them. Sera took the shovel and started to clear away the smaller stones while Ellen freed what rocks she could manage. The ground, she couldn't help noticing, was becoming rather damp.

'This can't be solid,' said Sera. 'there's cold air coming through the cracks.' They worked faster until only a few large boulders blocked the way, the middle one almost to the roof and wider than the mule. Through the cracks between them Ellen could see faint light; the end of the tunnel.

'We'll never shift these,' she said.

'We have to, there's no way back.'

She thought for a moment. 'Can you get a rope around this smaller rock at the front?'

Sera checked. 'The one jammed against the large boulder? I think so. But I already tried and it's stuck fast.'

'Humour me.'

Sera unpacked the coil of rope and secured it around the rock.

'I said there were two of us but I was wrong,' said Ellen. 'We have Hob.'

'I'm losing my touch.' Sera fastened the rope around Hob's chest; the mule already seemed to know what was expected of him and strained forward. The rock moved slightly and Ellen grabbed the rope. 'Come on! Pull.'

Sera joined her, and suddenly the rock seemed to leap out of the ground. The boulder wedged against it shifted and then tumbled towards them. Ellen grasped Sera's arm and dragged him to one side as the boulder came to rest just a foot away.

The blockage was around seven feet high now, smooth and sheer with no handholds. But behind the rocks the passage was clear, the path rising to the surface.

'I can't see any way round, but we can throw the packs over,' said Ellen. 'If I give you a leg up to the top you can pull me after you, but I don't think we'll be strong enough to haul Hob over, even if he's prepared to let us try. Which, knowing Hob, seems unlikely.'

Sera stroked Hob's neck, murmuring soft words.

'Sometimes you have to trust to luck,' he said. 'We'll get over and let Hob find his own way. If it's possible, he'll make it; I've seen him jump higher. Have faith.'

Sera was lighter than she'd imagined, and when he was straddling the top, he reached down for her. They looked at Hob waiting below, studying the rock as if to decide how to tackle it.

'I think we should get down.' said Sera, 'Now.'

They dropped to the ground and flattened themselves

against the side of the tunnel as they heard the clatter of the mule backing away, and then the start of his run. Seconds later Hob cleared the top of the boulder with inches to spare, his hooves almost to his chest, his head down and his ears flat.

'Told you,' Sera shouted.

THE EXIT from the tunnel brought them to a shallow depression bounded by straggly bushes with dull grey leaves and long spines, and beyond them the fringes of some woodland. They clambered to the top; a small ridge ran between them and the river, muffling the sound of the falls a few hundred yards away.

Ellen shivered in the slight breeze from the north. 'We need to get dry.'

'We could do worse than stay here tonight,' said Sera. 'The tunnel entrance is good protection and there's enough fallen wood around for a fire.'

The thought of travelling further that day had been weighing on Ellen's mind. And although she hadn't noticed it at the time, the work of clearing the tunnel had opened the wound on her arm and blood had seeped into its dressing. Brother Thomas would not be amused.

Sera relieved Hob of the packs and carried them to the entrance. Ellen collected fuel and lit a fire, and while Sera sat outside with his back to her, she stripped and changed into the only spares from her pack. No more boots, unfortunately. She spread her wet clothes to dry on small rocks and branches near the fire, and prayed that the rain would hold off, at least until morning.

They drew lots and Sera took the first watch; allowing something to come upon them in the night while they were both sleeping and helpless would be a risk too far.

The ground was nothing more than hard rock, but Ellen made a pillow from her pack and fell asleep within minutes. When she woke, it was still daylight, but with a different quality. A fresh morning light rather than the tired gloom of evening. Sera was feeding the last twigs from the wood pile onto the fire and turned as she sat up. 'Good morning, and don't look at me like that. You were exhausted, and I saw how you were holding your arm. We should check the dressing before we leave.'

'Damn you, Sera. You're no good to me if you collapse from tiredness and fall asleep while you're meant to be on watch.'

'I was a soldier, Ellen. We get used to staying awake at night, and the penalty for sleeping on duty was a damned sight worse than the angry tongue of Ellen Dust. I've seen men run through on the spot, and left to die with their guts spilling out. Trust me, no dreams are worth that.'

After breakfast they packed and moved off from the hollow towards the thin line of trees. The higher they climbed, the more the temperature dropped. Trees turned to bushes and bushes to sparse clumps of grass and heather amongst the rocks.

Mountains were deceptive, she realised. Scramble to the top of one rise and there was a higher peak hiding behind. And now the ground was turning from green and grey to white. The fine glazing of snow on the grass became thicker, slowing them down as they slipped on the icy track.

They'd been taking turned in the lead, and Ellen was in front when she heard Sera call.

'How much further until we reach the pass? Hob could find something to eat under the snow, but it's poor stuff and we need him to be strong.'

'I'm not sure,' she said. 'Unselm marked the falls along with the path we're on, but I don't know how far we've come.' She pointed to the map. 'I think we're somewhere about here.'

Sera shook his head. 'It's taken us three hours to climb this far and we're not even halfway to the pass.' They were no longer in the foothills but almost at the higher peaks, rising sheer and jagged ahead of them. The next few hours promised to be cold, very cold.

'Getting up here is only part of the problem,' said Sera. 'We still have to get down the other side. I don't know about you, but my immediate plans don't include spending the night above the snow line with no fuel for a fire.'

ARE YOU LOOKING AT ME?

The highest peaks disappeared as the ceiling of cloud sank towards them. Within minutes they were engulfed in a grey shroud so thick that the shape of the mule, only a few feet away, was scarcely visible. One day, she told herself, I'll find a place that has no rocks, no fog, no mist, and where my clothes aren't perpetually damp. She could almost smell the mould growing.

'We should stay close,' said Sera. 'Easy to lose each other in this.'

They carried on climbing. It wasn't just visibility that was reduced. Even the rhythm of Hob's hooves on the rocky track, usually a small percussion to accompany them, was muffled, as if sounds had lost the will to push their way through the murk.

They were moving more slowly. Too slowly. At this rate, they'd still be on their way to the pass when darkness fell. Sera took a turn at point, his body nothing more than a slight thickening in the cloud. He paused suddenly and pushed back past the mule to Ellen.

'There's someone ahead, I heard voices,' he whispered.

'Voices? More than one?'

'I can't say how many but yes, more than one.'

'Should we worry?'

'It depends. I can't imagine many people use this pass.'

'Perhaps they know how far to the nearest shelter, if there is one in this godsforsaken place.'

'Perhaps.' But he didn't sound convinced.

As if on cue, they saw figures condensing from the mist. One, another, and then three men. Not tall, not overfed, dressed for somewhere warmer. And knives in their belts.

She'd always prided herself on a sixth sense. Seeing the teeth behind the smile, the knife hidden up a sleeve. The downside was assuming danger existed where there was none. Tollin said to her once: *'You have to trust people sometimes. Not everyone is out to hurt you.'* But he hadn't grown up as a girl child on the back streets of Haefen.

The leading man held up his hand to stop his companions. 'Don't see many travellers up here on the mountain,' he said. 'An inhospitable environment, you could say. Tricksy paths, nasty drops. You folks lost?'

'We're heading for the pass,' said Sera. 'Can you tell us how far away it is?'

'Weather like this you'll be lucky to make it before midnight.' He lifted his head and sniffed the air. 'Going to be a cold one, that's for sure. Wouldn't like to spend the night up here if it were up to me. I mean, you might get through the night, you and that fine, sturdy mule. But as for your woman there, no sir. I wouldn't put a woman of mine through the freezing cold and dark.' He looked at Ellen and grinned. 'No, I definitely would not. Woman like that deserves to be kept warm, right boys?'

The two men behind him said nothing but stared at her. She knew what that look meant.

'I'm warm enough,' she said. 'If you could just tell us how far to the pass.'

'No offence, ma'am. Me and the boys here, we don't see too many people. Just trying to be pleasant is all.'

'The pass?'

'I'm telling you, that pass is a poor plan. You want to get over this mountain there's a better way. Not so far or so high, but the track does get a little exciting in places. The mule will be fine, those creatures almost like mountain goats. Let the beast go first, that's my advice. Always find a sound track, mules.'

'Where's this better way?' asked Sera.

'Me and the boys be happy to show you. Need to retrace your steps a way, you'll have passed it in the mist. A smaller track off to your right going back, curves round the edge of this hill. We were going there ourselves, anyway. Bit of advice though, don't look down if you scare easy.'

They turned back, one man leading, the other two bringing up the rear, with Sera, Hob and Ellen in the middle. After a few hundred yards, the man in front stopped. 'This is the turn off. Like I said, don't look down and careful where you walk. There's a spot a mile or so on where the track widens out for a while. We can rest up there if you need to.'

The track became narrower and narrower as the space between the chasm and the sheer rock face shrank. The bulk of the mountain rose on their right and when the swirling mist cleared for a few seconds, they were by the edge of a sheer drop with no ground in sight.

Swirling skeins of mist closed in again and they walked in silence, apart from the tuneless humming of the man in front. After what felt like hours with all her senses deadened, Ellen sensed a change in the air. The track widened and they found themselves on an area of stony ground a few yards across. Two paths led away, one heading down and one heading up.

'This'll do,' said the man. 'I regret to say that this is where we'll be relieving you of your belongings and your mule, he is such a fine beast.'

Ellen grabbed Hob's harness as if to protect him. The other two men had positioned themselves between her and Sera. Clever, she thought. they'd isolated him, trapped between the three of them. Deal with the bigger risk first, a good rule. Always assuming you're good at judging risks.

'We don't want any trouble,' said Sera. 'Just walk away now and we'll let you go.'

She had to give this to the man; he had balls. The trouble was, the other three men had knives and Sera's machete was stowed in the pack on Hob's back.

The main man laughed and ran his fingers through his thin, sandy hair. 'You, sir, are a comedian and I thank you for your humour, most sincerely. I mean that. But we all know there are only three people and a mule walking away from here, and you two aren't included in that august band.'

Sera kept talking, as if to buy some time. 'Why didn't you push us over the edge earlier?'

'That would have been a possibility, if downright discourteous. However, accidents happen to the best of us, specially during a struggle, and I'm fond of my boys here. Wouldn't like to see one of them go for a fall when there's an easier way. No sir, this is the right place and the right time and I'll tell you how it's going to go down. You seem like a brave man, and I appreciate that. So you can try to fight us all, in which case you'll die. Simple fact. Then, because we're lonely men with all the appetites that go with such a state, we'll take our pleasure with your woman, warm her up a little. We aren't animals, though, are we boys? We're gentlemen, and I promise we'll take our time. A thorough job, you might say.

When we're finished with her, she won't be walking anywhere, and that's another promise. I do so like to hear a girl squeal.'

One of the other two sniggered. Ellen caught Sera's eye and gave him the slightest of nods.

He picked up a small rock, little more than a sharp stone. A pathetic weapon. 'You'll have to get through me,' he said.

All three men had drawn their knives and circled him, as if Ellen didn't matter. And why would she? Three men with knives against one holding a rock. But he had their attention, which was all he wanted and all that mattered.

While they were closing in on him, Ellen reached into the pack, pulled out the machete, tested its balance, sent a prayer to the non-existent gods and threw it in a high arc, tumbling lazily over the heads of the men towards Sera. She and Annegret used to juggle with knives, back in the day, throwing them to each other for fun. Practice makes perfect.

The gods were kind, and Sera caught the machete by the hilt. Without pausing he dropped low and then slashed at the nearest man. The blade caught him on the wrist and his knife, as well as the hand holding it, both flew off in a spray of blood. As the man doubled over, grasping his arm in agony, Sera slashed again and opened the man's stomach, stepping away as the guts slithered out.

Ellen had never seen Sera smile like this; soldiering agreed with him.

'Definitely losing my touch,' he called, 'we used to collect the heads as footballs.'

Without her noticing, the main man had circled back towards her, and before she could reach her own dagger, he had his knife at her throat.

'Your choice,' he called to Sera. 'Throw down your weapon and she lives. If not, I'll bleed her out like a pig. And we'll still take our pleasure when she's dead, body will stay warm long enough.'

Ellen tried to call out, but the blade at her throat was already drawing blood.

Sera didn't move. 'I was a soldier,' he said. 'I've fucked more people in more ways than you've drawn breaths in the whole of your pathetic lives. And I promise you this, touch my friend and I will take my pleasure with you from here to eternity and back. You'll be fucked so hard you'll never walk again. That's my promise.'

Ellen's dagger was strapped to her leg, hidden under her skirt. But the man's grip around her neck was so tight there was no way she could reach it. Two on two, and she was out of the equation. Bad odds.

Although it went against the grain, if they thought she was a helpless woman, she might as well play the part. She groaned, fluttered her eyelids and let her body go limp so that the man had to support her weight.

He released her neck. 'Bitch has fainted,' he said, unnecessarily, and dropped her to the ground.

Hob had been watching the action with a stoic detachment, and he nudged her gently without looking at her. Mules, she'd found, were stubborn but protective, and over the past couple of days she and Hob had come to an understanding. Almost before she hit the ground, the mule turned, squinted at the man who dropped her and then kicked back with both hind legs. The crack of the man's pelvis breaking was crisp and clear as he collapsed next to Ellen, squealing in agony. Like a girl, she thought. He scrabbled around, trying to right himself and stand, but Ellen had her dagger out now and held it to his throat. Tables turned.

The man tried to push her away, but pain had made him weak. 'Stop playing, bitch, this ain't no women's game.'

'Believe me,' she said, 'I've played this game before. Many,

many times.' While he was still trying to get to his knees, she grabbed a handful of his hair, yanked his head back and stabbed him through his left eye as far as the blade would go. The iris was a watery blue colour, she'd noticed, not attractive. Looked better now.

The odds had changed; two on one, much better. But she was wrong again. Sera had been busy and found himself a football.

'I think that went well,' said Ellen. 'Shall we go?'

THEY DRAGGED the bodies to the edge of the cliff and tumbled them over. 'Tidier this way,' said Sera. The fight had given them both an appetite and they ate some dry biscuit and cheese, with a carrot for Hob.

'Which path do you fancy?' asked Sera.

'Perhaps we should have kept one alive, persuaded him to show us the way down.'

'Bit late for that now.'

Ellen wandered over to the end of the rocky platform. The right-hand path curved upwards, the left-hand one neither rose nor fell, but both were lost in the mist after a few yards.

'I vote left,' she said, 'not that I have an impressive record for choosing directions. We could try it for a while. If it drops, we'll know we're going the right way.'

'But what if it takes us round and back to where we started?'

'You want to try the other? It might take us to the top of the pass, the place we've been trying to avoid.'

'And we're assuming,' said Sera, 'that those bastards were telling the truth about a faster route over the mountain.'

'These paths aren't here for fun and one thing's for sure, we'll never find out by sitting here.'

They left the decision to Hob. He strolled to the end of the platform, considered for a moment, and then swayed along the path to the left. Is this what my life has come to, thought Ellen, letting a mule decide for me?

They hadn't gone more than a few yards when Sera said, 'The eye? Really? You couldn't just have slit his throat?'

'I didn't like the way he was looking at me,' she said.

After the first quarter of a mile they started losing height. It was still impossible to see where they were heading, but as far as Ellen could judge it was in the right direction. Half a mile or so later they stopped. The path carried on into a huge opening in the rock face, twenty feet high at least. A few small bushes with dark green leaves had rooted themselves in crevices around the opening, like garlands.

'Another damned tunnel,' said Sera.

'I can see that. At least there's no river this time.'

'No. But we'll probably disturb a family of bears. I don't like bears.'

'Do bears live in tunnels?'

'Only one way to find out.'

They had three precious candles left. Ellen lit one as they reached the limit of daylight from the entrance. The ground and walls were smooth, almost polished, and the roof arched high overhead.

'Why build it so big?' asked Sera. 'It must have taken an army years to quarry it out, and I don't remember seeing it marked on Unselm's map.'

'To be fair, the map was a bit vague after the mountain pass.'

They carried on slowly, the yellow glow from the candle only just reaching to the roof. After another mile or so, with the path always heading downhill, the flame fluttered and

Ellen shielded it with her hand. She sensed air coming in from somewhere, a warm breeze that reminded her of harvest time at home; hay in the fields and ripe apples.

A pale glimmer of light appeared ahead, growing brighter. They walked faster and within a few minutes they reached the end of the tunnel. The path fell away across a slope of rocks and scree, and a thousand feet below them a flat plain stretched for miles in a patchwork of green and yellow.

They'd made it to the far side of the mountain, and back to summer. A band of darker blue shimmered on the horizon. The sea. And before that was a mass of buildings, tiny from this distance but part of a town - a city - ten times or more the size of Haefen.

All her life Ellen had been used to houses built of wood and brick, a few of the grander ones from grey stone. But this place gleamed white in the sun which reflected off towers and domes, like something from a dream.

'I guess that must be Coria,' she said.

CHAPTER 6

Someone's Watching

AN UNINVITED GUEST

I decided to work on the conference paper back at the apartment. On the way home I paused on the small bridge and glanced down at the green water. A young duck floated underneath on a winding route through the lily pads and I wondered what that serenity would feel like, moving through the world with no apparent effort. No obvious streams entered the lake or flowed out, but perhaps there were unseen currents under the surface doing the hard work.

I'd learnt to dive a few years before on a coral reef off the Shukkanan coast and I knew about subaqueous rivers; invisible, but all too real. One carried me deep and far out of sight of my dive buddy. I almost ran out of air, but it never put me off. I loved the experience of sinking below the choppy, empty surface of the ocean to float through another world with its own mountains and valleys, its own rules. Completely separate, wholly alien.

As the duck reappeared on the other side of the bridge, I wondered who might be responsible for the break-in at the lab. It made no sense. Like a stolen work of art that could never be seen in public again, I could always prove that the research was mine. None of my colleagues would be able to claim it, and anyway, none of them were murderers. As far as I knew.

Shalmar hadn't been above a spot of industrial espionage in his time, but killing someone was out of his league. And what would a designer of veeyar games do with an arcane theory that had no obvious practical application?

I wasn't the only person to keep my research secret or drop red herrings to throw people off the scent. The data theft might have been a huge accident. Someone else's work was the target, and the thief broke into the wrong lab. An argument that would have made sense if not for my missing encryption key.

My mind went back to my twelfth birthday, the day my dad left home and never came back. The day my mum's mind wandered off in search of him and never returned either. That was the first day I realised I was alone and always would be. Childhoods define you, no matter what the existentialists say. Some choices don't exist.

But that was then. The duck drifted in towards the shore and I made my way home.

THE SUN WAS STREAMING in through the balcony windows as I punched in the code and let myself into the apartment. If I could only travel back in time. Not go to The Markdown, not drag that man here. What had he called himself? Mack? Not a Niyan name, so bound to be false. Why hadn't I noticed? That's the trouble with bodies when you're in a hurry, they lead you astray.

I stood in the middle of the room. Was it my imagination or did I still sense his presence? His cologne was one of the fashionable spices the younger men affected these days, but this was unusual, a dark musky scent like damp earth on a forest floor.

I've been hyper-sensitive to smells ever since I was a girl. I know why, an overabundance of olfactory sensory neurons in my nose, each with its own receptor, each able to react to any stray molecules in the air. And there were more than a few of those in the room.

My pulse had speeded up even though nothing obvious was out of place, the same as in the lab. I searched from room to room, like a scent hound following a trail. It was everywhere. And strongest in the bedroom - was that a slight indentation on my pillow? Not from me, I always make the bed before I leave.

I still wasn't sure. After the previous couple of days this was nothing more than old-fashioned paranoia which I could handle: see it, name it, forget about it. And then I opened the bathroom cabinet. Some people might call me obsessive; that's pushing it too far, but I like things to be in their proper places. Another good reason to live alone. And although the change in positions was minute, I would have sworn that the box of contraceptives had moved, ditto the new toothpaste and my body lotion.

Any last doubts were shrinking fast. Someone had got in without knowing the key code and trawled through my apartment. Someone who'd violated my safest of spaces. And unless my intuition was badly out of whack, it wasn't Mack, even though he'd been a big, big mistake. My pulse was still rattling along; how many more people did I need to worry about?

VOYEUR

Should he have been more careful? On balance, he thought not. The woman's reaction as she looked in the bathroom cabinet was priceless. He could almost smell the fear seeping out of her skin. He watched as she touched all the items he had examined; some of his skin cells were now on her, and the intimacy was close to unbearable. He almost envied the Niyan she'd taken home the other night, but consummation had never been his preference. Anticipation, gratification deferred; so much more elegant to slake desire. If he was lucky, she'd pick up someone new and this time he'd be able to watch. Real time, nothing beats it.

As for the Niyan, he'd fulfilled his purpose and it was inefficient to keep objects around when their usefulness was over. Almost an insult. The man had died quietly, just that pleasing warm struggle as he felt the wire tighten around his neck. His body was folded in a waste bin behind the mall; this time tomorrow it would be crushed and compacted beyond recognition. The men on the refuse disposal trucks earned so little, and he was happy to carry out his public duty and help them supplement their incomes. Nothing onerous, just turning a blind eye to an arm or leg sticking out of the rubbish. An investment, was how he viewed it.

A movement on the screen caught his attention. The woman was undressing in the bathroom while the shower was running. This was more like it. He'd hidden cameras in every room, no point in missing anything, but this promised to be good. Except that something was wrong; the image was becoming blurred and out of focus until he could see nothing but hazy blocks of colour. Steam from the shower had condensed on the tiny camera lens. No matter, he was a patient man, and this was all a bonus, even if he'd have to ping the recordings over to his employer. He would, of course, keep copies for his own archives. He'd known from the start, especially since he first saw Ashira in the flesh, that this job was going to be fun.

AN INVITATION

I called building security and had physical locks fitted to my apartment door. Whoever had found their way in knew how to hack an entrance code, and at least I'd see if anyone tried to force the door. But unless I was wrong, they'd already taken whatever they came in for.

That was three days ago. I'd finished the paper for the Metaphysics Society meeting since then, but there'd been no development on the break-in. Even Danu's contacts had come up with nothing. Perhaps the theft was speculative, but if so then the guard paid a high price for nothing.

Three weeks to the Society meeting, and I'd redrafted the paper more times than I cared to remember, trying to second guess the reaction. The findings still seemed fantastic, and I'd lived with my research for the past three years. Some of the audience would laugh, some would walk out in disgust. There would be mutterings, there would be disbelief. But however they reacted, they wouldn't be able to argue with the equations.

The lab was empty when I arrived; I'd given Danu the

week off. Soon though, when I published and the funds came in for the experimental phase, this place would be alive with activity. At least three more post-grads to assist Danu, four if the grants were generous enough. I sat at my desk and shuffled through the post I'd picked up at reception. The usual rubbish, but one envelope which stood out. The Eser Corporation logo, heavyweight paper. If Shalmar had something to say, why hadn't he messaged me as usual? I found a card inside, cream and green with gold borders and a lot of embossing; an invitation to the latest product launch. So he'd managed to get his act together at last; another opportunity to have his ego stroked, another chance for Shalmar to preen.

Then I noticed the date of the event; the day before I was due to present my paper. Typical. He'd expect me to come and applaud him, but I'd never seen him at one of my presentations. His loss this time. He'd hear about it soon enough.

But then I thought: why not go to his announcement? He'd talk about some new game, and the next day I would change the world. My name would be famous for generations, still talked about when Shalmar Eser would be forgotten dust. I didn't realise then just what I'd be famous for.

I put the card to one side, wondering why I'd bothered to come in today. Habit; the grant applications were ready to send at the click of a key, I had no teaching or marking. Why not take a few days off for some hiking in the hills? The idea appealed; I could travel alone and stay in a small hotel I knew, in the foothills of the Salas mountains with excellent trails. Maybe some scrambling to keep me in practice, but nothing too taxing.

I studied the invitation again, convinced that something hadn't gone to plan at Shal's last party. He'd been prepared to make an announcement, then someone threw tacks on the road. The day came, and he wasn't ready. Shal was always so organised, so aware of the optics. Something had changed since the opening of Eser Tower. The plans were on track, the timeline where it needed to be. He'd lost a few weeks, but I still wouldn't like to be the gameplay designers who missed the original deadline. Shal had never been known for his charity towards dead wood. In the last year alone, three of his employees had killed themselves, according to Danu. Hushed up somehow; those optics again.

With hindsight it's easy to see the links, the places where issues that seem a million miles apart intersect. But the world would be a different place if we were able to go back and change our decisions. The laws of physics are clear about that. As someone once said, time's arrow flies in only one direction.

I felt unsettled. A few minutes ago I was looking forward to a few days alone in the hills, now I wanted to camp in the lab like a guard dog, as if that would make any difference. My apartment didn't feel any safer. Memory plays tricks, and we're programmed to deny evidence we don't want to see. Perhaps the trouble at the lab had made me paranoid, imagining ghosts. Coincidences happen. Mack was a chancer who got lucky, and the encryption key was gathering dust down the back of a chair or under a rug.

On the other hand, I'd heard nothing following the theft of my research. The illogical part of my mind expected a ransom demand, but that would have been ridiculous. My project drives hadn't been wiped, there were always backups, and my data didn't come with non-fungible tokens. So a ransom was out.

I thought of Shalmar and his hazy concept of ownership, but the Ashira Field was a million miles away from anything he could use to make money.

I came back to the original theory. The break-in had been a catch-all, a general sweep for information. My research was simply caught up by someone hoping to stumble over a useable idea, a diamond amongst the dross.

None of this helped. My trip to the hills was over before it started, and my only option was to watch my back and wait.

CHAPTER 7

Coria

THE LADIES' ROOM

It was almost dark when they stopped at the first inn they came to on the outskirts of the town, not too grand. 'Unselm gave me more than enough gold', said Sera. 'The students pay for their studies but what would we spend it on?'

Ellen let him negotiate for the rooms. Their appearance had already caused stares as they made their way through the streets. The way people here dressed seemed completely impractical, both men and women in vivid greens, blues and reds, with hair teased into such bizarre towers and curls that it took her a while before she realised that most of them were wigs. She'd always felt different, but this was another league.

'Did you know Coria was like this?' asked Ellen.

Sera shook his head. 'My first time here. It's a disconcerting place.'

When Hob was settled in the stables, they each ordered a beef pie with sweet turnips and a jug of ale.

'How's your arm?' asked Sera.

'Sore. But it's healing.'

'The cut on your neck shows, you should find something to hide it. People will think I beat you.'

'Do I care what people think?'

'I do and you should. We don't know our way around, so I'd be careful what you say, especially about Haefen.'

'The whole point of coming here was to find answers.'

'Step by step. And we should find different clothes. We don't want people staring at us as if we're bumpkins, and you don't exactly smell like summer flowers.'

Sera went to his room after they'd eaten but Ellen couldn't wait to see more of the town, whether or not the inhabitants stared at her. The streets outside were wider than those in Haefen, and busier, even though it was dark. No fear of wolves here.

She walked to a nearby corner, past torches in sconces attached to the walls of buildings, and turned down a wider street lined with shops. The people who lived here must be more than wealthy if they could afford the goods arranged in the bow windows. A little way further on she noticed that almost all the people on the street were women, most of them with lace shawls covering their hair and faces. As they reached the entrance to an alleyway a hundred yards away, they ducked in and disappeared, as if deciding to change direction at the last moment.

Ellen reached the alley and peered down to where a torch was burning next to a small door. A woman pushed past her, apologised, and then said, 'Your first time? Come with me.'

Ellen followed her to the door where the woman knocked, three quick taps followed by two more. The door opened, and the woman beckoned her in to a large space with candlelit tables set around the edge. It was filled entirely by women; dancing, looking into each other's eyes, laughing, holding hands.

The woman who brought her in had disappeared and Ellen waited by the entrance door, not sure what to do. Strange, she thought, I can stab a man in the brain, but I'm lost in a place like this.

Another woman walked across the room towards her. She was older, maybe in her forties, and elegant in a dark yellow silk dress, her breasts almost bare above the bodice and a waist that would look too narrow on a ten-year-old. A confection of ivory clips and ribbons held her dark brown hair in place, piled high, but her skin was mesmerising, the reddish-gold of fallen leaves at the start of autumn.

'You appear lost,' she said. 'Can I get you something to drink?'

After all this time, to speak to another woman. The last was Annegret, and her bones must have crumbled to dust long since.

The woman found a table and returned a few moments later with a jug and two cups of decorated glass. 'You're a country mouse and no mistake.' She filled both glasses from the bottle. 'I'm Sophia. What do I call you?'

'Ellen. Ellen Dust.'

'A queer name, to be sure, but perhaps you think the same about mine. Here, taste this.'

'What is it?'

'Negus, girl. Wine, sugar, lemons, nutmeg, and a little gin to make it worthwhile.' She emptied her own glass. 'You're not from around here. And from the looks of you there's a story behind those blue eyes.'

'I've been travelling, with a friend.'

'And where is she, this friend?'

'He. In his room, resting. It was been a long day.'

'So you left him to his own devices while you came to see

what delights Coria offers. Well, you've come to the right place.'

There was nothing like this in Haefen. Sure, there were the men who never married and the girls who preferred kissing other girls to tumbling in the fields with lads. But this was a revelation.

Sophia reached for her hand and Ellen snatched it away.

'My apologies,' said Sophia. 'But please don't worry. In this room you can do as much, or as little, as you want. Be who you want to be.'

Ellen tried the negus, and the alcohol spread an immediate flush through her body. 'The last few days have been difficult. I should be the one apologising.'

Sophia pointed at her arm. 'You have a stain on your sleeve. If I had to guess, I'd say it was blood.'

'There was some trouble on the road. We dealt with it.'

'I don't doubt it.' Sophia sat back, cradling a fresh glass. 'There's much more to you than meets the eye, I knew as soon as I saw you. Dressed like a peasant from a history play, holding yourself like a street fighter.' She leant forward. 'I would love to hear your story.'

'My story would take too long to tell, and I should get back to my room. The journey here was tiring.'

'Where are you staying?'

'The Blue Boar. It was the first place we saw.'

'You came from the north then. Well, my home is just a couple of streets away. I receive visitors at ten every morning and bring your friend, he can keep my husband amused.'

Ellen tried, but couldn't keep the surprise from her face.

'Yes,' said Sophia, 'a husband. We have an arrangement; I pursue my hobbies, he his. A woman in this society needs the rank that only marriage brings. But we enjoy places like this to maintain our sanity.'

Sophia walked Ellen to the door. 'So, Ellen Dust, until

tomorrow. Don't forget, the blue door, almost exactly the colour of your eyes. You'll recognise it when you see it.' She took both of Ellen's hands in hers. 'And I have a sense you'll find we've a lot more in common than you think.'

BY THE LAKE

Sophia had been right, the house wasn't difficult to find. But why even consider meeting the woman from last night? She'd gone down the alleyway and into that strange building out of curiosity, nothing more.

As she'd realised during the night when she was lying awake in the unfamiliar bed, she'd never been so alone. If what she discovered at the Priory was true, then everyone she'd known was dead and buried, eaten by worms, with any remains under the waters that flooded her home. Sera was the nearest she had to a friend now, and he'd been in her life for less than a week. Although, she had to admit, a special bond developed quickly when you shared a killing spree with someone. So perhaps the loneliness was why she was here, outside the grandest house on the street with a blue door that, she had to agree, was the colour of her own eyes.

Sera had taken himself off early and left her a message with the innkeeper to meet back in their rooms at midday. A good thing; she hadn't been sure how to explain to him what happened the night before.

The blue door was still there the third time she passed as

she walked up and down the street. Half an hour, she told herself, and then I'll leave. The door opened at the second knock and a young woman invited her inside. Clearly she was expected.

'My mistress asked that you wait here,' said the woman, 'she'll be with you presently.'

The hallway was as wide as it was long, with pale green walls and ornate golden mouldings running along the top under the high ceiling. Haefen had never seemed so far away.

'Ellen, you came! How delightful.' Sophia swept down the curved staircase; her dress was red velvet today, with a dark cape. 'No man with you, I see. Probably best. I thought we might take the air - the park is close by and you won't be so noticeable there as on the streets. Forgive me, but is that skirt made of old sacks?'

To be fair, the journey hadn't been kind to her clothing. 'You were welcoming last night,' Ellen said, 'and I was tired. Exhausted, if I'm honest. But I didn't come to Coria for pleasure. And I'm here now to say thank you, that's all.'

'No, you're not. You came here for answers. This city isn't what you expected. It seems alien. You're all at sea, as if you've lost control of your own life. Trust me, I know how that feels.'

IN THE PARK a vast spread of grass, gravel and trees was arranged in geometric patterns around a lake. 'This is where one comes to be seen,' said Sophia.

'And that's a good idea for me, dressed as I am in rags?'

'I was trying to be amusing. And you must admit, your clothing is a little homely. But while you're with me no-one will say anything; my husband is one of the richest men in the city.'

They found an empty wooden bench overlooking the lake

and watched as a swan and her cygnets paddled up to a small island in the middle of the lake and clambered onto the bank. Was this what Haefen was like now, nothing more than a safe place for birds to nest among the ruins?

'You told me last night that we had something in common,' said Ellen. 'I don't agree. We're worlds apart.'

'Worlds apart, very apt. Yes, we are. Anyone can see that. But appearances can deceive, as you already realise.' She reached into the small bag she was carrying and pulled out a small decorated tin. 'Snuff,' she said. 'Do you take it? No, I thought not.'

She pinched a little brown powder from the tin, lifted it to her nose and sniffed it in. 'Ah, delicious. Just the thing after an evening of too much wine and company. I have this blend made especially for me, just a hint of jasmine to scent the tobacco. You're welcome to try, but the sneezing when you first take it can be tiresome.'

Worlds apart. In some ways Sophia was an alien creature, but at the same time there was also something familiar about her. The same confidence in herself, as if nothing could surprise her or catch her off balance. She is, Ellen thought, a little like me.

Sophia wiped her nose delicately with a small lace handkerchief. 'This isn't my home, you know, not my real home.' She laughed. 'You only need look at me to see that. I arrived here ten years ago, when I was about your age. By accident.'

'Why didn't you go back?'

'I never found the way. Believe me, I tried. This city felt like a trap, as if I was in a nightmare and I couldn't wake up.'

'Surely there were people who could have helped you.'

'I tried that too, at first. Has someone had ever locked you in an asylum? Kept you in a small room with bars on the windows and guards in the corridors? Said you were mad and dangerous? It happened to me, because I told the truth of who I was and where I came from. But I learned the rules of the game and persuaded them I was "cured".'

The swans were back in the water and paddled across in a line towards them, the mother gliding in front, small grey cygnets trying to keep up.

'I was lucky. A group of worthy citizens visited the asylum each month, salving their consciences by checking that we weren't actually being tortured. And to make sure that we couldn't escape, of course. One of them was taken with me. You know how men look at women and horses in the same way, trying to decide if they're a worthwhile investment. I was young, attractive, exotic. When I was released, he asked me to be his mistress, but I held out for marriage. I'd already seen how this place works.'

She rested a hand on Ellen's arm. 'You're a good listener. I don't talk about myself much these days.'

'You said you came here by accident, so what happened? Were you lost on a journey?'

'In a way. But I'm fascinated to know more about you and why you're here. Not by accident, I'm guessing. Humour me, Ellen, tell me about your home.'

Don't talk about Haefen, Sera had said, and it seemed like good advice. 'I don't want people thinking I'm insane too,' said Ellen.

'I already know you're not.'

Perhaps Tollin had been right; not everyone was out to harm her, and Sophia might have useful information. 'I come from a city called Haefen. A couple of weeks or more away on foot, the other side of the mountain. Well, we call it a city but it's small, more like a town by your standards. You wouldn't appreciate it much if this place seems hard.' She paused. 'The trouble is, I don't believe Haefen exists anymore.'

'Why on earth not? You must have been travelling for years unless there was a war or some sort of disaster.'

'I left home less than two weeks ago. Unexplained things were happening. Wolves reappearing centuries after they died out, attacking our children. A river swelling to devour our fields even when there was no rain. Summer turning to winter and back to summer, all in the space of a few hours.'

Sophia looked out over the lake to the island. 'And why does your mind tell you that your home doesn't exist anymore?'

Such a good question. What had she got; rumours from the brothers at the Priory, a traveller's tale from an ancient book. Haefen might still be there. Tollin and Annegret going about their business, Tollin still letting the cat steal food from the kitchen. For a moment she allowed herself to build the pictures in her mind, and then she remembered why she'd been forced to leave her home.

Her arm still ached where the wolf had bitten her, and she saw herself wrapping the baby in its shroud and burying it on the moor. She pictured the brother in the corridor with worms erupting from his living body. She remembered the river rising over the fields.

'Are you sure you want to know?' she said to Sophia.

SHIP WITHOUT SAILS

Sera was waiting for her back at the inn. She found him sitting in the large dining room, halfway through a platter of bread, cheese and pickles.

'How was your morning?' he asked.

'Complicated. You go first.'

The innkeeper came over, as suspicious today as he had been yesterday. The clothes again, she guessed. But gold was gold, and he took her order for mutton pie and small beer.

'I went to the harbour,' said Sera. 'Sailors come and go, they see and hear things and they're usually willing to talk for the price of some ale or a glass of rum.'

Ellen filched one of his pickles. 'Were they willing to talk?'

'Sailors are superstitious, always have been. Maybe it's living with death always just a few feet beneath the decks. Did you know that most can't swim? Seems like the first thing I'd learn if I were going to spend weeks at a time out of sight of land, not that I have that sort of death wish.'

'I can't swim,' said Ellen. 'Never needed to. In Haefen we

always saw it as something barbaric. We kept away from water, which is ironic given what happened.'

Sera flicked her hand away from the last piece of cheese and finished it himself. 'Something had spooked them. Everyone I tried to talk to just walked away.'

'You don't think it was anything to do with your appearance? Like you said, we don't fit in here.'

'I found someone in the end. An old boy, been on the rum for a couple of days by the smell of him. He was sitting in the back of one of the taverns on the harbourside, talking to himself.'

'Did he talk to you?'

'He'd been part of the crew of a fishing boat. They go out for a week or so at a time; don't ask me what they try to catch, he told me but it meant nothing. I've never liked fish; meat should be red.'

'We didn't came here to learn about the fishing business in Coria.'

'Sorry. He'd been out on a regular trip. Four of them as usual in the crew. The catch was good and they had a full haul. They were two days out, on their way back to port, when they saw something on the horizon. They knew it couldn't be land, and then they realised it was a ship.'

'Isn't that to be expected when you're out at sea? Ships, ocean, they sort of go together.'

'Not a ship like this. The way they described it, there were two short masts, one at each end, but no sails set. Two huge chimneys rose from the middle of the hull, almost as tall as the ship was long, belching out smoke. The man I talked to said he'd never seen anything like it.'

'Chimneys on a ship? You said he liked his rum; maybe he was drunk and seeing things.'

'My thoughts exactly. But he explained they never drink when they're working. Too easy to get something wrong and fall overboard; he lost his own brother that way. That's why they hit the taverns so hard when they came ashore.'

'He might still have imagined it.'

'But then another member of his crew turned up. Sober as you or me, told the same story. And I haven't reached the best part yet. There was a fair breeze blowing at the time and their boat was tacking backwards and forwards to get home. But this strange ship was coming right at them. Sailing straight into the wind, and all without sails.'

Not that she was an expert on nautical matters, but she'd seen enough ships in the days when they still came to Haefen. And they all had sails; smoking chimneys were for houses.

'So what happened when the ship got closer? Did they speak to anyone or find out where it was from?'

'Like I told you, sailors are superstitious. They were sailing as close to the wind as they dared just to get away. They'd convinced themselves that it was some kind of a phantom ship with a crew of demons, coming to claim their souls.'

'Evidently the demons failed.'

'You have no romance in your soul.'

'Demons are romantic?'

'Nothing matters to you but the evidence of your own eyes. If you'd been there and heard the fear in their voices; remember, this ship was sailing straight into the wind, bearing down on them faster than any ship had a right to. It came closer and closer, a dark grey hull and smoke from the two chimneys streaming out behind it. And when it was less than a mile away, it suddenly turned one hundred and eighty degrees and sailed back the way it had come, churning up its own wake. A few minutes later it had disappeared over the horizon.'

'No sign of demons? Fishermen's souls all present and correct?'

Sera sighed with exasperation. 'Think, Ellen, about everything that's going on. Why shouldn't there be ships without sails? We've experienced stranger things.'

No answers then, just more questions.

'What about you?' said Sera.

'Like I said, it's complicated. And there's someone you should meet.'

HOUSE WITH THE BLUE DOOR

They stood outside the house with the blue door. Sera looked over at the building, then back to Ellen. 'So you met her in some sort of secret tavern where there were no men?'

'You were a soldier, Sera, you've seen more of the world than I have. And you keep telling me to be open to new experiences.'

'Secret women-only societies wasn't quite what I had in mind.'

'You'll like her.' What Sophia would make of Brother Sera was another matter. This time the door opened before she could knock. No maid, just Sophia showing them into a room so highly decorated that it made the hallway look like a derelict stable.

'My husband returns in an hour,' said Sophia. 'He's very traditional. Likes to know where he stands, knows what he likes. Doesn't like surprises.'

'He chose you,' said Ellen. 'Wasn't that a bit out of the ordinary?'

'That was then. A brain silts up a lot in ten years.' She

looked from Sera to Ellen and back again. 'Ellen told me what's been happening with her town. And I gather your Priory's been experiencing strange events too.'

'You'll forgive me,' said Sera, 'but I'm not sure why you're so interested in the problems of a couple of strangers.'

He was being defensive, it was in the tone of his voice, the way he perched on the edge of his chair. And why not? From his point of view it must have seemed suspicious, this wealthy stranger with a penchant for other women, infiltrating herself into their affairs. And, thought Ellen, defensive about me too. It was obvious that Sophia's interest was personal and not just idle curiosity.

Sophia unclipped her two large, gold earrings and placed them on the small side table. 'You're not the only people to find yourselves in a strange place, out of time. I told Ellen that I came here ten years ago, which is true. But I've come to realise that, bizarre as it might sound, not all years last as long as others.' She picked up one of the earrings and turned it over in her hands. 'If by some miracle I get back home, I have no idea how much time will have passed. Perhaps one year, perhaps a thousand. But I know one thing - I want to find out, even if I've lost everyone I ever knew. I've been sleepwalking for the past ten years and you coming here has woken me.'

The suspicion of a tear ran down her cheek and Sophia wiped it away. 'Sorry. Every day's a performance, and it's hard to take the mask off. I've lived here so long that being Sophia has become comfortable. Safe. I could stay here until my last day, but if anyone mourns when I die, they'll be remembering someone who never existed. You understand.'

Is this what's waiting for me, thought Ellen. Exile for ever, loneliness, a sort of living death?

Sera looked agitated and uncomfortable. He fitted well enough in the Priory, and on the road he seemed like a man who'd found where he belonged. But in this elegant salon of civilisation and manners, he was out of place. The stained jacket and leggings weren't much help.

'You said you were trapped here,' he said. 'Why didn't you just retrace your steps? I could, so could Ellen, even if she believes Haefen has gone. So why not you? What makes you sure that the same has happened to your home?'

'If I could have retraced my steps, I would. But I didn't come here on foot and the way home wasn't possible.'

'A ship then?' said Ellen.

Sophia struggled to choose her words. 'It was a sort of ship, but not one that sails on water. Where I came from there were ships that sailed through the air. I know, it sound impossible. I told you, they locked me in an asylum the last time I said those words.' She focussed on the earrings again.

'You wouldn't believe it to see me now, but I was the captain of one of those ships of the air, ferrying people from one place to another. We were caught in a storm and my compass, I suppose you would call it, was damaged. The aircraft fell into the sea and sank. I was the only person to survive. Over a hundred souls lost when they were in my care, and never a day goes by when I don't grieve for them.'

She let the earrings drop to the table. 'I suppose you think I'm mad now.'

Sera ran his hands through his hair, the way he always did when concentrating. 'Ellen told you about the Priory. My brothers are good men, intelligent men, but they believe nothing unless it's written in an old book, and I can guarantee that there's nothing from the ancients about people in ships that fly. But there's nothing about ships with chimneys and no sails either, and I've spoken to people who swore on their children's lives they'd seen one. I believe them, and for what it's worth, I believe you.'

'I sometimes wonder if I am mad,' said Sophia. 'In this life

I have money and a fabulous home. I have a husband who loves me in his own way. I have standing in society. But within limits. There are unbreakable rules, especially for women. I can't become a ship's captain here, I can't start a business. I can't own property or earn a living. I depend upon the goodwill of men all the time.'

'And it was different, where you came from?'

'It hadn't always been. But I grew up knowing anything was possible for me as long as I put in the effort. No-one ever told me that I couldn't do something just because I was a girl.'

'I'd like to see your world,' said Ellen.

'It wasn't all easy. Here I'm given everything I want and my time is my own. There I had to work to live, but at least I was free. I'd choose that freedom any day compared with being the over-dressed slave I am here.'

'I've seen slaves,' said Sera. 'Their lives are nothing like yours.'

'Not all chains are visible,' said Sophia. 'But it's time I got rid of mine.'

'How? You've had ten years to get home.'

'You came to Coria hoping for answers,' said Sophia, 'but you won't find any. Not here.'

'So where?' asked Ellen. This entire trip to Coria was beginning to feel like a dead end.

Sophia turned to Sera, 'You talked about that strange vessel the fishermen saw. I've seen ships like that, in old history books back where I came from. Steamships, they were called. And the one seen here must have a home port. We should find it; if they have steamships, they might have more technology. And what other options are there? Come with me or turn around and go home, although who knows what you'll find when you get there.'

Sophia was right, what other options were there? Stay in Coria's gilded cage or keep looking. Home hadn't been an option for a while. 'How will you track down the place it came from?' asked Ellen.

'We'd need to charter a ship of our own. Sail on the bearings of the steamship they saw and hope it hadn't veered too far off a straight course from its home port.'

'Even if you find a ship, you still need a willing captain and crew and a huge helping of luck,' said Sera. 'And the means to pay for it.'

Sophia was silent for a moment. 'I have some money hidden away, but probably not enough. My husband does, but…'

'But you're planning to leave him,' said Ellen. 'In my experience, men don't take well to that news.'

'I brought gold with me,' said Sera. 'More than enough.' He sighed. 'Except that I won't be coming with you.'

Somehow this wasn't a surprise. She'd known all along that Sera was on a different journey from her, even if their paths had coincided for a while. It didn't make the words any easier to hear.

'I need to get back to the Priory,' he said. 'My task was to come here with Ellen and keep her safe, not that she needed much help. My part in this is over, at least for now.'

'Are you sure?' asked Ellen. 'We could do with a soldier around and you miss your old life; I saw your face on the mountain.'

'I left that life behind for a reason and nothing's changed. No, I'll go back with Hob to keep me company. But first, if you're set on this, we'll find a captain who won't dump you overboard as soon as you're out of sight of land, and charter that ship for you.'

THE BILLY BOY

The low ceiling in her room at the inn pressed down, and the bare floorboards had gaps she could slip her hand through. Was the pervasive, sour smell from her or the thousands of bodies that had passed through? Both probably, she was merely adding to the tally.

A small window looked onto the stables at the back of the inn. Hob was there, resting, eating hay, sleeping on his feet. She should be more like a mule. Go with the flow, dig her heels in sometimes, and not only for effect. Stop worrying about tomorrow. Except that for some people, tomorrow had already came.

She'd argued with Sera at first. Did he think she wasn't competent to find a ship and crew? Why was he still there if he was so eager to get back to his comfortable life in the Priory? But those were more by way of sulks than rational arguments. She'd came this far in life without leaning on other people, and she wasn't about to start now.

Sophia, though, was still an unknown quantity. Her story was a hair's breadth from fantasy, and yet there *was* something other-worldly about her.

And what about her own story; how would that sound to a stranger? Her old life in Haefen already belonged to someone else, not to her. The familiar hollow ache spread from the base of her throat; never look back, she reminded herself.

She glanced at the clothes laid out on the bed. As she'd pointed out to Sophia, the current fashion for women in Coria was predicated on them doing very little. Corsets, padded hips, skirts so full they made walking through doorways an exercise in geometry. Not altogether practical for a long sea voyage. But the clothes spread out on the bed included breeches, hose, shirt, drawers, jacket and heavy buckled shoes. After initial disbelief, she had to admit that it was an interesting plan. Sophia wanted to turn them into men. Both were tall for Corian women, and Sophia had assured her that without the corsets and stays her voluptuousness would evaporate.

'Cut our hair short and we'll fool them all,' she'd said. 'People see what they expect to see.' It didn't seem to have occurred to Sophia that she was one of the more recognisable people in the city, but time would tell.

Sera had been gone all afternoon. He'd been so confident about finding what they needed down at the port, but he should have been back by now. Unless he'd taken her at her word and left already, strapped his pack to Hob and left on the road north out of the city. Without his gold, there would be no ship and no answers.

Even if he came back now with good news, it would just be the beginning of another nightmare. The thought of trusting her life to some planks of wood, a pot of tar, and a few scraps of canvas made her stomach heave; gods only knew what it would be like on a rough sea out of sight of land.

Ellen threw the breeches to one side and sat on the bed.

She'd lost her friends, lost her home, and it seemed as if she was about to lose her own identity. Who would she be if not Ellen Dust?

The inn door downstairs slammed, someone ran up the stairs, and then her door flew open. Sera had never demonstrated a robust understanding of privacy.

'I've found one,' he said. 'A Captain Markus lost his wife a few days ago and doesn't want to stay here. Too many reminders, he said.'

'Does he own a ship?'

'The Billy Boy. I'm no sailor, but it looks seaworthy. He uses it to trade between ports but he's happy to go on what he called a "speculative voyage".'

'What about payment? And what did you tell him about us?'

Sera cleared another space on the bed and sat next to her. 'The man's no fool, Ellen. I didn't tell him everything or he'd put to sea within the hour to get away from me. But he'd heard about the ship with no sails, and he doesn't believe in demons. He's intrigued by the possibility of finding where it came from; he likes the idea of having a ship that can sail even when there's no wind.' He smiled. 'The gold helped.'

'So who does he think I am, and Sophia? You stuck to the story we agreed, two of your cousins?'

Sera picked up the jacket and held it against her. 'Very fetching. You'll carry it off well, they'll see a teenage boy. Sophia's another matter. I can't picture her without her flounces and curls. And she has a very womanly figure.'

'Are you saying I'm not womanly? Just because I don't wear silk and satin, paint my face, show my breasts to the world and totter around like a lapdog?'

'Ellen, of all the women I've ever known, you're the one I

would choose to spend my time with. True, you probably frighten most men away, but they aren't worthy. Men might desire women, and sometimes they need them, but they rarely respect them. You deserve respect. You demand respect. And I know you'll never settle for anything less.'

A BANTAM COCK

The rooftops were glowing with the first rays of the sun and the air still carried its pre-dawn chill as Sera and Ellen arrived at the harbourside. The citizens of Coria rose late, apart from the seagulls which dipped and wheeled over the water and marched in ungainly waddles along the cobbles, searching for scraps. No wonder sailors were superstitious; the shrieking of the birds sounded like souls in torment and who was to say that when sailors drowned, they didn't return as these malicious birds shrieking out their despair.

Captain Markus was waiting for them. 'I hope your companion's on time. We need to leave within the hour if we're to catch the morning tide.'

He was older than she'd imagined, in his fifties, with long grey hair tied in a pigtail that reached halfway down the back of his dark blue coat. The Billy Boy swung on her anchor chain a few hundred yards out in the sound, a brown and cream hull with two masts and a third jutting diagonally from the bow.

'She's a fine wee brig,' said the captain. 'Creaks a bit when the seas are high, but the hull barely works and you won't get your feet wet, that's a promise.' He slapped Ellen on the back. 'Your cousin here tells me you're not over-fond of the sea. Don't fret, we'll make you comfortable enough. I've given you my cabin, only place on board with a bed, and we've strung a hammock in there for your… brother, is it? Mister Sera here was a touch vague on that point. Anyways, I guess you'll just have to fight it out for who sleeps where. Me, I'd choose a hammock any time, but a captain has some dignity to protect.'

He stood back and looked Ellen up and down as if he was about to buy a horse. Sophia had been right.

'Bit of a slender flower, aren't you? Might be best if you kept to the cabin as much as you can. Although this ain't the navy I run a disciplined ship, but sailors are sailors, and a few weeks away from shore… let's just say that they tend not to be too discriminating when it comes to the natural urges. I don't want a pretty boy like you finding yourself in trouble, if you get my meaning.' He walked away, still talking to them over his shoulder. 'Most of the crew are on board except for the reprobates over in the Anchor Tavern. They should be sober this time of the morning. Better be or you'll be rowing us to the brig. I'll round them up and we leave on time regardless of whether or not your brother is here.'

He'd no sooner disappeared inside the tavern when a carriage raced towards them over the cobbles, and pulled up a few yards away. A man jumped down and stalked towards them.

'Where is she, that bitch of a wife?'

He was a small man, shorter than Ellen but pumped up like a bantam cock. Another Vlakas. She'd met men like him before; they hadn't caused her a problem then, and this one wasn't about to change that record.

'Do I know you,' she asked.

'You're the other one,' he said. 'Look at you, disgusting, women dressing as men. We don't stand for that sort of thing here.'

'I make a better man than you any day,' she said. 'Not that it's saying much.'

The colour of his face turned as red as his coat, threatening an apoplexy, and he threw a punch at her face. Easy. She stepped sideways, grabbed his wrist and used his own momentum to trip him, leaving him sprawled on his back on the cobbles. He reminded her a giant scarlet turtle on its back, trying to right itself.

He rolled onto his front, knelt for a moment to catch his breath, got back on his feet and backed out of her reach. 'You'll be sorry for that.'

A smaller carriage drew up, pulled by just one horse. At first Ellen didn't recognise the person who climbed down. A threadbare man's wig in need of powdering under a tricorn hat. Greasy green jacket and stained white hose. How she'd managed it, Ellen couldn't tell, but there were no signs of Sophia's usual soft curves. Even her face looked pale, and her eyebrows were dark and bushy.

'Returned to type, I see,' said the man. 'After everything I've done for you and all I get is this betrayal. You'll come home with me right now, take off those disgusting clothes and dress yourself as befits my wife. You will not shame me.'

Sophia ignored him and turned to Ellen. 'We need to hurry. One of the ships' crew must have said something, and whatever else my husband is, he has the cunning of a rat. He doesn't enjoy losing his property.'

'One of him and three of us,' said Ellen. 'And to be honest, that's two more than we need.'

'He's not that stupid,' said Sophia. 'He's called out the militia to arrest me and bring me back. You too, and Sera.'

Captain Markus had returned while they were having fun. 'Husband, is it?' he said. 'I reckoned the other one was a bit delicate. Well, it's your business and Mister Sera here paid well.'

Sophia's husband danced from foot to foot with rage. 'I'll have you arrested too, I'll have your ship seized. Everything you own will be forfeit.'

The captain seemed unworried. 'Catch me first, laddie. In my experience, the soldiers of the militia don't swim.' He turned to Ellen. 'All the same, we should be on our way.'

The narrow streets funnelled the tramp of men marching towards the harbour, getting closer. Ellen hugged Sera while Hob nibbled her hand.

'Thank you for everything, my friend,' she said. 'If you trust in any gods, I hope they protect you.'

'I can do that for myself,' he said.

'I know. Now leave, before you get caught.'

THE JOLLY BOAT rowed away from the harbourside as a squad of uniformed soldiers marched around one corner in formation, and Sera and Hob disappeared around another. A small dinghy in the harbour almost overturned as Sophia's husband attempted to pull himself out of the water, too out of breath to say anything.

'You're lucky he can swim,' Ellen said to the captain.

'The wee shite was annoying me,' said Markus. 'I don't like people threatening me or my Billy Boy.'

The officer leading the squad shouted out to them. 'Get back to shore now, on pain of imprisonment.'

'Pompous sod,' said Markus. 'Don't fret, those muskets couldn't hit the side of a house at this distance. Make quite a racket, but that's what soldiers like. Shouting, marching and running around. Makes them feel useful.'

A sudden crackle of noise reached them from the shore, along with a cloud of smoke and what looked like heavy raindrops hitting the surface of the sea yards behind them.

'Told you,' said the captain.

CHAPTER 8

Fescue's Challenge

A SUMMONS

⥈

Fescue Monad used the tongs to pick up another lump of coal and placed it on the glowing fire. A few sparks flew out along with a flurry of smoke. That was the trouble with the University; they gave you a decent study as part of your rooms, with Turkey rugs and heavy curtains to keep out the draughts, but they never kept the damned chimneys swept.

He took a cigar from the box on his desk. Baradan Bright Leaf tobacco, perhaps not the very finest grade but perfectly acceptable for a man in his position. He clipped one end, toasted the other with a spill from the fire, and then allowed the flames to caress the leaves as he sucked in the aromatic smoke and blew it out in a purple cloud. A ritual he permitted himself once a day, on good days. Sometimes bad days. But today had gone well so far, and he deserved his treat.

The clock on the mantelpiece showed five o'clock. Another hour and he could wander across the quad to the dining room for High Supper. Tuesday, that meant stew day. Thick mutton stew with herb dumplings, followed by jam roly-poly and custard. He'd always said that a chap needed ballast if he was to let the imagination run free.

Fescue poured himself a couple of measures of Hurrian whiskey, admiring the amber glow as he held the cut glass up to the light, sank back into his armchair by the fire, loosened another button on his favourite embroidered waistcoat, blew out a small cloud of smoke and tapped the ash into the fireplace.

Yes, a good day. Last night he had given a paper at the Science Institute on "Steam and Motion, an Ontological Perspective." There had been satisfying applause at the end, a flurry of notes delivered today to his rooms, expressing admiration, and not a few asking if he needed collaborators for his research. Nothing from Canterbury or Oliphant, but that was to be expected. Sometimes friends were the least charitable when it came to celebrating a colleague's success. And they were envious of his moustaches, he'd seen the looks. He picked up the small hand mirror from the side table and examined his face. A little more stiffening, perhaps, before supper?

He was interrupted by a knocking on the door. A knock that was sure of its place in the world. Not Canterbury, with his querulous tap like an impoverished blackbird. Or Oliphant, for whom doors were unnecessary impediments designed to keep everyone out except him.

No, this was someone else, and at this time of the afternoon everyone from the college would be preparing themselves for their evening meal. Fescue thought of pretending that he was out, but perhaps it was another admirer? He opened the door and saw the mutton stew, the dumplings, the roly-poly and the custard evaporating. The livery of the man standing there was all-too recognisable.

'Professor Monad?' The man handed over a slip of paper, cream parchment with a coat of arms at the top. 'May I present you with your invitation to meet the Princeps. At the palace.'

'His Highness? When…?'

'I believe that the word "Now" adequately reflects the expectations of my master.'

From delight to despair in the twinkling of an eye. The Princeps, ruler of the City of Forcello and the province of New Wallachia, had recently taken up occupation in his new palace, and there were rumours that not all guests managed to leave.

'Ah, the Princeps, of course. Happy to come, thrilled. And why, may I ask, has his Highness graciously extended this unexpected invitation to me. Not a mistake, is it, by any chance?'

'Dr Fescue Monad, Professor of Applied Ontology, University of Forcello? Your name *is* on the door.'

One escape route closed off. 'You couldn't, by any chance, give me an indication of the reason for this invitation?'

'I suggest a coat, Professor. The weather is inclement and the palace can be cold. And if I might also suggest that some alacrity in your actions would be expedient. The Princeps is not celebrated for his patience.'

And they said academics were long-winded. Fescue unhung his coat from the hook by the door, took one last, longing look at this welcoming study with its fire, its whisky, its armchair still warm from where he had been sitting, and shut the door behind him as he followed the messenger down the corridor, across the quad, past the dining hall, through the college gates and into the street.

THE PRINCEPS

The coat had been a good idea, not so much for the cold but against the damp, yellow fog that smelled of coal dust and caught in the throat. Fescue found himself breaking into an inelegant trot to keep up with the man marching ahead of him, and barely missed being knocked over by one of the new steam carriages that loomed out of the murk, faster than it had any right to be. The rider, in his goggles and leather cap, sounded the horn as if he were hunting foxes out in the fields.

And as if that weren't enough, he could feel his moustaches unfurling in the damp, their carefully curated curls wilting.

They crossed one of the canals leading from the lagoon to the old town and then started climbing, the street less crowded as they approached the palace that had been created on a hill bordering the edge of the city. The summit had been covered with trees once, a park for the citizens, but the Princeps had ordered that the top be cleared and flattened for his new residence, built from brilliant white marble. Whole quarries had been exhausted, said the stories, and legions of slaves worked until they dropped, all for this one folly. Stories told in whispers; no-one questioned the Princeps. Not in public.

The gates, easily the height of four large men standing on each others' shoulders, swung open at their approach. The messenger led him across a courtyard so wide that the actual palace buildings didn't appear until they had been walking for five minutes. A giant staircase wound up to the ceremonial entrance, and the wings to either side faded away into the fog. To Fescue's surprise, the man took him around the side of the staircase to a small wooden door. The tradesmen's entrance; at least that helped to manage his expectations.

The interior of the palace was a labyrinth of corridors and stairs, lit with the new gas lamps that were beginning to appear in the houses of the rich. Eventually they reached what looked like a banqueting hall, hung with immense oil paintings of the Princeps in various heroic poses; astride a horse, wrestling a mythical creature. Did the man never smile?

He had, of course, seen the First Among Equals at the obligatory processions, balanced more precariously on his white charger than the portraits showed. But never this close, never face to face. The man seemed somehow smaller in person, but perhaps that was the effect of the crimson dressing gown and velvet slippers rather than the usual uniform with its sash and epaulettes, and polished riding boots with silver spurs.

The animal at his feet didn't help. Approximately the size of a calf, with the body of a hunting hound and what looked horribly like the head of a giant cat, the beast gazed up at Fescue with eyes that blinked slowly, reflecting the yellow light from the gas lamps.

The man in the dressing gown was scratching the creature behind one of its ears, cooing to it, and then affected to notice his visitor. 'Ah, Professor, how charming of you to pop in. I hope you don't find yourself too discommoded.' His voice was barely above a whisper. 'I thought perhaps we could have a little chat, we men of science.'

He gave one last scratch to the head of the creature, which yawned, showing teeth at least two inches long. 'What do you think of my latest creation? Selective breeding with the teensiest help from a barber surgeon for the - how shall I put this - for the messy bits. A hobby, you could call it. Every man needs a hobby, even a prince.'

Now the coat was too much; sweat was running down his neck and soaking into the armpits of his jacket. 'Indeed, Highness, a wonderful creature to be sure. Not my field, of course, I bow to your skill and expertise.'

The Princeps handed the animal's chain to one of his servants, who led it away into the shadows at the back of the hall. 'Feeding time. She becomes very tetchy if she's late for a meal. And how about you, are you hungry?'

'Well, I have missed…'

'Splendid, let's get down to business then. I gather you gave a rather interesting presentation at the Science Institute the other day. People say you are quite the man of the hour.' He paused. 'I have a little proposition for you, a new project which I want you to head up, as it were. A journey of scientific discovery. Progress, where would we be without it.'

We'd be back home with a full belly and a glass of whisky, thought Fescue.

'Discovery, very good Highness. May I ask, a discovery to what end?'

'You really are a stickler, Professor. No messing about with your incisive brain. The thing is, and I say this with all humility, there appears to be a problem with the supply of food to the city. I know, I know. You're thinking, how can there be a problem when we have such an enlightened and omniscient ruler, the father of our people etcetera etcetera? But problem there is.'

'I hesitate to ask, Highness, but may I enquire as to the precise nature of this problem?'

'Precise nature. That incisiveness again. If I knew the precise nature, there wouldn't be a problem, would there?'

Eggshells and treading came to mind, and Fescue chose the next words carefully. 'So if I understand you correctly, and if I haven't the fault is of course mine, then you want me to go on a journey of scientific discovery to solve the problem of our food supply, the precise nature of which is currently a mystery.'

'Splendid, Professor, I knew I could rely on you. Mystery, an excellent word.'

'And were you thinking of a recompense for this journey? Something by way of expenses perhaps, or a little incentive?'

'Let me see. Incentive. Failure could entail being sent down the salt mines, what? What?' He chuckled at what Fescue could only hope was a joke.

'That might act as a disincentive, Highness. Might I suggest something monetary? I would, after all, have to put my academic duties to one side and the University can get very picky when that happens.'

'Money? Isn't that a little pedestrian? Where's the excitement in money? No, something more attractive. A tour of the palace, perhaps? How would that sound? An overnight stay in one of the guest bedrooms and a visit to the menagerie, followed by a slap-up meal. As for the university; the Vice-Chancellor is a personal friend, at least for now. Leave him to me.'

He couldn't use the word disincentive twice. 'Perhaps, I

might give some thought to the matter, Highness, and make a proposal to you when I'm ready with the other details.'

'Splendid! What day is it today, Monday? I'll see you back here on Friday. My man Tiro will collect you just in case you lose your way. Good chap, Tiro, knows what's what. And Professor, don't be late.'

TIRO EXPLAINS

The same man who had brought him led him back through the corridors to the main gate, stopped and then spoke to Fescue's right ear. 'In his zeal to protect the citizens from care and concern, his Highness occasionally omits to disseminate news that is less than optimal.'

'So you know about this less than optimal news? Something to do with the food supply?'

'His Highness is pleased to use my services as his secretary, in which role I necessarily deal with events that are best handled away from the gaze of the public. There have been some…' He paused for a moment and coughed gently. 'Some happenings. Unexplained happenings.'

'You'll have to do better than that, dear chap. Happenings doesn't give me a lot to go on and if the menagerie has more of the creatures I saw just now, I'd prefer to miss that particular tour.'

'Very wise, sir.'

Obtuse didn't come into it. 'These happenings and the food supply? We don't want to disappoint his Highness, do we?'

Tiro sighed, and his body sagged inside its livery. 'The city receives food from several sources; it's been many years since we produced enough to feed ourselves from the land surrounding the city.'

'I know that, everyone knows that.'

'Since the province of Kimit was pleased to place itself under the protection of the Princeps, we receive most of our grain from there, brought to the docks at Agaret no more than a couple of days from the city.'

'Again, this isn't news. Good grain, too. Best bread from their flour, nutty flavour.'

'Two weeks ago, a shipment failed to arrive on time. When the ships finally returned, they said that something had happened to Kimit. There were no docks, no towns. No shipments of grain.'

'The fools went to the wrong place. It's obvious. Their charts were wrong, or they had a navigator who didn't know what he was doing. Drunk perhaps? The sailors I see in town are always drunk. Mind you, so would I be if I spent weeks at sea with only stale water to drink and weevil-infested biscuits to eat.'

'We didn't send just one ship. It was a convoy of four and they all reported the same thing. It's as if the civilisation at Kimit had never happened. A small boat put ashore where the harbour should have been, and all they discovered were a couple of encampments of natives in tents with herds of goats. Lots of goats. Not enough to feed the city, sadly.'

'I still don't see how I can help. The ships probably found somewhere else to sell the grain they picked up, and for a better price. I'd start with the captains.'

'We did.'

'And?'

'One lasted more than ten minutes in the feeding chamber. Then again, he was a large man and his unusually meaty thighs kept the animals busy for a while. They usually save the genitals and entrails until last; I suppose they see them as a delicacy.'

Fescue tried to suppress a shudder. 'What about the crews?'

'My master's pets are exceedingly hungry.'

'How many of these bloody animals does his Highness have?'

'It depends on his mood. Sometimes he has six or seven in various stages of development.'

'Surely he keeps them locked away?'

'He has been known to take them hunting. The trouble is bringing them back again. For some reason they haven't proved exceptionally loyal.'

'So some of them are on the loose?' Fescue had a mental image of the creature he'd seen by the side of the Princeps, wandering through the streets of Forcello as it looked for delicacies.

'Indeed, in the royal forests. But don't worry, they have short lives. And, sadly, unhappy ones.'

The fog had thickened and Tiro's reassurances had done nothing to stop Fescue picturing a calf-sized beast with slavering jaws appearing from the murk, or hearing a soft padding behind him before being brought down like a wounded gazelle.

'Is there anything else I should know? Any other "happenings"?'

Tiro pulled himself upright again. 'I believe that I've imparted all you need to know, sir.'

'So let me get this right. A whole civilisation has disappeared, along with a great deal of our food supply, and I'm expected to find a way to fix this by Friday.'

'I believe your summary to be accurate, Professor. To the point. And if I may say so, I wish you luck, for all our sakes.'

CHAPTER 9

For the Avoidance of Death

SHARING THE PROBLEM

❦

A week to find an answer and no idea where to start. On the other hand, he was a professor, an intelligent man. Options, that's what he needed. Options.

The dining room would be closed now, so he called in at his favourite chop house on the corner of Magpie Lane and Plato Street. A mutton cutlet, baked potato and mug of ale wouldn't quite make up for losing his roast dinner, but needs must. He found an empty booth and checked out the other customers. No-one he knew, which was just as well. He wasn't in the mood for gossip about the Dean's latest mistress, or the inequities of who was in line for election to University Senate. A shame; he'd always been rather partial to the cut and thrust of college politics, but this evening's events had put that into the shade. The survival of the city had unaccountably been placed in his hands, and he wasn't sure they were big enough for the task.

A week. What on earth was he expected to accomplish in a week? He should have told the Princeps it was impossible. Held his ground like a man. Except that he'd be half-digested by now in the belly of one of the beasts.

The mutton chop tasted as if the sheep had died a century ago, and the potato of sawdust. Sleep, that was the thing. A good night's sleep and tomorrow he would enlist a little help.

Sleep there had been, but not good and not for much of the night. There was nothing for it but to rope in Canterbury and Oliphant. The doctor was another option, but he lived miles away in his clifftop retreat with that rather delicious wife, and he wasn't the best choice. If the Princeps had a problem with a sore throat, or wanted advice about foxglove-based medicinal remedies, the doctor was the right man. But disappearing cities and imminent starvation required more rigorous academic discipline.

Small boys were always hanging around the porter's lodge. He gave one a few pence to take messages to Oliphant and Canterbury, asking them to come to his rooms as soon as possible. Like him, neither of them were burdened these days with the need to give lectures, so they were bound to be free. Canterbury hadn't published in years, and Oliphant claimed he was researching something to change the world but was never quite ready to reveal it.

With the messages on their way, Fescue went back to his rooms and indulged in a glass of sweet sherry. He felt a little more content; a problem shared with two colleagues left him with just thirty three and a third of the original. Not snappy, but true.

They both arrived within half an hour. Oliphant first, determined not to miss out on any conversation, and then Canterbury, fussing with spectacles that steamed up as soon as he entered the room. A fine mind, Fescue reminded himself, once he got up to pressure.

'Bit of a summons,' said Oliphant as he pulled a chair over to the fire. 'Bit peremptory if you ask me.'

Fescue waited until they were both settled and then stood facing them with his back to the fire. 'Gentlemen, we have a problem.'

There was no point in dissembling or holding back any of the details. From the initial knock on his study door last night to Tiro's admonitions at the gates of the palace, they were uncharacteristically silent.

When Fescue finished, Oliphant cracked his knuckles, an annoying habit, and lifted himself from the chair. 'Menagerie, you say, and salt mines. I have to declare, possible starvation of the city's population notwithstanding, that I think I'll pass on this exciting opportunity. Exam papers to set, junior lecturers to admonish, you understand. But do let me know how it goes.'

Canterbury grabbed the hem of his jacket and pulled him back down into his seat.

'Don't be such an ass, Gregory. Fescue here asked for our help and we shan't let him down.'

'All I'm asking for is ideas,' said Fescue. 'Options, a starting off place. Something to tell the Princeps and keep myself alive. Not much to ask.'

'There's one obvious option,' said Oliphant. 'Run away. Take the railway to Hurria, or a ship to anywhere that isn't here. Because one thing is for sure, there's no way you'll solve this problem, not in a week. Are you sure the Princeps isn't playing some kind of joke on you?'

'He's not exactly known for his humour. And the creature I saw was most certainly not a joke.'

'I have another option then,' said Oliphant. 'Assassinate the Princeps. Get rid of the inciting issue. You'll be a hero in the city, they'll vote you a pension for life, give you a medal. No Princeps, no menagerie, no problem.'

'You can't talk like that,' said Canterbury. 'What if someone heard?'

'An infernal machine would do it,' said Oliphant. 'Those chaps in Partridge College are always messing about and exploding things. Right up their street. One of them would knock you up a little device in no time.'

'I don't want a little device. I'm not assassinating anyone. And although the running away has some attractions, it wouldn't solve the problem of no food for the city.'

'I agree,' said Canterbury. 'I think we have an obligation. If not us, then who? And Gregory, dear chap, do you really believe there is any better mind than yours in the city?'

'You always were a flirt,' said Oliphant. 'But a week is still too short. We need to persuade the Princeps to give us more time, and I think I have a solution.'

Gregory Oliphant wasn't known for workable solutions to anything, but it was worth the question. 'And your solution is?'

'We'll set up a conference!' he said. 'Look at it this way; you have to face our glorious leader in two days and you need to give him something. A bit like feeding a tiger to stop it feeding on you; chunks of raw meat usually do the trick.'

'You're not helping with that ill-advised analogy.'

'The conference is the raw meat. We'll put out a call for papers - always such fun - and use that to distract his magnificence.'

'What if no-one comes up with a solution?' said Canterbury.

'They won't. But we will.'

WAR CABINET

They tasked Canterbury with the call for papers.

'Are you sure I'm the right person? I've never done this before, not really sure where to start.'

'Telegrams,' replied Oliphant. 'Very modern, catch the imagination. Say that we mean business.'

'But what do I say in these telegrams? And who do I send them to?'

Fescue threw a pencil at Oliphant. 'Don't bully poor Gottfried, he'll only have one of his episodes.' He turned to Canterbury. 'The thing is, we're all working in the dark for now. In a mine without a lamp, so to speak. We need to keep things vague, allow for interpretation and imagination. Let's call the conference "Agricultural challenges and hyper-rapid urban decay." That encapsulates the issue rather nicely, should bring in a gallimaufry of ideas without scaring the horses overmuch.'

Canterbury looked morose. 'I still don't know who to approach. And don't look at me like that, Gregory. I'm a senior academic, not an events organiser.'

'You approach everyone,' said Oliphant. 'In an ideal world

we'd miss out sociologists, but they'll think this is right up their street and we don't have time to argue the point. We'll get reams of unintelligible waffle about the effects of social class on the growing habits of wheat or some such, but it can go straight on the "burn before reading" pile. Ditto critical theorists for obvious reasons.'

'That's settled then,' said Fescue. 'Send the telegrams to arrive just after luncheon. We don't want to over-excite the faculty on an empty stomach.'

AFTER THE WAR cabinet meeting broke up, Fescue stood in front of his window and looked down onto the quad below. He'd come here as a student at sixteen and was still here thirty-four years later. This was home. Snow College, second oldest in the University. He knew the hue of the lichen on every stone. He knew every archway, every corridor. He sat at High Table once a month, he was respected by his peers; at least, as much as anyone was. His papers were received with polite respect. He knew by heart the rotation of the meals in the Dining Hall. He belonged. And today he would leave it all behind, forever.

Oliphant had been so pleased with himself for thinking of the conference, and Canterbury trotted off happily once he understood his tasks. But neither of them had to make the journey to the palace on Friday. Neither of them had to face the Princeps and his pets.

Far better to take Oliphant's first suggestion and run away. A pragmatic, fact-based solution with the best predicted personal outcome for him. The People's Republic of Hurria was a twelve-hour journey by railway, and the Princeps had no authority there. Would probably be strung up from a lamppost if he even set foot across the border, or sent to a re-education camp somewhere cold and bleak.

Fescue rummaged through the top drawer of his writing desk. Under a nest of elastic bands and half-chewed notes on scraps of paper - the mouse had made itself a new home - he found a copy of the current timetable for journeys from Forcello Central station. Another of the Princeps' grand architectural follies; more white marble, more equestrian statues. But at least it had trains.

He ran his finger down the sheet of tiny print. Nothing direct until seven o'clock tomorrow morning, and the thought of spending another night where the Princeps could track him down was unsupportable. But there was a train this afternoon to Nikkal; the Apple Capital of Hurria, as the travel posters proclaimed. Three hours away and just on the other side of the border; from there he could pick up a connection to Hurria itself. A grey city, he remembered, that took itself far too seriously. But no Princeps, no menagerie and no salt mines. Perhaps illegal immigrants were condemned to the orchards, which couldn't be all bad.

He put the timetable on the desk and looked around his rooms. The fire needed more coal, but why bother now? So much to leave behind; his candlesticks, his decanters, his favourite crystal tumbler. The chair that had moulded itself to his shape over the years. The masculine smells of cigar smoke and lavender moustache wax, of carbolic soap and leather shoes.

But he would need to travel light to avoid suspicion. The Princeps professed such love for his subjects that it wounded him that any of them would be forced to live a life of deprivation and misery in another city. It explained the guards at the stations and ports, deployed there 'for your comfort and safety,' as the Princeps was fond of saying.

Fescue retrieved his leather portmanteau from under the bed and packed a few essentials. Moustache wax, shaving kit, some shirts and drawers, a spare pair of socks, a notebook.

And mustn't forget the stash of banknotes he kept hidden under a floorboard in the bedroom, drawn on the Bank of Fox and Fowler.

His books and other clothes could be sent for later as soon as he settled in. Gottfried or Gregory would see to that once they'd forgiven him. If they forgave him.

He was to become an exile, a stranger in a strange land. Once the Princeps learned he was in Hurria, there could be no return unless it was a one-way ticket to the feeding chamber of the menagerie.

The college clock chimed three o'clock. Fescue checked the pocket watch inherited from his father and corrected the time. Still losing five minutes a day, so all was well. Forcello Central was a brisk ten-minute walk, and the train for Nikkal was due to leave at five-and-twenty to four. Plenty of time to walk there without looking as though he was plotting to escape. And then freedom.

The streets outside the college gates were quieter than he had expected. Of course, Wednesday, early closing day and all the shops would have put up their shutters at one o'clock sharp. There were still students and the occasional don on a bicycle, and the new steam omnibus careered past him at a dangerous speed. Nasty contraptions, he'd always thought. Given the choice of fragrant horse droppings - good for the roses if he ever got around to having a garden - and the malodorous excretions of steam carriages, he'd choose the former any time. Oliphant would have disagreed, but Oliphant had always been attracted by new and shiny things, regardless of whether they were better than whatever they were replacing. Form over function, a strange predilection for a natural philosopher.

RAILWAYS AND REVOLVERS

※

He decided not to purchase a through ticket; no point in giving away his ultimate destination should anyone come asking. The train was standing on Platform One next to a booth selling tobacco, newspapers and boiled sweets. He took a box of cigars which would taste of cardboard, the afternoon edition of The Watchman, the only Forcello daily with a crossword he could complete without cheating, and a paper bag of lemon drops.

The first class carriage was at the front of the train and he managed to find an empty compartment. He sat by the window facing the engine, put his hat on the seat next to him, portmanteau opposite and coat next to that. The journey ahead would be long and tedious, and he could see no need to be burdened by tiresome companions who might have the temerity to engage him in conversation.

The guard's whistle sounded, the carriage jolted twice, and they were off. Fescue checked his watch. Three thirty-five exactly. Say what you like about the Princeps; his trains always ran on time.

He'd always thought that such a complicated operation as

running a railway was a catastrophe waiting to happen. Timekeeping, that was the essence. Get that wrong and there would be engines ploughing into each other all over the shop. His mind drifted to the conversation with Tiro and the port of Kimit with goats grazing where there used to be a city with a thriving port, the way it might have been centuries ago. A place running to the wrong timetable.

The outskirts of the city rolled by outside the window. Moments later they left the last house behind and passed through fields bordered by low hedges and the occasional tree. No-one ever celebrated Forcello for its landscape, and he could see why. Flat and green, with not even a hill in sight.

The noise of the compartment door opening interrupted his thoughts, and a young woman peered in. He'd never been sure about women. He knew that their strange shape was down to the clothes they wore, and the sound of a group of them together always reminded him of a flock of birds twittering; a lot of noise but no content. Not that he ever listened. And now the University Senate was considering a plan to allow females to study. Oliphant approved, of course, but he was a man who thought nothing of wearing brown shoes during the week.

This example of femininity was dressed in the modern fashion with a straight ankle-length skirt, tight jacket and almost no feathers in the hat perched on a confection of golden hair. 'Do you mind if I join you?' she asked. 'Some poor child threw up the contents of his lunch all over himself and his mother. Shrimp paste by the smell, and I felt decidedly queasy.'

She was in the compartment now, with a disconcertingly pleasant smile. 'Would you be awfully kind and move your rather delightful portmanteau and coat?'

He ran through all the objections to her suggestion, none of which had the slightest chance of holding water, then moved his paraphernalia to allow her to sit. Did it have to be opposite him?

The compartment was now filled, even more disconcertingly, with the scent of roses, and she was looking into his eyes as if expecting something. Conversation, probably, so he supposed he'd better take the initiative and control the narrative. 'May I inquire as to your destination?' he asked.

'I have a sister in Hurria City. She wrote to tell me she's joined their army.' She shook her head, causing the feathers to dance. 'A woman in uniform, what is the world coming to. What about you?'

'Me what?'

'I'm asking why you're on this ridiculously uncomfortable train.'

'Nikkal, short holiday. Very fine orchards, so I understand.'

'Surely it's the wrong time of year. The apples are long gone and there won't be any blossom for months.'

'I suppose there's always the cider.'

'True, very true.'

He allowed himself to picture the two of them on a blanket beneath an old oak tree with a picnic and an empty flagon of cider. A picture, he decided, that was best covered up and kept out of sight in a darkened room.

They subsided back into silence. After a while the woman opened the small bag she was carrying, extracted a pocket-book and pencil and began to write. Every few minutes she paused, stared out of the window and then returned to her scribbling. During one of these lacunae, she noticed Fescue studying her.

'It's a new novel. I compose romantic fiction for young women. So many end up married to crusty old men that their energies become blocked. Very unhealthy. The books provide an outlet for their passions. My publisher calls it poetic relief, but between you and me, no-one reads them for their literary value.'

He wasn't at all sure, but it appeared that she had winked at him. 'What about you?' she asked.

'I'm a professor at the University. Experimental Ontology, nothing to interest a young woman like you.'

'Ontology, the study of being and becoming. How fascinating.' She returned to her writing and silence fell again as the fields and hedgerows rolled by in a hypnotic progression of images.

He woke as the train slowed down. The woman had stowed the notebook and was staring out of the window. Fescue checked his watch. They were only a couple of minutes from Nikkal, so why stop here in the middle of nowhere?

The train guard opened the compartment door and saluted. 'Border inspection. Nothing to worry about, happens from time to time when the frontier police are bored. Shouldn't take more than a couple of minutes unless we have a dangerous fugitive aboard!'

Two men came out from a small hut standing by the side of the tracks and made their way across to the train.

'You seem disconcerted, Professor,' said the woman. She pulled down the window, leaned out and whistled in a manner that struck him as most un-ladylike.

'What on earth are you doing?'

'My job, Professor Monad, my job.' She opened her bag and pointed a small, sliver pistol at him. 'His Highness is a kind and thoughtful sovereign who asked me to keep an eye on you, for your own comfort and safety. Hurria is a dangerous place and we wouldn't want anything to happen to you there.'

The compartment door opened. The two border guards standing there, dressed in the livery of the Palace, could have been twins; both six feet tall, both with black monobrows and advanced five o'clock shadow. Perhaps the Princeps bred them in the same way he did his creatures.

The guard on the left smiled. 'My dear Professor, you'll be coming with us. A train's waiting to take you back.'

There was no point in arguing. At best he'd be allowed to carry on with the charade of a conference, at worst he'd soon be acquainted with the inside of the feeding chamber. But whatever happened, he would never experience the scent of roses in the same way again.

The guards escorted him down from the carriage and across the tracks to an engine attached to a single guard's van. No carriages. 'I apologise for the accommodations,' said the talkative one. 'Not quite up to your standards, but as my dear old Ma always says, it's the destination that matters, not the journey.'

THE GUARDS ACCOMPANIED him all the way to his rooms, and left him with an injunction not to leave the college grounds until his appointment with the Princeps.

The fire was out; the room was cold, and it was drizzling outside. He'd been gone for less than a day, and yet the room had a sense of abandonment. Perhaps, he thought, it was sulking at his attempted betrayal.

Betrayal. How would he explain his abortive flight to the Princeps? The desire to taste out-of-season Hurrian cider wouldn't cut it. He sat in the armchair and considered his options. Escape was off the table, which left the original plan of a competition or assassination. Or, and the thought felt for a moment like the answer, he could throw himself from the window and dash out his brains on the stones of the quad. But given his luck, he'd miss the ground and end up bobbing around in the air like a tweed balloon, waiting to be plucked by the Princeps' men.

The sound of laughter filtered up from outside and he went to the window and looked down. The talkative guard was standing next to a hay-filled cart strategically placed underneath the window. The guard looked up and waved cheerily, then turned back to carry on flirting with one of the first year undergraduates. As ever, thought Fescue, his comfort and safety were paramount.

He couldn't stay here in this belligerent room and he couldn't stray from the college. But Oliphant had chambers on the grounds, wasn't known for going to bed early, but was known for keeping an excellent cellar.

He wasn't sure if the guard's tuneless whistling was a deliberate attempt to unsettle him but at least the man walked a few paces behind so that he didn't feel like a prisoner under escort.

What had he done to deserve this? Pride, that was his downfall. So full of his own importance after his pathetic success at the Society a few days ago and this was where it had landed him, a walking menu item. Not that any creature would get much of a meal out of him. On the outside he looked whole, but inside was nothing, a vacuum. He had become a husk.

As expected, Oliphant was still awake. He invited Fescue in, sat him down and was about to pour a glass of his third best claret when he thought better of it and used the second best instead.

'Thought I saw you earlier on your way to the station. You seemed rather like an amateur spy, looking around every few steps to see if you were being followed. Not that you were very good at it, didn't even notice me. So what happened?'

The story gushed out as if this was a confessional. His fall was complete and Oliphant was triumphant. 'A girl, you say, sent to guard you? Sounds more like a nanny to me.'

'I didn't know what she was there for. She said she was a writer, women's stuff. Pleasant face, smelt like a summer garden. I didn't pay much attention.'

'What shall we do with you, dear chap? One sight of a pretty ankle and all your defences crash to the ground.'

Oliphant had a very unpleasant smirk when he was feeling buoyant, thought Fescue, not at all becoming. 'I didn't even notice her ankles,' he said, but the arrow fell lifeless from the bow.

'So Plan A failed,' said Oliphant. 'I assume you're still not on board with the whole assassination idea? Could be fun, lots of bangs and smoke. Those fellows from Partridge College really know what they're doing.'

'Fun? Perhaps for you, watching my public execution for high treason. You know what the sentence is for that, and being pulled apart by four donkeys is both slow and painful. Especially if the donkeys don't play ball. I'd rather be eaten, at least it would be over quickly.'

Oliphant topped up Fescue's glass and offered him a bowl of nuts. 'My last Kimit pistachios. And don't worry, we still have the conference. Gottfried sent the telegrams out earlier and I'm told there's already a veritable buzz around the college.'

'I thought you were less than sanguine about anyone finding a solution to satisfy his magnificence.'

'I am. But we have the advantage of knowing exactly what's happening, thanks to your man Tiro. Everyone else who knows about the problems with Kimit has been disposed of. Except him. And you.'

'Thank you for the reminder.'

'You've had a long day, old chap. Go home, get some rest and we'll reconvene in the morning. Fresh minds, fresh ideas, and we'll have two full days before your meeting at the palace. I'll bring Canterbury, he always cheers you up.'

'We won't solve the problem in two days.'

'I told you before, give the Princeps news of the conference as a tantalising starter. He'll see that you're beavering away and we'll have bought some time.'

'You always were a great one for prevarication, Gregory. We might buy some time, but at some point we need to find a solution that works or the city will starve. Apart from the beasts, obviously.'

'Go, dear boy, sleep. Until tomorrow.'

THE GUARD APPEARED to be dozing as he leaned against the wall at the bottom of Oliphant's staircase, but opened one eye as Fescue tried to creep past.

'Keeping late hours, Professor? Very sound, very life enhancing. His Highness likes to know that people take his suggestions seriously. Come on then, let's get you home.'

OLIPHANT AND CANTERBURY arrived at Fescue's rooms the next morning bearing a selection of pastries in a greasy paper bag.

'You won't believe what we had to pay for these,' said Canterbury, 'And Gregory had to push two old ladies out of the way to get the last apricot croissant.'

'First no pistachios and now no more pastries. Forget about the Princeps, this is getting serious.' Oliphant brushed the sprinkling of crumbs from his lap onto the Turkey rug where they instantly blended in with the pattern. 'And what is it with that hay cart outside your window? Not still planning an escape, are you?'

'You didn't notice the guard then. They want to make sure that my life ends when they say so and not a moment before.'

'Always doom and gloom,' said Oliphant. 'How about a more positive attitude?' He leaned across and prodded Fescue in the thigh. 'I've been thinking,' he said. 'No, don't look at me like that Canterbury. Believe it or not, my life is more than an endless round of gaiety and laughter, so listen. We've already started to arrange this conference and if the palace spies are all they're cracked up to be, his omniscience will already know what we're planning. Your job on Friday, Fescue, is to dress it up a bit.'

'And how do I do that?'

'Didn't you talk to him about paying you?'

'I wouldn't put it like that. It was more a case of the bank balance of my life dipping permanently into the red if I failed.'

'You won't, and that isn't the point. We're all men of the world - well, two of us are - and we know what gets our colleagues out of bed on a rainy Monday. Professional esteem is one thing, but if we turn the conference into a competition with a decent prize, we'll really get up a good head of steam.'

'What sort of prize?' asked Canterbury.

'I don't know yet. But think about it. Big competition, lots of entries from prestigious academics, splendid prize, and to top it all a huge ceremony when the winner is announced. A chance for his uniformed eminence to strut about on the stage and play the benevolent patrician. He won't be able to resist.'

They all pondered for a moment, and then Fescue said, 'You're right. The man's no intellectual, probably has no idea about research papers and conferences. But who doesn't like a competition?'

'Me for a start,' said Canterbury. 'But whatever you chaps think best.'

'That's settled then,' said Oliphant. 'Monad will sell the idea of the competition to the Princeps on Friday. How long should we give the entrants, a month?'

'You've never met the Princeps, Gregory, have you? He thinks more in terms of minutes than months. We'll be lucky to get two weeks.'

'Just do your best, old chap. And make sure you come back to us.'

'Just to be clear,' said Canterbury. 'Are we intending to enter the competition ourselves?'

'Not just enter it, old topper. We're going to win!'

Fescue sent them away, claiming a migraine. He'd barely slept, and when he looked out of the window at five in the morning, the moonlight shone on the figure of a new guard, stretched out on the hay in the cart.

For all of their discussions and Oliphant's breezy optimism, they were dancing around the problem like maids around a maypole. And yet something was tugging at the edges of his mind, something to do with railways. What was it, the rails? The engines? The carriages? None of those felt right. What about the timetable? Somehow that seemed to be the most likely candidate, but he had no idea what it had to do with disappearing cities.

Last night Oliphant had talked about fresh minds and there was one they hadn't used yet, one they could trust. The doctor always brought illumination to their discussions, even if his thoughts did go off at a tangent sometimes. There would be a full moon on Monday, which meant a meeting of their private and select philosophical society. And this month they were meeting at the doctor's house out on the coast. The perfect opportunity to dissect the problem and see it in all its naked glory from the inside. If anyone could come up with a diagnosis, it was the doctor.

Fescue sighed and rubbed his eyes. To get to Monday, he had to navigate Friday, and he wasn't sure he fancied the odds of still being alive after his audience with the Princeps.

CHAPTER 10

Pilchards for Breakfast

THE BATH HOUSE

&

*H*e remembered sleep. He remembered that wonderful prelapsarian time before the Princeps knew his name. He remembered when sleep came gently each night, bringing dreams that left him smiling even after he woke. Happy days.

The college clock struck six. He'd listened to each hour since midnight and now there seemed no point to staying in bed any longer. He put on a dressing gown over his nightshirt and looked outside. The stones of the quad glistened silver in the moonlight, like liquid silk.

Would Tiro arrive for him, or would one of the guards escort him to the palace this time? And when? Dawn was the usual time for executions he'd heard, and that was over an hour away. Or would his audience be in the evening like last Monday? He'd have a decent lunch if that looked like being the case.

Something was moving across the dark mass of the lawn in the middle of the quad. A cat, normal size. Stalking, almost snakelike as it flowed across the grass. A sudden flurry, a leap forward, and it trotted off with something limp dangling from its mouth.

The clock chimed the half hour. He wasn't sure if he wanted or feared the rising of the sun. This could be his last sunrise, his last dawn. For an ontologist, he had always steered away from thoughts of death, something he only considered as an abstract concept that happened to other people. His entire career had been about existence, about being and becoming. Now that he thought about it, the ultimate act of existence was becoming a corpse.

What would they do with his when the time came? The Princeps had banned the once-fashionable burials in the lagoon after bodies began to surface and float to shore. That undertaker had never been seen again.

Given a choice, he'd opt for a custom he'd read about once, of leaving bodies exposed on high towers for the bones to be picked clean by carrion birds. There was an elegant purity to that idea, to merge his remains with something that wasn't bound to the earth. Becoming something free.

The clock chimed seven - where had the three quarter gone? - and the last note coincided with a rapping on his door. Dawn it was then.

THE GUARD outside his building had disappeared along with the hay cart. Either they were trusting him not to self-destruct or they knew he wouldn't be coming back. Fifty fifty.

There was no fog this time, just the sharp cold of a late November morning. The sky was lightening; no colours yet, just a pale glow in the east where the lagoon met the sea. How long had it been since he'd taken a boat to one of the islands? A young man's game, but if he was still standing at the end of the day he'd arrange a picnic; a bottle of wine and some decent cheese, and spend the day looking up at the sky in a deserted bay.

Tiro was walking more slowly this time, rather than quick marching as if on manoeuvres, and Fescue caught up with him as they reached the canal bridge.

'How is his Highness this morning?'

'In the mood for japes.'

'Japes?'

'His Highness is celebrated for his practical jokes. They are very amusing.'

'Should I be worried?'

Tiro stopped and turned to face him. 'Always.'

When they reached the palace, Tiro led him round the opposite side to the entrance they'd used before, through geometric gardens to a rectangle of dense, high hedges. A small gateway led to a building that stretched for more than a hundred yards, built from the same marble as the palace but with a glass roof. Opaque floor to ceiling windows punctuated the long side, as if the place suffered from an advanced stage of cataracts.

'Where are we?'

'His Highness enjoys a little healthy exercise in the mornings before he starts on the labours of the day. This is his bath house.'

Tiro nodded at the two men guarding the door who let them in to what Fescue could only guess was a close approximation to the jungles of Poorim. Apart, that was, from the enormous pool which stretched the length of the building, with curves and steps and a waterfall halfway along. Now he understood the opacity of the windows; the steam-filled room was as hot as a Hurrian sauna. All around the edge, strange plants stretched up from giant tubs, dark green creepers covering the walls and reaching up to find the light percolating through the glass roof.

The far end of the room was lost in steam, but he could hear a strange sound, like a strangled barking. The sound stopped. He heard a loud splash and then saw two shapes under the water, sleek and grey, heading straight towards him.

So this was it. His last few moments, his last act of becoming. No longer being, just been. The grey shapes reared up out of the water in front of him. Round, almost human heads with whiskers. They made the barking sound again before hauling themselves up next to him on their giant flippers.

'I see you've met Pinny and Ped.'

Fescue swung round to see the Princeps in a one piece bathing suit embroidered with his coat of arms, holding a bucket of fish.

'My pet seals. We like to breakfast together each morning. May I interest you in a pilchard?'

THE PRINCEPS THREW some fish to the seals and then led Fescue to a couple of cane armchairs under the shadow of a palm tree. Fescue waited until his host was seated, and as he lowered himself into the damp chair Tiro arrived carrying a tray with a single glass and a bottle labelled with the drawing of an apple.

'Hurrian cider, from the Nikkal orchards,' said the Princeps. 'I understand you're rather partial to it. I'm a brandy man myself, but each to his own.'

The cider tasted as foul as he remembered from his teenage years, but he affected to drink with relish. 'I find, Highness, that a change of scenery helps to stimulate the creative juices. A temporary change, of course.'

'Of course. But the trouble with fresh sights is their seductiveness, don't you find? Out with the old, in with the new. Leave all your troubles behind, that sort of thing. All flesh is weak, Professor, even flesh as well-seasoned as yours, so it's a good thing I sent my daughter to keep an eye on you, for your comfort and safety.'

'Your daughter? She pulled a gun on me!'

'Just being playful, you know what women are like. Can't take anything seriously, minds like kittens.'

One of the seals flopped its way across and promptly fell asleep by the Princeps' feet. The smell of fish was overpowering.

'So Professor, to business. What have you come up with to address our little challenge? I have every confidence that you're the man for the job, isn't that right Tiro?'

'Indeed, my lord. Just the chap.'

'We're all very excited to hear what you have for us. Barely been able to contain ourselves, eh Tiro?'

'Containment has indeed been precarious.'

The Princeps leaned nearer, his breath smelling of pilchards. 'What's the answer, Professor? Don't keep us waiting. Do you know why Kimit disappeared from the map?'

'And how we'll supply the city with food?'

'You're being pernickety again, Professor. Of course the food's important, can't have starving people rioting in the streets. Always such a fag to put them down.'

It was showtime at last, and he had nothing to show. 'This has been a most intriguing challenge, Highness. Believe me, I have been thinking of nothing else, night and day.'

He studied the Princeps' face for any sign of a reaction, but the man was an accomplished poker player.

'I thought it politic to convene a small working party to address the issue. Two of my most experienced colleagues.'

The Princeps beckoned to Tiro who handed him a folder

of papers which he examined. 'Gregory Oliphant and Gottfried Canterbury, both professors of Natural Philosophy at Snow College. Not quite up to your standard, but I bow to your judgement. They will be discreet, I trust, I so dislike blabbermouths.'

'Very discreet, you have my word.'

'And what has this working party come up with?'

The ruler of the city was expecting caviar and all he had to offer was thin gruel. The best he could do was pour a little syrup on top. 'We decided at first to set up an academic conference and invite contributions.'

The Princeps yawned. 'And does this conference have a title?'

'We called it "Agricultural challenges and hyper-rapid urban decay." We felt it reflected the problem without giving anything away that might be seen as indiscreet.'

'Nothing about disappearing beasts? Are you sure you have the right focus? Every time I go hunting, another of my little pets goes missing.'

'I assumed your selective breeding hobby was a private passion.'

'True, very true. I must say, though, your plan sounds exceedingly dull to me. I was expecting something more exciting, more immediate. Please don't tell me I picked the wrong man for the job.'

'Far from it, Highness, there is more. The conference was our original idea, but to entice the very best to take part we felt that converting the conference to a competition would be just the goad needed.'

The Princeps leaned over and punched Fescue on the shoulder. 'You're a crafty wag, Professor. You pique my interest with talk of goads, and hidden behind is the need, I strongly suspect, for a substantial prize. We've been down this road before. I believe we discussed penalties for failure rather than rewards for success.'

'But think of the publicity, sire. Imagine a sunny day, banners flying, food on the shelves in all the shops and you, sire, handing a prize to the winner. Everyone will see how the city was saved through your generosity and wisdom.'

'And I'll have a full menagerie?'

'Without doubt.' Time to take a risk, press his advantage. 'We all know that the scurrilous Hurrians, detestable creatures that they are, have been a thorn in your side for years. Hurria, led by donkeys rather than someone of your wisdom, must be experiencing shortages too. When you are recognised by all as our deliverer from starvation, you won't need to invade with an army to put an end to their nonsense. Just send your police force over the border with a few cartloads of bread and they'll be welcomed as saviours. The government will capitulate without so much as a single shot being fired, and Hurria will be yours. A new empire will be born, with you as emperor. You could crown yourself.'

Had he gone too far? Oliphant always accused him of getting caught up in the net of his own rhetoric.

The Princeps leant down and flicked a bee away from the nose of the seal. 'What do we think, Pinny? Shall we become an emperor?' The seal opened one eye, blinked and went back to sleep as the bee circled round and landed, unnoticed, on the shoulder strap of the Princeps' bathing suit.

'I said to Tiro the other day when we were having a chinwag, I said, "That Professor Monad might dress like his grandfather's tailor, smell like a lavender bush and talk as though he has a mouthful of stones, but he won't disappoint. He knows his stuff".'

He pulled a raw fish from the bucket and began to chew at it absentmindedly, staring into the middle distance.

Tiro stepped across and tapped Fescue on the bruise left by the Princeps' punch. 'The audience has ended. Follow me.'

They left the bathhouse and went from a tropical summer to winter in the space of two steps. 'What just happened,' asked Fescue, 'what about my proposal?'

'His Highness has authorised me to inform you that the prize for your competition will be one thousand pounds, to be paid upon successful implementation of the winning plan.'

'That's more than ten times my annual salary!'

'Indeed.'

'But he said nothing to you just now, I was there.'

'His Highness made his wishes known yesterday. And I am instructed to tell you that the proposed solution - and the winner - will be announced in ten days' time. There will be a public holiday.' He sighed. 'And games.'

'So he knew all along what I was going to suggest.'

Tiro smiled, a little wearily. 'His Highness is nothing if not well informed. Look to your friends, Professor. And if I were you, I should put any travel plans on hold for a while.'

A LADY AND A PIE

❧

No escort home, which was a good start. His pocket watch showed three minutes to nine o'clock, but the streets were already crowded, the cobbles coated with a slurry of horse droppings. He wasn't ready to go back to his rooms, not yet. No doubt he was being followed and all his movements would be reported to the palace, but no matter. As long as he stayed in the city, nothing would happen to him now, at least not for another two weeks.

The realisation was dawning on him that he wasn't dead. He hadn't been taken to the feeding chamber. He hadn't even been punished for his escape bid, apart from the cider, even though he had no no doubt that the excuse of wanting to clear his mind failed to convince. But he was alive.

He passed a stall selling flowers and the scent of roses took him back to the woman in the railway carriage. The Princeps' daughter, who would have thought it? Such beauty emanating from the loins of a man who could easily have passed as the third seal this morning. The image of the Princeps in his bathing suit, cavorting with a wife or mistress, was too disconcerting and as he crossed Grocer Street towards Lampmaker Alley he heard a shout, looked up and saw a steam carriage bearing down on him just feet away. Part of his brain gave an instruction to his legs to move, but the legs weren't listening. The carriage was almost on him when someone grabbed his arm and pulled him to the side of the road. The carriage passed by, spewing steam and coal fumes, and he looked into the eyes of his rescuer.

'Good morning, Professor, you seemed a little distracted. Another few seconds and you would have been mulched down with the dung. Can you imagine my father's reaction? It doesn't bear thinking about.'

She straightened the lapels on his coat, which he realised still smelt of pilchards, and brushed his shoulders as if he were a child. It was strangely comforting. 'I hear you had breakfast with him this morning, but I'm guessing that you passed on the offer of raw fish; my father has quaint tastes and doesn't understand why no-one else shares them. Apart from the seals, obviously. What do you say to some jellied eels to settle the stomach?'

He wanted to speak but wasn't ready to trust his lips to form coherent words, so he simply nodded.

'Excellent.' She took his arm and led him along the pavement until they reached a food cart near the canal bridge. 'Would you rather have a pie? Perhaps eels weren't the most apposite suggestion.'

He nodded again with relief. The woman handed him one of the pasties; they climbed down the steps to the canal and sat on a bench by the side of the water. The food was nectar; two sorts of pastry, steaming minced beef and onion, thick gravy. A man need never eat anything else.

'How are you feeling now, Professor?'

'Better, thank you. A little discommoded earlier, but the pie has done the trick. You must let me recompense you.'

'No need, everyone knows who I am. They wouldn't dare charge their ruler's daughter.'

'But you have the advantage of me. I regret I don't know your name.'

'Lily Delacey. Daughter of His Highness Marino Delacey, Princeps of Forcello. At your service. And I apologise for the pistol the other day. I so rarely have a chance to use it.'

'I wasn't running away, you know. Just fancied a trip to clear my head.'

'And I'm the Empress of Hurria. It's all right, Professor. No harm done. But take a little more care in future; I won't always be around to look after you.'

'Were you really writing a novel for young ladies?'

'Someone has to.'

She walked back to the street with him and said goodbye with a smile that made his legs feel as if they were ready to give up the unequal struggle of keeping him upright. No fool like an old fool, he reminded himself. Lily was almost young enough to be his granddaughter.

He started back towards home, with one thing still worrying him. Tiro had said 'look to your friends.' What had he meant? That he would need their help, or that someone was spying on him? It could only be Oliphant or Canterbury, no-one else had been privy to their plan for a competition. But which one? It had to be Oliphant, always looking out for himself. Should he confront the man, call him out? Better, perhaps, to say nothing and let Oliphant think his betrayal had gone undetected. Quite how that would help wasn't clear, but if nothing else it would avoid an unpleasant showdown.

Unless, of course, there was no betrayal and he was being paranoid. An entirely justified reaction to his situation. He was almost at the entrance to the college when his colleagues hurried through the gate towards him.

'Fescue, dear chap, we were so worried about you.' Were those tears in Canterbury's eyes?

Oliphant nodded. 'We came to your rooms early, moral support and all that stuff, but the porter said you'd been taken away first thing. We thought the worst.'

'Let's get inside and I'll explain,' said Fescue. 'Too damned cold out here. And not my rooms if it's all the same to you, they've become decidedly cool towards me lately.'

'You're welcome to use my chambers,' said Canterbury, 'if you don't mind the rabbit.'

'Rabbit?'

'It belongs to my sister. She calls it Agnes, which strikes me as a strange name for a rabbit, but what do I know.'

'And why do you have Agnes living with you? Isn't that a breach of college regulations?'

'Technically. My sister's gone to visit a friend for a few days and I said I'd look after the creature. Wasn't prepared for the smell, but you get used to it after a while. And I have to be careful with the owl when it's at home. Seems to think Agnes is on the menu so I keep it in the bathroom.'

'The owl or the rabbit?'

'Rabbit, obviously.'

Canterbury's rooms looked out over Angel's Court. Not as fashionable as Fescue's but quiet and comfortable enough. Canterbury cornered the rabbit and locked it in the bathroom while Oliphant brushed some droppings and owl pellets from one of the chairs and settled himself.

'So spill the beans, Monad. I assume you met the man himself and put our proposal to him. And did you by any chance have kippers for breakfast? They must have been off, there's a strong smell of the fish market about you today.'

'They were pilchards, for the seals. Pinny and Ped. He swims with them every morning in a tropical bath house.'

'You had pilchards for breakfast?'

'Not me, the damned seals. And the Princeps. Raw.'

'Ghastly,' said Oliphant. 'The habits of the rich and powerful don't bear thinking about. But tell us what happened. You're still walking around with no obvious bite marks, so I assume it was a success.'

Fescue nodded. 'He agreed to the competition, winner to be announced in two weeks on a public holiday. And there's to be a prize of one thousand pounds.' Best not to mention Lily.

'Sorry old chap,' said Oliphant, 'I thought you said one thousand pounds.'

Canterbury was staring at him with his jaw hanging open.

'I did. Although I can't help feeling that there's a price to pay for failure as well as the possibility of a prize for succeeding. Those creatures of his…'

'We're going to win this,' said Oliphant. 'I just don't know how. Where do we even start?'

'I had an idea,' said Fescue. 'The doctor. We're meeting at his house on Monday and he always looks at problems from a different angle.'

'But he's a medical man, not an academic,' said Canterbury.

'So? Your specialism is strigiformes and we don't complain about that. Oliphant - well, he's a mathematician, so none of us know what he's working on. I don't suppose you know yourself, Gregory. But it doesn't matter. Whatever's happening is quite bizarre, and there are no experts to turn to. Just us. We shall go where no-one has gone before.'

'Better hope we don't get lost then,' said Oliphant.

Canterbury was fidgeting as if he needed to relieve himself. 'What do we do between now and Monday?'

'You're our public face, gods help us,' said Fescue. 'You need to send out more telegrams to all the people you contacted before, telling them about the prize. If we thought there was a buzz about the conference, we'll have a whole hornet's nest on our hands this time.'

'Just one, very minor point,' said Oliphant. 'A competition needs judges. And judges need to know what they're judging against. How will anyone know that their solution will work?'

'Easy,' said Fescue. 'We appoint the doctor. He's nothing to do with the university so he'll seem unbiassed. In reality, we'll tell him to choose our entry as the winner.'

'But that's unethical,' said Canterbury. 'He'll never agree.'

'Since when have ethics had anything to do with it? But as no-one else has the slightest idea what this is all about, our entry is guaranteed to be the best.'

Chapter 11

All at Sea

SETTING SAIL

Perhaps this wouldn't be so bad. The captain had introduced Ellen and Sophia to his officers as two rich gentlemen, engaged on a speculative voyage of discovery. They were, he explained, desirous of maintaining a degree of privacy, and their appearances on deck would therefore be rare. Indeed, so desirous were they of their privacy that any attempt to engage them in conversation would merit the strictest of punishments. In fact, he would set aside a period each day for the young gentlemen to take the air on the foredeck without suffering the intrusions of the crew.

'One advantage of being captain of my own ship,' he said as he showed them to their cabin. 'I'm like a wee god when we're on the water. I make the law, I'm judge and jury and executioner if need be. You can't run a ship without discipline. The men like it, they know where they stand. I've experienced a soft captain and weak officers; an unhappy ship that came to a bad end. Not a mistake I intend to make.'

The cabin was more spacious than Ellen had imagined, with large slanting windows looking out from the ship's stern. Small bed, hammock, a table that took up over half the space and a tiny room to one side. The quarter gallery, the captain called it.

'I'm imagining that it would be a touch embarrassing to have to share facilities for the natural bodily functions, so you'll be wanting your privacy. The men use heads near the bow and the officers have their own arrangements. Bear in mind that sounds carry on board ship, which also means that you'll want to be circumspect in any private conversations.'

He wiped a speck of imaginary dust from the table. 'I'll leave you to settle, but we'll need a discussion about our course once we reach open waters. I'll come back once we've weighed anchor and we can study the charts.'

'There's not much to settle,' said Sophia. 'But I'd much appreciate coming on deck to watch as we set sail.'

Markus considered for a moment. 'As long as you stay on the bridge and don't talk to anyone. You might pass muster to look at, near enough, but both of you have the voices of boys who balls haven't dropped. Once we're under way, come straight back to the cabin. No need to make life any harder for us than it needs to be.'

THE SUN above the roofscape tinted the white stone of Coria with a pale rose glow. From the Billy Boy's bridge the city seemed smaller, like a child's model, and the mountains Ellen had crossed with Sera were a distant line of snow-covered peaks far to the north, glowing with the same colour as the buildings of the city. Both places dangerous in their own ways.

Ellen and Sophia stood together at the rear of the bridge, looking at an exercise in chaos. Shouting, running, the noise of the anchor chain being wound up, sailors swarming across the rigging as if they'd been born in trees. The sails unfurled and filled with the light wind, and instead of rocking gently with the waves, the ship moved forward; the timbers creaking as the hull took the strain. A few minutes later they sailed past a headland and into the open sea. The motion of the ship changed almost immediately as it heeled over to one side and bounced over the white-tipped waves.

Ellen grabbed Sophia's arm. 'I think I need the quarter gallery.' But before she could move, she threw up last night's meal, just missing Sophia's feet.

Markus laughed at the sound. 'Welcome on board.'

'Is it always this rough,' said Ellen.

'Rough? Great gods, no. This is next door to a flat calm. Don't fret, you'll get your sea legs soon enough. But best you go below now, I'll be there presently.'

It was no better in the cabin. 'You'll get used to it,' said Sophia, 'I brought dried ginger root; if there's any hot water, I'll make a tisane to settle your stomach.'

When Markus returned, he pulled large sheets of rolled paper from a chest on one side of the cabin, and spread one of them on the table. 'I'll try to make sense of this chart for you. It's no more than a map of the sea, lets me know which direction to sail, the rocks and reefs to avoid.' He smoothed the paper. 'From what your friend told me, you want to go looking for that ship crewed by demons. Superstitious buggers. Tell you the truth, I wouldn't mind finding it myself. If the winds decide to play truant or blow from the wrong direction, I could lose a packet on a cargo if I land it late. But a ship that ignores the winds would take my business away overnight. Unless I had one of my own.'

He pointed at the chart. 'This here is Coria City, which we're leaving behind us now, and we're sailing on this course.'

'Why this direction?' Ellen asked.

'After I spoke to your friend yesterday, I looked out the

skipper of the fishing boat. Not hard to find, he's been telling his story all over the harbour. Man hasn't been sober since he landed. Anyway, I filled his tankard and he told me the same as he told mister Sera.' He drew a line on the chart with his finger. 'The ship they saw was on this bearing. Unless you disagree, I propose to follow its course and see where it leads. Could be a wild goose chase. Most people don't realise how vast the ocean is; I've often sailed for weeks without sight of land. And a wee word of warning, don't fall overboard, specially if the seas are high. A head bobbing around in the waves is well nigh impossible to see and I've lost more than one fool that way.'

'Where's the nearest land?' asked Sophia.

Markus spread another chart on the table. 'This is where it gets interesting. I know the seas and the landfalls around here, and I can't see the point of putting in at any of the ports. None of them berth anything like the ship we're chasing.'

Sophia shrugged. 'What about any ports you haven't been to in a while?'

Markus ignored her, patted the pockets on his jacket and pulled out a pipe and a small leather pouch. 'If you - gentlemen - don't mind, I like to take a pipe or two this time of day, specially at the start of a voyage. I might not believe in demons, but I'm still a sailor and we have our little rituals. Foolish, maybe, but it harms no-one and I like to think the gods enjoy the smell of good Hurrian leaf.'

He filled the pipe, tamped down the tobacco, then took a spill and lit it from a lamp that swayed from a hook on the cabin wall. He closed the glass door of the lamp carefully and puffed on the pipe. 'If it comes on to blow, we put out the lamps. Fire on board ship is a nasty thing. Wood, tar and canvas, we'd go up like a bloody candle.'

He traced a line on the chart. 'If the ship was on a straight bearing, it would have come from this direction. South east is Quidesh, and Vallaria's another week further down the coast. I've visited both in the past couple of months. They're the only places worth trading with. A few fishing villages dotted along the coast, but nothing that could provide a safe harbour for the sort of vessel we want. There's a large island much further on, mind you, due south. The seas around there are treacherous at any time of year, waves three times the height of this ship and the winds… it's like they want to play with you, northerlies one minute, coming from the west next, then southeast. No rhyme or reason. I was blown off course there once, never again. And they have floating mountains of ice that would turn us to matchwood in minutes. We won't find what you're looking for down south.'

Mountains of ice to crush them, fire to roast them. She'd been right, ships were best avoided. Ellen walked away from the table and sat on the bed. They should have taken the time to talk to Markus before leaving shore. If she'd known how hopeless this was, she'd have persuaded Sera and Sophia to look for another way. But after what had happened with Sophia's husband, turning back now wasn't an option.

Markus rolled up the charts. 'I called this a speculative voyage, and that's what it is. We'll follow this bearing for a few days, then swing by Quidesh and Vallaria just in case. If we find nothing in the next month, I'll put you ashore anywhere you like, although I'd stay away from Coria for a while to let the temperature cool.'

UNWELCOME ATTENTIONS

The ginger helped. After a week at sea, Ellen was almost accustomed to the motion of the ship. Each day, for half an hour in the morning and half an hour in the afternoon, the foredeck was cleared of men, allowing Ellen and Sophia to promenade around the deck. The captain took the wheel and only he could see them. It felt like being set free from a cramped prison cell; release for a few minutes from the miasma below deck and the chance to stretch in the space around them. It was what she missed most, the sense of distance, of being part of something vast. The moors, the mountains and now the oceans. Despite the hardships, she was more at home as an exile than she'd ever been in Haefen.

The wound on her arm had healed well, but thinking back on the journey made it ache, a sharp pain that disappeared as quickly as it had come. Did men forget pain as easily as women, she wondered? Perhaps it was a gift to make up for the miseries of childbirth, to remember only the aftermath of suffering.

They were heading south, according to Markus, and every day was a little warmer than the last. One morning

Ellen came on deck without a jacket, and thought Markus was about to collapse. 'The rumours have already started,' he said, 'though I hoped we might have been granted a longer respite. Some think you teenage boys, others have come closer to the truth. But for your own sakes, be careful.'

A few days later, Sophia woke with cramps and told Ellen to take her morning walk alone. 'I'll be fine, there's no reason you should miss the air because of me.'

As usual, the crew was confined below as Ellen climbed the short steps from the captain's cabin and crossed the main deck towards the foredeck. She liked it there, near the bow of the ship where the wind blew hardest and she could feel almost alone on the ocean. She walked as far forward as possible, then turned back along the other side. A number of large barrels were lashed together and stowed on the deck. She'd never asked what was in them; provisions perhaps, or fresh water.

As she crossed behind them, her legs were kicked away and she fell to the deck, out of sight of the captain. There was no way to shout for help; a hand was pressed over her mouth and the point of a knife pricked at her throat. The smell of the man was almost overpowering, sweat and mildew, and the stench of his breath as he whispered in her ear was worse than the smell from the maggots that had feasted on Brother William.

'Calm down and it will soon be done. A pretty thing like you, t'would be a sin not to give you what you need.' He dropped the knife and started to pull down her hose, ripping at the cloth.

Markus had said that sounds carried on board ship, but no-one was coming to help her, even though the crew must have been able to hear the noise of the struggle below deck. In his excitement, the man loosened the pressure on her mouth. She shook her head free and sank her teeth into his hand, tasting the warm, salty blood. He grunted, stopped fumbling with her clothing and punched her in the throat, a short hard jab. He'd done this before.

It was as if her lungs had forgotten how to breathe. She stopped struggling as she choked, unable to swallow or draw in air.

'You're a feisty bitch.' He pulled at the hose again. 'You only got yourself to blame. This would have been over long since if you hadn't set out to deceive decent men.'

Her lungs were working again, just. And her mind had never stopped. She was half sitting, half sprawling, backed up against the row of barrels. She could see where her attacker had dropped his clasp knife, probably thinking that it wasn't needed any more, and it was lying, still open, a few inches from her hand.

She relaxed her body as if she'd given up the fight and surrendered. The same trick as on the mountains; this was becoming a habit. As the man began to extricate his prick in triumph, she knew that all his focus would narrow on just one thing. She felt for the knife, and in one flowing motion picked it up and stabbed the at the back of his neck. Not enough leverage to deliver a killer blow and she would have preferred the throat, but it was enough to make him cry out with pain and surprise, and release her. She rolled away, scrambled to her feet and ran back towards the stern, hauling up the torn hose and shouting to Markus for help.

Back in the cabin, Sophia poured her a tot of rum and water and checked her over for damage. 'Sailors are good at sewing, so I'm told. I'll make sure they repair your clothes or run you up something new. Sailcloth is all the fashion this year. But you'll have a decent bruise where he hit you in the throat, and your thighs look like you lost a fight with an angry cat. And you need to wash, now. Gods only know what diseases that bastard is harbouring under his nails.'

Markus joined them half an hour later, looking like a someone who'd found his wife in bed with another man. 'The bastard lives, though you gave him a good blood-letting. He's locked up now, kicking and swearing.' He sighed and rubbed his eyes. 'This is a bad business, and the worst is that no-one came to help. Well, they'll soon see what waits for any man that steps out of line.'

He extricated a small silver flask from the pocket of his jacket, unscrewed the cap, and took a swig. 'I don't hold with drunkenness on board but there's a time and a place and this is one of them.'

He turned to Ellen. 'We all know what happened and who did it, but everyone has the right to face their accuser before I pronounce sentence. If this were the navy, the man would be up before a court martial. But on the Billy Boy, I'm the only law that matters. None of this is pleasant, least of all for you, but it must be done and done quickly. On deck, in an hour. I'll come for you then.'

After he left, Ellen looked out of the large slanting windows. The ship's wake stretched behind them, a straight line of white foam fading into the distance. Now the excitement and fear had subsided she felt the swelling in her throat, the burning of the scratches on her thighs. The rot on his breath was still in her nostrils, thick and cloying, along with the sweat and mould from his skin and clothing. The bruises and cuts would go, she knew, leaving only the memory. Perhaps she'd been wrong; bodily pain fades with time, but scars in the mind last forever. The trick was learning to ignore them.

. . .

THIS WAS the first time she'd seen him clearly, standing in front of her with his hands tied behind his back. A small man, with loose cotton trousers and a greasy jacket. She'd watched as he limped up to the quarterdeck, supported by two of his crew mates. His lips were cut and swollen, and one of his eyes was already turning purple, so she hadn't been the only one serving out retribution that day. The man glanced up at her and back down at the deck.

'Well, Stevens,' said the captain. 'You know what you've done and that I'll have no truck with a man who acts like an animal. Do you have anything to say?'

Stevens glanced up, spat a gout of blood onto the deck, and looked away again.

The entire ship's company had assembled below them on the main deck, as silent and apprehensive as if they were on trial. Markus raised his voice to carry the length of the ship. 'I will not tolerate this behaviour under my command. Stevens attacked a guest on our ship with a knife. There's only one penalty for this. Death by hanging.' He signalled to the men supporting Stevens, whose legs had given way. 'Take him down and let him reflect on his crime tonight. He hangs at dawn.'

As they led the man away, and the crew dispersed, Ellen said to the captain, 'I would have cut his throat myself if I could. But killing him in cold blood, that's a different matter. Is there no other punishment you could give him?'

'Everyone on the ship is under my care,' said Markus. 'If I let the men do as they please, we all suffer. So I have two things to consider; preventing this man from committing such a crime again and deterring others who fancy their chances. We still have weeks together on this voyage. I need - you need - for the men to understand that neither of you, whoever or whatever you are, can be touched.' He looked up to the tops of the mainmast, as if for inspiration. 'Yes, I could have him flogged, I could have him keelhauled. Either might kill him, and equally he would have a chance of survival. But hanging sends the right message to the crew. Under my command they know there's no appeal against the noose.'

As they reached the stairs down to their cabin Markus called out, 'Dawn tomorrow, you need to be there.'

CRIME AND PUNISHMENT

~~~~

She'd grown up with death. In Haefen, women would barely recover from giving birth to one child before they were pregnant again. A subconscious insurance policy; so many children died before their fifth birthdays, even more before they experienced their first, furtive kiss. And without children, old age was a cruel, lonely place.

It wasn't only the children that death stalked. So many men had younger wives, the previous versions having died during one of the multiple childbirths, bleeding out on a bed. A life for a life. It was a wonder any females were left in Haefen once they reached childbearing age, unless, of course, they were like her and managed to swerve away from marriage and the attentions of men. At least that way there was a chance of life, even if people whispered about her in the streets. Called her a witch, told their children to stay away. A small price to pay for freedom.

In the middle of the night she listened to the creaking of the timbers, the slap of waves against the hull and the sound of Sophia snoring lightly as she shifted position in the hammock, slung across the cabin from the bed. The sounds weren't enough to drown out the thoughts of what would happen at dawn. She'd seen death come in many forms, but never a hanging in cold blood.

Perhaps, in the end, death was more merciful than the alternatives. At least it would soon be over and Stevens' misery along with it. He would never attack another person, and his death might make the other men think twice before giving in to their fantasies, no matter how tempting. She wasn't innocent; the gods knew that, but the memories of the men who'd died at her hand caused her not a single sleepless night. Despatching them had always been done in the moment; self-defence and instant justice.

Perhaps people who believed in the gods had an answer, but she suspected their explanations depended on which god they chose. Or what the god's mood was on that day. No, right or wrong was something one had to choose for oneself. The trick was learning to live with the consequences.

Sleep came at last, but it was fitful, punctuated by sudden imaginings of someone creeping round the cabin, or of a shadow standing over her. Once she woke herself by crying out in her sleep, and had to reassure Sophia that the ship wasn't sinking and that all was well.

She was already awake when Markus knocked on the cabin door and called out. 'It wants but fifteen minutes of dawn. You should prepare yourselves and come on deck.' He sounded weary, as if his night too had been long and hag-ridden.

THE SKY WAS LIGHTENING in the east when they climbed the short steps to the quarterdeck. The sun was preparing to rise, a brilliant golden glow on the horizon cooling to pinks and reds as it spread out across the sky, tinting the grey clouds of the night. Once again the crew were assembled below them on the main deck and Stevens stood near the edge of the deck under a yardarm. His hands and feet were tied together, with two of the crew supporting his arms so that he didn't fall. A thick rope hung from a pulley attached to the yardarm, and the noose tied at the end dangled inches from Stevens' head, as if teasing him.

While most of the crew had dressed in jackets against the chill of the early morning, Steven was wearing nothing but a loose shirt and canvas trousers. Even from where she was standing Ellen, could see him shivering, great tremors that rippled down his body. She'd seen men fight to save their lives, daring death to catch them, but this man was ending his in fear. She almost felt ashamed for him.

Markus walked over to her. 'I passed sentence, but now you have a choice. I make no bones about it, hanging can be a slow business and painful to watch but it's in your gift to grant him some mercy.'

'You mean he doesn't have to hang?' Even as she said it, Ellen couldn't decide if she was glad to have this choice, or even which choice to make. For all the fine thoughts and words yesterday, did she want to see him cheat death?

Markus made it easy for her. 'No, either way he'll hang. But we can tie a shot to his feet, thirty pounds of lead weight. If he's lucky, his neck will snap as we string him up and the end will be quick. Mind you, it doesn't always happen and the weight pulling on him makes the agony worse. But choose quickly; the sun's almost up.'

Now she realised why Markus wanted her here. It was no longer just his decision, she was complicit and her choice would mean either a quick end, or an even more painful death for the man who tried to rape her. She wished that she'd been able to put up more of a fight, to kill him in the moment or topple him overboard. That would have been justice. But now she had to choose the degree of suffering for his last few moments on earth.

'The shot. If he has to die, so be it, but I won't torture a man no matter what he's done.'

The Billy Boy was no fighting ship but had a few cannon to defend itself against pirates and raiders. One of the crew brought a round shot up from the store, and tied it to Stevens' legs. Her attacker lifted his head for the first time and looked over in their direction, but his eyes were focussed somewhere across the waves.

As the noose dropped around his neck, Markus called out. 'Do you have anything to say, Stevens? These are your last moments, so if you have any words, make them worthwhile.'

Stevens was crying now, tears running down his cheeks, and his whole body shook as if he had a fever. He swallowed a couple of times and then spoke so quietly that the captain asked him to repeat his words.

'Tell my ma I drowned. She's a good woman, she don't deserve to know what I done. And there's two silver pieces in my chest for her; don't let these thieving buggers nick 'em.'

A team of sailors were waiting by the other end of the rope, and at a signal from the bosun they hauled away. Even though there were none of the usual chants to synchronise their efforts, they stayed in rhythm as they took up the slack in the rope. Stevens' body jerked as he rose in the air with the shot hanging from his bound feet.

'Too slow,' muttered Markus.

'What do you mean?'

'You weren't the only one to have a choice. Haul away quickly and with luck his neck would break, specially with the weight of the shot to help. A quick end. But haul slowly and he'll strangle to death. I've seen it take twenty minutes or more. The way these men are pulling him up, slow and steady, they're showing their disapproval of what he tried to do. There's shame there too, that none of them came to your aid.'

Stevens bucked and kicked as his body rose almost to the yardarm itself. The shot attached to his legs swung like a pendulum.

Markus sighed. 'Not a good sign. He'll be there a while and we must wait until the end. A heavier man might break his own neck with enough movement, but Stevens doesn't have it in him, poor little bugger. He'll be dancing the Pollian polka for a while yet.'

The ship had rarely been so quiet. Sophia, standing next to her, had said nothing throughout the entire morning and turned away from the sight, hypnotic though it was.

Every few moments Stevens stopped struggling and Ellen's pulse raced at the thought that it was over. Then he convulsed again, trying to jackknife his body, but each time the movements were weaker and every so often the breeze brought them the smell of the piss and shit that stained his trousers. This was an ugly death.

Finally he stopped moving altogether. After a few minutes the bosun looked up at the quarterdeck, Markus nodded, and one of the sailors stepped forward and sliced through the rope. Steven's body fell from the yardarm and hit the water with a splash. Ellen looked over the side, but there was no sign of him.

'We tie the hands and feet for two reasons,' said Markus. 'Stops them trying to escape, and when they hit the surface there's no way they can swim, even if they managed to cling on to life through the hanging. And with the shot to help, he's well on his way to the bottom, more than forty fathoms down. He's gone now.'

STORMY SEAS

A cry from the crow's nest interrupted them. 'Ship ahead, two points off starboard bow.'

One of the ship's boys scurried over and handed Markus a telescope. 'It's her, by all the gods, it's her,' said the captain. 'Two chimneys amidships, belching smoke. If I were a superstitious man, I'd think it was demons too.'

Ellen and Sophia took turns to look through the telescope. 'I guessed as much,' said Sophia. 'Steamship, fairly early design.'

'I thought young Sera was a queer type but you two make him seem positively normal,' said Markus. 'You know what this thing is?'

Sophia shrugged. 'I suppose it doesn't matter what I say now. You've heard about the steam engines used in mines to pump out water?'

'Aye, bloody great things they are too.'

'They don't have to be. That ship has a steam engine on board and it drives a device which propels the ship through the water. Doesn't need wind and can steer in any direction.' She paused. 'How fast does the Billy Boy sail?'

'With a fair wind, we've logged six knots. But we're built for capacity, not speed.'

'That steamship probably makes fifteen knots. And carries as much cargo as you, or more.'

Markus looked as though a vision of paradise had been snatched away from him. 'So you're telling me we stand no chance of catching her.'

'Not unless she wants to be caught. And she's sailing away from us.'

'But at least we have a bearing now.' Markus gave instructions to the steersman and the Billy Boy veered onto a new course, tracking the distant ship which was now nothing more than a haze of smoke on the horizon.

Ellen shivered in a breeze which had sprung from nowhere. She'd listened to the conversation between Markus and Sophia and tried to make sense of it. Steam she understood, but the rest might as well be a description of magic. The city of Haefen had been a very small world.

The early sun had disappeared behind a haze of cloud and the light was changing by the minute, as if someone was dimming a lamp. Where the distant ship was visible a few moments ago was now a line of dark grey cloud, racing towards them. The ship bucked like an unbroken horse, rising on a swell which had come from nowhere, and crashing down on the other side.

'You should go below,' said Markus. 'This is a storm, and a bad one by the look of it. Damn Stevens; if it hadn't been for him, I'd have paid more attention to the signs. But don't worry, the Billy Boy will see us through.'

Even in the cabin, out of the wind, the temperature had dropped dramatically. Sheets of rain swept across the surface of the ocean to batter the panes of glass in the stern window. Cloud and water had merged into one grey mass with the Billy Boy caught in the middle, and the wind groaned and wailed as it vibrated through the rigging. The jolly boat, which was always towed behind, had disappeared from view.

Sophia joined Ellen on the bed.

'Will the sails hold?' Ellen asked.

'I wish I knew, girl, but I'm no expert. Not on ships like this. I learned about them in history lessons when I was a child, objects from the past. But if I remember correctly, the crew should reduce the spread of canvas. They need to keep some sails so the captain can steer the ship, but too many and we could be blown on our side, or the sails could rip and be destroyed.'

'This isn't making me feel any better.'

'Markus knows what he's doing. We have no choice, just have to sit it out down here.'

'Like useless women? Still not helping.'

'You want to go outside and scramble up the rigging, be my guest. But I'm staying here until the storm blows over.'

They heard a sudden cracking noise from above, the sound of men shouting and then one piercing scream.

'Okay, perhaps staying here was a bad idea.'

The ship had been listing first to one side, then another, but now it was leaning over so far that they found it almost impossible to climb the steps to the deck. When they arrived, they were greeted by a scene from a nightmare. The mainmast had split halfway up and was hanging over the side of the ship, still carrying its sails, which were dragging in the water. The captain shouted orders to the crew as they hacked at the rigging and spars with knives and axes. Another cracking sound, like a minor explosion. The mast broke off completely, the sails dragged it over the side, and the ship immediately began to right itself.

Towards the bow one of the cannon had broken free and careered across the deck, hitting the same boy who brought Markus his telescope earlier. The wooden gun carriage had mangled the boy's legs beyond repair. The rain was beating into them like needles and the ship felt heavier somehow, righting itself more slowly each time it listed to one side.

Markus noticed them. 'There's nothing you can do,' he shouted over the whine of the wind. 'We're shipping water faster than the pumps can handle. If the storm blows itself out soon, we might come through.'

No mention of what would happen if it didn't.

Sophia grabbed her arm and shouted in her ear. 'Can you swim?'

'You're the second person to ask me that recently, and the answer's still no. Do I have a choice?'

'No.'

'I'd better learn quickly then.'

'If the ship founders find something to hold on to. A spar, a barrel, anything that floats. I'll do my best to stay with you.'

'That doesn't sound like much of a plan.'

'It's all I've got right now. Just pray we stay afloat.'

THE BILLY BOY had righted itself this time, but instead of the violent rocking from side to side it was wallowing now, sitting low in the water.

'I need to get back to the cabin,' Ellen shouted at Sophia.

'What for? You're better off here, you don't want to be trapped below.'

'Sera's gold. If we come through this alive, we'll need money.'

She made her way down the steps to the cabin door, but the floor inside was six inches deep in cold seawater with the level rising. Her knapsack was still dry on top of the map chest and she shrugged it onto her shoulders, but the cabin door had shut behind her and the weight of the water, level with her calves now, was keeping it closed. She pulled the handle with all her strength, but there was no movement. The only other way out was through the stern windows, but that led straight down to the roiling ocean, out of sight of anyone.

Ellen battered on the door, calling for help, and then heard Sophia's shout from the other side.

'Get away from the door! Stand back.'

Ellen waded away for a few steps; something hit the door from the other side, one blow after another, and a crack appeared in the timber. More blows, faster and frantic. Longer splits appeared in the dark wood and then Sophia was standing there, her hair no longer hidden under a cap but plastered over her face. She scraped it away from her eyes and swung again with the axe until the cracks merged and there was space enough to pass the knapsack, before she helped Ellen to scramble through herself.

'That, girl, was foolish.' Sophia could barely talk and bent over to catch her breath. 'I only hope the gold is worth it.'

A new noise was audible now above the wind and rain, the sound of something heavy shifting in the bowels of the ship. The hull listed again to one side, slow and inexorable, and this time the movement didn't stop.

Rain swept across the ship in grey sheets and anything further forward than the quarterdeck was invisible, hidden by rain and spray. Markus was nowhere in sight and then someone screamed, 'She's going down. Abandon ship!'

As if there was any choice.

'We mustn't get trapped beneath the hull or in the rigging,' shouted Sophia above the noise of the wind and rain. She and Ellen held on to each other as they scrabbled their way up the sloping deck to the side, which was rising higher in the air.

'When it goes, try to jump as far out as you can. You'll go under but don't panic. I'll be with you.'

The lower side of the deck was well under water now and as the hull finally turned upside down they clung on, waiting until they were nearly in the water before Sophia shouted, 'Jump!'

Easier said than done. The jump was more of an uncoordinated sprawl into the freezing ocean. Ellen splashed about more from instinct than design, trying not to sink or breathe in the salt water, and then her arm hit something hard. She grabbed it with both hands; part of the shattered yardarm from which Stevens had hung such a short time before. Death to him, but life to her, at least for a while.

The current had already swept her away from the broken body of the ship and as she watched it seemed to sigh, and then sink slowly beneath the surface. She was alone now, except for pieces of flotsam from the Billy Boy. How could so many people disappear so quickly?

What had Sera said about drowning; a peaceful way to die? Some people believed anything. Death never came easily and to spend her last moments breathing in cold seawater struck her as a particularly poor choice. But what was the alternative? Hang on to this piece of wood until her strength gave out and she slipped away, her body already as cold as a corpse? After all her fights and her victories and her dreams and her desires, to die alone in a featureless ocean; if she needed any more proof, this was it. There were no gods, there was no plan.

She tried to pull herself further out of the water, but the cold was already leaching away her energy. How long, she wondered, how long?

Her mind was wandering through images from her past when she heard her name called. 'Ellen, Ellen! Is that you?' Sophia's voice, and not too far away.

'Where are you?' Then she saw her friend, clinging on to the upturned body of the jolly boat. Now would be a good time to learn to swim. Using the spar as a float she kicked her legs and propelled herself towards Sophia who leant down, grabbed the end of the spar and pulled Ellen over.

'I should have known you'd survive,' Sophia said.

'Only just' She tried, and failed, to control the shivering that juddered through her body. A cough turned into a retch as she threw up a thin bile of seawater, and her arms and legs felt as if the bones had been removed. I am, she thought, getting too old for this kind of caper.

'One last effort, girl, don't give up on me now.'

'Don't worry, this isn't my day to die. What do you want me to do?'

'We need to get the boat upright. I tried, but I'm not heavy enough alone. The two of us might manage.' Sophia balanced on the keel of the jolly boat, horizontal to the surface of the ocean. 'You need to come up next to me, hold on to the gunwale - the top edge here - then we both lean back and use our weight to pull the boat upright.'

'Can't we cling on as it is?'

'We have to get out of the water, and soon. Trust me, I know what I'm doing.' She helped Ellen up alongside her and showed her how to hold on. 'We need to rock it backwards and forwards to build up momentum. When I say so, grip tightly and throw your weight back as far as you can. You'll fall into the sea so hold your breath and don't worry, I'll get you back.'

They rocked the hull down and up in a seesaw motion, moving it a little further each time until it sprung upright and floated, flinging them both into the water.

Sophia seized Ellen by the arm, helped her over the side into the boat and then hauled herself in, collapsing across the seats as if she'd exhausted her last reserves of energy.

THE NOT-SO-JOLLY BOAT

They were out of the sea but not, Ellen realised, out of trouble. They sat hunched on the bench seats, shivering in the rain with their legs pulled up to keep them out of the water rolling around in the bottom of the boat. Not that it mattered, there was barely any difference between the degree of wetness in the sea or out of it. But it seemed like the right thing to do, a small level of control over the elements.

The boat was empty of anything that could bale out the water, and if there were ever any oars, they'd long gone. Not that she knew how to row, so at least that was another embarrassment avoided.

The boat rose and fell on the swell, and neither woman had the energy to talk. After a while, Ellen noticed that the rain had stopped and the boat's motion was no longer so violent. It was as if some giant had poured oil over the surface of the ocean to calm it. But they were still alone. Now the clouds had lifted, visibility stretched for miles in every direction, and wherever she looked there was nothing but the grey sea. No other survivors, no sign of the Billy Boy's broken carcass.

A pale sun showed itself, little more than a veiled lamp behind a gauze of cloud. 'What time do you think it is?' Ellen asked.

Sophia was nodding in a half sleep. She lifted her head and peered up at the sky. 'Late afternoon. I guess it'll get dark in a couple of hours. Dark and even colder.' Her voice sounded pinched, as if it was an effort to form the words and force them out.

If they survived the night, it would be a miracle. Perhaps there were gods after all, teasing her with visions of salvation only to snatch them away again. 'There was land marked on the charts the captain showed us,' said Ellen. 'Remember? You can read a map better than me; how far away do you think it was?'

Sophia rubbed at a bruise on her calf, which was already turning dark purple. 'Could be somewhere over the horizon, could be only a mile away. But it wouldn't matter where it is. There's no way we can steer the boat, we have no oars, no sail. We're at the mercy of the ocean currents. For all we know they could take us further out to sea by the minute and there's not a thing we can do about it.' There was a bitterness in her voice Ellen hadn't heard before.

'The current could also take us towards land.'

'True. A fifty-fifty chance. But we have no food and no fresh water. And if we don't die of thirst, we'll likely freeze to death.' Sophia winced as if she was in pain and clutched at her side under the sodden jacket.

'What is it?' Ellen asked. 'Are you hurt?'

'I didn't take my own advice; something hit me when I went over the side.' She moved her hand away from the torn shirt to reveal a small piece of wood that had pierced her just under the ribcage.

'Gods, woman, you must be in agony. Why didn't you say something?'

'I couldn't feel anything until just now.'

'Your body's in shock. Let me see.' Ellen pulled the shirt open; blood oozed from the edges of the wound. This, at least, was in her domain. 'It's a fragment of timber. A couple of inches sticking out, but I can't tell how deep it's gone. The bleeding isn't too bad and the salt water will have kept it clean, but I wouldn't want to remove it till we have bandages and ointment. Hang on, you'll be fine.'

Sophia interrupted her. 'You told me this wasn't your day to die, but I think it might be mine. This wound's gone too deep, I can feel it now. If I were back home I could fix it, but in a boat on the open ocean with no field dressings, no painkillers…' Her voice trailed off as she gasped with pain.

'Remember what we were talking about earlier,' said Ellen. 'A fifty-fifty chance of hitting land. Try to hold on until we find help.'

It was as if the seawater had bleached all the colour from Sophia's skin, leaving it flaccid and grey. She allowed herself to lie back on the bench seat with her head in Ellen's lap and seemed to fall asleep for a few moments, but then opened her eyes and laughed quietly as if recalling a joke. 'Do you remember when we first saw each other? You, the country mouse from the past, me the glamorous vamp from the future, meeting somewhere neither of us belonged. I knew as soon as I saw you, the way you carried yourself. Out of time, out of place, but ready to take on the world for the right to belong. As for your hair, and your eyes… I always was a fool for a beautiful woman, but you had this aura around you like invisible armour.' Her voice had become fainter, as if she were drifting away. 'You were untouchable, yet I so wanted to touch. And here we are now, floating together on an empty ocean while I bleed my life away.' She looked up at Ellen, who stroked her hair.

'Don't you leave me now, woman, don't you dare. I need you.'

'I think, Ellen, that you will never need anyone. That's both your gift, and your tragedy.' Her body convulsed suddenly, and she coughed up a cupful of dark blood. When the fit passed, she sank back down and let Ellen wipe her face clean.

'I don't think your story's over, girl, even if mine is. Promise me you won't give up until you find what you're looking for. Whatever that is.'

'You know me, I never give up. Promise.'

THE BOAT CONTINUED to rock as the invisible ocean currents carried it along. On the horizon the clouds had split apart and the sun's rays reached out, turning the grey water to the colour of autumn leaves. Overhead a full moon had risen high in the darkening sky, and a few of the braver stars were already beginning to shine.

Ellen bent down to kiss Sophia for the first and last time, a brief touch of lips that were already as cold as the sea.

There should be a ceremony, she thought, a ritual. And what to do with the body? How can I throw her overboard like an object whose usefulness has ended? Something to be discarded, thrown away.

But perhaps, after all, it was better to give her to the waves. She'd cheated them once, when she fell out of her real life to this strange world. It was fitting for her to surrender to the ocean this time.

But practicality before emotion. Ellen checked the outside pockets on Sophia's jacket and found a small oilcloth packet with ten gold coins inside, enough to have bought Tollin's house twice over. Her friend must have taken them from the knapsack, knowing it was bound to be lost. If she ever found land, at least she could pay her way.

She stroked Sophia's hair, said a last goodbye, and then dragged the body to the stern and managed to tip it into the water without capsizing the boat. For a few moments Sophia floated, buoyed up by air trapped in her clothes, but then sank beneath the surface.

Alone again.

CHAPTER 12

Jetsam

ON THE BEACH

She woke to a different sound. Although night had long since fallen, the moon lit a scene that filled her with hope and dread in equal parts. A shadowy mass of land rose from the sea a few hundred yards ahead, a horseshoe bay hemmed in by cliffs. There was only one complication; jagged outcrops of rock guarded the approach to the shore, like sentinels with sharp spears rising out of the ocean. Spray showered her face as the craft drifted closer, and the swell broke itself on the rocks. If the boat foundered there, the frail timbers would surrender without a fight and its back would break. There was no way she could make it to the beach alive if she was thrown into the water here. Either the waves would crush her on the rocks or she would drown within sight of safety.

The tide rolled the boat towards the sharp outcrops and then dragged it out again, but with each cycle they came nearer. If those recalcitrant gods were kind, the current might sweep her through the narrow channel into the bay, but that would call for a significant transformation in their attitude.

The boat lifted again as a wave passed underneath and carried it forward. She half crouched near the bow; perhaps she could reach forward and grasp one of the spears of rock and try to pull herself round, but they were as sharp as blades and the current was vicious.

So close; just a few more yards and she would clear the rocks and be through into calmer water. The boat rose again as if a giant hand had come up from below to drive it forward. The bow snagged one of the rocks, and the abrupt cessation of movement toppled Ellen over the edge into the water. The undertow sucked her down and out to sea, and she struggled to hold her breath as the current changed direction and threw her forward again towards the rocks. Which way was up? She opened her eyes but found herself caught in a maelstrom of foaming water. Something sliced into her leg as she kicked out for the surface, and then the current slackened and she was in the stillness of the bay. She paddled her hands and legs in what she hoped was an approximation of swimming, struggling to keep her face above the surface as she breathed again. Now to reach the shore, just a hundred yards away.

Don't panic, Sophia had said just before the Billy Boy went down. The jolly boat had broken up when it hit the rocks and one of the benches was floating just within reach. Ellen splashed over and grabbed hold.

She drifted closer and closer to the small beach, and then her feet hit the bottom. She struggled to stand, but her legs refused to carry her weight and she sank back into the water. No matter. Using the wooden bench as a crutch, she staggered out of the water and collapsed onto the pebbles. A few moments to catch her breath, and then she crawled away from the water's edge. The tide looked to be coming in and there was no way to know how far up the beach it would reach. Such a cruel trick it would be, to bring her this far and then let the sea take her.

The cut on her leg was bleeding, but not as badly as she'd feared. Nothing to worry about, at least for now.

How long until daylight? The full moon cast silver shadows, but she elected to wait until dawn before finding a way off the beach. The cliffs ringing the bay seemed unbroken and high; it was one thing to clamber up a few yards to a cave in the forest, another to rock climb these sheer slabs.

Some fragments from the boat had washed up near her on the beach. She sat next to the wreckage and ran through an inventory of her possessions. A short list. The men's clothes she was wearing, soaked and torn as they were. The gold coins that Sophia had saved. And strapped to her thigh underneath the ragged breeches was the dagger gifted to her father for saving a sailor from drowning. She pictured Sophia's body sinking beneath the waves and thought; if only I could had saved you.

THE BEACH STRETCHED three hundred feet from the edge of the sea to the base of the cliffs. Halfway up, a slight ridge ran where the pebbles were larger, and even in the moonlight, they were darker than those nearer the shore. The ridge ran the length of the beach; with luck, it marked the limit of the high tide. Stay above that and she should be safe.

The cliffs were protecting her from the worst of the wind, but even so she was shivering from cold. Her wet clothes weren't helping, but it would be worse without them. A desire to curl up and sleep fought against the cold, and finally sleep won.

She woke from a dream of being towed along a cobbled street by a monstrous beast. A pale winter sun had taken over from the moon, but the sense of being dragged was still there. A small dog, creamy white with black ears, was worrying the tail of her jacket, growling and trying to tear the cloth to pieces with its teeth. Ellen sat up, shouted and shooed it away. The dog backed off and sat, its head on one side as if wondering what species of creature it had come upon.

Ellen and the dog studied each other. Some sort of terrier, Ellen decided, although dogs had never been a strong point. And it was wearing a leather collar. In Haefen, the dogs were left to roam or tied up with rope. Leather was for horses.

A dog meant there was a way off the beach. A collar meant an owner. An owner meant… Meant what? Rescue, food and water if she was lucky. Imprisonment or confinement in an asylum if not, or if she told the wrong story. It had happened to Sophia, it could happen to her. So what would she say to explain how she came to be on a deserted beach, damaged and bruised and dressed in dilapidated male clothing?

The dog wandered away, bored, chasing a scent trail across the beach to something left by the retreating tide. Sleep had restored some of her strength; Ellen struggled to her feet and hobbled over to see what it had found. The dog was dancing around the object now, barking for attention and Ellen looked down at the broken body of a sailor from the Billy Boy. No-one she knew, just one of the faces that had to turn away whenever she appeared. Like Markus, he'd tied his thick fair hair back in a pigtail, and a small gold earring glinted in his left ear. No shoes; perhaps he'd survived long enough to kick them off as he tried to stay afloat until the effort became too much and he no longer had the strength to keep his mouth and nose out of the water. Had he left anyone back in Coria? A wife perhaps, and children, who would never have recognised the moment when their hope became forlorn.

Ellen chased the dog away and it scampered across to the other side of the beach. She moved away from the body and checked the cut on her leg; sea-clean and no fresh blood. Still, only two more limbs to go and she would have damaged the full set.

She looked around the beach and noticed a figure emerging from the edge of the cliffs, running in her direction. Now the tide was out, there looked to be a way around the headland. The figure slowed to a trot as it moved closer and then stopped a few feet away. A child, perhaps eight or nine years old. She'd successfully managed to stay away from children for the most part; noisy and dirty and never where you wanted them to be. This one was male, by its appearance, turned out in strange baggy breeches with no hose and a coat flapping open at his knees.

'Hello,' he said. 'Have you seen Peterkin?'

'Who's Peterkin?'

'My dog.'

He spotted the creature and ran off to find him on the other side of the bay.

A most incurious child. Or perhaps he was accustomed to seeing strange women washed up on the shore. The boy collected his dog, which squirmed in his arms as he skipped back across the pebbles. When he was a few yards away, he let Peterkin jump to the ground.

'Is he dead?' He pointed over at the sailor's body. 'I've seen lots of dead people, they don't scare me. He didn't drown, did he. You can always tell when someone's drowned because the fish eat them, especially the noses. It's a fact. It's different when they get trampled by a horse or fall under a carriage. Then there's blood everywhere and they use sawdust to mop it up. I don't know what they do with the sawdust after. Or elephants. They make you go very flat, I expect. If they tread on you. I shouldn't like that. What's your name?'

'My name's Ellen. What about you?'

'I'm Alfred Edward Withering and I'm eight and a half years old. Nearly.'

'Do you live near here?'

'My papa's the doctor. I don't expect he could help that man, but your leg's hurt and you're very dirty. Shall I take you to him? He asked me to find you but we're late for luncheon and we don't want papa to get grumpy, that's what mama always says. Can you walk? You could lean on me, it's not far.'

She decided not to ask how the boy's father knew she was on the beach; answers could come later.

The journey across the beach to the headland was slow and uncomfortable; her whole body was tender with bruises. Alfred helped her scramble across a jumble of fallen rocks and around to the next beach, a mile or more of sand and pebbles, and the boy led her along a path between tufts of rangy grasses sprouting from sand dunes, winding and climbing until it reached a road that followed the contours of the coast.

'I need to rest a moment,' said Ellen. She leant against a dry stone wall, chest high, to take her weight. The pounding in her head was almost unbearable; the last water she'd drunk other than involuntary gulps of seawater was on the Billy Boy, just before they hauled Stevens up to swing from the yardarm. Twenty-four hours or more.

'How much further?'

The boy considered, peering at the ground and moving his lips silently. 'About five minutes when I run.'

'I'm not running anywhere.'

'But I could fetch Papa. He'll know what to do.'

'Go. Go now. And tell him to bring some water.'

THE DOCTOR'S HOUSE

Her clothes had dried somewhat while she slept, but still felt sticky with salt. She sat on the grass verge, her back against the stone wall. On the other side of the road behind another low wall, fields stretched across a flat landscape until they met a range of low hills in the distance.

The boy and his dog had disappeared around a bend in the road. She couldn't see buildings anywhere, but there was the suggestion of smoke from a chimney in the direction the boy ran. This was a lonely place, sparsely populated. But a doctor needed patients, so there must be a settlement nearby. The mud on the road was patterned with fresh wheel tracks and someone had filled in the larger potholes with pebbles from the beach.

How long had the boy been gone? Five minutes, he said, to his home. If he ran. Call that ten to allow for childish boasting, another ten to explain the situation to his father. And then the big question; would Alfred's papa believe him? Had he really known she was on the beach, or was that some childish invention. She could sit here for hours, waiting for someone who might never come, and she was ready to sell her body for water and a piece of bread. A wash to remove the salt on her skin would be a pleasant bonus. And clean, dry clothes.

More waiting. How long had the boy been gone now? She ran through the equations of time again. Ten minutes to his house, ten minutes to explain and persuade and fifteen perhaps for his papa to find her. Thirty-five minutes. Or he could be out with a patient, an early morning call. He could be hours away if he came at all.

She looked around for anything to use as a crutch. There was no point waiting for something that might not happen, and she'd feel better about taking control. It had been a while. With the wall as a support, she pulled herself to her feet. No branches in sight; she hadn't been thinking straight earlier, should had asked Alfred to find a suitable piece of driftwood from the boat's remains, something she could use to steady herself as she walked.

She considered her options. She could stay where she was, but how would that help? Or start walking, using the wall to support her, at least until the road curved away and inland, away from the coast. About a quarter of a mile. And then she would crawl if necessary.

The ground alongside the wall was overgrown and uneven, and more than once she stumbled, swearing at the shooting pain in her leg. She was almost at the point where the road and wall parted company when she heard hooves on the road. A few seconds later a pony trotted into view, pulling a small two-wheeled cart driven by a man wearing a jacket decorated with yellow and brown squares. A strange pair of thick spectacles hung around his neck like a necklace, and the tall dark hat looked for all the world like a miniature chimney. Sophia had talked about ships powered by steam. Surely people here weren't powered in the same way, not that anything would surprise her. Or perhaps she was hallucinating again the way she had on the moor.

'There she is! I told you I'd find her.' The contraption slowed to a stop, Alfred jumped down and ran over.

'It's all right, Papa's here. He can make anyone well.'

The man let himself down from the cart as the last of her strength drained away. She slid down the wall onto the damp grass and studied the man as he walked towards her. Dark wavy hair under the hat, grey flecked whiskers halfway across his cheeks. A lean man, she decided. On balance, she preferred lean men. If there had to be a choice.

'My dear lady, what on earth have you done to yourself? Alfred, bring my bag and flask from the trap.'

He took Ellen's wrist and felt her pulse. 'My boy said he found you in the next bay. Can you tell me what happened?'

'Do you have water? I asked the boy to tell you.'

Alfred handed his father a flask which the doctor uncorked and held to Ellen's lips, and when she was done he helped her across to the carriage and supported her as she climbed in, then shook the reins and drove the trap a hundred yards to where the road widened. He turned and touched the pony lightly with the whip. 'Come on, Bella, there's a girl. Step lively now.'

The dog jumped up beside her and Alfred ran behind, while Ellen focussed on trying to protect her leg from the jarring knocks as they bounced along the road.

They rounded the bend and there, a few hundred yards away, stood a large, red brick house with smoke rising from a chimney. Tall metal gates opened onto a curved driveway and the man pulled on the reins to bring them to a stop by a front door painted deep burgundy red; the door opened and a woman ran out. Younger than the doctor, much younger. Dark ringlets of hair under a lace cap and a simple dress tied high under her bust. An older child, perhaps, Alfred's sister? She shook her head in sorrow as she saw the man.

'Do you realise how you appear, Withering? Top hat and goggles, and that disgusting coat.'

'Forgive me, dearest. You're well aware that I was taking observations from the air yacht when I looked down and saw something in Gulliver Bay. After I landed, I tasked Alfred to investigate. This is what he found; would you rather I'd left her there while I took the time to change into a morning coat?'

The doctor and the woman helped Ellen down from the trap and into the house. 'I had Mary put the copper in the bedroom next to Alfred's.' The woman took Ellen's hands. 'He tells me your name's Ellen; welcome to our home. I'm Helena and this is my husband, Dr Antonius Withering. You've already met Alfred and Peterkin. Mary will help you upstairs and bring you fresh clothes of mine, we're much of a size. Then I suspect my husband will wish to examine you for any injuries.'

So even doctors lost wives; Helena was far too young to be Alfred's mother.

AFTER A BATH AND FRESH CLOTHES, the doctor came in and checked her for injuries. He was silent as he felt for broken bones and saw the scars, old and new, that patterned her body. When he was finished, he sat back and studied her face. 'You have not, I think, lived the life of a lady.'

'I lived the life I was given.'

'Not a straightforward task by the state of your body.'

'One thing my life has never been, doctor, is straightforward'

TYING THE THREADS

The smell of food trailed up the stairs. Meals on the Billy Boy had been basic, a type of stew with indeterminate ingredients and dry biscuits. 'If I'd had more notice, I would had arranged for some livestock on board,' Markus had said, 'but Master Sera impressed upon me most strongly that time was of the essence.'

He'd been right; any delay and they would had been at the mercy of the militia and Sophia's husband. Everything that took place on the Billy Boy would have been a possibility that never happened. Stevens would still be alive, so would the drowned sailor from the beach, so would Sophia. Markus would be loading cargo onto the ship and planning his next trading voyage. And me, she thought? I'd be in the asylum with Sophia, both of us locked away as dangerous mad women. A whole different future if they'd decided to wait just a little longer.

So much hung on the simplest of choices, which made living a somewhat precarious occupation full of 'what ifs'. What if I turn down this road rather than that? What if I decide to stay at home today? What if I smile back instead of turning away?

When the doctor had finished, Mary showed Ellen downstairs and into a large room where the doctor and his wife were already sitting at the table. Alfred had disappeared, but Ellen heard shouting and barking from outside. A boy and his dog; some things never changed.

'We're having a late luncheon today as my husband was gallivanting around in his aerial contraption.'

'An air yacht, my love, as I've described a hundred times. A chance to make some geological observations from the air.'

'And what if the balloon on your precious air yacht had been punctured, and you'd crashed to the earth hundreds of feet below? What would become of Alfred and me?'

'I'm safer in my airship than I am riding a horse. You know, the palace has expressed an interest in coming on one of my ascents. What d'you think of that?'

'I think he'd be as mad as you.'

When they'd finished eating and the table was empty of food, the doctor pushed back his chair and studied her. 'There's a strange story behind your arrival here. Wearing male attire from another century, but not cheap imitations for the theatre. Soaked as they were, I could see that they were beautifully made. Originals, but in an impossibly good condition. I ask myself, why would a young woman put these on? And why was she washed ashore after an unseasonable storm at sea?'

All good questions. People wanted the truth, but didn't like what they heard and preferred to make up their own version, trying to fit whatever happened into the shape of the world they already knew. Anything that didn't fit was knocked and moulded into a new shape or discarded. This was one of her truths.

A little dissembling first, she decided. 'My ship was wrecked. One of the sailors washed up on the beach along with me.'

'Alfred told us; I sent the undertaker to collect the body of the poor wretch. And you haven't answered my other questions.'

'Perhaps the answers are too complicated.'

'You're lucky that we found you,' said Helena, a little petulantly. 'My husband is a man of science and neither he nor I have any truck with superstition or dogma. Tell us the truth and we will believe you.'

'Perhaps I can help,' said the doctor. 'There have been reports lately, strange reports, of what fishermen are calling ghost ships. Sailing vessels from the past seen on the horizon. Ships of a design that no-one's used for the last fifty years or more. And then you and this sailor wash up on our beach wearing clothes from another age. You understand why we might see a connection.'

I should write my story, she thought, and hand a copy to each new person I meet. Save all the explanations.

'I'll try to make it simple,' she said. 'You know my name. Ellen, Ellen Dust. I come from a city called Haefen, a long way from here. My home was under threat, the people who governed didn't want to face the truth and they sent me into exile for questioning them. I've been on a journey since then, trying to understand what was happening to us. I failed, and all I've found are more questions.'

'And you sailed from this Haefen? Never heard of it. I assume you were on one of the ghost ships that was seen.'

'We sailed from Coria, a place I hoped would lead me to some answers. All it led to was death for the friend I was travelling with.'

'But why the clothes?' asked Helena.

'We chartered a ship, the Billy Boy. Sailors aren't keen on having women on board, they reckon it brings bad luck, so we decided to dress as men and keep to our cabin. The captain knew the truth, but others discovered it too. Didn't end well.'

'What was the purpose of your voyage? Where were you going?' asked the doctor.

Ellen couldn't help laughing. 'You mentioned ghost ships from the past, but we saw demon ships from the future. At least, that's what some people called them. Ships with chimneys instead of sails. I hoped that if we found their home port I might find some sort of explanation.'

'There was a storm at sea yesterday,' said Helena. 'I assume you were caught in that?'

'We didn't see it coming. The masts broke, the ship was taking water faster than they could pump it out and we sank. My companion and I got into the ship's boat, but we had no oars or sail. I was convinced we would die on the ocean. Instead, I was thrown onto the rocks outside the bay where you found me.'

'And your friend?'

'Injured in the shipwreck, a large splinter of wood under her ribs. She bled to death in my arms.'

They were all silent for a few moments and then the doctor cleared his throat, looked out of the window at the sea and then back to Ellen. 'We know only a fraction of the wonders in this world, and I wonder if you would humour me. There's a meeting here tonight of a small philosophical group, the Selene Society. We gather every month on the night of the full moon. Would you tell your story again, with more detail if you could? The ghost ships aren't the only strange occurrences troubling our society, and one of our number had been tasked with finding an explanation. Your story would intrigue him.'

Wherever she went, mysteries and trouble followed her.

'How many people are in your society?'

'Five of us tonight, including the man I mentioned. He's a little eccentric, but a dear friend. Fescue Monad, Professor of Applied Ontology at the University of Forcello.'

CHAPTER 13

The Selene Society

BEFORE THE MEETING

*S*he hadn't known a bed could feel like this. The doctor's wife had suggested she lie down after lunch and sleep came almost immediately. When she woke the curtains were closed. She drew one aside and looked out over the drive and the little garden towards the sea in the far distance, shimmering silver in the light of the full moon. This time yesterday she was adrift in an open boat on the ocean, with Sophia bleeding to death in her arms. And earlier that morning she'd watched a man die, kicking and struggling as he hung over the sea, fighting to breathe. A knife through the ribs would have been kinder, and more satisfying.

Time. Her life had been compressed, as if she were living months in a single day. It was exhausting. She'd left Haefen and crossed the river into the forest less than four weeks ago, but it felt like a lifetime.

She let the curtain fall back, dressed and went downstairs. The dining room was dark and empty, but at the back of the house she found a kitchen with Helena and Mary preparing plates of food. Helena noticed her by the doorway. 'Antonius prescribed rest and we let you sleep, but he asks that you join him in his study when you're ready. The others will be here presently.'

Mary showed her to a room with a fire burning in the hearth and six chairs arranged in a circle. The doctor was reading at a desk. 'Your arrival was timely,' he said. 'I just received a telegram from one of my friends; there have been other strange happenings to inform our discussions this evening.'

A headache from earlier had receded, but only to gather forces for another assault, and she winced as a giant fist seems to squeeze her brain.

'Are you feeling all right, dear lady? Is the cut on your leg causing you pain? Or that wound on your arm? I'm asking too much, you should go back to your room and rest.'

She heard the disappointment in his voice. 'It's just a headache. Something to eat and drink and I'll be fine.' She forced a smile. 'Who's coming to this meeting, apart from the man you mentioned earlier?'

'I already told you about Fescue Monad. Eccentric but clever. Strange sense of humour. Gregory Oliphant and Gottfried Canterbury are two of his colleagues, both professors at the University. Good men, although Canterbury can be a little vague and Oliphant's a law unto himself. And we have an occasional member who I've taken the liberty to invite this evening, John Tulliver. Bit different from the rest of us, more of a practical man. He owns a factory making components for railway engines. He can appear a little rough around the edges but he keeps our feet on the ground. Our digressions sometimes veer towards the realm of the scholastic.'

He noticed the expression on Ellen's face. 'I suspect that some words I use mean very little to you.'

'I learn quickly, doctor. I have to.'

They heard a carriage pulling up outside. 'They've arrived,' said the doctor. 'Wait here and don't be nervous.'

'I've been many things in my life, Doctor Withering,' said Ellen, 'but nervous has never been one of them.'

ELLEN LOOKED at the gaggle of men standing in the doorway, apparently working out whether she was dangerous. One in a brown tweed suit with an ornate moustache, next to him a bedraggled man with sad eyes, a large man who looked like the blacksmith back in Haefen, and a stooped one at the back with dark, flowing hair that reminded her of Sera. He pushed his way to the front and stretched out his hand.

'Dear lady, Gregory Oliphant at your service. You are, perhaps, a relative of the doctor? A favoured niece come to spend a few days in his charming house?'

Before she could answer, the doctor interrupted. 'While I was making observations from the airship this morning, I saw two bodies washed up on the beach. I sent my boy to investigate and there she was, along with one of the crew. Deceased, poor chap. They were shipwrecked in that storm a couple of nights ago. May I introduce Miss Ellen Dust, late of Haefen.'

Oliphant reached out for her again. 'Dear lady…'

She pulled away. 'I'm not your dear lady.'

'Oliphant means no harm,' said the man in tweed, 'just being gallant. Fancies himself with the ladies.'

This was a mistake. She was just a curiosity to them, something to be examined. An object. She hadn't put up with that in Haefen and she wasn't about to here. 'I have problems of my own,' she said, 'so I'll leave you to your discussions. Tomorrow I'll be on my way.'

'Probably for the best,' said the man with the moustache. 'I told you, Antonius, that we have a matter of importance to discuss. Matter of life and death. Confidential, very. Wouldn't surprise me if we're being spied on as we speak.'

'Don't be ridiculous, Monad,' said Oliphant. 'No-one is spying on anyone. And if the doctor has invited Miss Ellen Dust to join us, I'm sure he has a good reason.'

He turned to Ellen. 'My apologies for making you uncomfortable. Gallantry sometimes comes with the best of intentions, but can be misplaced. And I'd be honoured to understand how you came to be here.'

What else would she do? There was no point in leaving until daylight; the alternatives were her room or the wife's company. Or, gods forbid, twittering Mary. If she had to make a choice, this was the least worst.

FIFTEEN MINUTES later she stopped talking, and waited for a reaction, but there was nothing. Canterbury was actually trying to shift his chair back unobtrusively, to move further away from her. After a while Fescue broke the spell. 'If we thought things were bad before, they just got worse,' he said. 'We came here with a challenge from the Princeps; to say my life is at stake wouldn't be an exaggeration. And ignore Oliphant's smirk. He hasn't been summoned to the palace twice in a week. But after listening to Miss Dust, I have a feeling that whatever's happening goes much further than Forcello. Something connects all these events.'

'Why don't you tell me about your problems,' Ellen said. 'If there's a common link, we might be able to help each other.'

Fescue's explanation took less time than hers. 'As you can see,' he said, 'we bought some time by proposing a competition. All nonsense, we'll get nothing useful out of it. Regardless of Oliphant's optimism, the difficulty is finding a solution when we can't even formulate the problem.'

'You mentioned a town that disappeared,' said Ellen. 'Kimit? The port where your ships loaded food for the city? Tell me again what your captains found.'

'Not a lot,' said Fescue. 'No ruins, no sign that a city or a port ever existed. Just nomads and their goats.'

'The way Kimit looked centuries ago?'

'Centuries, even a thousand years or more. Why?'

'That's the opposite of what happened near Haefen. Our neighbouring city was in ruins, as if centuries had passed. When I got to the Priory, they told me that Haefen itself had been claimed by the sea lifetimes ago. I didn't believe them at first, but even before I left home I could see how the river was changing course and swallowing land too quickly. My arrival in Coria confirmed it; time was running at different speeds in different places, accelerating around me. Since I left home, each minute I've been on the road has taken me into the future. But your ships' captains saw the past, before Kimit existed.'

Fescue slapped the table in triumph. 'Railway time, I knew it!'

'What on earth are you talking about,' said Oliphant. 'Miss Dust don't want to hear about railways.'

Fescue looked at Ellen. 'I suspect railways are unknown to you; they're a method of travelling fast from one place to another. Been around a hundred years or so. Imagine a line of carriages pulled by a machine, a steam engine on wheels. The carriages and the engine run on metal rails which are laid like roadways between different towns and cities. At any time there are up to a hundred trains running along the same routes.'

After the ships without sails and all she'd experienced in Coria, nothing could surprise her. 'Don't they hit each other?'

'Exactly, exactly! We have timetables showing which trains are using a set of rails and when. The trouble is, people have always judged time by the sun, and that changes the further you travel. Ride a long way west or east, and you need to reset your watch when you arrive. Local time will differ from the time in your home. You probably had the same on board your ship - the captain would have taken readings each day to determine when the sun was highest in the sky, and that would have been noon. When railways started, accidents or near-misses were always happening because people got times mixed up.'

'How was it fixed?'

'Everyone agreed to use railway time in addition to local time. There are still differences - you can't change when the sun rises and sets - but railway time is shared, every place knows where it stands. End of accidents.'

'And that helps us how?' said Oliphant.

'It's obvious,' said Ellen. 'Different places in the world are running on different times. I don't know why, but they are. So the problem is bringing them back to your railway time.'

'What do you say, Tulliver,' said the doctor. 'You're a practical chap.'

'Don't know what use I can be,' said Tulliver. 'You're the men with the brains, I just build things. If you need a machine for something, I'm your man, otherwise I might as well go home. Not that I'll get a welcome there.'

Oliphant had wandered over to the window and was standing with his back to them, staring into space. 'A machine might be just what we need,' he said, almost to himself. 'I think it's time I talked to you about my research.'

'You mean you're actually doing some?' said Fescue. 'We all thought you spent your time playing golf and ogling the ladies, saving your presence, Miss Dust.'

'I've been working on something new, and you know how fellows at the college regard innovations. Challenge their paradigm and they call you a charlatan. I didn't want to say anything until I was sure of my ground.'

'And are you?'

'No. But if I'm right, I might have the skeleton of a solution.'

'Don't keep us in suspense then,' said Fescue. 'What's this skeleton? And if you mention equations, I'll hit you.'

'You see how I'm treated, Miss Dust,' said Oliphant. 'Monad here is a theoretical ontologist, sits around all day wondering whether the world is real or an illusion. Complete nonsense. If one of the Princeps' creatures feeds on him, he'll soon realise what's real when the first fang goes in. I, on the other hand, am an experimental ontologist.'

This must be what discussions were like back in the Priory. 'The words sound impressive, whatever they might mean,' said Ellen, 'but do they have any practical use?'

Oliphant sighed. 'Oh yes. I use mathematics to make models of the world. If my equations work, my very elegant equations, then the theory is correct. Probably. Which is more than Monad can say.'

'Models?' said Fescue 'I use words, you use numbers. Your theories are no more capable of being proved than mine.'

'Ah, that's where you're wrong. A couple of chaps from Partridge College were experimenting with electricity and magnetism and needed some help with the mathematics, so they asked me to help, obviously. As I worked on the equations - sorry Monad - to describe their experiments, I realised they overlapped with my own work. I've been thinking about how to describe natural phenomena through numbers, to quantify the qualitative, as it were. The only way the equations worked was to make time a factor as well as space. When I did that, everything fell into place, but there was an unintended consequence. My equations predict that the world we live in isn't the only one. In fact, there are an infinite number of worlds.'

'The man's gone mad,' said Fescue. 'Infinite worlds, and you accused me of illusory thinking.'

'Numbers don't lie,' said Oliphant. 'According to my equations, and I have checked them very thoroughly, some of these worlds will be almost identical to ours, others will be completely different.'

'So where are they, these other worlds,' said Ellen. 'Can we travel to them?'

'No. At least, not according to my work. They exist alongside ours, in a sort of bubble that encloses them all. Some are close, some are far away, but we can't move between them. At least, I didn't think we could.'

'I have a headache,' said Canterbury. 'Strigiformes are so much easier. You know where you are with owls.'

'I still think you're mad,' said Fescue, 'but even if you're right, I don't see how this helps us.'

'I think I do,' said Ellen. 'After I left the forest there were a lot of paths crossing the moors. Some were near, some were just tracks in the distance. The path I was following sometimes ran parallel to another for a while, or a track would come towards mine and the two would merge for a few yards, or even for miles, until they split again. They were all in the same overall landscape, but the details differed. Some ran through different coloured heather, some had standing stones alongside, some didn't. Some went uphill, some down. Isn't that what your worlds are like, Oliphant? Similar but different, running parallel to each other or in different directions. But now it seems like some of the paths are converging and merging into one.'

Oliphant jumped up and started pacing about beside the window. 'Paths, yes. Networks, topology, manifolds. Damn, I need a blackboard and some chalk.'

'Would a pencil and paper suffice?' asked the doctor.

Oliphant sat at the table and began to scribble. 'This works,' he said, 'but I'm still not sure about the effects of time.'

'Sometimes the paths go to the same place but take different amounts of time to get there,' said Ellen. 'Some take longer routes, or wind about a lot more. Does that help?'

They watched as Oliphant filled sheet after sheet of paper and threw them on the ground. At last he stopped and looked up. 'Dear lady, I believe you've just helped to elucidate a major question in chronological ontology.' He grinned. 'This is what's happening. For some reason, different versions of the worlds are merging with ours, but they're running to a different calendar, like Monad's railway time conundrum. If this continues, who knows what might happen. We could wake up tomorrow and find Forcello's become a village, or has goats grazing where Snow College used to be, or has flying carriages and buildings made of crystal.'

'Are you saying that time moves in different directions?' said the doctor. 'That we could travel to the future?'

'Don't like that idea,' said Fescue. 'What about free will? If the future already exists, then we wouldn't be making real choices about anything.'

'Not our future! My equations prove it; ontologically our future does not exist, time's arrow moves in only one direction. But we might be encountering the future of one of these other worlds.'

'Can we get back to reality,' said Tulliver. 'You talked earlier about a machine. How would that help?'

'I wasn't sure,' said Oliphant, 'but I am now. Remember those chaps at Partridge College?'

'The ones making bombs,' said Fescue. 'Are we back to assassinations?'

'No, idiot. The ones experimenting with electricity and

magnetism. My equations predict a sort of electro-magnetic field. You know when you get close to a fire? You feel the heat, but you can't see it. That's a field of energy, spreading out invisibly from its source. I think there are all sorts of fields around us, a soup of the damned things. What if they keep our worlds on their correct paths, to use Miss Dust's imperfect but rather useful analogy? A disturbance, a misalignment, could knock a world off course and send it careening into one of the others. Places and times all mixed up.'

'I need to understand,' said Ellen. 'Are you saying there's a world where Haefen still exists? And if there is, do you know how I could return there?'

'This is where it gets interesting,' said Oliphant. 'We need to knock all the worlds back onto their right paths. The trouble is, people like Miss Dust here have already moved between them. If we realign the worlds that converged, she could be stranded in a world where her home's in ruins, or never existed.'

'I long since accepted that I'll never go home,' she said, 'so how will you realign these fields?'

'That's where Tulliver comes in,' said Oliphant. 'We need a machine to generate energy, a field, to correct what's gone wrong. A large jolt to knock everything back into place. An Ontological Engine.'

Tulliver picked a speck of food from his teeth, conducted an examination and then ate it. 'If you want me to help then I'm going to need a lot more than this airy-fairy talk to work on.'

Oliphant picked up one of the papers and threw it back to the floor. 'It's no good, I need to get back to my rooms. I can work on the field equations, but I'll need help. Miss Dust will be best.'

'Me? What on earth can I do? If you need someone to

watch your back in a fight then I'm your woman, but all this talk of invisible fields is well over my head.'

'Who came up with the idea of worlds on different paths?' said Oliphant. 'You understand the concepts, and you have the experiences. I need to ask you what happened in Haefen; how quickly the events took place, what you saw. Details of your journey here. I can feed all of that into the parameters for the machine, but we need to work quickly before the worlds merge even more. Forcello's been mostly isolated from the changes so far, but now every day and every hour counts.'

MIST ON THE LAGOON

The doctor gave Ellen the choice of pony and trap or railway for the journey into town. Oliphant had demanded at least two days to work on the equations and draw up specifications for the Ontological Engine before he'd be ready for Ellen's input, and so she'd agreed to spend the next day with Fescue on a tour of Forcello.

A railway carriage sounded too much like a ship's cabin, too soon, so she opted for the pony and trap with the doctor driving. They left after an early breakfast for the one-hour journey, tracking the coast all the way through small villages and hamlets. The buildings appeared more frequently, the spaces in between fewer, until they were travelling through the streets of a city.

'I'll drop you by the college gates,' said the doctor. 'Fescue should be waiting there. And I'll be back at five o'clock, same place.'

'You don't need to. Doesn't the professor have a spare room?'

'No women allowed overnight in the college. The proctors are particularly strict.'

'Then I'll stay at an inn tonight.'

'I wouldn't if I were you. Don't worry. I have business in town so I'll be here when you're ready to leave.'

They pulled up by an ornate metal gate set in a stone archway. The college walls stretched the length of the street in both directions. 'Snow College,' said the doctor, 'most prestigious in the University, and the second oldest. You won't have realised it from last night, but Fescue and Gregory are both quite brilliant.'

'What about Canterbury?'

'Gottfried? A dear man, but obsessed with owls. He keeps one in his rooms, I once caught him trying to communicate with it by perching on his desk and hooting. Shame.'

As Ellen climbed down from the trap, Fescue appeared through a small wicket gate next to the archway. 'I fancied we might take a boat along the Great Canal,' he said, 'and then into the lagoon. It's unbearable in summer, but at this time of year the mists on the water are quite delightful.'

THEY BOARDED a water taxi by the steps down from the canal bridge. If she'd thought Coria was different, Forcello was worlds apart. Which, she realised, it was. A man at the stern propelled and steered the taxi with a giant paddle, and the buildings they glided past rose from the water, white and red marble carved into fantastic patterns, each with its own wooden jetty for boats to tie up.

'Who owns these?' asked Ellen.

'Old Forcellan families. Some are unbelievably beautiful inside. Frescoes on the walls and ceilings that are beyond price. Marble floors, views over the canal. But a nightmare to maintain; the cellars always flood and the canal's an open sewer in summer when it's hot. The families keep them as status symbols; most spend the year on their estates in the country.'

They passed under a decorated stone bridge, and the canal began to widen. 'We're about to come into the lagoon,' said Fescue. 'I used to take a boat to one of the small islands when I was a young man, and spend the day reading. In summer, obviously, bit chilly on days like this.'

A sheet of mist blanketed the surface of the lagoon, parting and coalescing again behind them as they moved across the water. Every so often they passed upright wooden posts, most with a seagull perched on the top.

'How deep is the water?'

'Not very. The Princeps keeps drawing up plans to drain the lagoon and reclaim the land, but like most of his ideas, nothing ever comes of it. Apart from his palace; you can see it if you look back.'

An enormous white building glistened in the sharp morning sun, sitting on a flattened hilltop that rose behind the roofscape of the old city. 'Is that where you had your meetings with the Princeps?'

'The same. Trust me, stay as far away from him as you can.'

'That won't be a problem.'

They eventually reached the shore of a large island, and the waterman steadied the boat as they climbed out onto a small jetty. 'Where to now?' said Ellen.

It was a long time since she'd seen a man blush. 'The last time I came to Altino with a lady, I was twenty-two years old. I convinced myself I was in love and made the mistake of telling her.'

'Why a mistake?'

'She laughed at me. Told me I was a boring goose and demanded to go home. Broke my heart. After that I decided books would be more congenial companions.'

'She sounds appalling. You were lucky.'

'Perhaps. But three times in the last few days I've found myself in the company of a young lady. Twice with Lily, even if she pulled a gun on me the first time, and now you. I've rather enjoyed the experiences.'

'Including the gun?'

'It had a strange sort of charm. Powerful women are most intriguing.'

'You think I'm powerful?'

'Oliphant and Canterbury are all very well but they don't exactly get the heart racing, and you don't smell of tobacco and tweed. A distinct improvement.'

'You're telling me I make your heart race?'

'I'm old enough to be your father, Ellen, and my intentions are strictly honourable. I simply had a fancy to buy lunch for an attractive and resourceful woman who wouldn't laugh at me.' He offered her his arm. 'Shall we?

CHAPTER 14

The Wrong Game

ANNOUNCEMENT

☙

I hadn't expected the President to be there. As a politician she was the opposite of a people person, and I didn't know anyone who openly voted for her, but Shal probably contributed to her campaign and he was going to get what he paid for.

The security for the event was insane. Each invitation card - mandatory to get through the doors - had an embedded personalised microchip which linked to AI facial recognition scanners. No gatecrashers here.

I eventually found my way to my seat in the auditorium; the Dean would have begged to have Shalmar's babies in exchange for a building half as impressive. The President had a row to herself at the front, joined only by her teenage son. A weedy creature, that boy, with his rat tail hair. I wouldn't be seen anywhere near him if he were mine, but mother love is blind. So I've heard. And their presence explained the security and the armed guards and my pervasive urge to do something criminal, just for fun. But was all this really necessary for the launch of a new game?

The lights dimmed and the wall-screen at the back of the

stage faded up to show a visual, with pairs of stylised figures joined by faint, pulsing lines. Each person was in a different setting from their pair; one in a bedroom, one skydiving, one sitting at a desk and the other wearing body armour and patrolling a city street. The images shifted and morphed, and the music sounded like the aftermath of the Big Bang. Amorphous, tuneless, unsettling. Knowing Shalmar, there would be something subliminal happening; I'd make him tell me later so that I could ignore any irrational purchase impulses.

The music faded, and Shal walked slowly onto the stage. I always thought it was no coincidence that 'shamble' and 'Shalmar' sounded so alike. He shuffled on, always in danger of tripping over his own feet. An accidental pizza sauce stain would be somewhere on the frayed tee shirt. Not that Shal didn't respect the status of his guests, he just thought his was the highest.

I don't like Virtual Reality, never have. At least, not for gaming. It has its uses in research, especially for manipulating complex topologies, and one of the establishments on Old Market Street provided it for some of their more discerning customers; that had been a fun night, but I prefer the real thing. Whatever Shalmar was about to announce wouldn't trouble my dreams.

Shal waited until the buzz died away and then spoke in his confected accent. He'd grown up two blocks away from me, but when we started our degrees, he affected a mangled drawl, stretching the vowels into shapes unknown in any language. Perhaps he thought it made him seem exotic, I told him he sounded like a knob.

I won't tell you everything in his speech as I'd like to keep your attention for a little longer; Shalmar always had a love affair with the sound of his voice. Of course, most guests had no idea about the quantum leap in technology he was describing. I did, unfortunately. And why? Because, as you already guessed, it was based on my work. My secret groundbreaking research. Specifically, he was trying to persuade people he'd achieved quantum entanglement at a macro level. In the real world.

Maybe you're a high energy natural philosopher and this is bread and butter to you. But in case not, entanglement happens at the quantum level when two elementary particles share a state, no matter how far apart they are. Change the state of one of the particles and the state of the other changes instantaneously, faster than the speed of light. A spooky phenomenon that breaks some fundamental laws of the universe. My research hypothesised that entanglement was possible, not just for elementary particles but - wait for it - for atoms, molecules. Even for life.

Only theory at this stage, of course. Without the maths it's hard to explain, but in simple terms I'd derived equations that postulated macro entanglement by interacting with one of the other predicted realities in the multiverse. I was years away from proving anything experimentally, but my colleagues would recognise I was on the right track. It would change everything. Whole new areas of research would open up. I'd have my own Institute, the Ashira uit Banipol Centre for High Energy Metaphysics. I'd already designed the logo.

And Shalmar Eser had announced that he was using my theories - not that he credited me in any way - for a new type of game. A game! Not Virtual Reality, but Embodied Reality. Players would actually live in their games, not just experience a virtual environment.

It wouldn't work, I knew that without even trying. He'd taken a theory expressed in the most ferocious equations I'd ever derived, with no practical or safe applications, and thought he could bend it to his own use. Building something to generate the right sort of energy field would be like crashing two lumps of plutonium together at high speed, just to see what happened. Not good, not good at all.

I couldn't speak up in front of all these people. I'd be restrained and marched out within seconds, probably spend a night or two in the cells for my trouble. But I had to see Shalmar and warn him. There was no way he understood the consequences of his plan, not in the short time he'd been in possession of my research. Whatever he believed, out of the two of us, I was the genius. Now it was my job to stop him.

I WONDERED if he'd told his people to keep me away from him, but when the presentation was over and the hubbub had died down, an assistant took me straight to his private office-cum-suite. I'd been trying to guess what line he'd take. Denial? Lies? Confrontation? Would he try to claim the work as his own? If Shal decided one day that the sun was a giant sky candle rather than an incandescent ball of nuclear fusion, he'd rubbish any evidence to the contrary and persuade everyone else that he was right.

On stage he'd looked wired, but close to I saw how much weight he'd lost, with new lines on his face. Twenty-nine going on forty-five. And I was right about the pizza sauce. He sprawled on a deep sofa by a wall of glass, fifty floors up; did he ever get used to the view?

I'd practised all the words I'd use, but none of them seemed adequate. As I was shown in, he put his drink down onto a small table shaped like a gold elephant and opened his arms in surrender.

'All's fair in love and research, Ash. You haven't published, so it's open season.'

'You killed a man to steal my work. Even for you that's a push.'

Shal stood and faced me. Classic defence stance. 'Not me. His death was an accident, he brought it on himself.'

'Your thug beat his brains out!'

'I don't employ thugs, and it wasn't supposed to be that way.' He sounded like a child caught out in a lie. 'It was an accident; arrangements were made, but the wrong guard was on duty. I'm sorry.'

'Sorry doesn't cut it. You'll go to jail for this.'

'There's no proof I was involved with his death.'

'How do you explain getting your hands on my research?'

His eyes flicked from side to side, anywhere but at me. 'It's your fault, Ash. If you worked for me, none of this would have been necessary. You realise that embodied reality is a game-changer. Literally. My competitors will eat my shit and beg for more.'

The man really was a slob. 'You have no idea,' I said. 'You've stolen something that's so far beyond you.'

Now he looked at me. 'You never did rate me, Ash. So full of your own importance and your ethical purity. I was never good enough for you. Which is strange, given the riff-raff you invite into your bed almost every night. And the things you do with them; the word purity doesn't quite fit anymore.'

Not just looking at me now, but smirking. 'You see, I know a lot about you,' he said.

Danu appreciates what I do for fun, but apart from her my life is private. So I like a little variety; that's my choice and no one else needs to trouble themselves about it. But apparently Shalmar did, and then I had a lightbulb moment. That day in my apartment, the sense that somebody else had been there; now it all became clear. I'd have to employ someone to sweep the apartment and look for hidden cameras. And what had possessed him to spy on me?

'I can see the neurones flashing in your brain,' he said. 'I thought you understood me, Ash, I thought you knew I was someone who doesn't take no for an answer.'

Still that smug smirk on his face. Every instinct was to hit him - he'd like that - but I denied him the pleasure. 'Why did you do it?' I asked. 'Jealousy, revenge?'

'Because I could. That's a good enough reason.'

I had to put the personal stuff to one side. Don't get me wrong; I have no problem with people watching me enjoy myself whens it's on my terms, but Shalmar would never be on the guest list. And bigger things were at stake here.

'How long before you put embodied reality into practice?' I asked.

'You'd be surprised. You academics, testing and retesting, you take years to do something we can achieve in days.'

'By cutting corners.'

'By being efficient. You spend all your time pottering away with that weird assistant of yours, while I put whole teams to work. The first person plays the game in two weeks' time. The president's son. Nothing like a high-profile player to shift product.'

'You can't!'

'I can. We've already run small-scale tests to generate what you charmingly call the Ashira Field. I can see why you like the name, but don't plan on it sticking. You'll just be a footnote in the history books. If that.'

I'd expected things to be bad, but this was worse than I imagined. 'Do you know what the Ashira Field does?' I said. 'If the field generation parameters are off by even the smallest margin, you'll create a breach between different realities.'

'I'm relying on it. Our players will be embodied, temporarily of course, in another one of the infinite universes. How else do you think the game will work?'

'Shalmar, you can't do this. I'm begging you. It would take

months of testing to tease out the consequences of your plan, but I tell you this, I already know they'll be devastating.'

He picked up his glass and looked out at the city. 'So what should I do, Ash? I have millions tied up in this, cancelling the game simply will not happen.'

There was no point. Shal would never be convinced, no matter what evidence I produced. I walked over to the door and tried to leave, but it was locked.

'I'm so sorry, Ash, but I really can't let you go. Not yet. You're an intelligent woman, you must've realised that you couldn't come here, accuse me of theft and murder, and expect to walk out again. Once the game is live, we'll reconsider what to do with you. In the meantime, I'll make sure you're comfortable.'

I SHOULD HAVE SPOKEN up during the announcement, at least people would have seen what happened. Now I'd disappear and no one would know where I was. Danu was right. I should have messaged her if I was about to do something dangerous. Or stupid. But how could I know today would be the day an old friend turned out to be a murderer and kidnapped me. I never expected to find myself living the 'man abuses woman' trope and I'd fallen into the trap of thinking I was invulnerable. Mortality is a hard lesson to learn.

At least they gave me a suite to myself. Bedroom, living room, even a desk to work at, not that I had a terminal or a connection, or even a pad and paper. Even the wall screen was dead. But apart from the isolation, I've stayed in luxury hotels that didn't come close to the way Shal treated himself. The difference was, I could walk out of a hotel anytime I chose. Here I was a prisoner, as much as in any jail. I could have used a battering ram against the windows and they would have been unmarked. Ditto the doors; the suite was a sealed unit with no way out. My com was gone, of course, the first thing they took, but at least they brought me meals; Shalmar kept an excellent kitchen and chef. He could afford to.

I keep fit, but I'm no fighter. Never have been. Perhaps in another reality all the energy I put into work and sex went into learning how to beat off the bastards and stay alive. But not here. So although I thought of trying to overpower the men who brought my meals, I remembered what happened to the security guard at the University. Shal had nothing to lose and everything to gain by keeping me out of the way and anyway, one of those guys could probably have lifted me above his head with one hand. Danu, I'll never ignore you again.

On the third day they bought me a change of clothes, and a reader from my apartment. I wondered why. Why feed me, clothe me, keep me entertained? Why keep me alive? If ever I was free, I'd tell the world what Shalmar Eser had done to me, so he must have had some plan in mind. Something to do with his game and embodied reality. I tried not to think about what that might be.

By my reckoning, this was the day the president's son was due to play. I'd not noticed anything strange, so perhaps this would be the first time they generated the Ashira Field at full strength. Then again, I didn't know what was happening in the world outside.

Shalmar came to see me at ten in the morning, the first time since he'd imprisoned me. He couldn't keep still, bouncing from foot to foot and grinning. Wired, big time.

'This is it, Ash. Are you excited? I know I am. Sometimes I think my entire life has been leading to this moment.'

'For the last time, please don't go ahead with this.'

'You worry too much. Anyway, I arranged a live feed so you can see what happens. The least I can do.'

'And then what? I assume you'll let me go.'

'According to you, the world will be fucked, so what's the difference?' He tapped something on his com and the wall screen flicked into life. 'We're due to kick off in an hour. Enjoy.'

It was the same auditorium as before, but this time the screen at the back showed a room with a machine in the centre. Without being there it was impossible to know what it was, but an informed guess said a generator for the Ashira Field. The machine itself looked unimpressive, a rectangular metal box. In the background two thick cables ran past a bank of monitors, up the side of the wall and through the ceiling. I guessed what they were too, carrying a signal to massive aerials on the top of the Eser Tower to propagate the energy field as far as possible. I had to admit; it was perfect if you wanted to maximise the destruction. Why on earth not limit the field locally, just in case?

The feed from the auditorium was a split screen, half showing the stage, the other half the machine and its monitors. Somebody entered the machine room and I recognised the President instantly. And on the other half of the screen her attenuated son was being fitted by Shalmar, still grinning like an idiot, with a thick, silver arm torc that must have been specially constructed for the boy's twig arms. That would be a transceiver to read the Ashira Field and relay back the energy states of the subject. I would have used inanimate test objects in my trials before moving on to single-celled creatures, and only if that was successful to larger animals. Not Shalmar. Straight to a human, and not one of the street sleepers who no-one would miss. No, he had to use the son of the most high-profile person in Mittani.

I checked the time, five to eleven. Just five more minutes and by the looks of it the President would turn on the machine to generate the Ashira Field, create macro quantum entanglement and generally fuck up everything.

CHAPTER 15

The Feeding Chamber

SUPPER WITH A GOD

They followed a path running alongside a small canal that led away from the lagoon. At first the island seemed deserted, but after walking for five minutes a clearing came into view. The building in the centre was as intricate as any in the old town; tables outside under coloured awnings and braziers to warm the diners sitting there.

'This used to be a cathedral,' said Fescue, 'but times change. I took the precaution of sending a chap here to reserve a table.'

'People come all this way to eat?'

'Wait till you taste the lobster.'

They'd barely given their orders to a waiter when someone spoke from behind her.

'What's this, Professor? Playing hooky with a beautiful companion?'

Ellen turned in her seat to see a man in a scarlet and blue uniform with gold tassels and silver spurs, even though there was no horse in sight. Fescue scrambled to his feet, his chair falling backwards into the path of a passing waiter.

'Your Highness!' He made a face at Ellen, trying to tell her to stand. On balance, she thought, she preferred to remain sitting.

The man moved around so that she could see him properly. About the same height as Fescue, although his boots had suspiciously built-up heels. His forehead was merely a backdrop to a row of carefully sculpted curls, and a retinue of liveried servants shuffled round behind him.

'Will you introduce us, Professor, you sly dog?'

'Your Highness, Miss Ellen Dust. Miss Dust, may I introduce His Highness Marino, Princeps of Forcello.'

She had no idea how to greet the despotic ruler of a principality. Not that it mattered; the Princeps reached out and took both of her hands in his.

'Miss Ellen Dust. Late of Haefen, I believe? Currently a guest of the esteemed Dr Antonius Withering. Your fame precedes you, dear lady, indeed it does. And you are just as striking as I had heard. Those eyes!'

'You seem well informed.'

He dropped her hands. 'I like to keep my finger on the pulse. And the Professor here is engaged on a rather pressing project for me. I do hope, Professor, that the charms of this lady aren't inciting you to neglect your duties? That would make me rather tetchy.'

'Not at all, sire. The competition we discussed is in hand, and Miss Dust has information that might be of value in our endeavours.'

'Mixing work and play, splendid. Good man, Professor, knew I could rely on you.'

He made a small bow to Ellen and turned as if to leave, then stopped. 'Forgot to say, Professor. Be so good as to convey Miss Dust to the palace this evening. Six o'clock prompt. She's to be my guest for a private supper; don't wait up.'

All the other customers were silent, staring at their plates of food until the Princeps and his entourage were out of sight. 'There's no way I'm eating with that man,' said Ellen.

'Keep your voice down, he has spies everywhere. I should have known.'

'Known what?'

'Probably the boy I sent to reserve our table, reporting back. Or someone watching where I go. I'm in a cage; the bars are invisible but I can't escape. And now I've drawn you into this nonsense.'

'He knew who I was and where I'm staying. What else does he know about me?'

Fescue unravelled a large red handkerchief from his pocket and wiped the sheen of sweat from his face. 'Whatever he knows, you'll find out this evening.'

'I told you, I'm not going.'

Fescue whispered; 'You don't understand. An invitation from the Princeps is a command. You don't say no.'

'What happens if I don't turn up?'

'You won't get far. Even if you escaped, I'd still be here. So would the doctor and his family, and Oliphant and Canterbury. You think we'd be safe if you defied the Princeps?'

'What gives him the right to treat people like this?'

'He's the Princeps.'

'Means nothing to me. Perhaps I should go to the palace after all; men like him bring out the worst in me. Could be fun.'

'Did you hear what I said? I used to wonder what happened to the people who disappeared, but after seeing that animal he created, I'm not sure I want to know.'

. . .

At five to six that evening - Fescue had insisted they be on time - Ellen saw a man standing outside the main gate of the palace as they approached.

'That's Tiro,' said Fescue. 'Not a bad chap but close to the Princeps, so don't trust him. And don't worry about the doctor, I'll tell him what's happened. After the Princeps is done with you - sorry, that wasn't meant the way it sounded - ask Tiro to bring you to the college. There's a porter on duty all night and he'll fetch me. We'll just have to improvise.'

Tiro stepped forward to meet them. 'Welcome to the palace, Miss Dust.'

'What time will I be leaving?' she asked. 'I have a long journey back.'

'I don't believe you need worry about that.'

'But I do worry. He can't order me here like a servant and then not say when I can leave.'

Tiro led her away from the gate towards the palace in the distance. 'If I might counsel you, miss. His Highness is unaccustomed to debates about fairness. Debates about anything. Such things make him… crotchety. I prefer not to see him become crotchety and I believe that would be in your best interests too.'

Ellen twisted round to see Fescue still standing by the gates. He waved tentatively, then turned and walked away. How did this keep on happening? No sooner did she meet someone she trusted than they deserted her. Or died. And now she was walking into the unknown again.

Tiro took her to a wide staircase that curved up from a lobby, bordered with marble statues of men and women in flowing robes.

'The gods and goddesses of Old Forcello.' He cleared his throat and took a deep breath. 'I should warn you that His Highness recently had a revelation in a dream that he is, in fact, descended from such a god. I understand that he intends to use the forthcoming prize ceremony to announce his own deification.' He sighed. 'A new god in the pantheon, such a delight.'

'He believes he's divine?'

Tiro shook his head. 'I long since learned that the minds of princes are beyond our comprehension.'

At the top of the staircase they entered a room where Tiro left her, empty apart from a table set for a meal; white tablecloth, silver candelabra, silver cutlery, crystal glasses. The walls were covered with tapestries of woodland scenes, except for one portrait of the Princeps standing with his arm around a woman, while a small girl sat at their feet. Behind them an oak tree was in full leaf and on a distant hill stood the palace, although there was no sign of any surrounding city.

'Do you like the painting? My wife was rather fond of it, but to my eyes it makes me look a little paunchy. What do you think?'

The Princeps had entered the room through a door in the far corner, disguised as part of the wall, and his uniform was different from the one he'd been wearing earlier on the island. A scarlet jacket this time, still hung with golden tassels, and tight white breeches which wouldn't look out of place in Coria.

Fescue had counselled her to show some respect, whatever she might feel. 'Your Highness,' she said, refusing to curtsy. There were limits.

'Please, call me sire. And the portrait, paunchy?'

'A good likeness. Sire.'

'I only keep it hanging because Lily admires it. I'd been abundantly clear in my instructions to the artist and he came highly recommended, which says something about the artistic sensibilities of the hoi polloi. I stood through interminable sessions while he painted the damned thing - "stand here sire, stand there sire, don't move sire". When I saw the result, I decided it wouldn't be fair to let him inflict his art on anyone else, so I relieved him of the temptation. Eyes or hands, his choice. Or the menagerie. No Miss Dust, don't look at me like that. I'm not a monster, nor a thief. I had the hands dried and varnished and set in a rather charming frame of oak, so he got them back in the end.'

He walked over to the table. 'Shall we? Oysters to start, such an evocative food. I like to imagine I feel their struggles as they slip down my throat. And after the oysters a stuffed roast to my own recipe.'

Even as he was speaking she imagined the oysters fighting back; clogging his throat, invading his lungs. She imagined watching him gasp for air, turning blue. She imagined him rolling on the floor, begging for help which never arrived. Sadly, life wasn't that kind.

'You asked me here for a reason,' she said. 'If you'd tell me what that is, I'll be on my way.'

'My my, aren't you the feisty one, giving me commands. Don't they teach manners to women in your Haefen? I asked you here for supper and to rescue you from that brown toad, Monad. There's something stomach-turning about seeing an old goat like him with a delicate flower like you.'

'I've been called many things, sire, but delicate isn't one of them. And I don't know the professor well, but he's doing his best to save you and your city.'

'Miss Dust, I've ruled this city and this Principality for many years. The burden is heavier than you can imagine, and we'd all be slaves of the ghastly Hurrians if I didn't take firm measures. As a barbarian from some misbegotten hovel in the wilderness, you might not understand this, but people like boundaries. Certainty makes them happy.'

'Boundaries? You call cutting off a man's hands, or threatening him with being eaten alive, "boundaries"?'

'So you've heard about my little darlings. I have to tell you, and I say this with great disappointment, I find your tone insulting and disrespectful. I invited you here as a special favour. I invited you to share my hospitality. And if you measured up, I was prepared to give you the honour of sharing my bed and bearing me a son. Just imagine, you could have been mother to another new god.'

She knew about cruelty. Cruelty was universal. Cruelty she could deal with, it was predictable. But the man in front of her was deeply, viscerally mad.

'This barbarian doesn't want your hospitality. And you're deluded if you think I'll share your bed, let alone carry a child of yours.'

She'd expected an argument, but the Princeps simply shrugged. 'Your loss, Miss Dust. In that case, perhaps you should leave.'

Ellen opened the door to find two liveried guards standing there. 'I shouldn't have expected any different from a foreigner; you're just another recalcitrant bitch,' said the Princeps. 'What is it with women these days? I should pass a law confining you to your homes where you belong.' He signalled to one of the guards. 'Tell Tiro to draft something appropriate and take this creature to one of the holding cells. One way or another, we'll eat together tonight.'

THE FEEDING CHAMBER

There was no point in reaching for the dagger under the swirl of skirts. The guards each took one of her arms and carried her down a labyrinth of corridors and stairs until they reached a small cell, the floor covered with filthy straw that smelled of stale piss and shit. They threw her in and locked the door behind her.

This was not good. No windows, only a small vertical slit at eye level in the back wall. Ellen picked her way across and looked down into a large pit with high sides and two gates, one large, and a smaller one on the opposite side. The scent of blood and raw flesh drifted through the slit, the smell of the clearing in the forest. So this was the feeding chamber, with ringside seats for the next meals.

What had Fescue said about the Princeps' creatures? She'd dealt with the wolf in the forest and if she was forced to defend herself against one of the creatures, she might have a chance, as long as she kept the dagger with her. But more than one would be challenging. And even if she killed the creatures, she'd still need to escape the pit and find a way out of the palace.

Tollin had often told her that her tongue would get her into trouble. She could hear him now: *'Soften your words girl, don't blurt out whatever's in your mind, It'll get you killed one day.'*

Perhaps today was that day.

Above the pit, on a level with her, she could see other slits in the wall, other holding cells. More poor victims waiting to be fed to the beasts?

Something was happening down below. The small gate opened and a man stumbled through. Middle-aged and balding, wearing trousers and a torn shirt, but no jacket or shoes. He looked naked despite the clothes, and the sound of his breathing reached her as he looked around the pit. His entire body was shaking, like Stevens waiting for the noose. And then she recognised him.

Gottfried Canterbury, terrified and standing alone in the feeding chamber. This was unfair. 'Not him,' she shouted at the door. 'I've changed my mind, take me to the Princeps.' There was no answer, but Canterbury looked up towards the sound of her voice.

'Miss Dust, is that you?'

'I'm here,' she shouted. 'Stay calm, I'll fix this. I just need to see the Princeps.'

As she finished speaking, the door to her cell opened and there he was, the smile twisting his face into a grimace. He'd been waiting outside. 'You wanted to see me? Have something to say?'

Revenge could come later. 'I apologise, sire, I realise I was disrespectful. Don't punish that man because of me. I'll do whatever you want, please let him go.'

'Whatever I want? Tempting. But what if I want to feed him to my darlings? They've developed quite a taste for human flesh, and they get petulant without it. What if I want to let them feed on you? It would be such fun to watch, and I suspect your meat would be especially sweet.'

'You can't harm me. Fescue needs my help to solve your problems with the food supply. You need me.'

'Somehow I doubt that. A raggle-taggle piece of jetsam vomited up on the tide, you're of no value to me. Except, of course, as entertainment.'

'What if you're wrong?'

'I'm a god, so by definition I can't be wrong about anything. Useful trait, don't you think? Wish I'd thought of it sooner.'

'But what about your people?'

'What about them? Poor, malodorous, never satisfied - I'll be better off without them. I'm actually thinking of burning the city to the ground and starting again. Fire can be so cleansing. And if there are no people, they won't need food. Perhaps I have no use for your professor after all.' He made as if to leave the cell but turned back before the door closed. 'Enjoy the show, the next act will be yours.'

The door slammed behind him, and Ellen rushed over to the slit. Canterbury had backed himself against the wall opposite the main gate. Ellen pulled up her skirt and unsheathed the dagger. If she could get it down to Canterbury, he might have a chance. If he was exceptionally lucky. But there was no way she could throw it through the narrow slit with enough force to reach him. It would fall to the ground below her cell and she'd be defenceless too.

The large gate rose, sliding upwards with the sound of chains being wound in. The shape of a creature appeared from the shadow behind it, something that made Fescue's description seem as if he'd been describing a kitten. Almost twice the size of the wolf from the forest, but with a head like a giant cat, its eyes blinked slowly as it scanned the arena, and the long black body undulated like a snake as it padded out to the centre of the pit.

Canterbury sank to the ground, his hands over his eyes,

and Ellen called down to him: 'You have to fight, man! Don't let it leap at you, try to move out of the way. Get it from behind, arm round its neck. Strangle it. Please, try something.'

But there was nothing he could do. He knew it; she knew it. The languorous creature knew it. It lifted its head to sniff the air, then continued on its way to towards the man cowering on the ground. There was no more to say, no words of hope or comfort. Canterbury was going to die, painfully. This was almost worse than being in the pit herself. At least there she'd be able to fight, but locked in this cell her body ached with impotence.

Canterbury got to his feet and looked up towards Ellen, even though she knew he couldn't see her. His breathing sounded calmer. Resigned.

'Good luck, Miss Dust. I never pretended to be brave, but I tried to do the right thing. I hope you find your way back home. And tell Fescue to feed the Agnes and the owl.'

The creature stopped its advance while it was still ten feet away, but then sprang forward, grabbed Canterbury in its jaws and shook his body violently from side to side, the way a cat shakes a mouse. As the fangs closed on him Canterbury whimpered once, a small, pleading sound, and then fell silent.

After a few seconds of play, the creature threw the body in the air, and as Canterbury landed on the ground, it pounced again and held his body down with one paw while it bit into his side and tore off chunks of flesh.

Ellen turned away. Please the gods, death had come quickly this time.

ESCAPE

How long before it would be her turn? This creature had feasted already, but there could be others. She'd realised that, dagger or no dagger, if she found herself in the pit the chances of coming out alive were close to zero.

Plan A had to be escaping from the cell. She tried the door, just in case, but it was locked. She peered through the small barred opening, but the passage outside was empty. No guard for now.

The Princeps would send two of them, almost certainly. With only a woman to collect, they wouldn't expect any trouble they couldn't handle. Her job was to give them an unexpected surprise and she tested the weight of the dagger in her hand. 'Bring me luck, my friend, I think I'm going to need it.'

What would the choreography be? Open the door and both come in to grab her, or would one stay outside while the other retrieved her? On balance, she'd prefer both at once. No chance for the one holding back to lock the door and fetch reinforcements before she could escape. But whatever happened, she couldn't allow them to get hold of her.

She was hungry and thirsty. No food on the island earlier - both she and Fescue had lost their appetites after the encounter with the Princeps - and none tonight. Something moved under the straw in the corner of the cell. A rat, sitting up and examining her. 'Not today,' said Ellen. 'I'm not that hungry.'

The rat scurried up the wall, through the slit, and disappeared. If only it were that easy.

When would they come for her? For all she knew, it could be days. The Princeps must have been relishing the thought of her languishing in this cell, filled with the scent of death. And if they didn't bring food and water, what state would she be in tomorrow or the next day? It would be a tragedy to end here after everything, and she owed it to Sophia to stay alive.

The rat returned, jumped to the floor and burrowed into the straw. Probably her nest; one person's death cell was another's home.

What was the time? She felt as if days had passed since Fescue left her at the palace gates, but it couldn't be more than three or four hours.

Were the creatures fed at night?

Just that morning she'd woken in a strange bed in the doctor's house, looked out at the sea which had claimed her friend and nearly been her own nemesis. Now she was locked in a cell, awaiting execution. She was tired, but falling asleep on the straw was unthinkable, if only to prevent her fingers and nose from being gnawed by a family of rodents. Worse, she might miss her chance if the guards came for her. Her one chance.

The only light filtered through the grating in the door, and the wall slit from the pit below, and the cold was almost tangible. She paced backwards and forwards, scuffing up the straw. Partly to keep warm, partly to be ready to take on the guards.

Another hour passed. Surely no-one would come for her tonight. Should she risk closing her eyes, just for a while? Even a couple of hours' sleep would help her stay strong. But it could turn into a mistake that might cost her life. If Sera stayed awake after they crossed under the river, she could do the same now.

She used her feet to pile up more straw in the rat's corner opposite the door. If someone came in they might think the mound was her, curled up in fear. Could buy a few precious seconds.

When she was finished, she went over to the slit in the wall. The pit was still illuminated, although she couldn't see what was lighting it. The creature had gone, along with Canterbury's remains, and both the gates were closed. But someone had swept the floor of the pit and put down fresh sand, ready for the next show.

She swung around at the faint sound of voices from the corridor outside, hurried to the door and peered through the grating. Two men were approaching, relaxed, chatting to each other. Unworried. So this was it.

She stood with her back to the wall next to the door, kissed the blade of the dagger for luck, and waited. The voices came closer, then a key in the lock, the door opening and one of the guards walking in. He peered around in the gloom for her, focussing on the shape in the corner where she'd piled up the straw. A big man, running to fat, smelling slightly of cheese. As he took a second step towards the shape, craning forward to make it out better, Ellen swung round and up and sliced the dagger across his throat. Easy enough, no need to stab through fat. Always aim to kill, not disable. As his blood sprayed out, she used all her weight to push his body back to stop the door from being closed.

The other guard was as bovine as the first. Some people reacted quickly to a sudden change in circumstances, like expecting a weak, weeping woman and finding instead a knife-wielding virago. This guard wasn't one of them. He was almost begging for the same quietus as his partner, Ellen decided as she trampled the first guard's body, and she obliged. More blood over the walls. She rolled the second body away with her feet, then took the set of keys from the lock. Who could say what other doors might get in her way?

ANOTHER BLOODY TUNNEL

Although she could hear no other sounds, someone would be expecting the guards to arrive with her in tow. And soon. She ran down the corridor, retracing the way they'd brought her earlier. This time she'd been lucky, next time might not go so well. The palace was enormous, covering more ground than some villages, and she would need a map to find her way out.

At the end of the passage she listened first, then peered around the corner. Another corridor, empty but with doorways dotted along the length. She walked quickly, pausing by each door to listen for the sounds of voices. One of these might be the guardroom, somewhere to avoid.

How long before someone raised the alarm? Not long, it could happen any minute. And then she heard someone. From the vibration of the footsteps, they were trying to walk quietly. She had two choices. Risk discovery and fight her way past whoever this was, or try one of the doors, hope it opened and that the room behind was empty.

The nearest doorway was a couple of yards ahead. She ran up and tried the handle. Locked. The footsteps were closer now, almost at the corner of the corridor, and going back towards her cell would get her nowhere. Her only hope was that surprise and luck would be on her side yet again.

She sprinted past the other doors, dagger in hand, not worrying about making a sound now. There was no point in waiting for whoever it was to come to her. Initiative was everything. As she reached the corner of the passage, a figure stepped out, hands up as if in surrender.

'Ellen, don't hurt me. My name's Lily and I'm here to help.'

The woman standing there looked familiar. Young, attractive, dressed for horse riding with breeches and boots. And a small, silver pistol tucked into her belt. She was an older version of the girl in the portrait, sitting by her parent's feet.

'We must hurry. When my father finds you've escaped, he'll lock down the palace and let his creatures out of the menagerie. You've already seen what they can do.'

Was she genuine, this woman who was barely more than a girl? Or was this a trap, part of the Princeps' entertainment? 'Why would you help me?' Ellen asked.

'It's complicated, I'll tell you as we go.'

Ellen followed Lily through a maze of corridors until they reached another door, disguised as part of the wall, which opened onto a staircase. Not grand, but narrow and dark. Lily took a lamp from the floor inside the door. 'The servants use their own network of routes through the palace. My father doesn't like to see them at work. Tiro's one of the few he can bear to have around him.'

'Where are we going?'

'My father's always been paranoid about his safety. When this place was built, he had secret tunnels made. Ways to leave the palace without being seen.'

'Surely they're guarded?'

'All but one. The builders added a tunnel that wasn't on the plans. I found out about it years ago.'

'Why on earth would they do that?'

They'd climbed up one floor, then another, then another. By now, they must be on ground level or above, out of the dungeons.

'You've seen what my father's like. He's always been strange, but over the past few months he's become much worse. It's bad enough for me, but it was terrible for my mother. They watched every move she made. She couldn't go anywhere without my father's permission, which he never gave. He told her what to wear, how to style her hair. Everything. When the palace was being built, she realised it was nothing more than a giant prison and she wanted an escape route.'

'And this was it?'

'I don't know all the details, she wouldn't tell me, but somehow she persuaded or bribed the workers to put in this extra escape route. My father knows nothing about it.'

At the top of the stairs they reached a narrow passage with a low ceiling and flaking plaster on the walls.

'We've been climbing a fair way,' said Ellen. 'Doesn't seem like a tunnel would be anywhere near here.'

'It isn't. The cells are separated from the rest of the palace. My father likes to keep his hobbies to himself.'

'How did you know where I was?'

'Once I heard you were coming here, it was odds on you'd end up in the cells like most of the "guests". I was coming to get you out if I could, hence the pistol. How did you manage to escape?'

'Let's just say there are two new vacancies for palace guards.'

She'd been trying to keep a map in her head of the route

they were taking, but it was impossible. So many passageways and staircases, all exactly the same.

'You were talking about your mother,' said Ellen. 'Did she escape?'

Lily stopped and turned. 'She killed herself in her bath. One of the maids discovered the body; she'd cut her wrists open and bled to death. My father told me she'd run away, but I knew the truth. Servants always gossip.'

'Why kill herself if she had a way to escape?'

'Think about it. If she managed to get out of the palace, then what? She had no money of her own, the servants locked away all her jewels the minute she took them off. Nothing belonged to her, and she had nowhere to go.'

'She could have tried.'

'I know my father. He'd have offered a reward, and someone would have given her up within hours. She would have been trapped again and when my father's angry - well, you've seen what happens.'

They'd dropped back down a few levels by now to where the air felt cold and damp, with mould growing in dark patches on the walls. Their shadows loomed and shrank as the lamp swung from Lily's hand.

'We're nearly there. Once we reach the tunnel, it gets messy.'

'I still don't understand why you're doing this.'

'I told you, my father's paranoid and he has reason to be. Have you heard of Free Forcello?'

'I've been here for two days, so no.'

'When my father connived to get rid of the senate, it was the last straw for people who wanted the republic back. Free Forcello works for a return to the old ways of governing the city. Proscribed, of course. Any members who were caught used to be executed publicly. Now they go to feed his animals.'

'And you're part of this group? The Princeps is your father!'

'Who drove my mother to suicide. After what happened to her, I'd do anything to bring him down. And I have an advantage; he thinks I'm like him. He trusts me, that's why I have so much freedom. Believe me, if I could see him trapped with one of his pets in the feeding chamber, my life would be complete.'

Lily held up a hand for Ellen to stop. 'We're here.' She placed the lamp on the ground and scraped away a layer of dust and mud to expose a trapdoor set flush into the ground, with two small hand-sized indentations.

'It's heavy, help me lift it.'

The trapdoor hadn't been moved for a long time, but eventually they managed to to pull it clear to reveal a shaft with a metal ladder fixed to the side. A cold draught flowed out, bringing a sour smell of stale air and subsoil.

'My experience of tunnels isn't exactly happy,' said Ellen. 'How long is it?'

'About a quarter of a mile. It ends in a copse just outside the boundary wall. Trust me, it's the only way out. I'll go first, and you need to pull the trapdoor back as best you can. If anyone comes down the passage after us, they might miss it. If we're lucky.'

Lily climbed down, the lamp swinging wildly as she held on to the sides. Ellen paused for a moment and then stepped onto the ladder behind her, scraping the trapdoor back into place.

They climbed down for what she guessed was about a hundred feet or more. At the bottom, a tunnel stretched into darkness. A very low, narrow tunnel.

'We have to get through that? Please tell me it doesn't go under any rivers.'

'None. But it's tight and we'll have to crawl. I was a child when my mother showed it to me and I haven't been back since.'

Crawling through this constricted space was hard enough for Lily with her smaller frame, but for Ellen it was torture, and within a few minutes her back and legs were burning. She had to fight thoughts of being buried there, unable to move as she inched along the damp earth surface, her back hunched and constantly knocking into the wooden beams which shored up the roof. How long had they been there? How many were rotten?

Suddenly Lily swore and the light went out.

'Shit! I dropped the lamp.'

'Can you light it again?'

'No. We'll have to go on in the dark. It's not as if we'll get lost.'

The darkness was absolute, like nothing she'd ever experienced before. It surrounded her, an all-enveloping black fog sticking to her face, clogging up her nose and mouth, invading her lungs. She had to remind herself to breathe.

Lily was still in front, crawling steadily along, seemingly not worried at all. Appearances were deceiving. And then Ellen noticed that the quality of the air had changed. A different smell, fresher. Not far ahead the darkness was no longer monochrome, but shades of grey.

Ellen crawled straight into Lily's legs. 'Sorry.'

'We've reached the end. Now there's another ladder to climb, and a trapdoor to open.'

She'd been worrying about this. 'You said it's in a copse. What if it's covered with earth, or something heavy's fallen on top? Rocks, a tree.'

'I made provision for that. Let's hope it worked out.'

Lily began to climb and Ellen followed, her legs and arms stiff and weak from the crawling. She sensed Lily stop, and then heard three sharp knocks, followed by three in reply.

The sound of something large being moved was followed by a shower of leaves and earth which fell onto Ellen's face.

Light, blessed light. Only from the moon behind thin clouds, but she'd never been so grateful to see again. Lily was already out, and an arm reached down to help Ellen up.

She tumbled onto the ground, barely able to move after being hunched up for so long. Lily was sitting nearby, along with two men squatting on their haunches.

'Filip and Volya,' said Lily, 'two of my comrades.'

One of the men handed Ellen a flask of water. 'We have to get away from here, and you can't go back to the college. I'll take you to one of our safe houses for tonight, tomorrow we'll move you somewhere else, out of the city. And don't worry about Professor Monad and his colleagues - we know about them and their work.'

In all the emotion of the past couple of hours, she'd almost forgotten about Canterbury. 'I have bad news; I saw someone die in the feeding chamber tonight.'

'Who? None of our people were there.'

'Gottfried Canterbury, a colleague of Fescue's. The Princeps knew he was helping with the project but I don't understand why he was taken, it makes no sense.'

'Nothing my father does makes sense,' said Lily. 'He kills for fun, just like his animals. He probably took an easy target and used him to scare you even more.'

A cloud passed over the moon. 'We need to go,' said Lily. 'Fescue should already be on his way to the safe house. We'll meet him there.'

THE SAFE HOUSE

She'd expected a house in a back street, but this was one of the grand homes lining the Great Canal in Old Forcello. Grand from a distance, but the decorations on the walls were chipped and blunt, with stunted ferns sprouting from cracks in the stone. The floor in the entrance hall, black and white squares of marble, looked as though a family of moles had been trying to break through.

'The ancestral home of one of our supporters,' said Filip. 'An old senatorial family; most of the time no-one lives here. They already lost two people to the Princeps and they don't want to lose anyone else.'

They showed her into an echoing room with blankets and cushions scattered on the floor. 'You'll sleep here,' said Lily. 'We'll bring food later and you'll leave before it's light.'

'Why can't I stay here?'

'Too much of a risk. You're recognisable, nobody in Forcello has hair your colour or blue eyes. I wouldn't count on escaping a second time if a patrol searches house-to-house and finds you. We've arranged for you to go to John

Tulliver's factory. It's miles away, should be safe enough for now.'

Fescue entered the room as Lily finished speaking.

'Why are you here?' asked Ellen. 'Is everyone in Forcello part of this organisation?'

'One of Lily's friends told me what happened to you - I'm so glad you're safe. And escaping the college without alerting the porter or the Princeps' spies was all very cloak and dagger.' He sounded almost excited.

'Do you know everything that happened tonight?'

Ellen glanced at Lily, who shook her head. So he hadn't heard about Canterbury, and there was no simple way to break the news. Like pulling an arrow from a wound, sometimes it was best done quickly. She decided not to describe every detail of the feeding chamber, just that Canterbury had died bravely.

Fescue seemed to crumple in front of her. 'Poor Canterbury. All he ever wanted were his owls. He lived for them.'

'There's more,' she said. 'I begged the Princeps to spare the Professor, but he refused and then told me - trust me, I'm not making this up - that he's becoming a god. He's completely mad, thinks he's invincible. And when I reminded him I was helping with the project to save the city, he said he'd burn everything to the ground and start again.'

'This has gone far enough,' said Volya. 'If we don't act soon, we'll miss our chance.'

'But it's impossible to get near him,' said Filip.

'I was close,' said Ellen, 'and he didn't find my dagger. I wish I'd used it on him when I had the chance.'

Fescue seemed to had recovered himself. 'When I told the chaps what happened in my meeting with the Princeps, Oliphant mentioned assassination as an option. A joke, I thought, but then he mentioned some people in Partridge

College who like blowing things up. What if we persuade them to make one of their bombs? We'd just need to get it close to him and boom! No more Princeps.'

Lily had moved slightly away from the others, and Ellen joined her. 'Should you be here, listening to this?' she asked. 'I know what you said about seeing him in the pit, but he is your father. This must be tough.'

Lily forced a smile. 'Tough, yes. But necessary. I understand better than anyone what he's capable of.'

'I might have an idea,' said Ellen, joining the others again. 'Fescue, you said there's going to be a ceremony to announce the winner of your competition.'

'The winner will be the Ontological Engine, obviously. Why?'

'The Princeps will want to be there, but he'll worry about his safety. When I first met the doctor, he mentioned the Princeps wanted a trip in the air yacht.'

'How does this help?'

'It's not enough to kill him,' said Ellen, 'it has to be done publicly so everyone can see he's gone. There can't be any rumours about him surviving. So what if we persuade him to arrive at the ceremony by this airship? Think about it. This will be an irresistible opportunity to show off, and he'll think he's safer than riding through the streets.'

'Still not understanding.'

'We hide one of your bombs in the airship's basket, set to explode while it's in the air. The best public execution ever, and there's no way he'll survive.'

'I like it,' said Filip, 'but I see problems. We have to persuade someone to make the bomb, then hide it in the airship's basket, then entice the Princeps to go up in the first place.'

'And whoever pilots the air yacht will die as well,' said Lily. 'Your doctor won't be too happy with that idea.'

Volya broke the silence. 'I'll do it. The doctor can teach me how to pilot the airship, and on the day he'll plead illness and say I'm his trained assistant. You won't even need a bomb, I'll just throw the bastard out when we're high enough.'

Lily shook her head. 'What if you fail, or he throws you out instead? The repercussions of a failed assassination don't bear thinking about - whatever we do has to be foolproof.'

'So we stay with the bomb idea.'

'But you'll be blown up along with my father,' said Lily. 'That's madness.'

'On the other hand,' said Filip, 'it's mad enough to work. We lose one person to save thousands - that equation works for me, and we all knew our lives were in danger when we joined the organisation. If Volya doesn't do it, I will.'

Ellen looked around at the little group, standing in silence as they came to terms with what they were planning. Fanatics, all of them, planning to murder the Princeps and sacrifice one of their own number in the process. Would she have done the same if this were her home? In a way, she already had.

'Well, if we're agreed on this I'll talk to Oliphant in the morning,' said Fescue, 'get him to speak to the chaps in Partridge. Tell them he needs a bomb for an experiment, something small and easy to set off.'

'And I'll talk to my father,' said Lily, 'assuming I get back into the palace with nobody noticing. Once the idea of the air yacht's in his head, he won't be able to resist.'

'How long do we have?' asked Ellen.

'Five days from today,' said Fescue. 'In that time we need to design and build the Ontological Engine, procure a bomb, and persuade the Princeps about the whole air yacht idea. And get the doctor to agree.' He checked his pocket watch. 'It's three in the morning, give or take five minutes, and I need to return to my rooms. A chap my age needs his sleep.'

'And I need to get back to the palace,' said Lily. 'Filip and Volya will take Ellen to Tulliver's factory, he's expecting her. When Professor Oliphant's ready with his designs, he'll meet you all there. Good luck!'

CHAPTER 16

The Ontological Engine

PUNCHED CARDS

They debated the best way to get Ellen out of the city; hidden in the back of a cart and hope it wouldn't be searched, or in plain sight. Taking a train was out of the question; the stations would be littered with guards.

Plain sight was the winner, in a steam carriage borrowed from another wealthy supporter. Filip driving, with Ellen sitting next to him in full view but with her hair pulled up under a hat, a voluminous travel coat meant for a woman of a certain age, and a pair of round, green-tinted spectacles to disguise her eyes. No-one trying to hide would choose to be so visible.

They passed the city checkpoints without a problem and followed the road Ellen had taken with the doctor the day before. She was becoming used to the noise of the engine and the rattle of the automatic hopper behind her, feeding coke into the small furnace. Even through the protective panel behind her seat, the heat warmed her back, and occasionally the wind blew smoke and fumes into her eyes. She looked across at Filip; his face below the goggles had turned piebald with black smudges of soot. *This is the future*, he'd said as they set off. Give her Hob any day.

When they were still a mile or so from the doctor's house, Filip turned off the coast road. They drove inland for another five miles until they reached a large brick building set in a small valley and surrounded by woods, with a stream bubbling through.

Filip shut down the engine. 'Tulliver's manufactory. He makes steam engines and carriages like ours, but most of the work's done by intelligent machines. Very modern, John Tulliver.'

The man himself came to greet them from an outbuilding set a little way apart, and he patted the side of the carriage. 'One of ours, I were proud of this design. Very economical on the coke.' He helped Ellen down. 'We'll go to my office; I keep it separate from the workshop, bloody noisy in there when the machines are running.'

He took them over to the furthest outbuilding, just one large room and a couple of anterooms. 'You'll sleep here, Miss Dust. Only a sofa, but there weren't much time to prepare. Your new friends always take things at a run.'

'So what's the plan,' said Ellen. 'I can't stay here for long.'

'Oliphant will be up later today, bringing his specifications. Fast worker, that man. Then we build the engine and we only have a few days. My supervisor's a good lad, though, and he makes the factory sing like a linnet in heat.'

'I thought the professor needed my help.'

'He'll need you, aye. Building the engine is the straightforward part, but once that's done he needs to give it instructions. That's where you come in. You'll have to wait for him to explain more, I'm only the metal basher.'

'How does he tell an engine what to do? It's just a machine.'

'Come over to the factory and I'll show you.'

. . .

Whatever she expected to see, this wasn't it. The building was vast, over one thousand feet long, with huge belts running across the ceiling, attached to different machines where they turned wheels and gears. The noise drowned out all thoughts and sounds. Above every machine a complex metal cage held a wide ribbon of large cards strung together, each card punched with distinct patterns of holes. The cards clattered through to the machine below the cage and then back up again.

Tulliver leant over to shout at her. 'What d'you think? Those cards tell the machines what to do and how to do it. They were invented to help in weaving designs on cloth, but the Professor saw they could be used in a factory like mine. Two hundred people worked here once, now I need only ten. That's progress for you.'

Oliphant arrived a few hours later carrying rolls of paper fastened with green ribbons. 'I have no idea if this will work. I got Monad to look over my calculations, but we're sailing into unknown waters here.' He handed the papers to Tulliver. 'These are instructions on how to build the engine. While you get on with the construction, I'll speak with Miss Dust to design the inputs - more cards, I'm afraid. We have little time; the ceremony's planned for next Monday and it's already Wednesday.'

She was becoming used to telling her story, but Oliphant made her go over it again and again, asking the smallest details. Describe the patterns in the river you crossed. What shade of green were the leaves of the trees in the forest? How tall were they? What shape was the wolf, what sounds did it make, what colour was its fur? How large were the snowflakes at the Priory? Describe the accents of the men who attacked you on the mountain. What did women wear in Coria?

On and on until she wasn't sure herself. 'Why does it matter?' she asked. 'I've told you everything I know.'

Oliphant stopped writing and put down his pen. He was tired, Ellen saw it in the lines around his eyes and the droop of his lips. No gallantry now.

'Once the Ontological Engine is built, we have to tell it how to produce an electro-magnetic field of the right frequency. The aim is to jolt the worlds back into alignment, so they return to their own chronologies, but the calculations are beyond anything I've done before. I'm building equations that combine the speed and locations of your travels with the phenomena you encountered, especially when there were anomalies like summer turning to winter in a few hours, or a steamship appearing in a world where it didn't yet exist.'

'What happens if you get it wrong?'

'Perhaps nothing, and the worlds continue to merge with all the problems that brings. Or it could speed up the changes. Or we might all disappear in a cataclysm of fire.'

'Then we have to hope you get it right.'

THE ONTOLOGICAL ENGINE

By Sunday evening the Ontological Engine was ready. Ellen had expected something like the machines in the factory, a mechanical beast that would need to be loaded into a cart with a crane. But the apparatus in Tulliver's office was a metal cube; three feet on each side, four round dials on the front and two large spikes attached to the top with a wire stretched between them.

'Aerials,' said Oliphant, who'd stayed to oversee the building of the engine. 'The cube generates the field and the aerials propagate it into the ether by sending out invisible waves.'

After all the discussions and work and worry, this felt disappointing. 'You keep talking about generating fields,' said Ellen, 'but I'm a simple woman from a simple time. Make it easy for me. And what was the point of taking the details from my journey here?'

'This is just the field generator,' said Oliphant, 'but we'll also take one of the card readers from the factory. The information about your journey has been coded onto punched cards. They tell the engine what to do; how strong a field to generate, what combination of frequencies. It needs to be a complex pattern in exactly the right order. As for power, Tulliver made an adapter for a steam carriage. Instead of turning the carriage's wheels, it'll turn a set of coiled copper wires inside the machine. They're surrounded by magnets of different strengths, and as the coils spin they generate the field. The punched cards determine which sequence of coils to activate, and how fast or slow to spin at any point. All rather clever, though I say it myself.'

'So what happens at the ceremony? Or should I say, what does the Princeps think will happen?'

'It'll take place on Antares Field, just outside the city. All the great and the good of Forcello will attend, as well as half the city's population. His Magnificence arrives by the doctor's air yacht and then mounts a stage, surrounded by a phalanx of guards. He announces the winner and the prize, and then the celebrations start. Games in the afternoon, fireworks in the evening.'

'So why all the rush to get this engine ready if he simply announces who's won, especially as the plan is for him never to get to that point?'

'Tiro told us the Princeps would command the winner to demonstrate their solution then and there. If they don't have something ready to put into effect immediately, he'll withhold the prize and throw them in the cells. We all know where that leads.'

'So this is being rushed just in case; I assume the bomb in the airship is still going ahead?'

'The chaps from Partridge College are finishing the device as we speak. They know it's for something I'm working on, but that's all. We've heard nothing from Lily; it's hard for her to get away from the palace sometimes. But the doctor's on board with the air yacht idea. Took a bit of persuading, though, he loves that contraption.'

'The plan seemed like a good idea when I came up with it,' said Ellen, 'but I'm not sure now.'

'It's our best chance. We can't allow that madman to burn the city, and even when he's gone, we still need to repair the breach between realities.'

'But Volya, sacrificing himself. I wish there was another alternative.'

'You'd rather it was the doctor?'

'I'd rather it was no-one. But I don't see any any other way.'

ALONE IN A CROWD

Fescue and Oliphant spent an hour trying to persuade her to avoid the ceremony but as she said, if they got her out of the city they could get her back in. With the same disguise and surrounded by thousands of people, she'd be as safe as anywhere.

The Ontological Engine started its slow journey to the city that evening, but Ellen left early the next morning in the steam carriage, with Filip driving again.

'When we're closer, I'll let you out,' he said. 'Most of the walls in the city are plastered with posters announcing the ceremony and there are bound to be crowds making their way to Antares Field, so you won't get lost. Don't talk to anyone. Your accent's peculiar and the Princeps will have spies everywhere; you don't want anyone informing the guards. And whatever happens, don't go near either of the professors.'

THE CROWDS WERE BIGGER than she'd expected, entire families carrying hampers for a day out. She stooped to disguise her height, easily the tallest woman around, and wished she could take off the heavy travelling coat. Driving along in the carriage had been fine but now, even though it was late November, the sun was hot and it felt more like early summer with a deep blue sky and no clouds. Sweat trickled down her back and between her breasts; the seasons were catching up with her again. Oliphant had been right, they didn't have much time.

She allowed herself to be carried along with the crowd, which became denser as they funnelled towards one of the checkpoints in the city gates. Ellen risked looking up; uniformed guards at a barrier were letting people through one family at a time. Not good. It was one thing driving through a checkpoint like an empress with guards saluting, another to be examined at close quarters as she walked through. She checked her hat to ensure that no tendrils of dark hair had escaped, and pushed the spectacles up her nose to hide her eyes completely.

She was getting closer, and the noise level was rising. People jostled her from all sides, bodies pressed into hers, and then she felt a hand reaching to touch her breasts. She'd learnt long ago that while the human body was resilient, leverage was leverage and everything had its breaking point. She heard a sharp cry and someone swearing behind her as she let go of his broken fingers. That was easy. Dealing with the uniforms would be another matter.

Closer still, with people shouting and complaining, children crying. Suddenly the crowd surged forward, the barrier cracked and snapped, and the guards retreated hurriedly into their shelter. All except one who tripped and fell, disappearing under the stampede.

She was through into a vast open arena, with a wooden stage so far away she could barely make it out. Antares Field;

fifty thousand people could come here for the ceremony, with space for that many again.

Ellen struck out, threading her way through the families and trying not to catch anyone's eye. Stay away from the professors, that was understandable, but no-one told her not to have a ringside view.

Closer to, she saw a large area cordoned off to one side of the stage. That must be where the airship would touch down at midday; by the position of the sun, there wouldn't be long to wait. She looked back towards the palace where the doctor would have arrived earlier in his air yacht. With luck, he'd persuaded the Princeps to let Volya take over as pilot. If not, all bets were off.

There was so much to go wrong, and this had been her idea. How much easier to react to danger in the moment than cope with these complicated plans. She'd told Oliphant she came from a simpler world; now every day was a struggle to understand this alien place with people using meaningless words and building machines indistinguishable from magic.

The sounds around her changed. The inchoate buzz of conversations had become a susurration, the sound of a summer breeze in woodland. People were looking up and pointing at something in the distance, floating in the sky and growing larger by the second.

Whoever else was with him, the Princeps was on his way.

BOMB AND BALLOON

❦

An hour earlier. Two hundred feet below the airship, the palace came into view, its white marble glittering in the sun. Doctor Withering checked the bandages on his wrist and instructed Volya to bring the airship down. First, stop the propeller connected to the small steam engine in the rear section of the gondola, then pull the cords to vent hot air from the balloon above them. A quick study, Volya. They made a perfect soft landing in the palace grounds where the Princeps was waiting, along with a company of his guards, one of them restraining an enormous animal attached to a chain.

Volya opened the gate on the gondola and helped the doctor out, while the Princeps beckoned to the guard holding the animal and walked towards them.

'What happened to your hand, doctor? I thought I'd made myself clear, I don't like surprises.'

'My apologies sire, a stupid accident this morning while preparing the yacht. I appear to have broken a bone in my wrist, which renders me unable to control the airship sufficiently to guarantee your safety. But my colleague, Volya, is supremely gifted as a pilot. Taught me everything I know about aerostatic airships.'

'Your colleague? Looks a bit rough around the edges to me. Not a beggar, is he? I don't like beggars.'

'Not a beggar, I promise. Fortunately, he lives not far from me and agreed to take my place today to avoid incommoding you.'

The Princeps looked Volya up and down, and then shrugged. 'Needs must, doctor. You'll come with us, of course.'

'I regret not. The yacht was built for two people, there's no space for me. I intend to make my way to the ceremony as fast as possible by other means.'

'Suit yourself. When you say "two people" I assume there's room for a child.'

'Possibly sire, if he were small enough. Why?'

'How about a boy of eight? Do you think he might enjoy the experience?'

The Princeps nodded to the guards who parted to show Alfred standing there, dressed in his favourite sailor suit, his hand tightly grasped in Tiro's.

'I thought to myself, how can I repay the good doctor for his generous offer of the airship? I know, I'll take his enthusiastic young son with me. Give him an adventure he'll remember all his life.'

Alfred's face reminded Withering of the cadavers he dissected from time to time; bloodless and drained of colour. The boy was doing him proud, trying not to cry.

'Highness, perhaps Alfred should remain with me. He's been poorly of late and is such a small child. They have a tendency to get in the way, you know how it is.'

'Indeed, doctor, I do. He goes with me, and he'll need to stay where he's put. I hope he learns quickly.'

The boy looked over at his father but didn't make a sound

as a guard placed him in the gondola. While Tiro helped the Princeps to board, the doctor leant in to Volya and gripped his arm. 'You have to abort,' he whispered, 'we'll find another way,' but Volya pushed him off and climbed into the basket, pulling the gate shut behind him.

Withering had heard people say their blood ran cold when they were afraid, but he'd never felt it himself until today. What to do? If he attempted to pull Alfred out, it would be obvious that something was amiss and the guards would seize him. Even if the airship remained on the ground, he'd have saved his son from danger now only to condemn him to a worse fate later.

Volya was a fanatic, like everyone in his organisation. Weighing one small boy's life against eliminating the Princeps, what judgement would he come to? Please the gods, Withering prayed, he'd make the right decision and not set off the hidden bomb.

And then the doctor remembered the fail-safe built in to ensure the Princeps' death, just in case the bomb failed.

WHAT GOES UP

⤬

*E*llen pushed through to the front of the crowd. Fescue and Oliphant were next to the Ontological Engine and all its accoutrements, installed on a platform next to the main stage. Fescue noticed her, but they avoided looking at each other.

The airship came closer, with two figures visible in the gondola hanging underneath the hot-air balloon. An incredible sight; the doctor had described it, but nothing could have prepared her for this. A bright green balloon with red vertical stripes, and above the basket a mechanism shooting flame into the wide base of the envelope; the hot air that kept it from crashing to the ground. A cloud of steam poured from a rear compartment, the engine driving the propeller.

Someone pushed his way through the crowd close to her, but the guards stopped him before he reached the stage.

'Tell Professor Oliphant I have important information,' the man said, 'I'm a colleague from the University and I really must have a word.'

Oliphant clambered down from the platform to the other

side of the security cordon. 'What is it, Mawdsley? Everything's in order, no need to worry.'

He was nervous, Ellen could hear it by the quaver in his voice.

'You pop on back to Partridge College,' said Oliphant, 'and I'll catch up with you later. Bit busy now.'

'I needed to explain about the "experiment" you asked for help with.'

'I told you, not to worry. I took delivery and everything's set up.'

'You don't understand. It was all rather rushed and by accident we left out one of the mechanisms. The device will fail.'

Not very subtle, but the guards nearby weren't interested. As if it mattered now. Volya would reveal himself when he tried to set off the useless bomb, the Princeps would stay alive and they would torture Volya to unmask the plot before he was taken to the menagerie.

Mawdsley shouldered his way back through the crowd while Oliphant whispered urgently to Fescue. There was nothing to do except go through with the ceremony, always assuming that the Princeps didn't realise there was a plot to kill him and have them arrested as soon as he landed.

The airship was overhead now, and another disturbance rippled through the crowd. The doctor this time, his face streaked with dust and sweat. He made his way over to Ellen.

'We're not meant to know each other,' she whispered. 'Go away.'

'You don't understand. Alfred's in the airship. My son's going to die.'

'No, he isn't, I'll explain later. The device in the airship won't work because a part is missing.'

'You still don't understand,' said Withering. 'In case something went wrong with the device, we put a plan in place.'

'What plan?'

But the doctor didn't answer. His gaze, like everyone else's, was fixed on the airship. It had been circling the landing site but instead of coming down, it was rising higher, the burner spewing out flame every few seconds.

'What's happening,' said Ellen. 'Why aren't they descending?'

'The burner's stuck and they can't turn it off. Our failsafe. The balloon will take them higher as it keeps burning, until the gas runs out.'

'And then what happens?'

'The balloon collapses and they crash to the ground.'

Summer was losing the battle with autumn and a chilly breeze had blown in from the north. She'd owned a skirt once, a present from Tollin. Deep indigo with a scalloped hem. She washed it so often the dye leached away to a pale blue, the colour the sky was now. A winter sky. The tiny airship was still circling but rising higher every second, with the flame from the burner a regular flash of orange, marking the moments until it failed.

It was too high to see the people inside. What were they saying to each other? Did they realise they were about to die? Did Alfred even know what death was? Of course, he'd told her on the beach, the day the ocean spat her out. *'I've seen lots of dead people.'* Now he would be one.

She wondered why the doctor was still watching; perhaps it was the fascination of abomination, an inability to turn aside from even the worst horror.

Another murmur from the crowd. Had the flames stopped, or was the balloon too high for them to see? Then the murmurs morphed into shrieks as something fell from the basket. The speck grew larger as it came closer, and gradually resolved into a person, arms and legs flailing as if attempting to fly. Ellen tried to make out what he was wearing, but the sun was in her eyes. All she could see was a silhouette tumbling through the air, heading for the stage. Time was speeding up; the figure seemed to accelerate, and then smashed through the wooden boards a few yards from where she was standing. She still hadn't recognised who it was.

The airship was hovering now, hanging in the sky as if gravity had called a temporary truce. And then the orange flare of the burner stopped, the laws of physics resumed, and it started to sink. The balloon, so full and bright on the ascent, collapsed in on itself, nothing more than a cylinder of silk stretching above the gondola and its passengers as they fell towards the crowd. Mothers and fathers tucked small children under their arms, deserted their hampers, and ran for the exits from the field.

It was close enough now to make out a figure. Just one, pulling in a package attached to the outside of the gondola. He disappeared, as if crouching down, and then the crowd gasped as he threw something out at an angle from the airship. Something attached to a cord. Someone. Someone small.

The figure tumbled through the air until the umbilical stretched tight, and then jerked to a stop. A mushroom of white spread out above him, the cord fell away, and the figure floated slowly towards the ground. Below him the airship continued its uncontrolled descent, the balloon still streaming out above. It was heading straight for the platform holding the Ontological Engine, but missed by just a few yards as it hit the earth, spraying fragments of bone and metal shards like tiny knife blades as it disintegrated.

CHAPTER 17

The Map is not the Territory

ALFRED EXPLAINS

Alfred reached the ground a few minutes later, floating down near the edge of the field as a freshening breeze blew him away from the carnage. The doctor was already gone, running through the thinning crowd to find his son, while Ellen made her way around and underneath the stage. The body of the Princeps was recognisable now, even though the uniform was stained with blood and brains where his head burst open with the impact. A shame, she would have liked to see him in the feeding chamber, but this was a good second best. She hoped he'd stayed conscious all the way down. She hoped he saw death rushing up to meet him. She hoped he recognised her standing there and realised in his last few moments that he'd failed.

There was no need to hide now. Some of the guards had seen the body, stripped off their uniform jackets and lost themselves in the crowd. Ellen ducked out from under the stage and climbed up to the platform where Fescue and Oliphant still stood guard by the Engine. They looked, she thought, like men who couldn't believe that they'd just cheated death.

'It was him,' she said. 'I would say he's not a pretty sight but actually he was, depending on your point of view.'

'Did I notice the doctor?' asked Fescue. 'I couldn't hear what he was saying.'

'Alfred was in the airship, along with the Princeps and Volya. Must had been taken as some sort of insurance. I think that's who came down attached to - what was he attached to?'

'A parachute,' said Oliphant, 'never seen one used before. I didn't realise Withering kept one on the airship; they tend not to work.'

From the platform, they could see over the heads of the people running from the devastation. The doctor half ran, half walked towards them with Alfred in his arms and Ellen scrambled down to meet him. 'Is he hurt?'

'That was amazing!' said the boy as his father set him down. 'Not the fight, that was scary. But I want to jump with a parachute again. Can Peterkin have one? We could jump together.'

'I'm afraid my airship is broken,' said Withering. 'Perhaps another time. And don't tell your mother.'

Ellen and the doctor each took one of Alfred's hands and walked him over to the platform, avoiding the wreckage. Oliphant was fussing with the Engine, checking that all the cards were in alignment. 'As there's no ceremony and no audience, we might as well turn it on now,' he said.

'It can wait a few more minutes.' Ellen knelt in front of the boy. 'I'd appreciate knowing what happened in the airship, if Alfred feels like telling us.'

'It was horrible when the men came to the house. Mama didn't want to let them in, but they pushed her out of the way. I tried to run, but they were too fast and one of them caught me and took me to the station and there was a train and it didn't stop anywhere until we got to the city and they took me to the palace. Papa arrived and I thought he'd take me home, but he didn't. That's when I was scared. He never allows me in his airship, so I knew something was wrong.'

'I'm so sorry, Alfie,' said the doctor.

'I know. We left the ground and went up really fast. The man in the uniform said horrid things about you, Papa, and your friends. When we were really high Volya said he had to make an adjustment and he pulled something out from one of the storage boxes and said to the other man that he was going to get his just deserts, but I couldn't see any deserts anywhere, which was strange. Volya swore at the thing he was holding, and the other man tried to grab him and they were fighting and I tried to be very small in a corner just like you told me to, Papa, if I saw people being bad.'

'What happened next?' asked Ellen.

'Volya hit the other man and knocked him out. He did something to the burner, but that went wrong too, and he kept swearing at it. Volya swears a lot.'

'The fail-safe,' said the doctor. 'We wanted a backup in case the bomb failed, so I rigged the burner to jam and keep firing. Volya knew, he must have been trying to fix it.' He turned to his son. 'What happened to the man who Volya knocked out? The Princeps.'

'He woke up while Volya was trying to fix the burner. They started fighting again, but Volya was stronger. He pushed the man to the edge of the basket and tipped him out.'

'But the balloon was still going up,' said Ellen.

'That's when it stopped. The burner made a sort of sputtering sound and the flame went out. Everything happened very fast. Volya leaned out and grabbed a satchel with all sorts of straps. He tied it to me very tight, told me to shut my eyes and not be afraid, and threw me out of the basket. He looked up at his father. 'Perhaps we won't tell Mama everything,' he said.

FIELD GENERATION

⁂

'I'd forgotten about the parachute,' said the doctor. 'It came with the yacht, but I saw someone jump from a cliff once, wearing one. It failed to open, and the chap using it smashed on the rocks at the bottom. I kept meaning to throw it away. But when I heard what a sacrifice Volya was making, I thought he could use it to escape. A slight chance but better than nothing.'

Alfred wandered over to the Ontological Engine. 'What does this do?'

'An excellent question,' said Oliphant, 'and I suppose we should find out. I recognise that circumstance have changed and I'm sorry about Volya, but there's work to do. Monad, if you attend to the steam engine I'll calibrate the field generation.'

A large wheel on the steam engine started turning, connected by a belt to a smaller wheel on the side of the Ontological Engine. As the small wheel span, picking up speed, the needles on the dials flickered.

'It's generating the field,' said Oliphant, 'but the strength is less than I'd hoped. Much less.'

Ellen stood back to allow the professors to work. The steam engine picked up speed, the wheels blurred and a sharp, bitter smell spread, reminding her of the tang of metal. But nothing else happened. What had she expected; mountains to rear up, or an invasion of the sea? Earthquakes? The dead rising from their graves? But there was nothing other than the spinning wheels and the strange smell. She'd hoped for more.

On reflection, she should had planned for this moment. Deep down she'd assumed that the Engine would fail. Not consciously; at the level of her thoughts she believed in Fescue and Oliphant, she believed they would succeed. But another part of her simply couldn't encompass the possibility of Haefen rising out of the waters, of Tollin's and Annegret's dust swirling back into the forms of their bodies. She hadn't believed in the possibility of going back. Hadn't Oliphant said that time's arrow flew in only one direction?

And even if some version of Haefen reappeared, what use would it be if she was stuck in Forcello? She looked at Fescue and Oliphant, Withering and Alfred. Good people, but not her people. She needed to find her home if it still existed somewhere.

Oliphant stepped back, shaking his head. 'Shut it down, Monad, it's no use. We'll need an engine a hundred times the size to generate a strong enough field. And before you ask, no, that would be beyond us. If I had a little more time…'

'So it failed?'

The doctor interrupted. 'Why such a powerful field?'

'There's no point in having an effect locally. We need to propagate the field over a wide area, very wide. Enough to jolt the realities back into alignment.'

'I might have a solution,' said the doctor. 'I correspond with friends in the airship community about developments in designs. My air yacht's used for geological observations, as you know, looking down at the land below me. But some other chaps have been investigating the atmosphere itself, with intriguing results.'

'I appreciate your dedication to your hobby,' said Fescue 'but their work is speculative at best.'

'Monad, you're a brilliant man and if ever I need help in understanding arcane concepts about what it means to exist, I'll be sure to consult you. But leave the practical stuff to me and Gregory.'

'Ignore him,' said Oliphant. 'What about these atmospheric observations?'

'They've discovered a phenomenon in the atmosphere,' said the doctor. 'It's called the Heavy Side Layer, for reasons that escape me, and it reflects electro-magnetic radiation, rather like a mirror reflects light.' He waved his arms around to encompass the platform and the increasingly empty space where the crowd had been. 'We're almost at sea level here. The fields generated by the Ontological Engine are too weak to reach high into the atmosphere.'

'They're attenuated by the ether in between,' said Oliphant.

'Exactly! But if the Engine's aerials are high enough, the waves of radiation it generates will bounce off the Heavy Side Layer and radiate for thousands of miles in all directions.'

'Could an airship like yours carry the weight of the Engine?' asked Ellen.

'Not like mine. We'll need to borrow a bigger version to float the Engine up. We could adapt the onboard steam propulsion for the propeller to run the Ontological Engine once we're up there, the same as we've done with the steam carriage here.'

'You're proposing high altitude electromagnetic field propagation plus an untested theory about invisible mirrors in the sky,' said Fescue. 'Believe me, I welcome paradigm shifts as much as the next man but there must be another way.'

'If there is, I can't think of it,' said Oliphant. 'Anyone else? No? Then I recommend you find us an airship, doctor, quick as you like. And we should get out of here. Once news about the Princeps spreads, things will get unpleasant. Doctor; will Helena accommodate us all at your house for a few days? The Engine needs adjustments and we'll be better off outside the city until things calm down.'

'What about Volya? We can't leave his body in the wreckage,' said Ellen. 'And doctor, don't you want to salvage anything from your airship?'

'We don't have time,' said Oliphant. 'Lily and the others will arrive soon. Much as we hated him, getting rid of the Princeps was their battle. We should leave the remains for them. As for your airship, doctor, I'm afraid that it's completed its last flight.'

GO OR STAY?

The streets were almost empty as they drove through the city. They stopped briefly outside Snow College for Fescue to collect a box of cigars and a bottle of whiskey, and then passed through a deserted checkpoint and on to the familiar road to the coast.

Withering drove the carriage with Alfred asleep on the front seat next to him. Oliphant was folded against the Engine, scribbling in his pocketbook, while Fescue seemed uncharacteristically quiet. Apart from the doctor, they were all unaccustomed to sudden death, she realised. Especially violent death. She'd seen too much of reality, that was the difference between them and her. They lived in a world filled with what people in Haefen would call magic, and they took it for granted. But they'd lost something as well. A broken connection. As for her, she was too inured to suffering and pain, and experiences couldn't be unlived.

She had decisions to make. It was as if the death of the Princeps had released her, given her permission to think about her future beyond searching for a reason. She could wait to see if the doctor's suggestion about the Heavy Side

Layer would work, but what would be the point? Either the Engine would repair the merging of the worlds and their different paths, or nothing would change. Whatever happened, one of her possible futures was a path that led out of Forcello. And if the Engine succeeded, she needed to be on the right path. The one that led home. Probably.

Summer had fought back. As the afternoon gave way to evening, they stopped at an inn on the edge of a village green where the surface of a small pond was a haze of flying insects. They still had a couple of hours or more to travel, but the doctor needed a rest from driving and the thought of beer and food was irresistible. They sat outside on benches next to long tables, glad to be quiet for a while. This could be almost anywhere, thought Ellen. Haefen, Coria, Forcello; cities grew and changed, but villages stayed the same.

The air was heavy with evening dew; although the sky had cleared, a thunderstorm was coming. She felt it the way she had all those weeks ago on the harbourside, wondering where the ships had gone. Oliphant took something from an inside pocket on his jacket. About six inches long, covered with tiny numbers and symbols and with a horizontal section in the centre which he slid along and back again before making notes in his pocketbook. She'd seen one of these before, or something like it. The object pulled from the water that day at the harbour.

'What is that?' she asked.

Oliphant looked up. 'This? A slide rule, helps me with calculations. Uses logarithms. Helpful chaps, logarithms.'

'I don't think we had logarithms in Haefen.'

'I know. A simple woman from a simpler world.'

On the other side of the table, Fescue drained his tankard. 'We should carry on. Don't know about you, but I prefer not to be in this contraption after dark.'

. . .

Darkness had fallen, and Ellen was in the same bedroom next to Alfred's; outside the window, clouds hid the moon and stars and there was nothing to see. Leaving would be hard. She sat on the bed and pictured the journey back across the sea to Coria, then over the mountains and the moors, through the forest and over the river. All in search of something that might not exist.

Or she could stay. Accept this fresh life as if it were a gift. Forcello was about to have a whole new set of challenges now that its ruler was dead, and who could say what opportunities there might be for a woman with her peculiar skills. More than in Haefen, that was for sure.

And yet.

She rose early next morning before anyone else was up, and walked along the coast road until she arrived at the beach where Alfred had found her. She sat on the wall and gazed out at the ocean; the threatened storm had passed them by and the sea sparkled in the shallow morning sun. From here it seemed beautiful, even welcoming. A siren voice, though. The memory of Sophia hurt too much; if she decided to leave Forcello, there had to be a way that didn't involve a ship.

Footsteps sounded along the road behind her; Helena, with Alfred and Peterkin in tow. The boy and his dog ran down to the beach and Helena joined her on the wall.

'Have you decided?' asked Helena.

'Decided what?'

'Whether to stay. It's on your mind, I've watched you stare into the distance.'

There was still so much about Forcello that she didn't understand. The people looked the same apart from their clothes. They spoke much the same language. But they were, literally, from another world. The longer she stayed, the more obvious that was becoming. In that moment, her decision was made.

'I have to leave. And I have to leave soon. Before the next attempt with the Ontological Engine.'

'You're worried about being trapped here. It's not so bad, especially now that maniac's dead. Stay with us for as long as you want; I'd appreciate having another woman around.'

'Forcello's your home, not mine. If I stayed I'd always be wondering, what if? Sometimes I wonder if I'm even meant to have a home.'

'I'm not sure what you mean. Home is everything.'

'For you. I used to think the same. I used to think I was happy, until I wasn't. I've seen things on my journey - let's just say that if I ever get back to Haefen, I won't be able to tell them what happened, not the truth. They used to call me a witch just because I was different; if I told them about steamships and machines that fly, they'd burn me at the stake.'

'And you want to go back?'

'It's not that I want to, but that I have to. Almost as if there's unfinished business.'

'What will you do if you don't find your home?'

Ellen glanced down at the boy and his dog, running up to the edge of the sea and jumping back to avoid getting wet. 'That's a good question. I guess I'll have to wait to find out.'

THE MAP IS NOT THE TERRITORY

The doctor found an atlas on his study shelves and opened it on his desk before setting off to speak to someone about borrowing an airship.

'You realise that this is based on Forcello's reality before the breach,' said Oliphant. 'What you'll find on your way could be very different. If my assumptions are correct, and if the Engine does the trick, the realities that started merging will be jolted back towards their proper paths.'

'You're assuming that every reality has its own course,' said Fescue, 'laid down like a railway track. If there are no predetermined paths, but each reality makes its own future as it goes along, anything could happen. There would be no "proper paths" and all bets are off.'

'Neither of you know the truth,' said Ellen, 'even if there is such a thing. Which I seriously doubt. I need to make my own future now, and if this Forcello moves away from the path Haefen's on, I'm guaranteed never to get home. Moving between the worlds will become impossible.'

'We all agree on that,' said Oliphant. 'Which begs the question, where will you go first?'

They looked at the map. There was no sign of anywhere called Haefen, or Coria. 'I took down the details of your route when I was programming the Engine,' said Oliphant. He traced a line across the ocean from Forcello. 'If I'm right, the Billy Boy would have capsized around here. And from your recollection of the direction of the sun, and the number of days you were at sea, I think you set sail somewhere here.' He pointed at a stretch of coastline hundred of miles away. 'I can't see any cities, and the scale's too small to show towns or villages.'

'That doesn't look right,' said Ellen. 'Coria was huge. If Forcello's big enough to be on the map, then Coria should be.'

Oliphant leafed through the atlas until he found a page with more detail. Halfway along the coast was a small village. 'Choria, has to be the same place,' he said. 'Or at least, it's in the same rough location. Never grew to be a city in our world.'

'We came in from the north,' said Ellen. They traced a route from the village towards a range of mountains. A river on the other side ran down from a stretch of high moors. She had the same feeling when Sera showed her the book in the library, back at the Priory. Peer hard enough, and would she see herself fighting brigands on the mountain pass? Or would Sophia be living in the village of Choria, wearing linen instead of silk, gutting fish landed by the boats in the harbour, dreaming of her own world? Sera had said to her when they first left the Priory, 'The map is not the territory', and it had never seemed more true.

The moors on the map dipped and merged into an amorphous area coloured green, the forest, and on the other side… nothing. No town, no village, just a river running down to an inlet of the sea. She felt a jolt of disappointment; she'd been so sure.

'Remember, this is our world,' said Fescue. 'Your map's bound to be different.'

He was right. But it didn't answer the question; where to go first. 'Is there any way I can get home without going by sea?' she asked. 'Even if it takes longer, I don't want to risk what happened last time.'

'Maybe,' said Oliphant. He turned to the first map. 'You could take the train as far as Nikkal and then head east on foot. You'd need to spend time away from any signs of civilisation. While you're in a town or city, or on a ship or train, you'll be tied to its world. It's why I didn't suggest an airship. It wouldn't have taken you all the way home, but it might have knocked a few weeks off the journey. But according to my equations, to swap paths, you need to be in places that stay the same over time.'

'Show me.'

'It won't be easy. You'll skirt round the borders of Hurria, before you come to the Empty Quarter. It's a desert and there are routes across, but you'll need a guide to take you with a group; no-one crosses alone. If they try, they never reach the other side.'

'So I'm on the other side of the desert - where then?'

Oliphant showed her on the map. 'The crossing will take at least a couple of weeks. Then you come to a set of foothills. These eventually rise to become the mountains you encountered on your way to Coria, but much further east.'

'Just foothills? Are you sure there aren't any lakes of boiling lava to spice things up?'

'They're treacherous enough. Wild country, no-one lives there, at least no-one you want to meet. And after you make it over the hills, you'll have the city of Kharuna on your right. If we've reversed the time breach, it might not even exist when you reach that point. You'll head north towards a lower stretch of the river you followed when you left the Priory.

Which would be here, except that it isn't marked on this map. From there you climb onto the moor, through the forest and in theory back to Haefen.'

'This is just a wild guess,' said Ellen, 'but that's going to take me over three months.'

'At least,' said Oliphant. 'It all depends what happens on the way.'

'Then I'd better get started. I'll catch the first train tomorrow to Nikkal and take my chances from there.'

'You need to be out of the city and past Nikkal before we make the next attempt with the Engine. It might not work at all, it might nudge the worlds apart so that they gradually meander back on course, or it might be a little more violent than that. Or there could be ripples in the field, one after another, rather than one enormous shock. I'm afraid the equations are rather hazy on that point.'

EVERYONE WAS at the station to see her off. Lily and Filip, the doctor and Oliphant. And Fescue, his moustaches waxed into total submission. 'I shall miss you, Ellen Dust. I hadn't realised how thin my life had become until I met you.'

He reminded her of Tollin. 'It's a new world for all of us,' she said. 'Or will be soon. Life is what you choose to make it, so take the right decisions.'

'What if I decide you should stay?'

'I confess that my theory falls apart a little when decisions conflict.'

'There's nothing I can say to persuade you to change your mind?'

The train guard blew his whistle and started shutting carriage doors. 'I've learnt so much from you, Fescue,' she said. 'None of us is a complete person, we're always in the process of becoming. You told me that. We each have our own unique journeys, and now I need to continue mine.'

She kissed him quickly on the cheek - the scent of lavender would never be the same - climbed into the carriage and found a seat by the window. As the train pulled off, she watched the little band of people waving at her, until the rails curved away and they were lost to sight.

CHAPTER 18

Time Breach

THE ASHIRA FIELD

Typical of Shalmar; he'd installed a huge red button for the President to push. All for the newsfeeds, of course, those optics again.

Eleven o'clock. The President looked at somebody for confirmation and pushed the button with both hands. I hadn't expected an explosion or for the tower to collapse. In truth, I don't know what I'd expected, but it didn't take long to find out. For a moment the air wavered, as if ripples were passing through the atmosphere. Only a couple of seconds and everything returned to normal with no obvious damage. Except, of course, for the other side of the split screen where the president's son was gone.

I don't know who else was in the auditorium. The great and the good of Mittani, reporters, people who paid for a front seat. Investors. Whoever they were, I heard a murmur growing to a hubbub. Someone shouted out, 'where did he go?' A couple of other voices shouted, 'it's a trick.'

I felt sick. If what I suspected had happened, every particle that made up that boy had been entangled with its counterpart in another part of the multiverse; his flesh and bones, the neurotransmitters between his synapses, his thoughts and his fears. He existed in another world now, and only the gods knew what sort of world that would be. Or if there was a way back.

If I'm honest, I really didn't care what happened to him. I didn't like the President; I didn't like her family. If they disappeared forever, it wouldn't have worried me for a second. No, the thing causing that hollow ache in the pit of my stomach was the realisation that Shalmar had caused a breach in whatever boundaries separated the infinity of worlds out there. A breach that would need to be healed. And neither Shalmar nor I nor anyone else in our reality knew how to do it.

A few moments later the live feed disappeared, and then the lights went out. From the window, I saw that power was down all over the city. The Ashira Field wouldn't have done that directly, but what did I know?

It was four hours before someone came to get me, one of the guards who brought my food. Something was definitely wrong. The man was skittish, still running round his home paddock but ready to bolt at any moment.

'What happened? Has the boy come back?'

'You should go.'

'Where's Shalmar?'

'Gone. Do you want to leave or not? Here, take this.' He handed me a key card. 'This works the doors to the stairs, they run on a backup battery. If I were you, I'd get home now.'

'Doesn't the building have generators?'

'You'd think.' He almost ran out.

Shalmar gone. What did gone mean? Surely he hadn't strapped on one of those arm torcs and attempted to embody himself somewhere we couldn't follow. But on second thoughts, it made sense. What better way of evading the consequences. No need to run and hide, not if he was in a different reality altogether.

I took the stairs, thirty-seven flights of them. At least I was going down, not up. From what I could see, the building was empty, bereft of the usual pervasive hum of business purring along. But people were milling about on the streets outside, a lot of people already breaking glass and looting shops. No sign of the police or military.

Still no power. Then I noticed something else. Aircraft were always flying overhead, night and day. High and quiet and painting lines in the sky with their contrails. But today there were none. The skies were clear.

I needed to get out of the downtown area, and there was no point hoping for a taxi. Even if I flagged one down, no way would it negotiate through the crowds. I kept close to the sides of buildings and took back streets where possible. While I was walking, I tried to think about what might have happened. I could just about imagine an energy surge knocking out one power station, but I knew the characteristics of the Ashira Field, so that didn't seem likely. More to the point, why were there no planes in the sky? The air traffic control centres were miles away from the city, which made me wonder how far the outage had spread. Four power stations served Mittani, all feeding into a grid. If the entire city was down, as well as the ATC centre at the main airport twenty miles away, this wasn't a failure. This was a catastrophe.

An hour later, I was close to my apartment. The streets here were quiet; this is the University district after all. Civilised people living civilised lives. Which made it even more bizarre to see a man driving a herd of cattle towards the University campus. He noticed me as I rounded a corner and reacted as if he'd seen a demon. He thrashed the hindquarters of the nearest beasts, forcing them to break into a run, and I watched as they stampeded away towards my favourite little bridge. Either I looked even worse than I felt, or he wasn't expecting to see someone like me.

I felt the same. He wouldn't have been out of place in the Mittani of five hundred years ago; no-one had driven cattle to market on foot for more than a century. It was obvious what had happened. My theories were right; a breach had occurred, the barriers were down, and my world, my Mittani, was converging with at least one other. And this was within just a few hours. I didn't want to imagine what the city would be like over the next few days.

Have you ever accidentally broken something valuable, something priceless and irreplaceable? That's how I felt. Because of my work, even if someone else had misused it, my world was broken. And right now I could see no way to repair it.

AN OBJECT OF DESIRE

❦

It's easy to lose track of time when there's no routine to punctuate the days. I remember when they blew up the Eser Tower. The crowds had been getting worse. Even though the police and the militia were back on the streets trying to keep order, I tried to stay indoors. That day I'd been collecting water from the river; nothing had been coming through the taps since the breach. The rumours said that the power stations had all disappeared, as if they'd never existed. Ditto the airport. A whole swathe of the country bordering the city was affected.

I was on my way back when I heard the explosions and looked over towards the capital. The Eser Tower seemed to judder, then to sink slightly as if someone had kicked its feet out from under it. And then, floor by floor, it concertinaed to the ground through a dust cloud that looked as though a small nuclear bomb had dropped. Please the gods, it was still empty then.

That was the same day I got home and found a man waiting for me in my apartment. I'd seen him before, the one who'd brushed past me on the bridge all those weeks ago, the day after the break-in. He had an anonymous face, no features that anyone would remember for long unless they had a reason, and I did.

He'd finished my last bottle of gin and was sitting in my favourite chair, grinning at me.

'I've always liked it here,' he said. 'Tasteful, if a little understated for my liking. Go big, that's my motto, maximise.'

A neutral voice, too. A Mittanese accent like millions of others, but from the other side of town where they'd built the projects to keep the poor away from decent folk. And you wonder why I'd happily see the President, her family and all her government disappear and never come back.

What do you say to someone who's broken in to your home? "Who are you," or "what are you doing here" both seem clichéd. And my heart was skipping double-time.

He crossed his legs and leaned back. 'What's the matter, cat got your tongue? Of course, I know you so much better than you know me, so I suppose that puts me at an advantage. Call me Parsha.'

Parsha, definitely a projects name. And talking was good, I'd heard. Make them see you as a person, not an object of desire. Something to be controlled.

'I had so much fun observing you and your friends every night. You are by many miles the most inventive woman I've ever watched as she took her pleasure. And then all this nonsense happens, thanks to my over-enthusiastic employer.'

'Your employer?'

'Shalmar Eser. He had the cameras put in. You found the first set, but not the second. Mr Eser doesn't give up easily, and nor do I. I suppose you could say I was addicted, which was fine by me. But like any addict, take away my recreational drug of choice and I get a tad twitchy. After the power went down, I thought, how can I replace what I'm missing? And then I realised, why put up with viewing on a screen when I can watch in person? So here I am, ready to play.'

'You put the cameras here?'

'And I was paid well. But I thought, why not sample the product myself? And what a product it was! I don't know whether Mr Eser realised I was making copies – to be honest, I doubt if he cared. Although I'm certain he enjoyed the shows you put on.'

His voice dropped to a stage whisper. 'Between you and me, if someone had taken out a contract on him and given me the hit, I would have carried it out with great pleasure. A strange man, but you know that.'

He emptied the glass, put it down and stood. 'In a way it's a shame there's only the two of us today. Given a choice, I prefer to watch rather than take part, but needs must. And like I said, I have been getting very twitchy.'

I think I told you before, I might be fit, but I'm not a fighter. I was sure of one thing, though; I wasn't giving in without a fight this time. Like my heart, my brain was firing at double speed. I ran through the options: I was closer to the kitchen than he was; could I get there before him and arm myself with a kitchen knife? Unlikely, and I suspected a struggle would be exactly what he wanted. Could I get out of the apartment? By the time I opened the front door, he'd be on me. And then I was out of options. Like I said, not a fighter.

'You know, Ash, may I call you Ash? I can almost see your thoughts. You people are so predictable. Go ahead, make a break. I'll count to five to give you a head start if you like.' He tilted his head to one side like a bird. Birds are descended from dinosaurs. 'I have no illusions about myself,' he said, 'men like me crave the hunt. And women like you, you're prey animals. Always were, always will be. You exist for our pleasure. You know it, we know it. The eternal, beautiful game.'

He took off his black leather jacket, slowly, as if daring me to take advantage and run. What was the point? I understood why women gave in at this point. Why risk broken bones or worse if you could let them take what they want. With luck, when it was over, there might be a chance to get away.

He really was reading my thoughts. 'Come on, Ash, try something. Don't make it too easy – where's the fun in that?'

As I backed off, he walked towards me and then we both stopped at the sound of the front door opening.

'Who the fuck is that?'

There were only two people who had access to my apartment other than me. My cleaner, who I hadn't seen since the breach, and Danu. Why her? Because she was the closest thing I had to a friend, even if the last time I saw her was the day of the game.

There was a reason I chose her as my postgrad. I'd always known I was bright, but she could see the answer before I had any idea what the question was. It took her a nanosecond to take in the situation.

For an academic, Danu often prefers action over words, and this time she didn't disappoint. I'd barely clocked who she was when she pushed past me, swaying around the man, grabbing him from behind with her exceptionally muscular, rock-climbing honed arm around his neck, and twisting with all her weight. The sound of a neck snapping, I now know, is quite unique.

CHAPTER 19

The Way Home

WAR ZONE

❦

Oliphant had called them foothills, but they might as well have been mountains. Ellen followed tracks laid down by wild goats, where she could find them, always heading north. The grass grew in tough, spiny patches and as she climbed higher, it gave way to creeping sedges, and then to peat hags. In places, the paths disappeared and she waded through black mud up to her knees.

The rain had been a blessing at first after the dust and heat of the Empty Quarter, but she barely remembered what the sky looked like after weeks of low grey clouds that sometimes reached the ground, surrounding her with a wet mist that soaked through everything she was wearing.

The last human she'd spoken to was the guide who led twenty of them across the Empty Quarter, a small caravan of camels and people. Oliphant had made the desert sound threatening, but she found it beautiful. Red and purple sunsets through soft, tired air. Sudden dawns, the air sharp and excited as the sun bounded up from behind hills of sand, throwing shadows towards them that retreated even as they formed. The night sky was littered with more stars than she could had imagined, and the simple solitude of the never-changing days was a balm after all she'd experienced. Even relinquishing decisions to the guide was a relief. A tall, self-contained man with copper skin swathed in white robes, he communicated with her in sign language. It was enough; all she had to do was walk, eat and sleep. She hadn't felt that safe for months.

After leaving the train at Nikkal, she'd been shedding civilisation step by step, day by day. The train was the last machine she'd seen. Then roads ran through rows of apple orchards, blossoming unseasonally, until the roads became paths and the paths became tracks and the days became dry and hot until she reached a settlement of parched bricks and drooping palms on the edge of the desert.

She remembered the day the Ontological Engine pulsed out, somewhere in the sky and a world away. An early morning; she'd slept the night on a bed of hay in a dilapidated barn, halfway between Nikkal and the beginning of the desert. After a breakfast of bread and cheese, she dusted herself down and was about to set off when the air trembled. Everything wavered, a reflection in water through the ripples after a stone had been thrown in. The disturbance lasted only a few seconds and the air settled again, but she smiled to herself. Whatever happened next, her friends in Forcello had done their best. Somewhere far behind her an airship was coming in to land, Fescue, Oliphant and the doctor were congratulating themselves, Alfred and Peterkin were running across a beach and Lily was probably the leader of the Senate.

A CAIRN ahead of her marked the high point of this particular rise. No-one had added new stones for decades or more, but it was a connection of sorts. People came here, once. Perhaps from Kharuna, the city Oliphant told her to avoid; if he was right it would had been somewhere on the plain below.

The slopes were different on the other side. Small stones littered the path, threatening to trip her, and the peat on either side had given way to outcrops of rock.

The cloud was lifting. She noticed a difference in the light; the mist becoming more translucent and then breaking up into wisps that curled and then evaporated. Within a few minutes patches of blue appeared through the grey, growing and merging until all traces of the clouds had disappeared.

She followed the course of a dried-up stream through a narrow gully. The first stunted trees appeared as she lost height, dwarf rowans growing from fissures in the rock. Still down until she noticed that the stones under her feet were dark with moisture. Another, living stream merged in. Now she was wading through water; shallow, but cold and fresh.

She filled her canteens and found a faint track running alongside the rill. The slope flattened out and within half an hour the rocks give way to clumps of grass, and then to what used to be meadows. Everywhere she looked the earth had been blasted into sour-smelling craters, some half filled with water, others with corpses the same colour as the mud that enveloped them. Any buildings had disintegrated into heaps of rubble and the only trees still standing were charred, skeletal stumps. Nothing was green.

Some of the priests in Haefen taught that people who led evil lives went to a place of eternal torment after death. She'd never believed their stories, but if such a place existed, it would look like this. She stood on the edge of one of the craters, wondering if the time breach had been reversed? If it had, and this was the result, then she'd lost all chance of finding her Haefen. But if the paths were still moving apart, trying to find their proper directions, she might yet make her way back home.

. . .

Dusk was falling when she heard the sound of running water, not the light dance of a mountain brook but the fat, lazy sound of a lowland river. A line of shattered stumps ahead signalled its course, and she rested on the bank near a solitary willow that had somehow survived, trailing its pale green branches in the water's edge. Small murmurations of evening insects clouded the surface of the water; the last time she'd watched a scene like this was outside the inn near Forcello, the day the Princeps died.

Her legs ached, and she studied the cuts and scratches covering her hands. Under the ragged clothes a patchwork of bruises ranged from yellow to purple; too many hard scrambles up rock faces, too many falls. But those were familiar sensations.

More troubling was a sense of hollowness in her chest, as if something was missing. So this was how loneliness felt. For the first time in her life, she missed the sense of being part of something. Of belonging.

Enough introspection; what was the point? Sometimes the path of her life intersected with someone else's for a while until they moved away from each other. You kept each other in sight for a while and then they disappeared. Tracks on an empty moor.

The sound of insects was louder than it should be. She looked along the bank; three uniformed bodies rose and fell as the water rippled through the reed bed that had become their final resting place. Clouds of flies surrounded the corpses; one was missing an arm, the second was a headless torso. The third floated face down and she preferred not to imagine what he'd seen.

She'd thought she was about to leave the killing fields behind, but these poor souls had floated downstream and she was about to head upstream, towards whatever happened to them. She'd been planning to fill her water bottles here, but who would want to drink from this river of blood?

There was no point in worrying. Tomorrow she would cross to the other bank and then walk the long stretch north, keeping the river to her left until she reached the base of the waterfall. If she came across hazards on the route, she'd deal with them the way she always did. Then to find a way up.

BOYS AND THEIR MOTHERS

A couple of miles from where she spent the night, well away from the bodies in the reeds, the land changed. Later that day she saw a group of soldiers in the distance, fanned out as if searching for something, or someone. No point in pushing her luck. She hunkered down in the nearest crater, clinging to the side so as not to slide down into the muddy pool at the bottom where an arm stuck out, as if trying to free itself.

After three days she eventually left the desolation behind; a line of cliffs gradually came into view ahead, as if part of the land had been sheared away in some ancient cataclysm. At least two hundred feet high, with a deafening cascade of water falling over the edge; rainbows shimmered in the clouds of spray. She recognised this place. Somewhere near the top of the cliffs a tunnel ran under the river bed, its entrance on the path that eventually led to the Priory. She stripped, then washed herself and her clothes in the pool at the waterfall's base. Time to spread the wet clothing on rocks and rest for an hour. They wouldn't dry much, but it was the thought that counted.

The falls looked as high from below as they had from above, but she wasn't in the mood for rock climbing. Would a set of steps carved into the side of the cliff be too much to ask? Time for the gods to back down for a change?

A well-beaten track led away from the pool and she followed to to where a rope looped down from the top, attached to the rock face every few feet by metal rings. The steps she'd hoped for zigzagged up the side of the cliff with the rope as a handrail. Not that she'd looked over the edge when she and Sera had approached from the other direction, but she'd bet her life these steps hadn't existed then.

All the same, no point in turning down an offer like this. She barely noticed the steepness and then she was at the top of the falls, watching the river as it rushed uncaringly to the edge. That hadn't changed, still the choppy white water of before. But something was new, a broken wooden signpost that had snapped halfway up. The upper part, carved to the shape of a pointing finger, lay a few feet away on the ground. 'Fenmaen Moor 5 miles'. It hadn't been here before, and yet the sign was bleached and faded by years of spray. People had carved sets of initials into the upright, some with hearts against them. Once this had been a wild, rough country, now it was a place for lovers; things had changed.

The wide path leading away from the falls was dry and packed hard as iron, nothing like the faint track she followed all those months ago, and a little further on she found the entrance to the tunnel. There was no need to search for it this time; the bushes that used to hide the location had long since disappeared, but a metal grating was blocking the entrance, with a sign in red: 'Do not enter'. Fair enough, not that she would had been tempted a second time.

She remembered this trail, could almost feel the ghosts of Sera and Hob walking behind her. After a couple of hours she reached the edge of the moor and another wooden sign. 'Fenmaen Priory 2½ miles'. Why was it that going back never took as long as leaving?

The path led past the place where she'd rested with Sera and Hob, and after a while the buildings of the Priory appeared in the distance. Something wasn't right, but she kept on walking until she had a better view. Nothing remained of the outer wall and its gatehouse and the buildings still standing were roofless, some only a couple of walls that look ashamed of their uselessness. The Priory was a ruin, Lannick all over again. At first she wondered if this destruction was a result from the war, but small plants had long since made their homes in the cracks between the stones. Whatever happened here had taken place centuries ago; nothing about this was recent.

She roamed through the stubs of walls; this was the library where she first met Sera, there the infirmary where she came to after being rescued from the moor. The cloisters ran around this bare clearing of stone, and across there was the corridor where she found Brother William dying from an infestation of worms.

She sat by the remnants of what used to be the main gate, now nothing more than a few stones and a rusted hinge. Unselm had waved them off from here as they set out for Coria. All gone, all the lives that were lived and lost between these walls.

A part of her had hoped that she'd find Sera, someone to compare stories with, but if he'd arrived at the Priory before Oliphant sent out the pulse from the Ontological Engine, then he'd be one of the sets of bones in the ossuary. Had he waited for her, she wondered? Ever stood where she was sitting now, looking down the track towards the mountains, just in case?

A voice broke her reverie. 'Hello, what do we have here?'

Five skinny teenage boys, two wearing torn, bloodstained uniforms which hung loosely from their narrow shoulders. Looted from corpses; they still carried the sourness of death. No weapons apart from a rusted metal rod in the hands of the lead boy; seventeen, at a guess, the others a little younger. What was most on their minds right now? Food or sex if they were like most boys their age, and she wasn't about to let them take either.

She appraised her situation. They should have come closer before speaking, would had given them more of an advantage. At least now she had time to stand, slowly, and face them. No need for aggression though, not yet. They were so young.

'Afternoon, boys.'

How would this play out? The one in front was the most confident, him and his weapon. The others hung back, waiting to see what happened.

'You got anything to eat in that pack?' He sounded even younger than he looked, with a nervous catch to his voice. Good. He was't experienced in these situations, except perhaps in his dreams. And now she knew what was on their minds; food first, but sex wouldn't be far behind. Sad but true, the way of the world. Hunters and prey.

'Whatever food I've got, I need. Sorry.'

'I ain't asking. Just throw it over here.'

'Boys, I've had a long journey and a rough day, and I'm feeling a little grumpy. You want my pack, come and get it. But my advice is, go away and don't come back.'

If they had any sense, they'd fan out and try to surround her, attack from all sides at once. But that would be asking too much. The leader started to run towards her, unable to stop himself even as he saw her unsheathe the dagger. His attention faltered, he stumbled over his own feet and as he fell Ellen sidestepped and stabbed up into his side below the ribs, twisted, and out again. Less blood that way and she was filthy enough. Bless Tollin; a good blade. The best.

The boy grunted and rolled over, clutching at the tear in his side. Blood covered his hands. The others hadn't moved except to shuffle around where they stood.

She looked down at the boy's writhing body. She really hadn't wanted this, but in situations where she was outnumbered there was no choice but to hit first and hit hard.

'He'll almost certainly die,' Ellen called out to his friends, 'and I'm sorry about that. The next time someone gives you friendly advice, take it. Now, anyone else want to try their luck? Like I said; long day, still feeling grumpy.'

Loyalty was clearly not high on their personal set of values, given the way they turned and ran. Ellen knelt beside the boy on the ground, pulled his hand away and examined the wound. If Brother Thomas were here with his poultices and cordials and bandages, there have might be a chance. As it was, the boy wouldn't last the night and the next few hours were going to be extremely unpleasant. For him. She rolled him onto his back, as carefully as she could, and studied his white face, twisted with pain. One day, if she was lucky, she wouldn't need to fight any more.

'What's your name?' she asked.

'Ezra.' Not even seventeen, probably didn't shave more than once a week. 'It hurts so bad.'

'I'll be honest with you, Ezra, you're not going to make it. Your friends left so now it's just you and me, and I have somewhere else to be.'

'You can't leave me here.' He started to cry, and she sat behind him with his head in her lap, stroking his hair.

'Actually, I can. But as I told someone once, I try not to be cruel.'

Her favourite cut this time, across the throat, and after

the first high spurts of blood she held him while what remained of his life bubbled away. Food, sex and their mothers. She always forgot the last.

CHAPTER 20

An Ending of Sorts

FABER EST SUAE QUISQUE FORTUNAE

*Danu stayed to help me get rid of the body. We got it outside and dragged it a little way from my building; just another victim among so many. She told me she'd been staying with her parents out in the country, about fifty miles from the city. It was bad there, she said, but nothing like in Mittani itself where the streets were little more than middens.

Part of her reason for coming back was to check on me, the other was to see what we could do to reverse the damage. It didn't take long to realise that there was nothing. Both of us are theoreticians, we leave practical applications to others. My new set of postgrads would have been helping with that, but they were an entire life away. Never going to happen now.

After a couple of days, Danu left to go back home. She was a late baby and her folks are old; they need her more than I do. But I miss her.

. . .

THE GOVERNMENT IS GETTING its act together at last, and official food banks are operating throughout the city. Actually, that's not quite true. There's one near me, even if the rations are barely enough to live on. But I've heard rumours they've fenced in the projects and turned them into ghettos. No-one in, no-one out, and anyone who tries is shot. Saving food. When this is over, the authorities will probably bulldoze the entire area, melding buildings and bodies together and starting again. Just another equation; one I really wish I didn't know.

And now the war has begun.

I'm surprised it didn't start earlier. Mittani can't be the only place affected by the breach, and when people feel threatened, they lash out. Try to find a culprit, an enemy. Who started the fighting? I have no idea, and it probably doesn't matter, but I've seen war drones streaking overhead on their way to destroy whatever it is they see as a threat, as if there hasn't been enough destruction already. I don't even know if the drones were ours or theirs.

After what happened with camera man I couldn't sleep at my apartment. I realised I wasn't being filmed any more; I knew his body was food for flies, but I needed to be somewhere else and so I moved into my lab. The motto above the main entrance is curiously unscathed, probably because no-one outside the University knows what it means. "*Faber est suae quisque fortunae*"; "Every man is the maker of his own fortune". Not quite true for all the poor bastards whose fortunes I ruined, not to mention their lives.

Various mobs trashed the campus grounds long since. Most of the buildings have broken windows and the walls are pockmarked and stained with soot. What is it with rioters and fires? Their need to break down what they don't understand like impatient children. Once people realised what caused the problem, all experts were suspect and therefore fair game, and the best place to find experts is a University. Back to hunters and prey.

I worry the gangs will come for me. Not because of my involvement, which is, I hope, not public knowledge, but simply because I'm one of 'them'. People who live by their brains. People who should know better. Hard to gainsay them; what with my theories and Shalmar's application of them, misused though they were, the mob is right. Between us, we've brought countless worlds to the edge of the end.

No-one else is around on campus, which suits me fine. I might as well be here as anywhere. I thought if I was in my lab surrounded by all the paraphernalia of work, I could dream up a way to repair the breach. As usual with my boundless arrogance, I failed. Although I understand all the parameters, I simply don't have the skill, nowhere near it, to build the sort of machine that Shalmar used to generate the Ashira Field.

I only hope that someone, somewhere in another reality, will do what I can't. And I still don't sleep as I wonder about the consequences, the infinite consequences, of what I started.

I was outside earlier, taking one of my usual runs around the campus, from Life Sciences to Humanities to Business, each one a village of its own on the vast University site. Then past the Senate building with the Dean's residence next door - she'd been one of the first to make tracks to another of her other houses, a long way from trouble.

I'd stopped to catch my breath when everything seemed to ripple, as if a wave were passing through the buildings, the trees, the burnt out sheets of cars. Me. As if we were floating on the surface of a pond when someone threw in a stone.

I recognised this phenomenon, the same as the day Shalmar turned on his machine to start the game. Handles and manifolds; the topology of reality had shifted and rearranged itself in an instant. For the first time since that day, I felt a small spark of hope.

Someone, somewhere, has achieved what I couldn't and generated the Ashira Field. I don't know how far they've repaired the damage. Will we go back to normal, whatever that might be? And what about the President's son and Shalmar and anyone else who went through the Breach to some other existence? Something tells me they'll never be back. They've left this world forever, trapped in another life, and gods help the people who live there.

THE WAR'S COMING CLOSER. Even as I write this, the sound of distant artillery shakes the building like thunder. Which probably means we're losing. I have no idea if that's a good thing or a bad thing. Bad, I guess, though I have no allegiance to our current rulers, whoever they are now.

I could run, I suppose, but to where? Is anywhere safe? Win or lose, the mob will be back. I've been lucky so far, hoarding food and water, but when things get really bad, they'll find me.

I HEARD VOICES OUTSIDE. If I go to the window to check, they might see me so better stay out of sight. If I'm lucky they'll pass by, at least this time. Like I said, not a fighter.

But I've waited long enough; staying here is too much of a risk. Tomorrow I'll pack a bag, sufficient food and water for a few days, and make my way out of Mittani to search for a sanctuary where I'll be safe. Maybe head up country and find Danu.

Funny, a week or so ago I was looking through books in the History Department library - I've had more than enough time on my hands - and I came across a history of the city. Did you know Mittani was built on land reclaimed from the sea, on the site of a settlement that disappeared a thousand years or more ago? I wonder about the people who lived there; who they were, how they passed their time. Why they deserted their home. I wish I knew its name.

CHAPTER 21

Time's Arrow

YOU CAN NEVER GO HOME

The last time she crossed the moors, a winter storm had caught her. Now the scent of honey perfumed the air. This path up from the Priory must be the one the shepherd carried her down after she collapsed, seeing visions. After a while it merged with another track running from the forest in the distance, where the heather dipped down to meet the trees.

Eventually she reached the edge of the forest, which was less dense than she remembered. Lighter, as if there were fewer trees. The paths were the same as the one from the falls; wide and well-kept. Somehow she knew that any wolves had disappeared for good, a long time ago. She passed through the rocky gully and looked for the small cave where she spent her first night away from home; at least that was still there.

Her pace slowed; she'd reached the clearing where she discovered the bodies and fought the wolf. She wouldn't have been surprised to see the corpses lying here; would she always feel guilty that she didn't bury them? She propped herself against what was probably the great-granddaughter of the tree where she found the woman and the baby, and pictured all the people who must have crossed through here over the centuries; none of them knowing what happened, walking across the spots where people died and their blood seeped into the earth. This was one of the days when she felt the weight of all the lives she'd lived, and all the choices she'd made.

* * *

Time to go; the shadows were already lengthening and Haefen beckoned. This time the way home was clear, heading down towards the river. But long before it should, the forest thinned into open woodland and then ended. One moment in amongst the trees, the next out in the open. The land sloped down to where the river should have been, but buildings and gardens now covered the ground that a few weeks ago was carpeted with autumn leaves, and what used to be a river was now a lake. Not wild but tamed, covered in waterlilies and surrounded by landscaped gardens that seemed a little unruly, as if neglected for a while. The remains of the stone bridge over the river had been transformed into a miniature wooden version of the ornate bridge in Forcello, a folly, crossing the narrow end of the lake. Beyond the bridge, several large buildings in strange geometric shapes stretched across a couple of acres. The entire front of the nearest was glass, five storeys high and in the distance, a few miles away, slender towers of crystal pierced the sky.

She walked slowly between the deserted buildings; absence hung heavy in this alien place. Behind the ground-floor windows, the rooms for living in were empty. Some of the glass had been smashed, and the contents of drawers and cupboards scattered across the floor. Not a single piece of furniture that hadn't been turned to firewood.

This wasn't as bad as the killing fields near Kharuna, but something had caused the people to disappear. She left the buildings and made her way towards the water. The objects on the other side of the bridge reminded her of the steam carriages in Forcello, but wrecked and burned, and she was about to cross when she heard a voice.

'Ellen? I wondered when you'd get here.' Sera and Hob ambled towards her as if this were an everyday occurrence.

'I had a few things to sort out,' she said, matching their casualness. 'How long have you been here?'

Both man and mule looked exactly the same as when they'd left her at the harbour. 'A couple of hours. Why?'

'Where did you go after Coria?'

'Nowhere in particular.'

'You came straight back?'

'Yes. I avoided football games in the mountains this time, two easy weeks on the road. Everything seemed normal until I reached the Priory - I guess you saw what it's like now. I don't know how to explain it.'

'I can help with that. But just to be clear, the last time we saw each other was a fortnight ago in Coria. Is that right?'

'Markus threw Sophia's husband in the water; I'm glad I was around for that. But I guess you decided not to go sailing after all.'

She studied his face in case he was having fun with her, but he was serious. 'Since you left Coria, I spent weeks on the Billy Boy before we were shipwrecked,' she said.

Sera stared at her. 'Weeks? Shipwrecked?' He looked around. 'Where's Sophia - is she with you?'

'She was injured when the ship went down, didn't make it.'

'Gods, Ellen, I'm sorry. A strange woman, but brave. You survived, though.'

'Only just. When we were a few weeks out, a sailor attacked me. Bastard caught me with my guard down. No harm done, luckily, not to me, but he wasn't so fortunate; Markus hung him as a punishment.'

'Your disguises didn't work?'

'It was always a risk; Sophia couldn't help swaying her hips as she walked.'

Sera was looking at her as if she were a ghost. 'You said the ship went down?'

'I nearly drowned when the Billy Boy capsized in a storm. Sophia rescued me, but died of her injuries before we reached shore. The jolly boat broke its back on rocks and I washed up on a beach near a city.'

'The gods were looking out for you.'

'Oh no, they were still having their fun. At one point I was a heartbeat from being thrown to a wild beast by a madman. I watched a young boy float to earth from an airship. I've travelled on machines you couldn't imagine. I helped build an engine to repair a breach in reality. I spent weeks crossing a desert. And now I'm here, looking for Haefen.'

'I guess this place doesn't count; it doesn't match with what you described.'

'No. But I came to terms with losing my home a long time ago.'

Sera shook his head slowly. 'And I used to think I'd led an interesting life. But I don't understand how you could do all that, and get here, in the two weeks it took me to travel back from Coria.'

'Months, Sera, months. I've lived a life in the time it took you to wander back.'

'I didn't exactly wander. I feel that time is continuing to play games with us.'

'Not arguing with that. But those games might be coming to an end. If I'm right, the worlds are moving back to where they should be.'

'Worlds?'

'It's complicated.'

* * *

As they crossed the bridge, a flying machine, more like a bird than Forcello's airships, streaked past them a few hundred feet above. A few minutes later, an explosion shook the ground. One of the towers in the distance shivered and then collapsed slowly in a cloud of dust.

Sera stopped and stared. 'What was that?'

'There's a war going on. Didn't you meet any soldiers on your way back?'

'No. Just retraced my steps the same way we travelled out. Saw no-one.'

'I came back overland, didn't want another ship in my life. I was caught up in some fighting briefly. Well, not so much fighting as the aftermath.'

'You're a trouble magnet. And there's fresh blood on your sleeve.'

'Not mine, nothing to worry about. Just a few lads who took a step too far.'

'Let me guess; there are fewer lads now than there were to start with.'

'I told them I was feeling grumpy.'

'Is no-one safe when you're around? Remind me not to annoy you.'

They passed the burnt out carriages, one with the charred remains of a person sprawled across the front seats, and reached the building with the glass front.

Ellen pointed up to an inscription in stone above the main doors. 'What's that writing?'

Sera read. '"*Faber est suae quisque fortunae.*" It means something like *"Every man is the maker of his own fortune."* An old, dead language from another land. I learnt it from the books in the Priory's library.'

'What about women; didn't they make their own fortunes in that old, dead land?'

'Not usually. Then again, they never met you.'

* * *

THEY LEFT HOB OUTSIDE, munching on a shrub, and entered the building, stepping over the broken glass doors lying on the ground. 'Someone was in a hurry to get in,' said Sera. Several trees in enormous pots were dying and one had fallen over, stretching twenty feet or more across the floor. They found stairs behind a door and climbed to the next floor. A corridor stretched ahead, strewn with fragments of broken furniture.

'What happened here?' she said.

'A mob. I've seen it happen before when law and order break down. Makes you realise we're all animals inside, waiting for a chance to rip and tear.'

'Speak for yourself.'

'I've seen you with a knife.'

'Self-defence, Sera, always self-defence.'

Each floor was the same; deserted corridors with lifeless rooms that looked as though a tornado had blown through. On the third floor Sera said, 'Have you seen enough? There's nothing here for us.'

'I lived in this place once, when it was somewhere else. Just this floor and then we go.'

A door halfway down the corridor stood half-open.

'"*Professor Ashira uit Banipol, Head of Experimental Teleology.*" You have any idea what that means?' said Ellen.

'Teleology, looking at purposes rather than causes. Like saying a stone falls because its purpose is to reach the centre of the earth, rather than because I dropped it.'

'Ridiculous. You think you have a purpose?'

'Me? No. Things happen because there's a cause. You left Haefen because you were exiled, not because your purpose was to go on a journey.'

'I wish I knew what caused all this nonsense in the first place.'

They pushed through the half-open door. On the far side of the room, below the window, the body of a young woman lay sprawled on the floor. Her blue eyes stared at the ceiling and sticky blood matted the raven-black hair on the side of her head.

Sera looked between the body and Ellen. 'You never said you had a sister.'

'Not in my world.' Mirrors had never featured much in her life, but she recognised the face staring up. So many worlds, so many chances. So many lives. How had this one been lived? She knew she should feel something, an emotional response, but there was no point. Life happens, and then it ends. All she hoped was that this version, whatever her name, had a good life. And a quick death.

She knelt down. No pulse, although whatever happened was recent; the limbs were still stiff with rigor. 'You think she was the professor? Ashira uit Banipol, a weird name.'

'She'd probably say the same about yours.'

Ellen closed Ashira's eyelids, then walked over to the end wall and studied the equations covering a large whiteboard. 'Oliphant would probably know what these mean,' she said.

'What ever she was working on, she thought it worth dying for.'

'Nothing's worth that.' She looked around suddenly. 'What's that noise?'

They peered carefully out of the window. A crowd was cavorting around a bonfire of books, shouting and cheering. 'We need to leave as soon as we can,' said Sera, 'Being incinerated always struck me as a poor choice of death.'

'I'm not sure there is a good choice.'

They went back outside after the fire died down and the crowd had dispersed. 'Where's Hob?' said Ellen.

'He'll find us.'

They returned to the bridge where Ellen paused for a moment when they were halfway across, looking down at the waterlilies to a duck negotiating its way through the foliage. Once they'd crossed and reached the cover of the trees, Hob wandered out to join them.

'What now,' said Sera.

'Whatever this place may be, it isn't Haefen,' said Ellen. 'Someone told me once; time's arrow only flies in one direction, you can never go back.'

'There's a small town called Aktiki I always meant to visit,' Sera said. 'It used to have a reputation for learning. If we track back to the moors but turn in the opposite direction from the Priory, we could reach there in a week or so. What do you say?'

'Will there be books? I've never been good with books; too much sitting down.'

'Probably.'

'We won't be staying though.'

'Probably not.'

They headed back along the track into the forest. Just before they reached the clearing, Hob wandered a few feet away to investigate something in the undergrowth. Not worth his time; he headed back, twitching his ears. The right one brown, the left one white. A mirror image of the Hob she first met at the Priory. She glanced at Sera, but all his features seem much the same as before. What had Oliphant said? *'Some of these worlds will be almost identical to ours, others will be completely different.'*

Sera noticed her look. 'You okay?'

'Never better.' They walked through the clearing, still empty of bodies, and carried on towards the gully.

'By the way,' Ellen said, 'were you ever going to tell me why you gave up the soldiering game?'

'It's a long story.'

'No problem, I think we have time.'

* * *

The End

Printed in Great Britain
by Amazon